THE ORPHAN TRAIN SAGA

Enjoy the Journey

SHERRY A. BURTON

Dorry Press

Also by Sherry A. Burton

The Orphan Train Saga
Discovery (book one)
Shameless (book two)
Treachery (book three)
Guardian (book four)
Loyal (book five)
Patience (book six)
Endurance (book seven)

Orphan Train Extras
Ezra's Story

Jerry McNeal Series
Always Faithful (book one)
Ghostly Guidance (book two)
Rambling Spirit (book three)
Chosen Path (book four)
Port Hope (book five)
Cold Case (book six)
Wicked Winds (book seven)
Mystic Angel (book eight)
Uncanny Coincidence (book nine)
Chesapeake Chaos (book ten)
Village Shenanigans (book eleven)
Special Delivery (book twelve)
Spirit of Deadwood (a full-length Jerry McNeal novel, book thirteen)
Star Treatment (book fourteen)
Merry Me (book fifteen)

Clean and Cozy Jerry McNeal Series Collection
(Compilations of the standalone Jerry McNeal series)
The Jerry McNeal Clean and Cozy Edition Volume one
(books 1-3)
The Jerry McNeal Clean and Cozy Edition Volume two (books
4-6)
The Jerry McNeal Clean and Cozy Edition Volume three
(books 7-9)
The Jerry McNeal Clean and Cozy Edition Volume four
(books 10-12)

Romance Books *(*not clean* - sex and language)*
Tears of Betrayal
Love in the Bluegrass
Somewhere In My Dreams
The King of My Heart

Romance Books *(clean)*
Seems Like Yesterday

"Whispers of the Past" (a short story)

Psychological Thrillers
Storm Series
Surviving the Storm (book one, contains Sex, Language, and
Violence)
Sinister Winds (book two, contains Language and Violence)

Patience

Book 6 in The Orphan Train Saga

Written by Sherry A. Burton

Copyright Page
Patience, The Orphan Train Saga Book 6 © Copyright 2023
by Sherry A. Burton

Published by Dorry Press
Edited and Formatted by BZHercules.com
Cover by Laura J. Prevost
www.laurajprevostbookcovers.myportfolio.com

A special thanks to:

My editor, Beth, for allowing me to keep my voice.
My cover artist and media design guru, Laura Prevost, thanks for keeping me current.
My proofreader, Latisha Rich, for that extra set of eyes.
To my amazing team of beta readers, thank you for helping take a final look.
To my husband, thank you for your endless hours of researching, your help with all things genealogy, and for allowing me to bounce story ideas off of you.

Dedication

*The orphan trains and the children who rode them are my passion. My goal with each book is to keep the memories of the children who rode the orphan trains alive.
Remember, without a past, there is no future.*

~ Sherry A. Burton

Chapter One

Scholars have spent a lifetime debating what was the greatest book ever written. Some proclaim it to be the Bible; others have their own opinion. I, too, have given this a great deal of thought and have thrown my own selections into the mix a time or two. But what if the best books are the ones that are never considered? Simple journals written on a whim that document a person's life and set forth stories of one's past so that all the history that was them is not lost when they are no longer here to tell things they've seen. Should we not honor those storytellers who are so adept at showing us their worlds that we laugh, cry, and mourn along with them as we read? I am not saying my words are the best ever to have been written; they are far from poetic prose. However, my hope is that I've done my life justice and you will enjoy them all the same. My name is Howard Paddy Moore, although my birth name is of no matter, as I left that life long ago.

***

Cindy placed the journal in her lap and heaved a heavy sigh.

"You either read those at lightning speed, or you're already disappointed," Linda said, setting her own pile aside.

"Sorry. I didn't mean to pull you from the story. I just thought that Grandpa Howard would shed some light onto who I really am."

Linda eyed her over her glasses. "You mean besides my daughter?"

1

Cindy smiled. "I mean like my real last name."

"Your real last name is Moore. That's what it says on your birth certificate. It doesn't get much more official than that," Linda assured her. "What gives? It's not like you to give up so quickly. You have a whole stack of your grandfather's words in front of you."

"Maybe that's what I'm afraid of. I've always held him in the highest regard. What if something in here changes that?"

"You're right," Linda said, rising from her chair. "Give them to me; I'll burn the lot of them."

Cindy laughed. "Yeah, right. You'll hide them until I'm not home and then read them by yourself."

"Probably. Won't be hard to do, as much as you've been gone of late."

Cindy felt the heat of a blush rise in her cheeks as she thought of David and all the time they'd spent together lately. "Whose fault is that? You're the one who set us up," she said playfully.

"No, I wrote the man an apology. I never told him to send you flowers, nor did I tell you to agree to go out with him." Linda nodded to the picture frame on the table next to Cindy. "But I'm glad you did."

Cindy followed her mother's gaze to the framed photo of Linda, herself, David, and his seven-year-old daughter Stella, taken at the school's Christmas program. "Me too. And you're right, the last name doesn't matter."

Linda's eyes grew wide, and Cindy laughed. "Slow down, Linda. Just because you have Stella calling you 'Grandma' doesn't mean David and I are getting married any time soon."

Linda pushed her bottom lip out. "It's not nice to dash an old woman's hopes. So, you're okay reading the journals?"

Cindy nodded. "I'm 'Moore' than okay."

Linda smiled. "That's my girl."

"That I am," Cindy said, picking up the journals and finding the place where she left off...

I am the seventh son of a seventh son. Some would consider that to mean something special, but I was never privy to the good of it. My papa was a mean old coot with brilliant red hair and freckled leather skin. His only redeeming quality was that he loved my momma something fierce. While he was quick to raise a hand to me and my brothers, I never saw him lay a hand on my mother. That was probably the reason my mother didn't hesitate to stand up to him when she thought he'd taken my punishment too far. While my momma could be heavy-handed, she never doled out a punishment I didn't earn. My papa, on the other hand, never needed a reason to lay into me. I used to wonder why the man hated me so much, then one day, my mother confessed I was her favorite son, and things kind of made sense after that. I've often wondered what my life would have been like if I weren't her favorite. I guess I'll never know, but one thing was certain, while my papa whooped on my brothers, he never laid into them the way he did me.

Maybe it was because I had a hard time holding my tongue. I knew sassing the man would raise his ire, but the knowledge never stopped me from going toe to toe with him, and that left Momma to be the referee. While she didn't hesitate to jump in between us, she'd wait until she had me alone to scold me for my wrongdoings. More than once, she pulled me aside to tell me my temper was going to get the best of me, further assuring me that if I were just to bide my time, Papa would cool down. I learned that lesson way too late, as being patient didn't come naturally to me in the early years of my life.

My wife Mildred reminds me a lot of my mother, with the same dark hair and eyes and the same self-assured way she carries herself. That I'll-persevere-or-die-trying attitude was the first thing I noticed about Mildred. It was at that very moment I heard my mother's words, "You can have what your heart desires if you just find the patience to wait." It was as if all her years of trying to teach me to be patient smacked me right in the head at that exact instant, and I knew all I had to do was wait, and I'd marry her one day. Okay, it might not have happened quite that quickly, but I saw a fire in her, and that reminded me of my mother, and I never could put her from my mind.

I had no idea what troubles would ensue between that moment and the time I actually married the girl, but in the end, it all worked out for the best. It turns out that self-assured girl needed me just as much as I needed her. By the time she and I were married, Mildred had lost two sets of parents and was pressured into marrying a man she barely knew. I'd like to say that our marriage was born out of love, but it would be a lie. While I loved her, by the time she returned to me, she'd lost faith in the world around her and married me simply because she thought she had no other option. But then, I'm getting ahead of myself.

I've already told you I was the seventh son. There were nine years between me and my oldest brothers, John and Elijah, who were twins. Momma had gone five years without bearing any children by the time I came along. One of my brothers told me birthing me nearly killed her and went on to claim Momma had not been the same since I was born.

We were a family in the sense that we were related by blood. But I never really felt as if I belonged. The oldest two boys had moved out west by then, so I never met them. The other boys were older and just seemed to know things I didn't. Like how to talk to Papa, so he didn't whoop on them. I wish they would have taught me that bit of advice, but I always felt they rather enjoyed watching me get my licks. Perhaps that's because my mother coddled me so. I guess I was kind of oblivious to that at the time. I got a rude awakening to the way of things when my momma fell pregnant again. My sister died coming into the world, and in some strange way, she took a part of me with her when she went.

I still recall that day as if it were yesterday. Momma was heavy with child and had not felt well for some days. I thought to cheer her up by bringing her some coins I planned on fishing out of the grate. I grabbed my fishing string and took off to do just that. I was seven at the time and well accustomed to going out on my own.

***

Paddy took the stairs two at a time, heading to the roof. Several of the women from the building were hanging clothes across lines that stretched to the next building. They were deep in discussion and didn't pay him any heed as he ran the length of the building, gathered his feet under him and leapt to the next roof. Once landed, he started his run to get enough speed to make the next jump.

Jumping buildings didn't scare him. He'd been doing it since his brothers had tried to ditch him last year. They'd thought him too chicken to follow, but he'd shown them and further surprised them days later by climbing up the side of a two-story building after seeing another kid do it. While he and some of his friends could climb, he was one of the youngest kids in the neighborhood who could easily climb all the way up the side of a tenement building and onto the rooftop. Perhaps it was because his brothers often sat at the table reading news stories out loud telling about a man named Harry Gardiner, whom the papers called "the Human Fly." His brothers' voices were often filled with awe, further igniting Paddy's desire to outclimb the man as he imagined the smiles on his brothers' faces when they read stories of their own brother climbing to new heights.

Paddy saw the edge approaching, so he gathered his feet and landed with his feet already in motion. A good thing, as he was able to scramble to the other side before the dark man noticed him. While jumping from the rooftops of buildings didn't scare him, he didn't have any desire to tangle with Big Joe, who, according to his brothers, had once killed a man with a single punch. Reaching the next building, Paddy slowed, opened the door that led to the stairs, and stepped inside the stairway. Instantly, the smell of dirty bodies and human waste invaded his nostrils. Holding his breath except for small intervals, he hurried down the stairs, not stopping until he pushed open the outer door and rewarded his lungs with gulps of clean air.

Paddy walked the short distance to the corner store and waited near the edge of the building for the right moment to enter. It didn't take long until he heard the rustle of a skirt and turned to see a woman in a floor-length green dress heading his way. She paid him no heed as she approached and didn't seem to notice as he stepped up behind and followed her inside. He stayed close as she browsed the aisles and was careful to slip into the shadow of her long skirt any time she turned. When the time came for her to pay for her purchases, he slipped up beside her, listening as she chatted with the clerk, then smiling as she told the man to place the merchandise on her account.

Paddy tipped his hat to the clerk and left the store in the woman's shadow, only to return a moment later. The clerk raised an eyebrow when he hurried to the counter.

Paddy smiled a freckled grin and pointed to the gumball jar. "Momma forgot to get me a gumball. I'd like a red one, please. She said to tell you to put it on her account with the rest of her things."

Nodding his understanding, the clerk wiped his hand on his apron, then used a long metal spoon to fish out the preferred gumball, placing it in the palm of Paddy's hand. "You sure you want just one?"

Paddy plopped it into his mouth, smiling as the sweetness filled his senses. "I thank you, sir. I'd like another, but my momma only agreed to pay for one."

"That's what I like to see, a boy whose mother is raising him right. We have enough heathens running amok and living on the street these days. Coming in here and trying to steal from me right under my nose. It's a good day when I get an honest lad inside my store." The clerk smiled and fished out another gumball. "You take this one and slip it into your pocket for later."

Paddy started to take it, then pulled his hand away without accepting. "My momma would not be happy paying for two."

The clerk's smile broadened. "This one is on me. A reward for your honesty."

Paddy grinned, pocketed the second gumball, and hurried outside before the man had a chance to change his mind. He was walking along enjoying the flavor when his friend Buster stepped in front of him.

Nearly double him in height, Buster was three years older than him and the one who'd wised up Paddy and some of his friends to the ways of the street.

Buster sniffed the air. "Where ya going, Paddy?"

Paddy reached into his mouth and pulled out his gum, showing it to the boy. "Fishing in the grates. Wanta come watch?"

"Nah, me and the boys are gonna go do some real fishing," Buster said, looking over Paddy's shoulder. "There's a big to-do at the park. You should come."

Paddy rubbed his backside. The last time he'd tried to pickpocket, one of his brothers had found out and took great pleasure in telling their papa. "Nah, I'm not too good at dipping pockets. I got caught last time."

"You're not going to get good if you don't keep practicing," Buster countered.

"I best be hanging around here. I think Momma's going to have her baby today. She was feeling pretty sour when I left." Paddy shoved his hand into his pocket, felt the gumball and started to offer it to Buster to change his mind about fishing in the grates.

Buster shrugged. "My ma said your mom is too old to have another kid. Said she could die."

It wasn't the first time Paddy had heard that. He'd overheard his papa telling one of his brothers the same thing. Paddy pulled his hand from his pocket, leaving the gumball inside. "Yeah, well, she's having the kid, and there's nothing to be done about it now."

Buster raised his hands. "Don't go getting sore at me. I'm just telling what my ma said."

"Just 'cause she said it don't make it true. Why don't you go on and get out of here?"

"Suit yourself. You see Tommy and the twins, tell them where to find me," Buster said, turning on his heels.

Paddy wished he hadn't run Buster off. Tommy was a simple-minded kid who did what others told him to do. The twins were a bit more level-headed. Maybe that was because they were so much alike and always at each other's side, making it seem as if the two of them were a single entity. So much so that while the boys each had a name, everyone, including Paddy, simply called them the twins.

While Paddy agreed to tell, he knew it was a lie, as he had no intention of telling any of them where Buster was. He had no qualms about dipping pockets; he just didn't want the guilt of having sent them there if they were to get caught. He'd just turned to go in the opposite direction when he saw Tommy and the twins heading straight toward him.

Tommy lifted his arm and pointed past him. "There's Buster!" he said and took off in a sprint.

"You coming?" one of the twins asked when they saw him.

Paddy shook his head. "Nah. I'm staying closer to home today. I have a bad feeling."

"A bad feeling about going or something else?" both boys asked at once.

The feeling had come just as Buster asked him to dip pockets, and while he'd blamed his reluctance on his mother, now he wasn't so sure. He shrugged. "Just a bad feeling."

The boys looked at each other. "Okay."

Paddy didn't know what they meant by the word, as they took off without explaining. He didn't care that they went since it wasn't he who had sent them. Not wishing to follow, he turned, walking back in the direction he'd just come. He stopped at the first grate he found and peered into the hole. *Nothing.* He did the same at the next one and the one after that. He got lucky at the next stop when he peered inside and saw a shiny new dime. Hiding his excitement, he kneeled in front of the grate, pulled the string from his pocket, and spat out his gum. The string was tied around a washer, which when covered with gum, would help fish the coins from the grate. He pressed the gum tightly onto the washer so there was no chance of it falling off. Once he was sure it was secure, he started feeding it through the grate, letting the weight of the washer pull it down. He moved his hand to get a slight swing in the line, then worked to lower it onto the dime.

The moment the gum touched the dime, he pulled it toward him. Halfway up, the dime let go, falling back to the ground beside a second coin he hadn't previously seen. Determined to win his prize, Paddy scrunched up his face and lowered the gum once again. It connected with the coin, and he stuck out his tongue, biting it between his teeth to remind himself to bring the coin up slowly. It worked. Paddy pocketed the coin and lowered the wad once more. This one came up without issue. He slipped the coin into his pocket with the other, smiling a jubilant smile when the coins jingled together.

Pushing off his knees, he pulled the gum free of the washer and plopped it into his mouth, chewing off the dirt to get it sticky once more. Feeling rather pleased with himself, he stopped at each grate he came to, searching for coins. By the time he was ready to go home, he'd found two dimes, a nickel, and six whole pennies.

Paddy dropped the last coin in his pocket, brushed off his knees, and started for home. As he did, the feeling of dread intensified. He looked around to make sure he wasn't being followed by someone who'd seen him pocketing the coins. "Quit being a dope," he said, scolding himself for his insecurities. He'd just opened the door to his tenement building when he heard Tommy calling his name. Paddy stopped and waited for Tommy and the twins to catch up, a chill racing up his spine when he saw tears in the twin's eyes. He let go of the door. "What's wrong?"

"It's Buster," Tommy sobbed. "He got caught with his hand in a lady's purse, and the police hauled him to jail."

"It's true," the twins said, bobbing their heads. "Buster bit the policeman and kicked him in the shin. The copper just smiled and told Buster they'd be sending him off to prison with the murderers and rapists come morning, and how he'd better not try to take something that belonged to one of them or he'd see what he'd get."

Paddy swallowed his gum. He'd heard tales of them sending kids to prison, but up until this moment, he'd never known if it were really true.

Chapter Two

Paddy stood firm as Tommy and the boys ran along the street, spreading the word about Buster's plight. He himself didn't find joy in relaying such news, mainly because his mother always told him to be wary of spreading gossip. Whether true or not, she had held firm in the belief that something like that was sure to come back on a person.

He leaned against the building, revisiting his earlier conversation with Buster and wondering if he had gone with his friend, if he could have warned him of impending danger. *Don't be a dope*, Paddy thought to himself. *If you had gone, you could have ended up in the joint with him.* While true, the knowledge of it didn't make him feel any better. In fact, just thinking of Buster being hauled off by the coppers brought tears to his eyes and made him so upset, he forgot all about taking the coins to his mother.

Tears brimmed his eyes as he turned and walked blindly down the street, imagining all the atrocities a street-smart seven-year-old kid could muster. Not having led a sheltered life, his mind was running amuck, which was precisely why he didn't realize Milo was standing in front of him until it was too late.

Tall and lanky with dark, shaggy hair, a crooked nose, and rags for clothes, fourteen-year-old Milo stood blocking his way. According to Paddy's brothers, Milo once lived in the same tenement building as them and, at the time, was a halfway decent kid. All that changed five years ago when the boy's parents died of the fever, and Milo was cast into the street to fend for himself. It didn't take long for the nine-year-old to surround himself with a small gang of younger boys, each eager to do his bidding. Under the angry orphan's instruction, the gang set out to terrorize the neighborhood where Paddy lived.

Paddy subtly scanned the area. While Milo appeared to be alone, he knew it was only a matter of time before others joined him.

Milo squared his shoulders. "Where ya going, squirt?"

Normally, Milo's appearance would have him quaking in his shoes, but not today. First, he wasn't wearing any shoes, and second, because Buster's predicament weighed too heavy on his mind. Sure, Buster could be a dope at times, but he never minded that Paddy and the others wanted to hang around. The truth of the matter was Buster was a bruiser, and his size kept boys like Milo from messing with them. Without that layer of protection, Paddy and the others would have no chance. Why, they might as well never set foot outside again, as doing so would likely get them pulverized. That, or be forced into doing the one thing Paddy swore he'd never do – join Milo's gang. *Not a chance.* He'd seen some of the things Milo had made the younger kids do, and he'd have no part of it.

His momma always told him all a person needs to learn what's good for them is time. *I just need to do what Momma said and be patient.* She'd also said there was nothing better for the soul than a good night's rest, and his soul sure needed some rest at the moment. He sniffed. Milo might be bigger than him, but without his gang, the boy didn't seem so intimidating. "Go away, Milo. I'm not in the mood." Paddy sniffed.

Milo took hold of Paddy's jaw, tilting it from side to side. "What ya crying about, Red?"

"I ain't crying about nothing," Paddy said, batting his hand away.

"Sure you are, and I know why. It's on account of your friend Buster got hauled off to the clubhouse," Milo said, referring to the police station. "He ain't going to be around to protect you no more 'cause they won't be letting him out. One of my boys got yanked off the street three years back, and I ain't seen hide or hair of him since. Word on the street is the dope got sent to Sing Sing. Poor sap. Can you imagine getting caught stealing a loaf of bread and being sent to a place where they serve you nothing but bread and water?" Milo arched his back, howling with laughter.

Paddy gulped. While Milo might have seen the humor in the situation, he did not. Furthermore, if Milo knew about Buster, it meant his being here was no accident. *Better think of something, Paddy, and make it quick before the boy does what he came here to do.*

Paddy used Milo's moment of levity and took off running. Knowing he was no match for him on foot, Paddy cut into the first alley he came to, did a quick search of the building, and jumped. Digging his fingers into the brick, he pulled himself upward, hand over hand, not bothering to look down until he was safely out of reach. When he did, Milo was nowhere in sight. Not wishing to chance things, he continued his climb, working his way to an open window on the second floor.

Paddy peeked inside, breathing easier when he saw the room was empty. He couldn't see into the other room, so he ducked inside and hurried to the door, leaving before anyone saw him. He ran to the stairwell and opened the door, debating his choice. Milo preferred staying at street level. While he'd seen the kid on the roof plenty of times, he'd never actually seen the boy jump. If he could make it to the top before Milo got there, he could jump to the next building to get home. Deciding that would be the best course of action, Paddy ran up the stairs, pausing only when he opened the door to the roof. There were several clotheslines strung across the flat rooftop, each holding freshly laundered sheets that flapped in the breeze. On any other given day, the subtle snap of the sheets wouldn't bother him, but today, each snap had him jumping. He hurried to the side, made ready to leap to the next building, then caught himself just before making the jump. Why he'd balked, he wasn't sure, as he'd made the jump many times before without issue. Now, something gnawed at him, warning him to proceed with caution.

"Dang it, Howard, stop being a coward," Paddy said, using a phrase his brothers often used to egg him on when they wanted him to do something he didn't want to do. Ignoring both the sheets and his own apprehension, he ran to the other side, stopped at the edge, and turned to face his fear. Taking a deep breath, he charged toward the edge. As he neared, he pushed off the roof, stretching his right leg forward in an invisible step as if doing so would help him close the distance. As he landed, his ankle curled, sending him skidding across the tar roof and tearing the hide off the palms of his hands as a searing pain raced up his leg. "Now you gone and done it. How are you going to explain this one?" Paddy said, scolding himself.

He stood, pressing down on his foot, grimacing as tears spilled from his eyes. Not having any other choice, he lifted his leg and hopped to the door of the stairwell. The moment he opened the door, the stench of the enclosed space invaded his nostrils. Knowing there would be no running to escape the smell, he began the slow trek down.

By the time he reached the fourth floor, the pain in his ankle was so bad, he was nearly oblivious to the smell. Just as he turned to head down the last flight of stairs, he ran smack into the last person he wanted to see.

Paddy gulped. "Milo, what are you doing here?"

Milo plunged his fist into Paddy's nose, the force of it sending him flailing to his backside. Paddy felt the warmth of the blood and cupped his hand underneath in an attempt to keep the blood from ruining his shirt. Milo reached for him, and Paddy scampered out of the way.

Milo laughed.

Paddy scrambled to his good foot and wiped the blood from his nose once more. Lowering his injured leg, he bent his head and ran forward, plowing headfirst into his nemesis. Milo's eyes bugged as he sucked in a breath. Not giving the boy a chance to recover, Paddy began bombarding him with open-handed slaps to both ears. He might not win this fight, but Milo might think twice before cornering him again.

Just when he thought he was gaining the upper hand, two sets of hands clamped firmly on each shoulder, pulling him away from Milo. Paddy knew without looking that the rest of Milo's gang had shown up, and instead of getting the upper hand, he was in serious trouble. He fought to get loose as the boys' fingers dug deeper into his shoulders.

"We got him. Now give him what for," one of the boys who'd grabbed him sang out as Paddy struggled to free himself.

Millo moved forward.

Paddy lifted his bad leg, kicking Milo away, silently cursing himself as tears streamed down his face.

Milo stood glaring at him. Then the crook of his mouth began to curve upward. He squared his shoulders and bent to look over the rail. "I'm done with this crybaby. Throw him down the stairs."

Paddy's mouth went dry as fear washed over him. *The stairs! I'll die for sure.* He summoned all his strength and twisted free of the boys' grips. Lowering his head once more, he plowed straight into Milo, sending him backward. Somehow, he found it in himself to keep going, stepping on Milo's hand as he ran headlong up the stairs. Only seconds ahead of the gang, he opened the door to the hall and ran straight into his papa. Never in his life had he been so happy to see the man.

The happiness was short-lived as his father took hold of his arm, pulling him along as he headed to their apartment.

"Papa, wait up. My leg hurts something awful."

If the man heard his cries, he didn't acknowledge it. By the time they reached the door to the apartment, Paddy's whimpers had turned to sobs.

The last thing he saw before his father yanked him into their apartment was Milo and the boys standing in the doorframe that led to the stairs, staring at them as if they'd just seen the devil himself.

His father turned to face him with disheveled hair and a scowl that sank deep into his forehead. Instantly, Paddy wondered if he'd have been better off letting the boys send him to his demise.

"Stand up straight!" his father bellowed.

Paddy looked at his brothers, who each sat on the sofa staring wordlessly as his father towered over him. Not wishing to look like a baby, he lowered his leg to the floor and fought off a whimper as he lifted it once more.

His father glared at him. "Your mother is near death, and I find you fighting like a mad dog."

"Momma's dying?" Paddy scanned the boys' faces, saw their red-rimmed eyes, and knew his father was telling the truth. He started for the bedroom, and his father doubled his fist. "I wasn't fighting them. They were fighting me," Paddy said, scrambling out of the way.

"You almost killed her once. Seeing you like this will surely do her in this time," his father said, moving forward.

"Kavan," his mother called from the other room.

His father lowered his hand, hurrying to the bedroom on

the other side of the room. Paddy followed at a distance, hopping on one foot, trying to land as quietly as possible. He pushed open the door just enough to peek inside. His mother was lying on the bed. Her dark, sweat-soaked hair lay plastered to her head, and her face was as pale as a waning moon.

Paddy gasped at the sight of her.

His father whirled, then stopped when she called to him once more. She whispered something he could not hear, then patted the man's hand. "Kavan, leave me with my son."

"No."

His mother grimaced while trying to pull herself onto her elbow.

"Let me help you, Bridget." Kavan stooped and gently helped her into a sitting position, then carefully placed a well-worn pillow behind her back and pushed the hair away from her face with a tenderness reserved only for her.

His mother placed her hand on his briefly, then reached for the bundle at her side, bringing it to her chest.

"Momma! You had the baby!" Paddy said, forgetting his pain as he hopped into the room.

His father looked at the bundle, and for a moment, Paddy thought the man was going to cry. Instead, he hung his head and walked from the room without a word.

Paddy took this opportunity to move closer to his mother's bed. He glanced at the bundle and saw the blanket covering the infant's face. "Is the baby dead, then?"

His mother nodded as fresh tears streamed down her face. "She is."

"She? What was her name?"

"She didn't live long enough to be given a name."

Paddy sniffed and wiped his nose with the back of his arm, leaving a trail of blood.

Fresh tears brimmed his mother's eyes. "Did your papa do

that to you?"

Paddy shook his head. "No, Momma, this was Milo." He started to add that the boy was happy that Buster was going to prison but knew his mother didn't approve of him hanging out with the older boy and decided against it. Instead, he reached into his pocket and pulled out the change. "I have money for you, Momma."

She shook her head. "Not this time, Paddy. You keep it."

"But, Momma, you need it."

She closed her eyes momentarily, then opened them once more. "Put it in your pocket, Howard, and don't tell your papa you have it."

His mother rarely called him by his given name, and when she did, he knew she meant business. Paddy returned the change to his pocket, and his mother rewarded him with a faint smile. "Are you okay, Momma?"

She heaved a heavy sigh. "No, Paddy, I am not. The doctor said there's something broken inside of me."

"Broken? Did he fix it?"

She shook her head. "No. He said it can't be fixed."

Paddy glared at the bundle his mother was holding. "Did she break you?"

"I was already broken."

Paddy swallowed. "Papa said…"

His mother firmed her jaw. "Don't you pay any heed to what your papa said. You did not do this to me, and I'll not allow you to take the blame."

Paddy frowned. "Then who should I blame?"

His mother patted the bed beside her. "Sit with me."

Paddy hopped to the side of the bed and sucked in his breath to ease the pain as he climbed up beside her.

"You want to see her?"

He wanted to say no, but his mother seemed to want to show

him, so he nodded his head and watched open-mouthed as she gently pulled the blanket from the baby's face. He wasn't sure what he expected to see, but within the bundle was the tiniest baby he'd ever seen. Her eyes were closed, and her head was covered with dark peach fuzz. He knew without a doubt it was the most beautiful baby he'd ever seen. He longed to touch her but didn't dare ask. "What will you do with her, then?"

"Your papa will take her to the undertaker."

Paddy was incensed. "You mean they're going to put her in a box?"

"Yes. They will bury her in the ground, and when I die, they will bury me with her."

"Then I'm glad you're going to die." He felt her stiffen beside him and instantly regretted his words. "It's not like I want you to die or nothing, but I don't want her to be buried all alone."

"Paddy?"

"Yes, Momma?"

"After I'm gone, I won't be around to see that your papa doesn't hurt you."

He sighed. "I know."

"I want you to leave."

Fear gripped him. "Where would I go?"

"You find yourself a policeman, and when you do, you tell him your momma and papa are dead."

Paddy swallowed. "Why would I do that?"

"Because if he thinks we are dead, he will take you to the asylum to live. It won't be an easy life, but they will see that you are fed, and it will be better than living here or fighting to survive on the streets."

"You want me to lie to the policeman?"

"You must. If you don't, he will bring you back here, and your papa will punish you for leaving." She pulled his chin up and looked him in the eye. "I won't be here to stop him."

Paddy thought about this for a moment. "He doesn't like me, does he?"

"No, Paddy, he does not." The hurt in her voice was evident.

"I didn't mean to hurt you, Momma."

"I know, Howard. I didn't mean to hurt you either."

Paddy jerked his head up. "You never hurt me. Well, sometimes, you spanked me kinda hard, but mostly, I needed it."

"I'm not talking about the spankings. I'm talking about not keeping your papa from beating on you."

"That's okay. He's bigger than you too."

"Promise me you'll go."

"I promise."

"Good. Now go tell Papa I need him to send for the doctor."

"Are you gonna die, Momma?"

She wrapped an arm around his shoulder and pulled him close. "Not tonight, Paddy. I want the doctor to look at your leg. But don't tell your papa that, or he won't go get him. It's best he thinks the doctor is for me."

His mother had never lied to him before, so he didn't think she'd start now. He scooted from the bed and hopped on one foot until he got to the door. Opening it, he saw his father sitting in the chair, whiskey bottle in hand. "Papa?"

"What do you want, boy?" Kavan growled.

"Momma wants you to fetch the doctor."

"Then go fetch him."

"I can't run," Paddy said, glancing at his bum leg.

His father started to get up, then reconsidered, shaking the bottle at the boys instead. "You heard him. Go."

Each of the boys fled the room without a word.

His father took a drink from the bottle and narrowed his eyes at Paddy. "Come out of there and leave your mother alone."

"She told me to come back," Paddy said, ducking back inside the room and closing the door. It was a lie, but at the moment, he really didn't care.

Chapter Three

Paddy sat on a low stool on the rooftop in the shade of an adjoining building as Tommy and the twins scrutinized his leg.

"Is it broke, then?" Tommy asked, poking the bandage with grubby hands.

Paddy batted his hand away. "No, it's not broke, but it hurts a bunch. The doctor said I have to mind it a bit, and it will be good as new."

Tommy lifted a lanky leg and scratched at his ankle. "Was your pop mad about you jumping roofs?"

"Do you think I'm a dope? I didn't tell him the real deal. He thinks it happened when Milo and his boys jumped me."

"I wish Buster was here so that Milo and the boys would get what's coming to them," the twins both said at once.

While Paddy agreed, he also knew it was Milo and his gang who'd invertedly prevented his papa from pounding on him. "If it weren't for Milo, my papa would know the truth."

Tommy frowned. "You mean you're not sore at Milo?"

"Of course, I'm sore. But I'd be a lot more sore if my papa knew I'd been jumping roofs. Why, he'd probably be mad enough to toss me off himself. Probably take great pleasure in it, truth be told."

"Your pop's one ornery cuss," Tommy agreed. "I ain't seen anyone more ornery in all my years."

One of the twins looked up at him. "I heard some of the ladies talking on the stoop. They said your momma's sick."

"Ma ain't sick. She had a baby."

The twins looked at each other, their brown eyes full of doubt. One of them turned and asked the question they already knew the answer to. "The baby died. Right?"

Sadness washed over him at the thought of his sister being underneath all that dirt. He nodded.

"One of the ladies said a baby dying makes a person sick. Said she knew a woman who went mad on account of her baby dying."

"My ma's not mad at anyone. She's just sad."

"Not the kind of mad that gets a person yelling. The kind of mad that makes a person lose their mind," the boy clarified. "You know, like Crazy Mike."

Paddy knew the man the twin was speaking of. Even Milo crossed to the other side of the street when Crazy Mike was hanging around. No one he knew wanted to be around someone who was squirrelly, including him. "My ma's not crackbrained!" Paddy said heatedly. "Her sickness is not in her head. The doctor told her she's broken on the inside and can't have any more babies. My brothers say that's a good thing on account of me and my sister nearly killed her."

"We ain't gonna tell no one," Tommy said when Paddy grew quiet.

"That's 'cause there's nothing to tell," Paddy fumed. Only, there was. He kicked at the ground with his good leg. "My ma told me something."

"What'd she say?" all three boys asked at once.

Even though they were alone on the roof, Paddy looked to make sure no one else was listening. "She told me I should run away."

Tommy blew out a whistle. "Why would she tell you that?"

Paddy looked around once more. "She's sick, remember? She said she won't be able to keep my papa from beating on me if I stay." Okay, it wasn't the whole truth, but he didn't want to think about his mother dying.

"Where does she want you to run off to?" Tommy asked.

"She told me to find a policeman. Said he would take me to an asylum where they'd feed me." It was no secret that most kids lived in fear of being sent to the asylum, but since he didn't see another choice, Paddy said it to gauge his friends' reactions.

Tommy's eyes bugged. "Are you going to go?"

It was a question he'd given a great deal of thought to over the last few days. It had been a week since his mother had made the suggestion. While she hadn't died, she spent most of the time in bed. To make matters worse, his father's rage grew with each passing day. So much so that he'd even taken to beating on the older boys when he tired of taking his anger out on Paddy. Maybe going into an asylum wouldn't be so bad. Sure, he'd heard stories about how kids went inside and never came out, but it wasn't like it was prison or nothing. He knew how to climb, so he was pretty sure he'd be able to climb his way out if things weren't to his liking.

Paddy recalled the night before when his papa had laid into him for not moving out of the way in time. Unlike times in the past, he wasn't trying to irritate the man; he had a bum leg, which made moving out of the way difficult. He swallowed to prevent the tears that threatened. Anything would be better than being beaten all the time.

"Well?" Tommy said when he didn't answer.

Paddy shrugged. "I'm thinking on it."

Tommy and the boys blinked their surprise. It was Tommy who jumped on the statement. "What do you mean you're thinkin' on it? I've heard of fellows trying to get out of the asylum, but I don't know no one who wants to go in."

Paddy laughed. "I was just funnin' you guys. I'm only thinking of the running away part, not the whole policeman part. I ain't got no time for no coppers – specially' not since they took Buster away."

Tommy shook his head. "You'll not last a week on the street. Milo and the boys will pummel you."

"Milo ain't gonna bother me none," Paddy argued.

"You're not planning on joining Milo's gang, are you?" one of the twins asked.

"I wouldn't join his gang for nothing, and he can't make me," Paddy said and spat on the ground.

The other twin spoke up. "But you have to join a gang if you're going to survive the streets. We used to have Buster…"

"Buster's gone!" Paddy said, interrupting him. "The dope went and got himself locked up and there's nothing to be done about that."

"Who's going to protect us from Milo?" Tommy looked like a rabbit about to run.

"I'm tired of worrying about Milo. I ain't scared of him or any of the other gangs. I got you guys and don't need anyone else," Paddy said, trying to sound more confident than he really was. "We can be our own gang."

The twins traded looks, then one of them shook his head. "We like you well enough, Paddy, but we ain't no match for Milo and his boys."

Paddy faked a smile, hoping to charm them into acceptance. "Not yet. But we can get more boys to join us. Then we won't have to be scared no more."

"I d-don't know," Tommy stuttered.

Paddy squared his shoulders. "Well, I know. I'm tired of being pummeled by my old man. If I'm going to be in a fight, I at least want to have a chance to fight back. I'm not going tonight. But as soon as my leg is good enough to jump and climb, I'm leaving. So, you chumps better think about it. Because when I leave, I'm not coming back here."

"Where will you go?" Tommy asked.

To the asylum if you don't agree to go with me. Paddy shook off the thought as he stood and leaned on the wooden crutch the doctor had given him. "I don't know for sure. But no way I'm gonna hang around here and let my papa find me. So, you can either come with me or not. I'm going, and that's that," he said, heading for the rooftop stairs.

He didn't need to look over his shoulder to see if Tommy and the twins were following, as he knew they were not. He wouldn't have followed either if the shoe was on the other foot. He'd be standing there talking with the others. What he didn't know was if the boys were currently trying to talk each other into following him into the unknown or making a case for staying with their family. As he entered the stairwell, his heart began to race. He shook off the fear and slowly began the trek down the stairs while trying not to feel guilty at having asked the boys to leave their homes to accompany him on the street. He thought of Buster and all the times the boy had guilted them into doing something they knew was wrong. If not for his wanting to take some coins home to his mother, and a little nagging voice warning him not to go, he would have followed Buster the day he got nabbed dipping pockets.

Once again, Paddy shook off the thought. This was different. He wasn't trying to get them to dip pockets. This was a bid for survival, as the boys had been correct when they told him he wouldn't last on the streets alone. Getting them to agree to join him was first and foremost on his mind. How they would survive once they were there would have to be worked out later.

He felt Tommy to be a sure thing. Even though the boy was older and taller than him, he was more of a follower than a leader. The twins, on the other hand, could go either way. While they were easily persuaded on their own, together, they had brains enough to know they were better off staying with their family than living life on the street.

Paddy stopped when he got to the place where he'd tangled with Milo the week prior and looked over the rail as he'd done multiple times since the incident. Milo's boys had been seconds away from tossing him over the side when his father showed up. If not for the fact that his father came looking for him when he did, he'd likely be dead right now instead of contemplating life on the street at the hands of Milo and others like him. Paddy gulped. "Papa saved my life." Somehow, the thought of his father doing something nice for him calmed the churning in his gut. By the time he made his way to his apartment, he'd almost convinced himself to stay.

Paddy pushed the door open and looked to make sure his father wasn't inside, then hobbled across the room and stood listening at his mother's door. When he didn't hear anything, he pushed it open and saw she lay facing the wall. He started to circle the bed, but something made him stop. "Momma?"

"What do you want, Paddy?" Her voice was barely audible.

Paddy thought it was perhaps because she had barely eaten anything since the baby died. "Are you hungry? I can get you something to eat."

"No, Paddy."

"But you have to eat, or you'll waste away."

"Go away," she snapped.

Something was wrong. Unlike his father, his momma had always had patience for him. He couldn't recall her ever raising her voice to him unless he'd done something to raise her ire.

Maybe if I make her a little something to eat, she'll eat a few bites. Paddy slipped from the room without another word and went to the kitchen to find something for his mother to eat. Opening the cabinets, he found sugar, flour, lard, cornmeal and a handful of other things he wasn't quite sure of. He closed the door to the cabinet and lifted the lid to the bread box, only to find it empty. There had been Johnny cakes left over from the evening meal his older brother Joseph had cooked. *Papa must have taken them for lunch.*

Paddy had watched his mother make them dozens of times. It didn't look that hard. He used a match to light the stove and pulled the skillet with lard to the burner the way he'd seen his mother do. Next, he pulled a bowl from the cupboard and strained to recall if his mother used cornmeal or flour. He couldn't recall, so he added both. He returned them to the cabinet and pulled out the sugar, adding some to the bowl. He started to put the bag away, then added a bit more. The oil in the skillet started to pop, so he knew he needed to hurry. He took two eggs from the bowl on the counter and broke one into the mixing bowl. He repeated this step with the second egg, frowning when sections of the shell fell into the bowl.

Paddy laid the eggshell on the counter and then went to work digging the broken pieces from the bowl. He'd just dug the last bit out when he turned to see black smoke rolling out of the frying pan.

"Momma! There's a fire!" he yelled as he pulled a glass from the cabinet and filled it with water.

"Paddy, no!" his mother said as she grabbed his arm, pulling him away. As flame rose from the skillet, she covered the pan with a lid. "You can't put water on a grease fire."

"Why not?" Paddy asked, fanning the smoke.

"It just isn't done." She sat heavily in the chair, coughing and batting at the smoke. "What are you doing in here anyway? You could have burned the whole building down."

Paddy's stomach ached as he took in the dark circles under her eyes and noted how her cheeks had sunken in. "You haven't been eating. I was trying to make Johnny cakes for you, so you'd feel better."

His mother used the table to pull herself up from sitting and walked to the counter. Unable to stand upright, she looked into the bowl and then dipped her finger into the mix. "How much sugar did you put in there?"

He held up a spoon. "Three of these."

She arched an eyebrow. "They're going to be sweet, but I think we can save them. I'll see to this: open the window so we can air the place out before your papa gets home."

Paddy used the crutch to limp across the room to open the window and returned to his mother's side as she moved about the small kitchen, working to salvage the mess he'd made. While he wanted to enjoy her being there with him, it was evident in the way her face screwed up each time she moved that she was highly uncomfortable.

"Momma, are you still going to die?"

Her brow furrowed. "We are all going to die someday."

Until recently, he'd never imagined himself dying. Now, he pictured his demise each time he stepped into the stairwell. "Momma?"

"Yes, Paddy?"

"I thought I was going to die that day with Milo. I still think about it sometimes, and I get scared, but I guess I wouldn't be so scared if you were already dead on account of I'd know you were with me being dead."

She turned from the stove, her eyes brimming with tears. "I don't want you to think about dying, Paddy. I want you to think about living."

Paddy felt tears well in his own eyes. "I don't know if I want to if you're not here."

"That's why I want you to leave," she said softly.

He started to tell her he'd been thinking of staying, but the look on her face kept him from doing so. "Momma? How come you didn't tell my brothers to leave?"

She looked him in the eye. "Who said I didn't?"

Paddy sucked in his breath. "You mean you did?"

"I did." She grew quiet for a moment. "But I didn't tell them the same thing I told you."

"What did you tell them?"

"I told each of them they are old enough to make their own way now. I told them they should leave the city and go west to seek out their brothers. I've written John and Elijah and told them to look for the boys and, if they make their way to them, asked if they would look over them and help them get jobs."

"How come I can't go with them?"

"Because you're too little to be on your own."

Paddy firmed his chin. "There are boys younger than me living on the street."

"There are boys younger than you going to jail," his mother countered.

He thought of Buster and eased his stance. "Then why can't I go with my brothers?"

"Because I had you too late."

What's that supposed to mean? "I don't understand," he said, echoing his thoughts.

"It means that your brothers don't think kindly of you, and they won't go easy on you if you were to slow them down." She removed the first batch of Johnny cakes from the stove and placed two on a separate plate to cool before sitting at the table and motioning him to join her. "I'm sorry for the life you've led, Paddy."

Once again, her words confused him. "What do you mean?"

"I mean, a boy should be loved. Something happened the day you were born, and that something took the love out of the house. Your papa was once a good man and a good father to our sons. But something soured him."

"It was me, wasn't it, Momma?"

She blinked, and more tears followed the trail that already flowed. "No, it was me. I knew you would be my last baby, and I loved you so much that, at times, I didn't have room for anyone else. Your papa saw it too, and he was fiercely jealous of the love I have for you. That is why he is harder on you than the other boys. And it is why the boys never accepted you as one of them. I'm sorry, Paddy. I wish I could undo all the pain I've caused, but it is too late for that now." Tears trickled down her face. "I hope someday you will find it in your heart to forgive me."

Before he could answer, the door opened and his father came in. Kavan sniffed the air and glared in Paddy's direction. "What have you been up to, boy?"

Paddy opened his mouth to apologize for almost burning down the building.

His mother placed her hand on his shoulder. "I guess I'm out of practice. I decided to make some Johnny cakes and the skillet got too hot. Before I knew it, the whole place filled with smoke. We might have lost the whole building if not for Paddy's quick thinking."

Kaven raised an eyebrow. "How so?"

"He ran to the stove and put the lid on the pan," she lied.

"Is that the truth of it, son?" his father asked, holding his gaze.

The last thing he wanted was to get his mother in trouble for lying to his father, so he nodded his head, silently echoing his mother's lie.

Chapter Four

May 1916

Paddy woke, turned on his side, and remained perfectly still as he stared into the darkness, trying to figure out what had pulled him from sleep. He heard soft footsteps in the dark and held his breath as the steps paused beside his sleeping pallet.

"Are you awake?" Joseph whispered.

Something told him not to answer, so he lay there unmoving. Just as he thought he would explode, Joseph walked away, and he quietly let out his breath.

"The kid's still asleep. Now pipe down before you wake him. The last thing we need is for him to rat us out to Papa. The old man finds out we're leaving, and he's bound to figure out a way to stop us."

Leaving! But Momma isn't even dead. Paddy was just about to say as much when Benjamin spoke.

"What about Paddy?"

"What about him?" Joseph replied. "You heard Ma. She said we're not to take him with us."

"That's because he's her favorite. She won't be around much longer. Are we just to leave him to Papa?" Benjamin said.

"Ma said to leave him be, and that's what we'll do. It'll be hard enough to find food for the four of us. I, for one, don't want to listen to no baby crying on account of he's hungry," Joseph said.

Paddy swallowed his tears. *I'm not a baby.*

"So how do we know when to leave," Michael asked, pulling him from his thoughts.

"You heard Papa. The doctor said she's given up. He didn't tell you, but he told me how the doctor wanted to take her away, but Papa said how he didn't want her to go to one of those places."

"What kind of place?" Michael asked, echoing Paddy's thoughts.

"The doctor called it something, but Papa got mad and said they weren't taking his wife to no nut house," Joseph replied.

"A nut house? You mean like for crazies?" Daniel asked.

"Sure, what other kind of nut house is there?" Joseph asked.

"You mean Ma's crazy?" Michael's words were loud and clear.

Joseph shushed him. "Must be if the doctor wants to put her in the nut house."

Michael blew out a low whistle. "Well, what do you know about that?"

"So, when do we go?" Benjamin asked.

"Not until Momma's gone." Daniel's tone left no room for discussion.

"Yeah, it won't be long. But we'll stick around until she's in the ground and buried," Joseph said.

A knot formed in Paddy's stomach. His ma wasn't crazy. She was just sad. He'd just decided to tell them that when the outer door slammed.

"Papa's home!" Joseph said in an excited whisper. The bed squeaked as all four boys scrambled to get in.

The room grew quiet. Paddy lay there in the darkness, waiting for something to happen. It didn't. Sometime later, sleep overtook him.

***

August 1916

Paddy hurried down the stairs, eager to put the coins he'd been saving in the sock under his pillow. He opened the door to the hallway leading to their apartment, when he saw Joseph leaning against the wall.

Joseph stepped in front of him. "You been on the roof?"

Paddy nodded.

"The leg good enough to jump?"

Though his leg was perfectly fine, and he'd been back to jumping roofs for over a month, it wasn't like his brother to take an interest in him, so Paddy nodded once more.

Joseph looked him in the eye. "Big Joe's back in town. Papa told me he killed a man. Killed him dead with just one punch."

Paddy gulped. "Who'd he kill?"

"Papa didn't say, but you best make sure Big Joe doesn't catch you on his roof. A person steals a soul once, they won't be afraid to do it again."

Paddy cocked his head at Joseph. "What do you care if my soul gets took?"

"I'm your brother," Joseph replied.

Paddy narrowed his eyes. "Brothers look out for each other."

Joseph laughed. "I just told you about Big Joe. If that ain't looking out, I don't know what is."

"I guess," Paddy said with a shrug. "But it's not the same as really caring."

"I told you about Big Joe and asked about your leg. What more do you want?"

"I want you to take me with you when you go," Paddy blurted.

Joseph took hold of Paddy's shirt and slammed him into the wall. "Who told you about that?"

"No one," Paddy said, struggling to get free.

"What do you mean no one?" Joseph's breath was hot

against his face.

Paddy stilled. "I heard you all talking about it that night in the room."

Joseph leaned in and twisted the neck of Paddy's shirt as his words came out in a menacing whisper. "You tell anyone, and you won't have to worry about Big Joe. I'll throw you off the roof myself. Then I'll tell Papa you tried to jump and missed."

Paddy kicked up his knee and connected with Joseph's privates with such force, the boy groaned and let him go.

"See, I'm not a baby. I can take care of myself," Paddy said as Joseph struggled to stand up straight.

"Too bad. We're not taking you with us, and that is that," Joseph said between breaths.

"You'd rather leave me here with that monster."

"Just stay away from Big Joe." Joseph's words were coming easier now. "You can run faster than him. He can't hurt you if he can't catch you."

Paddy looked his brother in the eye and held his gaze. "That's not the monster I'm talking about. Papa hates me and will kill me for sure if I stay. You know it's true. Momma believes it too, and that's why she told me to leave." Paddy slapped a hand to his mouth. He had not intended to tell of his conversation with his mother.

Joseph glanced over his shoulder. "You mean Ma told you to leave?"

The cat was out of the bag, so there was no use pretending he hadn't said it. "Uh-huh."

"She told us not to take you, and she wouldn't want you living on the streets. Where'd she tell you to go."

"She told me to find me a policeman and tell him to take me to the asylum."

Joseph's eyes widened, then recovered as a slow smile spread across his face. "That's good."

Paddy frowned. "It is?"

"Sure, it is. What are you, a dope? Why, if you were to go with us, you'd have days of having to go to bed hungry. But not if you're in the asylum, because they have to feed you in there."

Paddy scratched at his head. "They do?"

"Sure they do. They can't lock kids up and not feed them after all. You're probably going to get all kinds of food. My mouth is watering just thinking about it."

"It is?" Paddy studied Joseph's face, trying to see if his brother was fooling him.

Joseph clamped him on the shoulder. "I'm telling you, you'd better not tell the others about this, or they won't want to come with me."

"You mean they'd want to come with me instead?" Paddy's voice was hopeful.

"Yes, but that's not the way of it, on account of they have to come with me."

"Why?"

"Because Ma said so. You trust her, don't you?"

Paddy nodded.

"Then you have to trust she knows what's best for us all. And if she told you to go into the asylum, then that's what you are supposed to do, and going to find our brothers is what me, Michael, Benjamin, and Daniel are supposed to do." Joseph looked down the hall and lowered his voice. "I don't want you talking to the brothers about this."

"How come?"

"I've already told you, we can't let the thought of good food stop them from doing what Ma told us to do."

"What's the other reason?" Paddy asked.

"We can't let Papa overhear that we're planning on running away after Ma dies. We'll all have to leave at the same time on account of if we don't, he'll be watching us. He won't want us leaving, so he'll find a way to make sure we can't leave. Why, he might be so mad, he locks us in our room."

Paddy firmed his chin. "He does that, I'll climb out the window."

Joseph shook his head. "There you go, just thinking about yourself. You'd climb out that window and leave the rest of us there to fight the old man."

It was true. While Paddy had no problem climbing the building, his brothers had never been able to. "Joseph, how come you and the brothers never learned to climb?"

Joseph shrugged. "Probably because no one ever told us to try."

"I've told you plenty of times," Paddy reminded him.

"Yeah, but by then, it was too late. Once you get old like me and the boys, you learn to be too scared to do stupid things."

"Climbing buildings isn't stupid. It keeps Milo and the gang from getting to me."

"It's not stupid if you can do it, but if you can't, then you end up dead. I used to think you were the daftest person I knew, the way you climb up the side of buildings, but that's because I was always too scared to climb more than a few bricks. But not you, no sir. From the very first time, you just dug in your fingers and toes, and started climbing, without even worrying about falling."

Paddy laughed. "Sure, I was scared. But you always read me stories about the Human Fly, and I thought if he could do it, then I could too. Then I told you I was going to try, and you all were watching me, so I couldn't back out. I didn't want you to think me a baby." Paddy recalled them saying that very thing only months before and felt his face grow hot. "Why are you being so nice to me?"

"Because we're brothers."

"Yeah, but you're never nice to me."

Joseph sighed. "I guess it's because once we leave, we probably won't ever see each other again."

The comment hit him so hard, tears welled in his eyes. Paddy hurried to brush them away.

Joseph placed a hand on his head and roughed his mop of red hair. "It's okay, kid. I won't call you a baby if you cry."

***

Cindy stared at the journals in disbelief. "Do you think Grandpa Howard really climbed up the side of buildings?"

Linda looked up over the paper she held. "It's written in his hand. Why would he lie?"

Cindy sighed. "It's a building? He was just a kid."

Linda took her glasses off and rubbed the side of her nose. "I remember a kid in my class used to climb. Of course we were in high school and the girls were having a sleepover, and he wanted to see things he shouldn't have been seeing. One of the girls saw him peeking in the window and screamed."

"Mom, I'm being serious."

"So am I," Linda assured her. "Scared him so bad, he let go and fell. Broke his leg in three places."

"It's scary to think that if Grandpa had fallen, I wouldn't be here," Cindy replied.

"You'd have been here," Linda assured her. "You just would have had a different last name."

Deciding not to start with that again, Cindy picked up her papers and began to read.

Percival, a kid we called Slim on account of he was, proved to be one of my best friends. Maybe it was because I met him at just the right time. I still recall that day as if it were yesterday.

***

Paddy ran across the roof, smiling as the coins clanged together in his pocket. He'd been lucky to find enough pennies to match all his fingers and most of his toes today—pennies he planned to add to the sock hidden under his pillow. He jumped and landed on his feet just as Big Joe turned. Not giving the man time to snatch his soul, Paddy took off running and leaped to the other building, landing with a soft thud. He was about to take off again when he stopped and stood watching a boy float about the roof. The kid was several heads taller than him, probably because he was mostly legs. His dark hair was cut short, and looked as if he'd been to one of the barbers where people actually paid money to have it done. His eyes were closed, and his arms waved about, causing him to look much like a puppet gliding through the air being pulled by an invisible string. Paddy had seen the kid before but had never spoken to him, mainly because the boy was always with his mother, a good-looking dame who often wore clothes that left little to the imagination.

Paddy felt a blush creeping up his cheeks as he recalled the time he'd been ogling the woman's gams, and his own mother had snatched him by the hand, dragging him across the street as if being on the same side of the road would somehow corrupt him.

Paddy shook off the memory and felt the flush leave his face. The woman wasn't here now, and neither was his momma, so there was no reason to leave. If anyone else had been with him, he would have had no option but to laugh, but since he was alone, he stood staring in awe at the way the boy floated around the roof without a care in the world. The kid must have felt him watching, as he opened his eyes and looked at him as if he'd just got caught dipping his hand in a policeman's pocket.

Paddy laughed then narrowed his eyes. "Whatcha gaping at?"

The boy blinked several times before speaking. "Are you magic?"

Paddy scratched at his head. "Magic? Why, whatever gave

you that idea?"

"My momma told me leprechauns are magic." The words were no sooner spoken than the boy started dancing in place. He continued talking as if nothing were amiss. "Said they granted farmers wishes."

"Yeah, well, I ain't no leprechaun. Even if I was, you sure don't look like no farmer, so I wouldn't be granting you a wish no how." Unable to ignore the boy's legs, Paddy pointed at them. "You're the one hopping around like a toad in the rain. Maybe I should be questioning you. What makes you think I'm a leprechaun anyhow?"

"Because you've got red hair and the door to the roof's over there," the boy said with a backwards glance.

Paddy realized the boy hadn't seen him land on the roof. "I got red hair 'cause I'm Irish. Least that's what my momma says. She says I take after my papa. I don't, though. My papa's an ornery soul. Drinks too much and likes to beat on me and my brothers. Momma said he's got the devil in him, said I gots it in me too on account of I have red hair."

The boy stretched his neck, looking him up and down the way Paddy had seen his momma do when inspecting vegetables she bought from the wagons. Paddy frowned. "Now whatcha gaping at?"

The boy shrugged. "Trying to see the devil, is all."

Paddy waved him off. "You can't see the devil."

The boy sighed. "You can't?"

"No, the devil is in the actions." Paddy scratched his head once more. "Least I think so."

The boy's eyes grew wide. "You don't know?"

"No, but when my papa gets mean, my momma says the devil's in him, so I figure that to be true."

"Do you think the devil put you here?" the boy asked.

"Why, I never thought of that. Do you think he did?"

"He must have, 'cause you didn't use the door," the boy replied.

Understanding washed over him, and Paddy laughed. "Oh, that. No, it wasn't the devil. I jumped."

The boy's mouth dropped open. "Jumped?"

Paddy yanked his thumb over his shoulder and smiled a wide smile. "Yeah, from the other roof. I do it all the time."

The boy's face paled. "You do?"

"Sure, lots of kids do it, especially at night. It's safer than walking the streets. Why, a kid gets caught on the streets at night and," he thought of Milo and his gang, "well, it can be real bad."

"Ain't you afraid of falling?" the boy asked.

"Nah, you just have to know the ones to jump. We've done it enough, we know. Like that side there," he said, pointing to the far side. "Only experienced jumpers would try that. And then only the ones with long legs. You got ya some long legs, and they seem to like to move, so you could maybe make it. I wouldn't try it until you've jumped a few of the easier ones. 'Cause if you get scared, you might not jump so good, and you'd end up splattered on the street. That happens, and they'd scrape your body into a wagon with a shovel. I've seen it happen."

The boy swallowed. "I've slept up here at night. Why ain't I never seen ya?"

"We've been here, my friends and me. We know to be quiet."

The boy seemed satisfied with his answer. "You got a name?"

Sheesh, the kid's daft. "Course I got a name. Everybody's got one."

"Well, what is it?"

"My name's Howard, but everyone calls me Paddy on account of I'm Irish and have red hair."

"What's that noise?" the boy asked, staring past him.

Paddy tilted his head toward the sound. *Big Joe.* "Nothing you need to concern yourself with."

"But what is it?" the kid pressed.

"It's Big Joe. You don't want anything to do with that guy. I heard he stole a man's soul, that one. My papa said Big Joe kilt the man with just one punch. You ever see him, you run," he said, echoing his brother's warning. Just knowing Big Joe was near made his skin crawl. While he liked talking to the boy, he wanted nothing to do with the man. "I best be going."

A frown flitted across the boy's face. "Will you be back?"

"I might. Tomorrow." Paddy took off without another word, running the length of the building, leaping just as he reached the edge. Having distanced himself from Big Joe, he slowed and revisited his conversation with the kid. He laughed, remembering how the boy thought he was a leprechaun. Dang it, all that talk about Big Joe, and he'd forgotten to get the kid's name. He stopped, intending to go back, when he heard the door to the stairwell open, and he saw Milo and the gang. Milo was looking over his shoulder, laughing at something one of the other boys said. Paddy sprinted across the roof, leaping to the other side without a backward glance.

Chapter Five

It was the middle of the day, and his mother had yet to get out of bed. Paddy tiptoed into her room and stood staring at her from the edge of her bed. "Momma?" The word was barely audible even to his ears.

Several moments passed until her eyelids fluttered and then opened, focusing on him with sunken eyes. "Howard, my favored son. How difficult this all must be for you."

"Yes, Momma."

"It will all be over soon, my wee lad."

"I don't want it to be over." Paddy's voice cracked as he spoke.

"I know, but this is the way of it. And when I'm gone, you will be free to be a boy again."

"I don't understand."

She patted the bed beside her. "Sit with me." Paddy did as she said and leaned into her touch when she brushed the hair from his eyes with trembling fingers then rubbed at the space between his eyes. "There is too much sadness in your eyes these days. I want you to promise you'll remember me as I was and not as I am."

"How do I do that when I feel so sad?" Just talking about his sadness brought tears to his eyes.

"It might take time, but you'll overcome it and find your happy place once more. Do you remember what I told you before about getting things you want?"

"You told me I had to believe."

"That's right. You can have whatever your heart desires if you just find the patience to wait."

"I don't want to have patience if it means watching you die!" Paddy blurted.

"You don't have to, Howard."

"But?"

"No buts. I want you to leave."

"I know; you already told me."

"No, I mean today. Right now. I want you to take the money you've been saving and go find the policeman like I told you. That way, when you think of me, I will be alive." His mother struggled to pull herself up to a sitting position and smiled a strained smile. "This is the way you will remember me. And when you think of me, you will know that you were my favorite son. Now go, gather your things before Papa and the boys get home. GO!" she said when he hesitated.

"Okay, Momma," Paddy said, scrambling from the bed.

"And make sure you don't come back here, as the only thing you'll find in this apartment is pain."

Paddy raced from the room, battling fresh tears as he shook the pillow from its case. He then retrieved the change he'd been hoarding and added his extra shirt and trousers to the cloth bag. His resolve wavered as he looked at the bed where each of his brothers had slept for as long as he could remember and recalled Joseph's words. *Once we leave, we probably won't see each other again.* Paddy firmed his chin and spoke to the room. "It doesn't matter; they don't like me anyway. I'll go just like Momma said. Who cares if Papa gets mad and locks them in their room? Momma's right, I have to go, or Papa will keep me here forever." *Or kill me.*

The thought had him running from the room and bolting out

the door with no thought other than getting as far away from the tenement as possible. He reached the stairway, started downward, then decided against it and sprinted up the stairs. Once there, he raced across the roof, jumped to the next building, and continued to the one after that. He wasn't sure where he was going, only that he wanted to get as far away as possible so that his papa and brothers wouldn't find him.

Paddy landed on the roof of the building where Big Joe lived and saw the glistening silhouette of the boxer standing under the structure. Facing the opposite direction, the man's skin was so dark, he looked much like a shadow.

He doesn't look like all that much. Paddy had no sooner had the thought than Big Joe raised his arms and pounded his fists one after another into a bucket-size leather bag hanging from a board at the top of the rooftop shanty. While Paddy had seen the man on the roof plenty of times before, he'd never actually seen the boxer in action. Intrigued, he crept to the corner and hid in the shadows, watching the hulk of a man beat the bag with fists double the size of a normal man's.

The bag fought back, coming at him after each punch, but Big Joe didn't seem to care, as he kept pounding it away again. Paddy remembered what Joseph had said about Big Joe killing someone with a single punch and decided to take his leave. Just as he stood, he heard yelling coming from the roof next door. Big Joe must have heard the commotion too, as he stilled the bag and started off in the direction of the voices.

Paddy followed at a distance as the man crossed the roof in long, confident strides, then felt his mouth drop open as Big Joe easily made his way onto the next building without a running start.

Intrigued, Paddy crouched, peeking over the side and shivering as Big Joe's voice boomed a warning for all to hear. He crawled to his right to get a better look and gulped as he saw what had gotten the man so riled. Milo and his gang had the boy with the dancing legs surrounded and looked very much as if they planned on tossing him off the roof.

Paddy recalled his own encounter with the gang months earlier and shivered once more. *That Milo. Someone needs to throw him off the roof.*

As if hearing his thoughts, Big Joe called the long-legged boy over and asked him if he wanted the man to do just that. Much to Paddy's chagrin, the boy declined the offer. *Man, where was Big Joe when Milo tried that with me? I would have told him to toss him over the side and not be a bit sorry for it.*

Big Joe placed his hands on the long-legged boy's shoulders and told Milo and his gang that the kid was now under his protection, and if anyone messed with him, they would answer to him. Paddy gulped as he realized this was the answer to his prayers. The kid liked him, or at least he thought it to be true. If he could get the boy to ask Big Joe to protect him as well, all his troubles would be over. Not only would he not have to go into the asylum, but his papa was afraid of the guy. If he ever found him, all he'd have to do was tell his papa that Big Joe would steal his soul and his father would leave him be. *Maybe I should go over there right now. No, that won't work. They'll think I saw the whole thing and call me a coward for not helping. But I didn't see the whole thing, so I couldn't have helped even if I wanted to.* Paddy frowned. *Would I have helped if I'd known?* "No." He knew the answer even before whispering it aloud. He would have stayed rooted in fear and then lived with the guilt until his dying day.

Humbled by the knowledge, he sank to the ground with his back to the edge of the low wall, which was a good thing, as seconds later, Milo and his gang landed not more than a few feet away. Not that they were looking for trouble, as they were off the moment they landed. The fact that they had landed was troubling, as none of the boys were known to frequent the rooftops. Paddy knelt and looked over the wall to the other side, watching as Big Joe and the boy with the long legs entered the stairwell. He turned once again, sitting with his back to the wall.

Now, what am I to do? While he wanted to honor his mother's wish, he wasn't quite ready for dinner and, therefore, didn't feel the need to get himself locked into the asylum. *Where will I sleep?* Paddy scanned the rooftop, his gaze landing on the open structure where Big Joe was practicing his punches. Until today, he and everyone else he knew never dared look in that direction for fear of the man snatching their soul. Paddy got up and walked to the shanty. It wasn't much, but it would keep him off the street and keep the rain off of him if need be. *What if Big Joe catches me sleeping there?* He shrugged off the thought. *Then I'll lie and tell him I'm afraid of Milo and didn't have anywhere else to go.* Only it wasn't a lie, and the knowledge of that scared him more than having Big Joe discover him sleeping there.

***

A week had passed since his mother sent him away, and he still hadn't turned himself in to the police. He'd spent his evenings in the rooftop shanty on top of Big Joe's building, leaving just as the sun rose to keep from encountering the man. Most of his days were spent next door on the rooftop of the building where he'd met the long-legged kid, hoping the boy would come up. So far, that hadn't happened. And since Paddy didn't know which apartment the kid lived in, it wasn't as if he could go knock on the boy's door. What he did know was something better happen soon, as he was nearly out of coins and would be in danger of going hungry in the coming days. He kicked at the tar roof and blew out a sigh as he dipped his hand into his pocket and felt the weight of the washer he kept tied to the string and the gumball he'd purchased the day before when he noticed his coins dwindling.

"I may as well go fishing for pennies." Paddy looked across the roof, then decided to take the stairs instead. He hated the stairs, as they reminded him of Milo and his gang. But, unless he wanted to climb down the building, he didn't have any other options. Plus, if the boy was on his way up to the roof, he didn't want to chance missing him. Paddy hurried down the stairs, stopping at each landing, opening the doorway, and searching the hallway for any sign of the kid. Not seeing him, he closed the door and raced to the next level and the one after that until he'd reached the first floor and pushed his way outside, sucking fresh air into his lungs as he surveyed the street for threats.

Normally, the main threat would be running into Milo and his gang, but somehow, after Big Joe put the fear in them, they felt like the least of his worries. Instead, his gaze snaked from side to side, looking for his Papa and brothers, knowing running into them could prove disastrous. He came to an alleyway and hesitated, waiting for several men he'd passed earlier. As they strolled past, he fell into step beside them. The men continued forward without conversing. If the fellow next to him noticed him tagging along, he must not have cared, as he never said a word to dissuade him. After several blocks, he saw Tommy and the twins heading his way and slowed, allowing the men to move forward on their own.

"Where've you been?" Tommy asked as he neared.

Paddy shrugged. "Around."

"Around where?" Tommy pressed. "You haven't been to school. Joseph came looking for you. Said he'd give me a whole penny if I told him where you were."

"You don't tell him nothing!" Paddy said, whirling on him. "He don't have a penny to give."

Tommy glanced at the twins. "That's what they said, and besides, you know I'm not a snitch."

"Sure, I know you're not. I just don't like Joseph checking up on me. What'd he want anyhow?" Paddy said, easing his tone and fishing for information.

Tommy shrugged. "He didn't say what he wanted on account of I didn't have nothin' to tell him."

Somehow, the boy's answer, or lack thereof, appeased him. If his mother had died, Paddy felt certain Joseph would have used that information for leverage. "Good, on account of my doings are none of his business!"

"Then there's nothin' to be sore about. You're here now. Are you coming to school, then?"

"Nah. I'm gonna go fishing for dimes," Paddy said, hoping it to be true. While they all wanted dimes, mostly they found pennies and nickels instead. He pulled his fishing line and washer from his pocket to entice them. "Wanna come?"

The boys looked at each other, and for a moment, he thought they'd say no. Finally, Tommy bobbed his head. "Count me in."

The twins smiled and nodded their agreement.

***

Paddy knelt over the grate, biting his tongue as he concentrated on placing the wad of gum directly on the dime. Though they'd found a few pennies, the dime would ensure he could eat for at least a handful of days if he were careful what he spent it on. Just as he was lowering the line, a feather floated across the grate. He looked up, his eyes widening at seeing a woman with the best set of gams he'd ever laid eyes on. She caught him looking and smiled a painted smile so broad, he nearly let go of the line. He tightened his grip just in time to see under the woman's coat. Feathers. Lots of them, barely covering things a boy his age could only dream of seeing. Someone whistled, and the woman's smile disappeared. Another whistle, along with something that made him blush, had her looking around and responding to the comment just as she stepped off the curb. Her ankle turned, and she fell. Tires screeched and someone who sounded a lot like him screamed.

Paddy scrambled to his feet and raced to where the painted woman now lay covered in feathers that were quickly becoming the color of her lips. He stared at the scene for way too long, taking in the mangled mess. Someone grabbed hold of his shoulder. Only then did he realize he was in the street, standing in her blood. He felt the color drain from his face and pushed his way through the crowd that had gathered, the only thing on his mind to outrun the image in his head. He raced down the street for some time before pulling open a door, hurrying into the building, and climbing the stairs without knowing where he was going. He forced himself to keep running. He had to get as far away from the street and that image as possible. He heard someone calling his name, and still, he kept running and leaping from one roof to another until, at last, the words seeped through the fog that had clouded his brain.

"Slow down. The man's not out here," Tommy called after him as he jumped to the next roof.

Paddy landed on Big Joe's roof and saw the boy with the dancing legs standing there with his fists at the ready. Before he could ask him what he was doing, the boy began to laugh. *The simple action was all that was needed to pull Paddy from his shock.* "What's so funny?"

The boy swiped at a tear without speaking.

The twins stepped up beside him. "You know this kid, Paddy?"

Paddy nodded his head. "Yeah. I don't know his name, but we've talked some."

"The name's Percival," the boy replied. "They call me Slim."

"This is Tommy, Jacob, and Joshua. Don't worry if you can't remember their names; we can't tell them apart, so we just call them both 'twins'." Paddy saw the color on the boy's cheek that matched the color of the blood and felt a wave of nausea. "You been smooching a dame?" he asked to cover his unease.

Slim shook his head. "Nah, it was my momma doing the smooching."

Paddy blew out a low whistle. "Ain't no ma I never saw that wears paint like that."

"We best be g'tting. I don't wanna be round here no more," Tommy said, looking over his shoulder.

"Don't worry," Paddy said. "Big Joe's not gonna be up here anytime soon. I saw him and a bunch of others in the crowd. They'll all be busy gawking for a while yet."

"That dame was messed up," Tommy replied.

"Shut up, Tommy," Paddy said, silencing the kid.

"You were scairt too. That's why you ran. Not that I blame ya, seeing sumptin like that…"

"I wasn't scared," Paddy lied. "I just didn't want to stick around, is all. You know what my pop will do if he finds out I didn't go to school."

"What happened?" Slim asked.

The boys all looked at each other, fidgeting as if deciding who would tell the tale. Paddy hoped one of the others would tell what happened, but they seemed to be waiting for him. He swallowed the bile that threatened. "The boys and I were fishing in the grates when we heard someone whistle. We looked up and saw a dame coming down the street. Now, this wasn't any dame. She was a real looker. And those legs, they were fine gams, to be sure."

"She was a looker for sure," Tommy said, agreeing with him. "Downright shame."

One of the twins elbowed him. "Pipe down, Tommy. Let Paddy tell it."

Paddy went on to describe what happened in great detail.

"What was her name?" Slim asked as his legs drummed the ground, seemingly on their own.

"Drug her down the road he did, feathers flying everywhere," Tommy said sadly. "Kilt her dead."

"WHAT WAS HER NAME?!" Slim's legs moved from side to side as if they didn't know which direction they wanted to go.

Tommy blurted out the wrong name. Paddy shook his head. "No, Tommy, that wasn't it. He called her Margareta."

At the mention of the woman's name, Slim's legs seemed to quit working as he crumpled to his knees without a word.

"What's wrong with him?" one of the twins asked.

"Maybe his legs were hurting. They were jumping sumptin' fierce," Tommy offered.

Paddy shook his head. "Nah, I think maybe the story made him sad."

Slim lifted his head and cried out through his tears. "The woman, she's my mother."

A knot formed in the pit of Paddy's stomach, and he blew out a long whistle. Is that why he came here? Had something told him this was where he needed to be? "Of all the dumb luck."

"I want to see her," Slim said, finding his voice.

Paddy recalled the sight he'd just seen and struggled to figure out a way to get out of returning to the scene.

"You can't," Tommy said, shaking his head. "It ain't right a kid seeing his momma that way."

"Not right," the two smaller boys agreed.

"I've got to make sure," Slim said, staring directly at Paddy. "Please show me."

"I don't know. Maybe you should get your pop to take you," Paddy said nervously.

"My papa's dead," Slim said, narrowing his eyes.

"You got any other family?" Paddy asked.

Slim shook his head. "Momma has kin in Italy, but that's not around here."

Paddy looked at the others as they realized what the boy had said. "You don't tell no one else that. They find out you don't have any kin, and they'll take you to the asylum."

"Or in prison. That's where they took Buster, remember?" one of the twins said.

Paddy shook his head. "Buster was different. He got caught dipping pockets. They wouldn't throw Slim in the big house for being an orphan. They'd toss him into the asylum."

"I heard tell it ain't so bad. At least they'll feed ya," Tommy said.

Paddy started to agree with him.

"I'm going. With or without you," Slim said, batting his eyelids against the tears.

"I'll go with you." One of the twins stepped forward. "I don't want to, mind ya, but ain't no one should see that alone."

"I'm coming too," Tommy said, and the other boy nodded his head.

Paddy was out of luck. If he didn't agree to return, he would forever be looked upon as a coward. "I'll go."

"What about your pop?" Tommy asked. "He nearly kilt you last time."

"I ain't afraid of him," Paddy said, jutting his chin. He thought to tell them he'd run away, so he never had to worry about his papa anymore, but it didn't seem like the time. Instead, he turned to Slim and apologized for looking under his mother's coat. When the boy didn't say anything, Paddy took off running across the roof, easily making it to the other side. Starting for the next, he looked over his shoulder and realized the boy wasn't among them. He stopped. "Stay here, I'll go see what's up with the dope." He ran across the roof and found the kid right where they'd left him. "I thought you wanted to see if she's your ma?"

"Can't we just take the stairs?" Slim asked.

Paddy shrugged. "This way's faster."

"I'm scared. I've never jumped the roof before."

"You don't live in this building." Paddy knew it to be true, as he'd slept here for the last week. "How'd you get over here?"

"I used the stairs. I was coming to see…"

"It don't matter," Paddy said, cutting him off. "We've got to get going before the meat wagon comes to take your ma away. They do that, and they'll not let you see her."

Slim's eyes bugged. "I've got to see her. I need to be sure."

Paddy wanted to tell the boy he understood. The thought of his own ma dying was bad enough. He had no clue how he'd feel at learning she'd been hit by a truck. He softened his tone. "Then you need to come and see for yourself."

Slim nodded his readiness, and Paddy turned toward the building. "Whatever you do, don't look down. Keep your eyes on where you want to go, and just keep running until there's no roof left, then jump. Don't worry 'bout nothing. You got yourself some long legs that like to move, so you'll do just fine," Paddy said, hoping it was true. He started to tell the boy if he didn't make it, he'd tell the men who came to scrape him from the sidewalk to put him in the same box with his momma but decided against it. Sometimes, things like that were better left unsaid.

Chapter Six

Watching his friend Slim break down after seeing his mother wrenched his soul and reminded him of his own plight. Not wishing to revisit the pain of either, he'd distanced himself from the boy, the guilt of which tormented him further. He spent his days aimlessly walking the streets and his nights in smelly stairwells. Once, he'd even approached a policeman with the intention of turning himself in, only to run away the minute the man asked him why he wasn't in school.

Now, he wanted nothing more than to return home to his mother, even though he knew it meant dealing with his papa's abuse. Paddy hid in the shadows across the street from their tenement building waiting for his papa and brothers to leave. Each time the door opened, he let out a frustrated sigh until, at last, his papa stepped out and placed his hat upon his head. The man looked in his direction, and for a moment, Paddy thought he'd seen him. He held his breath, letting it out once more, when his papa stepped off the stoop and turned, walking up the sidewalk without a backward glance. Paddy stayed in his hiding place for several moments, expecting his brothers to follow, and frowned his confusion when they did not.

Could it be true? *Has Papa really locked them in the room like Joseph said?*

He looked to the window, expecting to see them staring out at him. *Nothing.* Paddy wasn't sure if he should be disappointed or relieved. What he did know was he needed to go to the apartment and see his momma. He pushed off from his hiding place and darted across the road.

Dodging around a wagon pulled by a swayback horse, he sucked in his breath as he stopped short of being mowed down by a buggy on the other side. He waited for it to pass, then ran to the tenement, hurried inside, and rushed up the stairs while praying his mother would be more relieved to see him than angry about his return.

Eager anticipation mounted as Paddy opened the door and stepped inside. Confusion replaced anticipation as he looked about the room, saw nothing as it should be, and his senses screamed a warning that he was in the wrong apartment. He scratched his head, then stepped back into the hallway, pulling the door closed behind him. He hurried to the stairway, checking the number to see if he was on the correct floor. He was. Even though he'd lived in the same place all his life, he retraced his steps, walking slower this time to be sure he entered the correct apartment.

His hand hovered over the doorknob as he gathered the courage to open it. As he pushed the door open, he was greeted by a slight woman with reddish-brown hair who held an infant, which stared at him with brilliant blue eyes. The woman hiked the child up on her hip as she looked him up and down. "Ye be Paddy, I presume."

Paddy nodded.

"Ye papa said how you might show up. Said you ran off right afor' ye ma died."

Paddy blinked as tears stung his eyes. "Momma's dead?"

"Not more than a week since. Ye papa brought me in to care for her right after ye ran away. My husband died when he fell from a building he was helping build. After Mrs. Bridget was gone, ye papa said since I needed a husband to care for the babe and he no longer had a wife, I should stay."

Paddy walked to the room he once shared with his brothers, opened the door, and looked inside. "Where are they?"

"Run off same as ye. Only the boys had the decency to wait until she was gone. Barely. They never came back after they laid yer ma in the ground. Kavan will be wanting to have a word with ye when he comes home. I'm sure ye know him not to be a patient man." There was a hint of a smile in her words.

Paddy walked to check out his parents' room just to make sure the woman was telling the truth. A wave of nausea hit him as he pushed open the door and saw the empty bed.

"I told ye she's gone." The woman stepped up behind him and placed her hand on his shoulder. "Things have been good since she and the boys left."

"You should go and take the baby with you," Paddy said, shrugging out of her grip. "My papa is a monster."

She smiled a mischievous smile as she hugged the infant to her chest once more. "Kavan said it was ye who had the devil inside. I'm beginning to think he bore the truth. I don't want the likes of ye rubbing off on my bebe. It's best ye go on now and give Kavan and me a chance to raise this child in peace." As she spoke, she caressed the baby's back, and for the first time, he saw she was wearing his mother's wedding ring.

Unable to control his emotions any longer, he bent and vomited on the floor, then wiped his mouth with the back of his arm and left the apartment without as much as an apology for soiling the floor.

He ran up the stairs and sprinted across the roof, jumping and running until, at last, his lungs would not allow for another jump. He looked about and realized he was standing on the roof where Big Joe trained. The man wasn't there, so he went to the rooftop shanty, curled into a ball, and cried himself to sleep.

His dreams were filled with images of his mother, Big Joe, and Milo and his gang. When, at last, he opened his eyes, a small part of him was surprised to be alive. He rose, stepped into the sunlight, and instantly felt the sorrow dissolve as if he'd left it within the confines of the shanty. He looked toward the structure, somehow knowing if he returned there today, the sadness he'd previously felt would suffocate him.

His stomach rumbled, reminding him he was out of coins and hadn't eaten since the morning prior. He'd used up the last of his gumball and would need to either find a wad of gum that was still usable or steal a gumball, which would prove to be even more difficult as store owners normally kept their candy jars near the counter where they could prevent such thefts. If he was going to get one, he would need a distraction.

Instantly, Slim and his dancing legs came to mind, and for the first time, thinking of the boy didn't make him queasy. On the contrary, he couldn't wait to find him and convince him they would make a great team.

Paddy ran across the roof, jumping to the other side with ease. As he landed, he saw Slim standing on the far edge of the building. "Slim?" *What's he doing over there?* Paddy wondered when Slim didn't acknowledge the greeting. His concern mounted when the boy walked closer to the edge. While Paddy had made the jump once, he'd sworn off leaping that direction because the vast gap between buildings had frightened him so. Not only was Slim an inexperienced jumper, he wasn't even giving himself a running start. *The dope will never make it.*

The thought of watching another person die had him racing across the roof and looping his arm about Slim's waist, sending them both tumbling across the hot roof.

Slim pushed him off and jumped up, his feet moving from side to side. Paddy rose more slowly, steadying himself as he brushed the soot from his knees. "Don't go getting all flustered; I was just trying to stop you from jumping."

"I wasn't going to jump," Slim replied.

"No? Well, your legs were. Why, if I hadn't stopped you, you'd be flat as a flapjack by now."

"What business is it of yours anyhow?"

"You're my friend. I don't want to see them scraping you off the sidewalk." *Like your ma.* He kept that part to himself.

Slim narrowed his eyes. "If you're my friend, then why haven't I seen you around?"

"I thought to come by, but I didn't know what to say. I get mad at my ma, but I wouldn't want to see her dead. My pop maybe wouldn't be so bad, but seeing my ma like that, that's not something a boy should see." Paddy realized what he'd said and felt the blush creep up his cheeks. Trying to change the subject, he looked over the edge of the building. "Were you really going to jump?" Slim answered with a shrug, and Paddy blew out a long whistle. "You must be some kind of sad."

"Yep," Slim replied.

"The landlord letting you stay, then?" Paddy asked, hoping it to be true.

"He doesn't know my mom…is not here," Slim replied.

"What about the rent?"

"I paid it."

"You?" Paddy gasped.

"My momma had a bit of money saved up."

It was the answer to his prayers. Paddy smiled. "So you live there all alone?"

"It ain't so good." Slim sniffed.

"What if you had someone to share it with?"

"Like who?"

Paddy yanked his thumb to his chest. "Like me."

"You?"

"Uh-huh, seems that just this morning, my pop told me how I've become too big for my britches and how I need to move out." It was a lie, but he wasn't yet ready to share his story with others.

"Why don't he just buy you some new pants?"

Paddy laughed, and he realized it was the first time he'd done so in weeks. "My pop would rather see me naked than buy me new pants, but that's because he's as ornery as a stubborn old mule." At least that part was true.

"Won't your momma be sad when you don't come back?"

The comment pulled at Paddy's heartstrings. He made up a lie to cover his feelings. "My momma has enough mouths to feed without worrying about me. The only thing she'll be sad about is when I don't bring her the dimes I fish out of the grates."

Slim hesitated a moment then nodded his acceptance. "Alright, you can stay, but we have to be quiet so the landlord don't send us away."

"Haven't you eaten nothing?" Paddy asked when Slim's stomach rumbled.

His friend shook his head.

"Got money?"

This time, Slim nodded.

"Come on, then."

Slim stood his ground.

"What's the matter?" Paddy asked.

"I promised I wouldn't let the landlord see me."

"Promised who?"

Before Slim could answer, Milo and two of his gang landed on the roof only steps in front of them. Paddy sucked in his breath. *This is bad. Not only are Milo and his gang jumping roofs, but they appear to have mastered the dangerous side as well.* Paddy sucked in his breath as Milo grinned. He tugged on Slim's shirt when the kid had the audacity to take a step forward. "Don't be a dope. They'll throw you off the side for sure."

Milo nodded his agreement.

"What about Big Joe?" one of Milo's boys asked.

"Big Joe's gone and Percival here is on his own," Milo sneered. "Word on the street is he came into some money and left for good. Cleared out his apartment and everything." He gave the slightest of nods, and the boys pounced on Slim, wrestling him to the ground.

Paddy didn't have a chance to react to the situation as Slim scrambled to his feet, ducking and pummeling the two that had jumped him. If that wasn't enough, he turned and faced Milo as if daring him to step forward.

Milo glanced at the fallen boys then took off in a sprint, running the length of the roof and jumping to the other side without a backward glance as the two boys hurried to their feet and chased after him.

Slim turned to Paddy, smiling as if he'd just found a handful of dimes in the grate.

Paddy blinked his surprise. "Where'd you learn to fight like that?"

"Big Joe taught me."

A chill raced down Paddy's back. "You mean the murderer?"

Slim narrowed his eyes. "I mean my friend, Big Joe."

Paddy blew out a long whistle. "Well, if that don't beat all. You sure are something, Percival."

Slim froze and leveled a look at Paddy. "My momma called me Percival. My friends call me Slim."

Paddy thought of his own mother and nodded his understanding. "Do you think your ma would mind if we use some of her money and get something to eat?" he asked when his stomach rumbled.

Slim smiled. "I think she would want me to eat."

Paddy sighed. "Oh."

"You can come too if you want," Slim said.

Paddy matched his smile. "Do I ever. And I know just the place!"

***

Paddy raced down the street, ducking through an alley, then back into the street before entering a building and racing up three flights of stairs. Not the best idea after having eaten more than he'd ever eaten in one setting. Never in his life had he felt so full. He stopped and looked at Slim. "Good to know your legs are good for more than jumping in place. I shouldn't have run after eating so much." Slim was about to respond when Paddy heard a noise and placed a finger to his mouth. He leaned in, whispering to Slim, "Someone's coming. Maybe more than one. I'm going to puke if I run anymore. We're going to have to fight."

Slim nodded.

"Are you scared?" Paddy asked when Slim's legs began to dance.

Slim shook his head. "Only wish I knew who it is we're going to be fighting."

"Won't be long now," Paddy replied.

"Wait up!" a voice called out.

"It's Tommy," Paddy said with a sigh. "The twins are probably with him."

"Who's chasing you guys?" one of the twins asked as they came into view.

"We thought you were." Paddy laughed.

"We saw you running and thought there was trouble, so we figured we'd come help," the other twin replied.

"You didn't see anyone following us?" Paddy asked.

Tommy grinned. "Way youse was running, no one could have caught you even if they tried. We only found you 'cause we know'd which way you was going. Knew you'd be jumpin' roofs the rest of the way. Who ya running from anyhow?”

"We thought we saw Slim’s landlord coming,” Paddy lied.

The twins looked at Slim with newfound curiosity. “Slim? I thought your name was…”

“It’s Slim,” Paddy said, cutting the boy off.

“Fits him,” the other twin replied.

“Fits him just fine,” Tommy said, wiping sweat from his brow. “I figured you’d be running from your pop. I heard him yelling at you this morning. Heck, I think the whole building heard him. What’d you go and do to get him all riled like that?”

Paddy, who had not been home to be yelled at frowned his confusion. “I didn’t do nothing.”

“Well, you’d better stick a pillow down yer pants afor you get home. Your brother said yer pop gonna lay into you the minute he sees ya.”

“He ain’t going to see me,” Paddy said once they reached the rooftop.

“He gonna see you sumtime,” Tommy argued.

Paddy wasn’t sure what was up with Tommy, but he decided to put an end to it. “Nope, my pop’s done giving me whoopings, on account of I’m not going home.”

“You’re not?” both twins said at once.

“Nope. I’m a man now. Just like my pal Slim here.”

“I’m a man?” Slim asked.

“Sure you are. You pay a man’s rent, don’t you?” Paddy replied.

Slim nodded. “Yeah, but that’s only because my momma’s not here to pay it.”

“Don’t matter the reason. Just matters the doing. You have man responsibilities, that makes you a man.”

“Where’d you git dough to pay?” Tommy asked.

“Big Joe gave it to me,” Slim said.

Tommy gasped. “Big Joe? You mean the…”

"Leave it be, Tommy. Big Joe is Slim's friend," Paddy warned.

"Friends?" Tommy said, ignoring Paddy's warning. "Why ya wanta be friends with someone who kilt a man, much less a…"

Slim pressed Tommy against the stairwell wall. "He's not a killer. He's not any of the things people say he is. Big Joe's my friend, see. I'll not have you talking bad about him. Got it?"

"Sure, Slim, whatever ya say," Tommy sputtered.

Slim released Tommy and looked at the twins, who nodded their agreement and took off up the stairs.

Paddy hung back as Slim followed. He turned to Tommy, grabbed hold of the front of his shirt and lowered his voice. "What was all that stuff about me and my pop? You know it ain't true."

Tommy bobbed his head. "My ma might have mentioned that your ma died, so I stopped by your place, ya know, to see how ya was. Your new ma was there and told me you and your brothers done run off. The twins didn't say nuthin' about it, so I guess I didn't think you wanted anyone to know. I figured you might be running a number on the kid, so I thought I'd help you out."

Paddy let go of Tommy's shirt. "Well, they know now, so pipe down with the lies. I ain't trying to pull the wool over no one's eyes. I just left and I ain't going back. Got it?"

Tommy bobbed his head once more. "Sure thing, Paddy. And, Paddy?"

"Yeah, Tommy?"

"I'm sorry 'bout your ma."

Paddy heaved a heavy sigh. "Me too."

"I won't blab about your ma to the others."

Paddy smiled a weak smile. "Thanks, Tommy."

"I had a brother once. Pa said he left when I was born. Is

that why you left? On 'count'a your new ma has a baby?"

"Yeah, that's the reason," Paddy replied, because in the end, it was easier to lie.

"I figured it was sumptin' like that," Tommy said as they made their way up the stairs.

***

Paddy looked around at the meager room with nothing more than a bed, with a side table. "This is it? Why, you don't even have a kitchen. How'd your momma cook your supper?"

Slim switched on the overhead light. "She brought me food."

Paddy frowned. "Didn't she know how to cook?"

"Sure she did. My momma was a fine cook. I used to help her when we had a kitchen. She even has a book where she wrote down all her recipes." Slim fished out a book and showed him words inked into the margins. "See, my momma wrote these."

Paddy glanced at the pages as he sat on the edge of the bed and bounced up and down. "At least you have a proper bed," Paddy said.

"That's my momma's bed." Slim's voice was cold.

Paddy stilled. "Where do you sleep?"

"On a pallet of blankets under the window. It's cooler over there."

Paddy leaned back on the bed. "It seems a shame to sleep on the floor when there's a perfectly good bed right here."

Slim shrugged. "Go ahead if you want."

Paddy couldn't believe his luck. "You want me to sleep in the bed?"

"No, but I won't stop you," Slim said as he returned the book to the table. He opened the closet door to retrieve the pile of blankets he used for his pallet.

Paddy pushed off the bed and helped him spread them under

the window, then glanced longingly at the bed before joining his friend on the floor. "I've never slept in a real bed before. I guess there's no need to start now."

"I had a real bed before we moved here," Slim replied. "Had my own room too."

Paddy yawned. "Why'd you move?"

"Had to when my papa died," Slim said, copying his yawn.

"How'd he die?"

"Jumped from the roof. Big Joe says my papa was brave for what he'd done on account of most men don't have the courage to go through with it."

"You were thinking of jumping today," Paddy said. "Are you brave, Slim?"

"No. I can't do what my papa did."

"I don't want to speak ill against your friend, but I think it takes more courage not to jump," Paddy said, thinking of his momma and her battle. She knew she was going to die and could have easily gone to the roof and been done with it. But she chose to stay and he thought part of that was so she could be there to protect him.

"You think so?"

"Well, if you jump, your pain is gone the moment you hit the ground. But if you stay, then you have to face your pain a lot longer. I think that makes a fellow who chooses to stay a lot stronger." Thinking of his mother made him sad. He was glad when Slim didn't comment on his musings. He was also glad he didn't have to sleep alone this night. He closed his eyes and fought back tears, relaxing only when sleep came for him.

Chapter Seven

The jiggling of the doorknob pulled Paddy from a deep sleep. His first thought was his papa was coming into his room looking for a fight, then he remembered where he was. "Slim, wake up. Someone's fiddling with the door."

"Stay here," Slim said as he sprang to his feet and hurried to the door. The door squeaked open, and a man stuck his head in through the opening.

Instantly, the stench of alcohol filled the room. "Where's your ma, boy?"

"She's at work," Slim lied.

"That ain't how I hear it." The man pushed his way into the room, his words slurring as he spoke. "I hear you've been giving my nephew Milo a hard time."

"Milo?" Slim replied.

Paddy struggled to remain hidden, as he wanted nothing more than to jump up and tell the man he was lying. Milo didn't have any family. He'd been living on the street since his parents died.

"That's right. He's my nephew. Ain't right to be messing with a man's family," the man said before Paddy could call him on the lie. "Now tell me where your momma really is."

"She's at work," Slim said, sticking to his story.

"You wouldn't be lying to me now, would you, boy?" the man said, moving forward. "The way Milo tells it, she's dead and has been that way for some time."

That Milo, he sure has some nerve ratting Slim out like that. Why, when I get hold of him…

"What's it matter to you? You got your rent," Slim said, pulling Paddy from his musings.

Paddy smiled from his hiding place. *That a boy, Slim. You tell him.*

"It matters on account of I don't rent to no kids," the man grumbled.

Paddy worked his way backward as the man started moving toward the bed.

"You've no right to be in here!" Slim shouted.

Paddy knew his friend was trying to warn him the man was moving closer.

"My building."

Paddy flattened himself against the floor as the man lifted the edge of the mattress, then gulped as the guy tossed both the mattress and box springs against the wall. Paddy looked up, saw the landlord staring in his direction, and attempted to scoot out of the way. Too late, the landlord bent and clamped his hand around the back of his neck, lifting him off the ground. He swung at the man, kicking his hands and feet behind him in a desperate attempt to make contact. It was no use. The man slapped his hands and feet away at each thrust. Paddy peered at the window, knowing if the man would only let go, he would be able to climb up and find help.

"Take another step, and this one goes out the window," the landlord fumed.

Paddy didn't know if Slim was doing what the man wanted or if he was too much weight for him, but at long last, he lowered him to the floor. Unfortunately, that was the only break he got as the hand held firm to the back of his neck.

"Where's the loot, kid?"

"I already paid you the rent for this month."

"I'm not looking for a measly ten dollars. I want the jewelry. I know what kind of dame your ma was. Lookers like that always have jewelry. Now tell me where it is, or the boy goes out the window."

Jewelry? So that's the guy's game. All Slim has to do is give him the baubles, and he'll be on his way. Continuing his struggle, Paddy managed to turn his head just in time to see his friend shake his head no. The landlord tightened his grip, dragging him kicking and screaming to the window.

While Paddy wanted to get to the window, his current predicament was a death sentence. *Not like this! I need to turn around so I can grab hold of the ledge.*

"Tell me, or I let him die," the man growled.

Slim must have agreed as the landlord pulled him forward and turned him enough so that he could grab hold of the windowsill. The second he did, the man released his hold and turned to face Slim. That was all Paddy needed as he dug his feet into the crevasses between the bricks and inched himself over, then, using his hands and feet, began his climb up to the roof. His heart was pounding as he clawed his way upward. He wasn't scared of the climb; he'd done similar climbs many times. He was worried about what was going on back in the room. Slim had shown he could pack a punch, but the landlord was a mountain of a man and Slim was just a kid.

Paddy sank his fingers in the crevice, placed his foot, and was about to extend his other hand when his foot gave way. Instantly, he heard his mother's voice in his head. *Easy, Howard, you must have patience. Take your time. Rushing will do you no good.* The calming memory of her words worked to settle him. He replaced his foot and made the rest of the climb without issue. He threw his leg over the top, intending to take off running to find help, and was surprised to see Slim kneeling on the rooftop, sobbing as if reliving his mother's death.

Thinking to console him, Paddy placed a hand on the boy's shoulder.

Slim called out as he scurried out of the way.

"Hey, Slim, I didn't mean to scare ya."

Slim's jaw dropped open. "Paddy?"

"In the flesh." Paddy grinned.

"But you're supposed to be dead," Slim whispered.

Paddy chuckled. "Says who?"

"Says me. Are you really a leprechaun, then?"

Paddy waved him off. "Again with that? No, I'm not a leprechaun."

"Then how?"

"I climbed up the side of the building," Paddy replied with a wide grin.

Slim's eyes bugged. "Weren't you scared?"

"Only of what that man was going to do to me if I stayed. Besides, I do it all the time."

"Get thrown out of windows?"

"No, ya dope, climb buildings. We all do it, Tommy and the twins, though not so much since they are almost too small to reach some of the footholds. But lots of us kids do it, all hoping to be famous like the Human Fly." Paddy beamed.

"You want to be a fly?"

"Not a fly, the Human Fly. Don't tell me you never heard of him?"

Slim shook his head.

"His real name's Harry Gardiner, but they call him the Human Fly. He goes all around the world 'buildering'." Paddy jabbed a thumb toward his chest. "That's what they call us folk that climb buildings. Course, the most I've ever climbed is five stories, but not the Human Fly. That guy climbs skyscrapers. There's a guy around here named George who's pretty good. I think he's gonna take Harry."

"Take him where?"

"He's going to beat his record. That's what he says anyway." Paddy thought about telling his friend that he, too, hoped to break the record one day, but decided against it since he didn't seem to believe him. "Hey, how'd you get away?"

"I hit the guy," Slim grinned.

Paddy blinked his surprise. "You must have clocked the guy pretty hard if you were able to get away."

"Caught him with an uppercut," Slim said, demonstrating the blow.

"No kidding? And you were able to clock him in the jaw?"

"Not exactly," Slim said and stared at Paddy's pants.

Paddy shifted in place and whistled his understanding. Still, it didn't make sense that Slim came to the roof instead of running away. "So if you know the man's going to have it out for you, why didn't you get outta here?"

Slim's legs began to dance as he considered the question. "I didn't know where else to go. I couldn't go to the street."

"Why not?"

"On account of I thought you were lying on the street, and I'd know it was me who put you there."

Paddy toed the ground. He'd hated seeing his mother's ring on that woman's finger, but he would have hated it even more if someone like the landlord had taken it from her. Nor would he have been keen to give the man his mother's money. "I can't say I blame ya. I wouldn't want to turn over my loot neither."

"It wasn't the loot. It was the memories. Those things belonged to my momma. But in the end, he almost got them anyway," Slim said.

Paddy lifted his head. "Almost?"

Slim patted his pants pocket. "Yep."

Paddy rocked back on his heels. "Then I expect you owe me a debt of gratitude."

"I do?"

"Sure, because I helped you keep your momma's jewelry."

"You did?"

"Course I did. I kept you from jumping off the roof, didn't I? If you would've jumped, your landlord would have cleared out your room and taken the jewels. The way I see it, I saved you and your momma's jewels."

Slim reached into his pocket. "How much do I owe you?"

"I don't want your money," Paddy said, waving him off.

"What do you want?"

"I think I'd like to hold on to that in case I need something from you later. Right now, we have bigger problems. I can't go home, and you don't have a home, so we'd better find us a place to spend the night. What's wrong?"

"I thought I'd stay here," Slim replied.

"We can't stay here. It's too dangerous. The landlord will be looking for you. He's probably already sent Milo to find ya."

"I ain't scared of Milo. He's scared of me. I fixed him a good one the other day."

"That explains it."

"Explains what?"

"If he was sore at ya, that's why he told your landlord about your momma. He was lying about being Milo's uncle, by the way. But if Milo and his boys are using the rooftops, the best thing we can do is go to the ground and get Tommy and the twins to help us."

"Help us what?"

"Put Milo in his place, of course."

Slim shook his head. "Big Joe said I shouldn't go looking for trouble."

"We ain't looking for trouble. Trouble found you. Now, I could just walk away since they think I'm already dead, but I'm willing to stay and help you. You'd like that, wouldn't you?"

Slim nodded his head.

"If we don't let Milo know we mean business, then he'll make big trouble for you. You don't want that, do you?" Paddy knew it wasn't the total truth, but he didn't want his friend to think he was using him. Sure, it was a gamble, but if they didn't do something to back Milo down, he wouldn't have any other choice but to go to the asylum. "We don't have to pound on him none. We just have to make him think we're ready to pound on him if he don't leave you alone."

"Aren't you worried about him making trouble for you?" Slim asked.

"Yep, I'm taking a big risk," Paddy admitted. "You know why?"

"Why?"

"Cause we're pals, you and me. I wouldn't let you face Milo alone any more than you'd let the landlord drop me out the window. Well, you almost did, but you came through." Paddy looked from side to side then leaned in close. "Now, Milo, he'll be surprised. You see, if you were to show up by yourself, he would send one of the boys to go get his uncle. But if Tommy, the twins, and me are with you, then he'll know you mean business."

"I don't know. Big Joe said—"

"Big Joe's not here," Paddy interrupted. "Besides, didn't Big Joe tell you that if trouble came looking for you to do something about it?"

"How'd you know that?" Slim asked, scratching his head.

I didn't. I was just taking a guess. Paddy kept that to himself. "Because Big Joe's smart, and that's the smart thing to do. So, it's a deal?"

Slim nodded.

Paddy spat into his palm. "Now you do the same."

Slim did as told. "Now what?"

"We shake on it, and that makes us blood brothers. Some people become blood brothers by cutting their hands, but we'll use spit 'cause I don't have a knife," Paddy said, leaving out the fact that he wouldn't use a knife even if he had one on account of he didn't like the sight of blood, especially his own.

"What now?" Slim asked, wiping his hand on his pants.

"Now we go find Tommy and the twins and get them to join our gang," Paddy replied.

"Big Joe said I shouldn't join a gang," Slim said, standing his ground.

Paddy nodded his agreement. "That's good advice and he's right. You shouldn't."

Slim scratched his head. "But you just said…"

"I never said I wanted you to join a gang. I said we were going to get the others to join our gang."

Slim frowned. "What's the difference?"

Paddy smiled. "You are the gang. You know how to fight, and you have the money and jewels. So we will be joining you, not the other way around."

"What's my mama's jewelry have to do with anything?"

Paddy smiled. "Nothing, only that you have it. When the boys find out you didn't let your landlord take what belongs to you, they will know you are someone they can trust. I'm not saying you are, but if you were looking to join a gang, wouldn't you want to join someone you could trust?"

Slim nodded. "Big Joe did tell me to be a good judge of character."

Paddy bobbed his head. "Well, there you go. If we can get Tommy and the twins on board, then you'll be doing exactly what Big Joe told you to do."

Slim heaved a sigh. "Boy, Paddy, I wouldn't know any of this stuff if not for you. I'm glad you're my friend."

"Me too, Slim," Paddy said in return. "Why, we are going

to be so close, people will think we are brothers. Aside from the red hair and dancing legs, of course."

***

"Whatcha thinking?" Linda asked when Cindy finished.

Cindy placed the papers in her lap and smoothed them with her hands. "Honestly, that Grampa Howard was a little stink butt."

Linda laughed. "That's putting it mildly."

"The question is, was he sincere or playing the poor kid?" Cindy mused.

"You have more experience with kids than me. What do you think?" Linda pressed.

"I think probably a bit of both. He's scared of being alone and is grasping at straws. Sounds like he spent more time listening to his older brother manipulate the others than he wants to admit. It just sucks that these kids even had to deal with any of this."

Linda raised an eyebrow. "Careful, daughter, your motherly instincts are starting to show."

"Just read your journals, Mom," Cindy said, trying not to laugh.

Chapter Eight

Cindy tucked her legs underneath her and began to read....

We all have that one person that gets under our skin, and for me, that was a kid called Mouse. I knew that boy would be trouble from the moment I laid eyes on him. I'd like to say I wish I'd never met the kid, but if I hadn't, I might never have met my darling Mileta. It was Mouse who introduced me to her in a roundabout way, but there I go, getting ahead of myself again. Where to start... I believe it was August of 1916, a few months after I'd convinced Tommy and the twins to join up with Slim and myself. Things had gone well enough when Slim still had a small bit of dough, but when it ran out, we were forced to live off our wits. Fishing for coins in the grates only went so far, and we were all too afraid to dip pockets after watching Buster get nabbed by the coppers. Summer was waning, and we went to sleep hungry more often than not, and though I wanted to be the leader of our little gang, I wasn't very good at maintaining control—something that became obvious when Tommy and the twins started grumbling about going home.

***

"We're all hungry," Paddy said when faced with the comment one too many times. "We'll have our supper; we just have to go fishing for dimes."

"I saw someone else by the grates earlier," Tommy replied.

"Then we'll go somewhere else. It's time we moved on anyhow. Been two weeks and not a sign of Milo and his gang."

Paddy started walking, hoping the others would follow. "Tells me we don't have to worry about him no more."

"But we always fish around here," one of the twins said, tugging on Paddy's shirt.

Tired of being questioned at every move, Paddy whirled on the boy. "You want to stay, then stay." Paddy nodded to Big Joe's shanty, where they'd been sleeping each night since joining together. "But I say we go and be done with this place! It's not safe for us on this side of town. We can't even jump the roofs without worrying if Milo and his friends are going to come after us." The thing was that even though they'd spent the better part of two weeks roaming the streets during the daylight hours, they hadn't seen any sign of Milo or his gang. In some ways, not seeing them was as bad as knowing where they were. At least knowing where to find them would help them avoid haplessly running into the boys. Instead, they were on constant alert, watching the shadows for any sign of a threat.

"You said he would protect us," Tommy said, looking at Slim. "Said that's the reason you asked him to come along. That, and on account of he had money."

Great, not only was he losing control of the younger kids, but he was also in danger of losing what little protection they had if Slim learned the real reason he wanted him to join them. "I asked him to come because he had no place else to go," Paddy countered.

"But you said…"

Paddy glared at Tommy. "He's with us, and that's the end of it."

"It's not the end of it. We can't even find enough for us," Tommy argued.

Slim's legs began to dance and he started back in the direction they'd just came.

Paddy knew the boy was upset and with good reason. Aside

from him, Slim was the one that contributed most to their little gang. The lanky boy was as loyal as a puppy, but sometimes, even dogs grew weary. While they didn't actually mistreat him, the younger boys didn't fully appreciate all Slim had done for them. As such, Paddy feared it wouldn't be long before Slim found himself recruited by another gang that would offer him something other than a bunch of sniveling kids who contributed nothing but expected everything in return.

Paddy felt his control dwindling as Slim made his way through the crowd. If Slim was truly leaving, the others would surely follow. Then what? The grates had been empty of late and he didn't even have a few pennies for a loaf of bread. *I have to stop him!*

Paddy brushed through the crowd trying to catch up with Slim, falling further behind as his friend turned into an alleyway and hurried on his way. Paddy called out to him, "Slim, where the devil are ya going?"

Slim didn't answer, so Paddy hurried after him, gasping his surprise when the boy stepped out of the shadow and put a finger to his lips. "What is it?" Paddy whispered when he and the others caught up.

"Milo," Slim said just as softly.

"What ya doing following him?" Tommy's voice held an edge.

"They're up to no good," Slim whispered in return.

"They're always up to no good," Paddy replied. "Let's get out of here."

"What do you mean get out of here?" Slim sounded surprised. "We've been looking for them all week."

"We didn't actually mean to find him," one of the twins explained. "Paddy said how you can fight. He wanted to make sure Milo didn't pound on us if he saw us."

"Why would Milo pound on you?"

"Milo pounds on all the kids," the other twin replied.

"Except you." Tommy grinned. "It's all over the streets how you whooped him. Ain't that right, Paddy?"

Before Paddy could answer, shouts filled the air.

"Sounds like Milo and his friends found who they were looking for," one of the twins gulped.

"Where you going, Slim?" Paddy asked when the boy started toward the noise.

"To help," Slim said over his shoulder.

Paddy caught him by the arm. "What's going on back there ain't our business."

"That boy wasn't no bigger than you," Slim said, pulling his arm free. "Those boys are likely to hurt him bad. What happened to all of us standing up to Milo?"

Paddy gulped and kicked the dirt with the toe of his shoe. The truth was he was terrified of Milo, and was perfectly content slinking through the streets, praying he and his gang didn't find him. "I don't know, Slim. They sound pretty worked up."

Instead of agreeing with him, Slim's face turned crimson as his legs beat the ground as if he were running in place. He turned and headed toward the ruckus.

"Slim, don't go." His words fell on deaf ears as Slim never looked back. Paddy remained frozen in place for several moments, fighting his inner thoughts. On one hand, he wanted to run as far away as possible to avoid the conflict. On the other, he felt a loyalty to his friend, now that he knew Slim would not turn and run if the roles were reversed.

Tommy stepped up beside him, pulling him from his turmoil. "What are we gonna do?"

Paddy's eye twitched as he made up his mind. "We're gonna do what we promised we'd do." Without waiting for a reply, he took off running toward the chaos, glad when he realized the others were following his lead. He and the others stopped short of joining the fray, mostly because it looked as if Slim and a well-dressed boy he'd never seen before looked like they were handling the situation just fine.

"Milo!" Slim's voice sang out. "My beef is with you."

Milo laughed and motioned to the others. "You'll have to get through them first."

Paddy gulped as Slim singled out the biggest kid in the group, motioned him forward, and pounded him to the ground with a single punch. Another boy stepped forward. Tommy and the boys cheered as Slim made short work of him as well. Paddy, on the other hand, felt nothing but guilt, which increased when the kid Slim had been protecting joined in the fight. He looked at the others. "It's not right them doing all the fighting. We promised Slim if he found Milo, we would all fight him together." Paddy balled up his fists and raced to where Slim and the boy stood looking over several boys they'd taken down.

"Do you really think they need our help?" Tommy asked when he and the twins moved up next to him.

Paddy looked at all the kids lying on the ground, then burst out laughing when Milo looked at them and took off running.

"You look like you enjoyed that," Paddy said when Slim turned toward him.

Slim smiled. "Not at all."

"You didn't even get to punch Milo, and you're smiling," Paddy said, watching the kids pick themselves off the ground. "So you must have enjoyed it a little."

"Maybe a little," Slim admitted.

Paddy looked in the direction Milo had run. "What about Milo?"

"That's the second time I disgraced him in front of his friends. He won't bother us again."

Paddy wasn't convinced. "How can you be so sure?"

"I can't. But if he does, we'll take care of him together." Slim lowered his eyes. "I thought…"

"That I'm a coward? I am, but I figured if that boy could stand with you, then so could we. Who is he anyhow?" Paddy said, glancing at the boy, who seemed to be the same age and height as himself.

Before Slim could answer, a boy from Milo's gang approached. He looked in Paddy's direction before directing his comments to Slim. "If you're looking for people to be in your gang, the boys and I wanna join ya."

Paddy did little to hide his disappointment when Slim sent the boy away. "Why'd you send them away?"

"I don't need a gang," Slim replied.

"Boy, Slim, you sure can be a dope. You're living on the streets now. You need all the help you can get."

"Give me a minute," Slim said when the new kid called him over.

Paddy started to go with him but decided against it. He was mad. Mad that Milo's gang hadn't recognized that he was the one who was in charge and mad that Slim hadn't asked him to walk with him to see what the boy wanted. Sure, he'd told Slim he was in charge, but no one actually believed it to be true. The more he thought about it, the angrier he became. Still fuming, he decided to go over to have a listen to see what it was the boy wanted.

"So you'll do it, then? Teach me how to throw a punch?" the boy asked as Paddy neared.

Paddy wasn't sure why, but there was something about the boy that grated at him. They were the same height and build, but that was where the similarities stopped. The boy had dark hair and eyes and a self-assured confidence that said "I can handle anything life throws at me." Unlike Paddy, the boy's attitude wasn't a charade and Paddy took an instant dislike to the kid.

Slim bobbed his head. "I'll teach you."

The boy pulled a wallet out of his pocket. "How much is it going to cost me?"

Paddy heaved a frustrated sigh as Slim waved the kid off and told him to put his wallet away.

"Ah, I should have known you were putting me on," the boy grumbled.

"I'm not, but a friend told me not to give something without asking for something in return."

Paddy couldn't hold back his frustration any longer. "He tried to pay you, ya dope."

"I don't want his money," Slim replied.

"I do," Paddy said, reaching for the boy's wallet. The boy slapped his hand away, and Paddy doubled his fist.

The boy narrowed his eyes and matched Paddy's stance.

"Stop it, the both of you," Slim said, coming between them.

"Who put you in charge?" Paddy fumed, knowing good and well it was of his own doing.

"I'm not in charge of nothing, but if I'm going to teach you both to fight, then you'll have to listen to me."

"Will you teach us too?" the twins asked, stepping up.

"Me too?" Tommy asked.

"I'll teach him, and everyone can watch. That way, you'll learn too," Slim said.

"Why are you going to go and teach him for?" Paddy asked.

"On account of he's going to teach us something in return."

"He is?" Paddy and the others asked at once.

"I am?" The boy seemed just as surprised as the others.

"You're going to show us how to dip pockets."

The kid rocked back on his heels. "Who said I know how to dip pockets?"

"I did. I saw you doing it just before you ran from Milo and his pals. I saw you." Slim's legs began to dance, showing he was getting riled.

The boy looked at Slim. "Do those legs ever stop?"

"Not for long."

"Didn't think so. Might be a problem with the dipping, but we'll try."

"Good," Slim said making introductions.

"Ain't they got names?"

"They do, but we just call them 'the twins' since no one can tell 'em apart. My name's Percival, but my friends call me Slim."

Paddy glanced at Slim, wondering why he felt the need to give the boy his true name.

The boy took off his cap, ran a hand through his hair, and then returned the cap to his head. "My name's Tobias, but my friends call me Mouse. You're a real smart fellow, Slim. I think we're gonna get along just fine."

Perhaps it was how self-assured the kid was. Or maybe it was simply the way Slim looked at the kid as if he'd follow him anywhere. Whatever it was, Paddy's senses were screaming, warning him this cocky boy with the charming smile was going to be big trouble.

***

Paddy stood with the others, gaping at the tree-lined street.

"You mean they don't have to share?" Tommy asked.

Mouse smiled. "Nope. Only one family to a house. Some of them only have two or three people living in there."

One of the twins whistled. "They must all be rich!"

Mouse shook his head. "That they are, which is why you shouldn't feel bad stealing from them."

"And you've done this before?" Slim asked.

Mouse nodded. "Lots of times. Now, when it is just me, I find myself a mark that looks to be the same size as I am and

83

follow them home. Sometimes it takes a day or two but eventually, the clothes show up on the line, and I get something to wear."

"That sounds easy," Tommy nodded. "Why can't we do that now?"

"Because there are too many of us," Mouse replied. "We are going to have to go through the yards and hope we find something that fits."

"Why do we need new clothes anyway? What's wrong with what we are wearing?" Paddy grumbled.

Mouse shrugged. "Nothin', if all you want to do is fish for dimes. But if you're going to dip pockets of people who live in houses like these, then you have to look like you live in houses like these. A copper finds you hanging around looking like you do, they'll haul you in, but if you look like you belong here, they'll tell you to run along home before they rat you out to your momma and papa."

"How do they know I have a momma and papa?" Tommy asked.

Mouse waved a hand to encompass the street. "Easy, on account of rich kids always have a momma and papa. The mommas take care of them and make sure they have food in their bellies and clean clothes on their backs, and the papas work to see that there is money for such things."

"How do we know what houses have kids?" Tommy asked.

Mouse thought about it for a moment, then looked at Slim. "You and Paddy take that side of the street, and I'll take Tommy and the twins with me. Stay to the back of the yard, away from the house, so there's less chance of being seen. If anything happens, we'll all meet up back at the church."

Paddy moved up beside Slim as soon as Mouse led the others to the backyard. "You doin' okay? We can go back to the roof if you're scared."

Slim shook his head. "I'm not scared. I was just thinking about my momma. She said one day we would live in a house like this with windows on all sides. She seemed happy 'bout that, as she said we'd have curtains that would blow in the wind."

Paddy looked at him in awe. "You mean your ma was rich?"

"No. But she must have planned to be because she told me about how we were gonna live in a house just like this," Slim said as they walked into the backyard.

"I'm sorry your ma died," Paddy said, not knowing what else to say to his friend.

"You're a good friend, Paddy. I know you don't like Mouse so much, but he's done right by us, teaching us how to dip pockets and all. We haven't gone to bed hungry since we met him."

Paddy couldn't argue that point, but it still troubled him they had no clue where Mouse spent his nights. "Where do you think he lives?"

Slim was in the process of picking through clothes strung across a line. He stopped and pondered the question. "I don't know. Where do you think he lives?"

Paddy shrugged. "Maybe he lives in one of these houses, and that's how he knows so much about the people who live here."

Slim removed a wooden pin and pulled a pair of trousers from the line. "You think Mouse is lying to us?"

Paddy sighed and watched as Slim pilfered a shirt so white, it looked as if it came straight from the store. While he did have misgivings about their new pal, Slim was right. Mouse had not done anything but help them since they'd met. He shook his head. "Nah, I was just thinking is all."

Slim draped the pants and shirt across his shoulder and nodded to the next house. "Good, on account of I'd hate to have to choose between you two."

The statement felt like a punch in the gut and let Paddy know he needed to watch his step. Being friends was one thing, but in the end, no one wanted to go to bed hungry, not even him.

Chapter Nine

Dressed in knickers, a white shirt and black socks that wouldn't get him a second glance from the upper class, Paddy followed behind a well-dressed couple chatting merrily amongst themselves as they casually navigated the busy sidewalk. The woman had her gloved hand tucked into the crook of the man's arm as he pushed a hooded baby carriage.

Paddy waited until he was near, then began whistling a tune as if he didn't have a care in the world. As he neared, the woman smiled at him and then returned to her conversation. He waited for the right moment, then dipped his hand into the pocket of her vivid green skirt, nimbly retrieving her coin purse. He dropped back and emptied the contents of the purse into his pocket before discarding the purse and slipping back into the crowd unnoticed. Not having anything better to do, he had been at it all afternoon and had a pocket full of change to show for it.

He might not think as highly of Mouse as the others did, but if not for him, he would still be spending his days crouched on his knees fishing coins out of the sewer drain. For this skill alone, he owed Mouse a lifetime of gratitude – unsettling, as he still couldn't think of the boy without clenching his jaw, and didn't know why the fellow got under his skin or why he felt the need to challenge him at every turn.

He was still pondering this when he saw Slim move alongside a robust woman and attempt to snatch her purse. As his hand neared, she stopped and clutched her hand to her chest.

The dope's been caught. Paddy was about to run to help, when a hand took hold of his arm. He yanked it away, cocking his fist to fight.

"Good reflexes," Mouse said, letting go of his arm. "You remembered what Slim taught you."

Paddy shrugged off the compliment and nodded to where Slim now stood talking to the woman. "Yeah, well, he needs to remember. I think she's onto the dope."

"I've been watching them. Slim seems to be doing okay for himself," Mouse countered.

"What if she calls the coppers?" Paddy asked as the others joined them.

"If we go butting in now, we'll only make things worse," Mouse replied. "If things go sour, we'll create a distraction. Until then, we wait to see how this plays out."

While Paddy knew Mouse to be right, he didn't like the boy telling him what to do. Especially in front of the others. He narrowed his eyes at the boy. "Easy for you to say. Slim's my friend."

"Slim is my friend as well, and I say we wait," Mouse said, firming his chin.

Paddy knew he'd crossed the line, and if he didn't concede, Mouse would put him in his place. While Slim had shown him and the others how to fight, Mouse was a natural, and he knew if push came to shove, the street-smart boy would come out ahead. Paddy splayed his hands to show his concession. "I didn't mean nothin' by it. Besides, we can't help Slim if we're fighting each other," Paddy said, relaxing when Mouse backed down. They stood in silence, watching to see Slim and the woman conversing until, at last, Slim ran to meet them. Paddy handed him the cloth pillowcase he'd been holding for him. "Boy, Slim, we were getting worried. What did the woman talk about for so long?"

"She was sad that I was living on the streets," Slim said, tying the bag around his waist. "I guess she's never seen a kid living on the streets before."

"She must not get out of the house much. There are kids all over the place. We thought she was gonna rat ya out," Paddy said.

"Rat me out?"

Tommy nodded. "She caught ya, didn't she?"

"I didn't steal anything," Slim said, shaking his head.

"Oh," Paddy said, sighing his disappointment. While the others were excelling under Mouse's instruction on dipping pockets, Slim just couldn't seem to get the hang of it. Paddy worried if the boy didn't catch on soon, the others might give him a hard time for not contributing.

"But she gave me this," Slim said, holding up a bill. "On account of I told her I was hungry."

Paddy blew out a long whistle as his worries dissipated. "You mean to tell me all we have to do is give a sap story, and people will hand over the loot?"

"It works sometimes," Mouse agreed. "Mostly with the dames. The men aren't so gullible."

Paddy took the bill and held it up to make sure it was the real deal. If they could get their hands on a few more, it would go a long way to keeping them warm in the coming days. "She must be loaded to have given you this. Come on, boys, let's go see if we can get her coin purse."

"NO!" Slim lowered his voice. "Some chump has already taken everything; this was all she had left."

"Why'd she give it to you if it was all she had?" one of the twins asked, scratching his head.

"Maybe 'cause she had more at home," Slim replied.

"Too bad we don't know where that is," Paddy said, heaving a sigh. "At least it's enough to pay for a room at the Newsboy's

Lodging House tonight." Paddy started walking, and the others fell in behind him. He got to the end of the second block and looked to see Slim and Mouse lagging behind. "You guys coming or what?"

"We're coming." Slim jerked his thumb toward Mouse. "He said we can stay at his place."

"You got a place?" Paddy said, narrowing his eyes. "Why didn't you tell us before?"

"I wanted to make sure I could trust you first," Mouse said, stepping around him. "A fellow don't just invite anyone into his home."

Paddy couldn't believe his ears. All this time sleeping in the shed on Big Joe's roof worrying about Milo, and they could have been sleeping in a house. *Boy, that kid has some nerve.* He'd just about summoned up the nerve to call him on it when Mouse stopped in front of St. Paul's Chapel. Paddy and the boys stared open-mouthed at the enormous church looming on the other side of the black gates.

"You live here?" Tommy gulped.

Mouse pointed to the side yard. "Around back."

Paddy followed behind the others as Mouse led the way through the bushes and into the graveyard, dropping to the ground in front of a massive monument. "This is where I sleep. You boys can take your pick from the rest. Find a big one. It'll hide you if someone comes and will help keep the rain off you some."

"You live here!" Tommy repeated, only this time, his words held fear. "Aren't you afraid?"

"Nah, the caretaker doesn't mind as long as we don't make a mess of the place. Just make sure to stay out of view when people come to pay their respects to the dead."

Paddy heard the others talking but couldn't focus on their words as he scanned the cemetery, which boasted large stones with etched lettering telling who was buried beneath them. It wasn't that he was afraid of ghosts. It was that all he could picture was his mother and baby sister lying there covered in all that dirt.

Mouse's words penetrated the recesses of his mind. "The way I hear it, if you don't speak ill of the dead, the dead won't bother you none."

"My momma used to say the same thing," Slim said, looking about.

"I don't know," Paddy said softly.

"Listen, I don't give a rat's tail where you go. The caretaker don't bother me, and I don't bother him. You just have to make sure you're back here before it gets dark. He closes the gates then, and if you aren't inside, you're in big trouble," Mouse replied.

"Cause of the ghosts?" Tommy asked, sliding his eyes from side to side.

"No, I told you there ain't no ghosts, but there are gangs, lots of them. The caretaker shuts the gates at dark so they don't come in, not that they would."

"Why not?" Tommy asked.

"Cause they're scared of the ghosts."

"You just said there aren't any ghosts," Paddy replied.

Mouse smiled. "I know that, and you know that, but they don't know that. Sometimes, when I hear them coming, I make some noises and watch them run away."

Paddy looked at the ground, picturing his mother lying at his feet.

"Aren't you staying?" Slim asked when he turned to leave.

Paddy didn't want his friends to see him like this. "Nah, I've got some things I need to do."

"Want me to come with you?"

"No, I'm going to go see my momma and my pop. He don't

like me bringing strangers around the place." Why he'd said it, he did not know. All he knew was he needed to be alone so his friends wouldn't think him a baby for not wishing to spend the night here.

"You make sure you're off the street before dark," Slim said, catching up to him.

Paddy forced a laugh. "I thought I was the one who was teaching you about the streets." He lowered his voice. "You make sure to keep an eye on Tommy and the twins. I don't trust your new friend so much." Paddy couldn't breathe. It felt as if there was something balling up inside of him, threatening to rip him apart if he didn't get far away from there.

"I'll watch out for them."

"Good," Paddy said and took off running, racing through the front gate as if someone was chasing him. Whether there was or not, he did not know, as he never once looked over his shoulder to see. He had no clue where he was running to, only that he wanted to get as far away as possible. Dusk was upon him, the streets were growing empty, and he knew he was in danger of being caught on the streets after dark. Mouse had been right to want to be off the streets before the gates were closed.

As he ran, he recalled waking one night to his brother's whispers in the dark. Joseph's voice had drifted down from the bed, telling stories about what happened on the streets after dark and ending the tale by telling the others that even boys like Milo feared the gangs that roamed the city when the darkness brought the devil to life. Thinking of Joseph only made things worse as he recalled how nice the boy had been in the days before his departure. Tears stung his eyes as he ran, his only thought going home.

It was dark by the time he reached his building. And while he'd not seen any gangs, he'd never in his life been so glad to step into the smelly stairwell of his early childhood. He slowed and made his way to the third floor, letting his breath catch up to him as he went. He opened the door and walked down the hall, pausing just outside the apartment. Just as he reached for the doorknob, he heard his papa's booming voice on the other side of the door. He could not decipher the words that were spoken, but the tone of his voice sent chills racing down Paddy's spine. *I won't do it.* Tears flooded his eyes once more as he pulled his hand away.

Not knowing where else to go, he made his way to the rooftop, thinking he would jump the roofs to go to the shack. Only he hadn't ever jumped in the dark. While he'd jumped them enough to do it with his eyes closed, he was feeling extra vulnerable at the moment. Giving in to the fear, he went to the far corner of the roof and sat with his back against the wall.

Ya big dope, you should have stayed with Slim, Tommy, and the others. Heck, even Mouse's company would be better than sitting here all alone. He thought about Mouse and how the kid had rubbed him the wrong way since the moment he laid eyes on him. *What's that about anyway? The kid hadn't even said boo to you when you decided you didn't like him. Why is that? Everyone else likes him. Probably because he is smart, self-assured, and doesn't seem to need anyone and yet, Tommy and the gang accepted him as their leader straightaway, following his instructions and learning how to dip pockets without worrying about anyone catching them. And he can fight. Slim only had to show him something once.*

As Paddy went over Mouse's attributes, a sudden realization struck him. Mouse was everything he wasn't. Okay, he was smart, but Mouse had still outwitted him at every turn. While Paddy had excelled at dipping pockets and shadowing a mark, he still wasn't nearly as good as the boy who'd taught him. Mouse was good at everything, and yet he needed no one. He, on the other hand, had spent every minute of the day trying to keep Slim, Tommy, and the twins close so he wouldn't have to be alone. Paddy pulled his legs to his chest and wrapped his arms around them. "Ya dope, look at you now, ya dope. You sure showed him."

Sometime during the night, sleep found him, and he woke curled in a ball. He stood, ran to the edge, leaped to the other side and chided himself for being such a coward the night before. He made his way to Big Joe's shanty, happy to see it untouched from when he and the boys left. He went inside and sat debating his next move. He'd spent the last few weeks thinking Mouse was the problem, but now, in the light of day, he thought perhaps the boy was the solution. Maybe it was time to be more like Mouse. Mouse didn't need anyone. He thought back to the day they'd met the boy. Instead of crying and begging for mercy when confronted by Milo and the gang, he'd stood in that circle ready to fight Milo and the boys. And that was before Slim taught him how to throw a punch. And instead of begging them to let him join their gang, Mouse went back to the cemetery and continued to sleep there on his own while he, Slim, and the others stayed together.

His stomach rumbled, and Paddy patted his pocket, smiling when he felt the weight of the coins he'd collected the day prior. He went to the stairwell, started to run, then thought of Mouse and walked down the steps one at a time. Reaching the bottom, he looked around to make sure the coast was clear. *Ya dope. Remember what Mouse said. If a boy looks like he belongs, no one will pay him no mind.* Paddy pulled himself taller and walked down the sidewalk holding his head up high and forcing himself to look straight ahead. At the corner, he went inside the market and slapped a nickel on the counter. "I'd like a meat pie, please."

The man behind the counter scooped up the coin, replacing it with the pie, which sat atop a white plate. Paddy stared at it, realizing he hadn't eaten off a plate since the fancy meal he'd shared with Slim.

"Did you need something else, boy?" the man asked.

Paddy shook his head. "No, sir."

The man nodded to a counter facing the window. "You can eat it over there. Bring me back the plate when you're finished."

"Yes, sir." Paddy took the plate to the counter, pulled up a stool, and sat staring out the window watching as people walked down the street. He'd nearly finished when he saw his papa walk by with his lunch bucket in his hand. Paddy started to hide, then picked up the remaining meat pie, taking a bite as he watched his papa climb onto the trolley. As the trolley pulled away, a boy who looked to be a year or two younger than himself, dressed in rags, stopped in front of the window. The boy's sandy blonde hair fell in front of his eyes as he stood staring at him.

The bell on the door chimed and the man from behind the counter shook a broom at the kid, shooing him away. Paddy fought the urge to run after the boy so neither had to be alone, then remembered his quest to be more like Mouse.

"Are you doing okay there, son?" the man asked, stepping back inside.

Paddy nodded. "Yes, sir. I'm doing just fine." He dipped his fingers into the crumbs and then handed the man his plate. "If it wouldn't be too much trouble, I'd like two purple gumballs, please."

The man nodded and fished two out with a pair of tongs, handing them to him without waiting for him to pay. Paddy handed the guy a penny and plopped one of the gumballs into his mouth. "Anything else, son?"

"No, sir." Paddy pocketed the second gumball, went outside and stood in front of the window scanning the street for the boy. Seeing him, he ran to catch up. "Hey."

The boy cowered. "I didn't do nuthen."

Paddy shrugged. "Didn't say you did."

"I ain't lookin' for a fight neither."

Paddy smiled. "Neither am I."

"Good, on account of I'd whoop you for shor," the boy said and continued on his way.

Doubtful. Paddy caught up to him and pulled out his fishing line and washer, showing it to the kid. "You know what this is for?"

"Of course I do."

"Do you want it?"

The boy frowned. "What do you want for it?"

Paddy shook his head and handed it to the kid. "Nothin'."

The kid rocked back on his heels without accepting. "What's the catch?"

Paddy shook his head once more. "No, catch. I just don't need it anymore."

The boy held out his hand, his eyes growing wide when Paddy placed it into his hand.

"What's the matter? I told you I'd give it to you."

The kid shrugged. "I thought you were fooling."

Paddy pulled out the gumball. "Nope, and I ain't fooling about this neither."

The kid snatched it from his hand and shoved it into his mouth before he had a chance to change his mind. "Thanks."

Paddy smiled and started to walk away. He stopped and turned to the boy once more. "If you can find your way over to St. Joseph's Church, there are some boys living in the yard behind it. Make sure you get there before dusk and ask for a kid named Slim. He'll do right by you. Don't worry about the cemetery. If you don't speak ill of the dead, they won't do you no harm."

The kid took a step and then hesitated. "Why are you being

so nice to me?"

Paddy smiled. "You just looked like you needed a friend."

Chapter Ten

October 1916

Paddy walked down the sidewalk, recalling Mouse's instructions. Nod to the gentlemen, tip your hat to the ladies, and if a person scowls at you, offer them your best smile. More often than not, they will return the gesture. If not, keep walking and don't give them a reason to question your presence. So far, it was working. While he'd seen people scoff at other children running the streets wearing little more than rags, no one had given him a second glance. A few had even gone so far as to initiate the greeting. He saw a woman stop at the corner flower cart, and he held back, watching the exchange. The flower girl reached for a bouquet, and the woman shook her head and pointed to a different arrangement. The girl pulled it free from the cart, handed it to the woman and cupped her hand. The woman dropped a few coins into the girl's palm then dropped her coin purse into her pocket. She missed and the purse dropped to the ground, spilling its contents. Paddy raced to her side and began picking up coins, handing them to the woman.

"Oh, what a nice young man. All these heathens around here ready to steal a person blind and here you are helping me with my coins."

"Yes, ma'am," Paddy said, handing her another coin. He slipped a coin under his foot, and the flower girl smiled at him and winked.

At that moment, the flower girl sneezed and continued for several more.

The woman tsked and handed the girl her handkerchief, at which the girl put on a big show of blowing her nose. When finished, she attempted to hand it back, and the woman told her to keep it, as she obviously needed it more than she did.

Paddy stood and handed the woman several more coins.

She smiled and offered him one.

Paddy waved her off. "Oh no, ma'am. I have plenty of my own."

The woman nodded and placed them into her coin purse with the rest before walking away.

As soon as she was out of earshot, the girl turned to him. "What are ye, daft? You should have taken her money."

Paddy pulled back his foot to show a small pile of coins. "I did. I gave her all the pennies and nickels and kept the rest for us."

The girl's eyes grew wide. "Us?"

Paddy nodded. "Sure. If you wouldn't have sneezed, I wouldn't have been able to keep so many."

"Perhaps, but since you were here to distract her, I was able to get this when she handed me her kerchief." The girl smiled a brilliant smile and held out a shiny green stone bracelet.

Paddy scooped up the coins and slipped them into his pocket and the girl frowned. "Hey, I thought you said we're going to share."

He laughed. "Are you planning to share the dough you get from selling the bracelet?"

"Of course not. Why should I?" she said, hiding the bracelet in the basket under the flowers.

Paddy frowned as he watched her cover the bauble with the flowers. "It would be safer in your skirt."

"Yes, but not until I know the woman won't come back looking for it."

Paddy tilted his head. "You mean you want her to find it if

she does?"

"Of course not, but if she comes back today and finds it on me, then she will think I stole it, and rightly so. But if she thinks me a thief, she would most likely bring a policeman along. I would make a show of looking in my basket and finding it and then say how it must have slipped off the woman's arm when she was looking at the flowers. Since it is not on my person, who is she to say for sure?" The girl shrugged. "Who knows, she may even offer me a reward for helping find it."

Paddy bobbed his head. "Pretty clever."

She beamed under the compliment then looked him up and down. "You're dressed pretty sharp for a street kid."

He frowned and looked at the clothes he was wearing. "What makes you think I'm a street kid?"

She smiled once more. "It's not your clothes, it's your fingernails. You got dirt under them."

He held out a hand and inspected his nailbeds. "Don't rich kids get dirty?"

"Not too much. Not the ones I've seen anyhow."

He looked at her hands and noted the cleanliness of her nails and the lack of dirt on her dress. "Are you rich, then?"

"Course not. I just know how to dress like a lady." She spat on the ground and wiped her mouth with the back of her arm. "I'm Dorthia."

"I'm Paddy."

She looked at his hair and smiled. "It fits."

"That's what everyone says," he said, bobbing his head. "So where do you get the flowers?"

"From the flower man. I get a couple of pennies for each bouquet I sell."

Paddy looked at the basket. "Maybe I could sell some."

Dorthia pulled her basket close. "Only girls can sell them."

Paddy scratched his head. "How come?"

She shrugged. "On account of people don't want to buy flowers from a boy."

"How come?" Paddy pressed.

Dorthia eyed his hands. "Maybe it's because your hands are grubby."

Paddy cocked his head. "What if I wash them?"

She laughed. "Nope. You're a boy. They'd only get grubby again."

He splayed his hands and looked at them. "Yeah, you're probably right."

Dorthia wrinkled her nose. "Course I'm right. I'm a girl. Girls are always right."

The only girl he ever really knew was his momma, and she was one of the smartest people he knew. Plus, Dorthia had managed to strip the woman's bracelet from her arm right under both their noses and Paddy had been trained to watch for that. Paddy nodded his agreement. He realized he hadn't seen her on the streets before. "Where do you sleep?"

She narrowed her eyes at him. "Where I go and what I do is none of your concern."

"Geez, I didn't mean nothin' by it. I just ain't seen you around is all."

"Yeah, well, I'm still not telling you." The words had no sooner left her mouth than she turned on her heels and stormed off.

"Dames," Paddy said as he walked off, shaking his head. He stopped at a cart, bought some sausage from the vendor and stood eating it while contemplating his next move. *I could go to the lodge.* He took a bite and debated his choice. He, along with Slim and the boys, stayed at the Newsboy's Lodging House a couple of nights before Slim's money ran out. *Even without dipping, I have enough to pay for a cot for at least a week.* Paddy shook off the thought, knowing Mouse would not pay for such foolishness. At least not when he had another option.

Paddy looked to the sky to judge the sun, then wrapped the remaining sausage in the paper and placed it in his pocket before heading to the nearest tenement and jumping roofs until he got to Big Joe's building. Once there, he stood looking over the side as he ate the rest of his sausage. Alone with his thoughts of the direness of his situation, loneliness set in. He filled the time thinking of his momma, wondering of the fate of his brothers, and aching to join his friends and beg them to welcome him back into the fold. The fear wasn't from his friends rejecting him; it was the fear he'd felt that day in the graveyard. He'd been scared before, like when his father singled him out, or when he raced past Big Joe hoping the man would not turn and see him, or that day he thought Slim was going to jump off the roof. He'd been really scared that day. But the day in the graveyard was a different kind of scary, one that had kept him from breathing and made him feel as if the devil himself had plucked the air right out of his lungs. What if it happened again? What if the next time he never found his air? Then what would become of him? Would they bury him right there or just let him rot the way he'd seen happen when a horse died in the street?

Don't be silly. They wouldn't let you rot; they'd throw dirt on you. The thought conjured up an image of his mother and a chill raced the length of his spine.

Paddy shook off the chill.

While he'd done well walking the streets, dipping pockets and scrounging a few coins at the flower cart during the day, he couldn't chance returning to the cemetery until he'd overcome the insecurity of being alone at night. Not that he thought he would ever be alone in the graveyard, but if he was scared, his friends would know it the moment he started jumping at each little sound. He thought about Slim and smiled. *Boy, that dope is pretty darn lucky. No one would even know if he was scared on account of his legs never stop jumping.*

Paddy thought back to the night before and how he'd cried himself to sleep and how he couldn't even sleep alone on a rooftop without crying like a scaredy-baby. The boys would laugh him out of the graveyard for sure, and there he'd be standing in the dark at the mercy of the gangs who ran the streets at night. "I can't go back. Not yet anyway. Not until I can stay on my own without being scared."

As if speaking the truth aloud would give away his secret, Paddy turned from the edge and walked to Big Joe's shack, stepping inside without hesitation. Unlike before, when he used to race across the roof to avoid the big man, the shack now felt like a safe haven. Big Joe hadn't been seen in weeks, and the others who roamed the rooftops at night knew it belonged to the fighter. When he and the others were staying there, they'd made sure others knew of the stories surrounding Big Joe and that the shack on top of the roof was not to be messed with. As such, no one had ever bothered them there. He went inside, lay with his back pressed to the far corner of the wall, curled into a ball, and closed his eyes. As he drifted off to sleep, he prayed if death came for him, it would take him without his knowing.

Paddy woke in a panic, looking around and wondering what had pulled him from sleep. Hearing nothing, he closed his eyes once more as tears trickled down his cheeks. It wasn't fair. He could dip pockets and fight well enough that he could walk down the street without fear. He no longer had to fish the grates or worry about going to bed hungry if he couldn't find a penny or two. He had enough money to eat and was wearing clothes that would allow him to get more, but he still couldn't get through the night without being afraid. Paddy sat batting at the tears. As he did, he thought about the last conversation he had with his mother and her telling him to turn himself over to the policeman so he could go to the asylum. "I'll go, Momma." He sniffed and drifted off to sleep, secure in the knowledge that tonight would be his last night sleeping alone under the stars.

***

On any given day, it would be no problem finding a policeman, but today, Paddy roamed the streets, searching to no avail. Growing hungry, he stopped at an apple cart to grab him a lunch apple. Just as he plucked the apple from the cart, he looked up, relieved to see a policeman walking up the street. Not wishing to miss him, he took off running to greet the man.

"Stop thief! Someone catch the varmint!"

Paddy looked to see the apple man standing at the cart shaking his fist in his direction. *Thief? Who, me?* He glanced at the apple in his hand, then looked to see the policeman running toward him. He wanted to tell them he hadn't meant to steal the apple, but the scowl on the policeman's face told him the man was not likely to listen to him. *He won't take me to the asylum; he'll throw me in prison with the murderers and rapists!* At the thought of going to prison, Paddy's survival instinct kicked in. He tossed the apple aside and ducked out of reach just before the officer nabbed him. Paddy looked over his shoulder to see the man stretching his hand out. Paddy swallowed, knowing it was only a matter of time before the policeman nabbed him.

A kid cut in between him, throwing the policeman off balance, then grabbed Paddy by the arm, pulling him along. Paddy's hat flew off. He started to retrieve it and the boy tightened his grip.

"Leave it!" the kid growled.

"Mouse, what are you doing here?" Paddy asked, recognizing the voice.

"Shut up and keep running unless you fancy yourself in prison," Mouse replied. They ran for several blocks before Mouse finally glanced over his shoulder. He stopped, whirling on him. "Didn't I teach you nothing? What were you thinking stealing apples? You could've easily dipped a pocket and had enough money to buy a whole sack."

"I wasn't stealing the apple," Paddy said, denying the accusation.

Mouse spat on the ground. "Lies. Why, I saw you with my own eyes."

Paddy sighed. "I was planning on paying for it and then I saw the policeman."

Mouse's frown deepened. "You're telling me you wanted to go to prison?"

Paddy shook his head. "Of course not. I thought he would take me to the asylum."

"Boy, Paddy," Mouse sighed. "I thought you were smarter than that. Coppers don't take kids to the asylum for stealing apples."

Paddy ran a hand through his hair. "I told you I wasn't trying to steal the apple. I was gonna pay for it until I saw the policeman, then I guess I kinda forgot."

Mouse cocked his head to the side, eyeing him. "You said you wanted to go to the asylum?"

"No, but my momma told me to go there before she died." Paddy clapped a hand over his mouth.

"When'd she die?" Mouse asked coolly.

"Not long afor Slim's momma was ran over."

"Slim didn't mention it."

"That's because I never told him. He was sad that his own momma died. I didn't want to make him more sad by telling him about mine."

"Yeah, I guess that makes sense." Mouse crossed his arms, sizing him up. "That's why you run off like you did. Because you were picturing your momma under all that dirt."

Paddy started to lie, but this was Mouse. Mouse had a way

of knowing if a fellow was telling the truth or not. He nodded and started to walk away.

"Well, where are you off to?" Mouse asked.

Paddy shrugged. "I figured you'd want me to go, knowing I'm a scaredy-baby and all."

Mouse chuckled. "You think people would think that just because you don't want to think of your momma under all that dirt? I thought the same thing about my momma the first time I went in there."

Paddy's eyes widened. "You did?"

"Sure thing, how do you think I knowed what you were thinking?"

Paddy swallowed and lowered his voice. "How'd you get over being scared?"

Mouse shrugged. "My momma once told me it's not the dead you have to worry about; it's the living. And that night, those boys were surely looking to hurt me, so I went in there, and truth be told, it was the best night's sleep I'd had in weeks. I still don't like the thought of my momma being covered with all that dirt, but if she were in there, I guess I kind of thought maybe she'd be looking over me."

Paddy scratched his head once more. "I didn't think of that."

Mouse jutted his thumb to his chest. "That's what you got me for. To tell you the way of things, and I think you should come home."

Paddy frowned. "You do? I kinda thought you didn't like me."

"I don't, but that's okay because you don't like me either."

"That's true."

"Yeah, but just because we don't like each other don't mean we can't have each other's back. That's what life on the street is all about."

Paddy sighed. "Boy, Mouse, you're a tough one to figure

out."

Mouse shook his head. "It's like this, see. You might not like the guy you're fighting alongside of, but if you're fighting with them, you're not fighting against them."

Paddy thought to tell him he was smart, but he would have figured it out in time. Besides, the last thing he wanted was for Mouse to think he was smarter than him. "Mouse?"

"Yeah, Paddy?"

"If it's all the same to you, I'd rather not tell the guys about what happened today."

Mouse grew quiet for a bit then nodded his head. "Show up at the church this afternoon and I'll make sure the fellows know I don't like you."

Paddy smiled. "You know, Mouse, you're pretty okay for someone I don't like."

"Take that back before I punch you in the nose," Mouse said, narrowing his eyes. A second later, he winked and then raced away without another word.

Even though he knew the others wouldn't return to the church for some time, Paddy started off in that direction. As he walked, he knew something inside of him had changed. He was no longer going because he was scared of being alone; he was returning because he now knew it was where he belonged.

Chapter Eleven

The cemetery was empty when Paddy arrived. He was grateful, as it gave him time to gather his courage to step inside. His heart began to race. *Easy, Howard, no one's going to hurt you.* Paddy stopped and looked about the graveyard. He wasn't sure what surprised him most, that the voice inside his head sounded very much like his mother or that the voice had used his given name, which he hadn't heard in so long that it almost sounded foreign to his ears. Either way, the combination worked to soothe his trepidation. He circled the graveyard quickly at first, then slowed and took his time walking through the yard and reading each stone. By the second pass, he gathered enough courage to touch each stone while reading the names on the granite. By the time he'd finished with his fourth pass, he was comfortable both in walking amongst the stones and touching them.

He sat facing a stone carving of a large, winged angel. As he stared at the woman's face, he pictured his mother standing there. "I wish I was with you, Momma."

Instantly, he recalled a conversation they'd had before his mother grew ill. He'd wanted to go off and do something, and she'd taken him into her arms, kissed him on the forehead, and whispered, "You are too much like your father, Howard. It's not your fault; it is the curse of red hair that will get you in trouble. You must learn to be patient. Just because you want to fly doesn't mean you can grow wings."

Paddy swallowed and wiped at tears until, at last, there were no more. Sometime later, he brushed himself off and made a final walk about the headstones, then returned outside the gate and waited for his friends to return.

***

He heard the small group long before seeing them. Slim walked slightly ahead of the others as the procession neared. The boys must have noticed him standing there, as they grew quiet. Then, in a show of solidarity, each boy moved up alongside Slim. Paddy smiled and removed the hat he'd pilfered along the way. As soon as his flaming locks were exposed, Slim grinned and ran to greet him.

"Where ya been?" Tommy asked when he arrived a second later.

"Around." Paddy scanned the group, looking for Mouse, who'd promised to put on a show. "Where's Mouse?"

"He's doing his thing," one of the twins said. "Boy, will he be surprised to see you."

No, but he would pretend to be. Paddy smiled. "I'll bet."

"We best get inside," Slim said, glancing down the street. He turned to Paddy. "You coming?"

"May as well; I ain't got no place else to go." Paddy pushed away from the fence, waited for the others to go inside, then stepped up beside Slim. "I see you picked up some more boys. I thought you weren't interested in starting a gang."

Slim shrugged. "We're not a gang."

"They seem to listen to you."

Slim shifted and looked to the others. "No one else stepped up when Mouse was away."

"He away a lot, is he?" Paddy wondered if that was why Mouse had asked him to return. Maybe he wanted him to come back and take charge of things in his absence. He had to admit, the thought appealed to him.

"Sometimes," Slim replied.

109

"Where's he go?" Paddy asked.

"Can you believe it? He's got him a dame."

"A dame?" Paddy hadn't expected that.

"A girl," Slim said as if he was too daft to understand.

Paddy shook his head at his friend's lameness. "I know what a dame is, ya dope."

Without warning, Slim grabbed him by the arm, pulling him backwards. "Listen, Paddy. I know you don't mean nothing by calling me that. But Mouse, see, he don't like when people disrespect us. He ain't going to be so happy about you coming back, but I can handle him, so you don't have to worry about that. But you got to stop with the names, or he'll boot ya right back out of here, see?"

Paddy felt his face grow red as the rest of the boys stood in rapt silence, watching. "Yeah, I see how it is," he said, jerking his arm away. "I thought we were pals."

Slim gave a nod. The boys moved into the graveyard and sat going through their pockets. Once they'd moved away, he looked at Paddy. "We are pals. Don't you go getting all sore on me. You never liked Mouse no how and he don't like you none either, so it's best to play it straight and follow the rules. And the rules say show respect."

Paddy wasn't sore because Slim was in charge; it was to be expected since he himself hadn't been around. It was that the others had witnessed Slim chastising him that grated on him. No way would they now see him as anyone to look up to. If only he'd stayed that day, it would be him they all looked up to. Not that he had anything against Slim; it was just he was better suited for the job. Paddy shrugged off Slim's comment. "So you're loyal to Mouse now, I get it."

"I'm loyal to my friends." Slim nodded toward the others. "Unless something's changed, that means you too."

Before Paddy could answer, Mouse stepped up beside them,

catching them both unaware. "What's he doing here?"

"Jeesh, Mouse, you about scared me to death," Slim said, then added, "Paddy's going to be staying with us."

Paddy returned Mouse's glare, then when Mouse made no move to give his opinion of the matter, he turned his attention back to Slim. "Want to introduce me to the gang?"

"Slim?" Mouse said, calling after him. "Make sure he antes up with the rest."

Slim hesitated, then bobbed his head.

"What was that all about?" Paddy asked when they were out of earshot.

"We give our loot to Mouse for him to hold."

Paddy frowned. "How much does he take?"

"All of it."

Paddy stopped in his tracks. "What do ya mean all of it? What if you need something?"

"We get our clothes from the lines, eat before we come back, and it doesn't cost nothing to stay here," Slim replied.

"What does Mouse do with the dough?"

Slim shrugged. "I guess none of us ever thought to ask."

Paddy sighed. "Of all the harebrained…" Not wishing to raise Slim's ire, Paddy checked himself. "It's not right, Slim. I can understand a little, but not him taking it all."

Slim glanced nervously over his shoulder. "Don't talk like that. If you don't give it to him, he won't allow you to stay."

Paddy looked over at Mouse, who had joined them in the cemetery and was now holding his hat, watching them out of the corner of his eye as the younger boys emptied their pockets. While he didn't relish handing over the fruits of his labor, the thought of returning to the rooftop alone had him nodding his agreement. "Okay, Slim, I'll give him my dough."

His friend released an audible sigh before turning and walking toward Mouse and the others. Paddy moved in behind him, using him to block Mouse's view as he quickly moved some of his money into another pocket. When he stepped up in front of Mouse, he emptied only one.

***

Paddy watched for Mouse to enter the graveyard, then hurried to be first in line to pay his dues. He reached into his pocket, scooped out his dough less the coins he had moved to the other pocket, and made a show of placing everything into Mouse's cap. When finished, he sat and watched as the others came forward one by one and emptied their pockets as they'd done each day since his arrival two weeks earlier. It wasn't that he'd come to grips with turning over loot he'd stolen. On the contrary, he'd now made it his mission to discover what Mouse was doing with the money he collected. Especially since as far as he could tell, Mouse never contributed any money of his own. Since he was first in line, he knew the hat was empty when he started collecting, and he'd yet to see the boy reach into his own pocket to add anything.

While watchful, Paddy had never voiced those concerns aloud, mostly because no one else seemed to have a problem giving Mouse everything they collected. Nor did they bother to question why the boy disappeared for hours on end, leaving them alone when it was he who trained them to work as a team so they could create a diversion if any of them found themselves in a pickle. As the last boy moved away, Paddy watched Mouse reach into the cap, scoop up the day's earnings, and place the money into his pocket before returning his hat to his head. Mouse then went to his sleeping place without another word. Paddy lowered to his side, blew out a breath, and closed his eyes. *It's just not fair.*

***

After spending a dream-filled night fighting and arguing with Mouse, Paddy had feigned being too sick to move and now stood in the shadow of the building, watching as the boys left the graveyard. He shadowed everyone from a distance, then followed when Mouse waved goodbye and headed off in the other direction. If he was aware he was being followed, he didn't let on, nor did he seem worried about being followed as he walked down the street as if he didn't have a care in the world. He stopped at a tenement building on Ludlow Street, pressing himself against a building while appearing to watch an apartment building on the opposite side of the road. The door opened on the building, and a woman stepped out with a girl who looked to be their age in tow. Mouse ducked, and Paddy craned his neck, trying to get a closer look while also trying to stay out of sight.

The woman was tall and wafer thin and dressed no different than most women who lived in this neighborhood. The girl looked like a smaller version of the woman with dark, stringy hair and a rail-thin body. Both woman and child wore ill-fitting dresses, and the girl plodded along beside the woman, seemingly oblivious to the dirt beneath her dirty bare feet. The duo started down the street, and Mouse followed. Paddy pulled his cap low to hide his hair, then sank into the shadows as he'd seen Mouse do when tailing a mark and followed at a distance. As he walked, he wondered who they were and why Mouse had set his sights on them. Mouse didn't target the poor, and these two looked to be as poor as you can get. Could they be family? Paddy frowned. No, Mouse's mother was dead. Unless he lied, could that be it? Could these two be his family? It all made sense.

***

Paddy stepped up to Mouse and dropped the money into the hat. As he did, he thought of Mouse's momma and sister and smiled.

Mouse narrowed his eyes. "What's so funny?"

113

Paddy froze. The last thing he wanted was for Mouse to know he'd been spying on him. He shrugged. "I don't have a problem."

Mouse took a step forward. "Sure you do. You've been a thorn in my backside since you got here. You got a beef with me. Tell me now."

Not having a better answer, Paddy told him the truth. "I don't think it's right us giving you all our money."

Mouse narrowed his eyes. "You're forgetting that, if not for me, you'd be rotting in jail right now."

Though he hadn't expected Mouse to out him, Paddy couldn't argue with that.

Obviously looking for a fight, Mouse didn't let Paddy's silence stop him. "Have you gone to bed hungry even once since you met me?"

Paddy shook his head.

"That's right. On account of I showed you how to dip and told you not to come here unless you had food in your belly."

"It still doesn't give you the right to steal from us," Paddy said evenly. He started to tell him he knew about him giving the money to his mother and sister when Mouse laughed a taunting laugh.

"I have never stolen a penny from any of my boys – even you."

"But…"

Mouse cut him off. "Not once! You could have told me no. Instead, you're always the first in line to turn it over."

The statement was true, and the others knew. His cheeks burned as the others nodded their agreement. Not fair; he'd only been first in line to see if Mouse was contributing to the pool. He stumbled for an answer. "Because Slim said I couldn't stay if I didn't hand it over," he said without looking at his friend.

"Slim's right. But you could have said no."

"Maybe I still will," Paddy replied.

"Typical redhead. My papa always said boys like you have the devil inside," Mouse fumed. "Go on and go now. We'll be better off without you, then."

As he heard the words, Paddy pictured the woman who'd taken his mother's place. Anger balled up inside of him, and he spat right in Mouse's face.

Mouse dropped his hat and dove at Paddy, pounding on him as they both rolled about the ground like a couple of mad dogs. Paddy wrapped his legs around the boy and matched him punch for punch until Slim and Tommy wrestled them apart. Paddy wiped blood from his lip with the back of his arm as Tommy held on to the back of his shirt collar. Slim held a hand in front of Mouse's chest while the others looked on with eyes so wide, they looked as if they would pop.

Paddy sighed, knowing there'd be no hope of staying now. While he knew he should be sore at Mouse for antagonizing him, he wasn't. On the contrary, he felt relieved. It was as if all the anger he'd felt from what life had dealt him had disappeared. Paddy wiped at the blood once more, looked at Mouse, and smiled.

Mouse wiped the blood from his own lip and returned his grin.

"Does that mean Paddy can stay?" Tommy asked, releasing his hold on Paddy.

Mouse didn't answer. He simply bent, picked up his cap, and returned to what he'd been doing before the altercation.

Slim stepped up beside Paddy and lowered his voice. "Are you staying, then?"

Paddy mulled over the question. "I don't reckon I have anyplace better to go."

"It felt good, didn't it?"

Paddy raised an eyebrow. "What?"

"Getting the anger out."

Paddy smiled and nodded his head. "It felt real good, Slim."

Slim nodded his understanding. "Big Joe told me it's okay to get mad, but you let that madness build up inside, and it will rot your soul. I think your soul has been rotting, causing you to be mad at Mouse for no good reason, and you had to get it out."

Paddy blew out a whistle. "I think Big Joe must have been right since I'm not mad anymore." It was the truth, while he'd been sore at thinking Mouse was stealing from them, he didn't mind handing over his dough if it meant giving it to family. He went to his sleeping place and lay on his back. As he lay there, he thought about his own family and wondered where his brothers had ended up.

Chapter Twelve

November 1, 1918

Paddy sat in a circle with the others, listening as a nasal-nosed kid named Lefty told of a trip he and his family had taken on the train. While they'd all stolen rides on the subway before, Lefty was talking about a real train coming all the way from Boston and how his father had actually paid for the family's tickets. Paddy had heard the story before, as Lefty seemed fond of telling it. It must have been a good trip, as it was the only memory the boy ever chose to tell of. Paddy had asked him about his family once, but the boy refused to tell him why he'd left home. It wasn't unheard of for the boys not to want to mention their parents, as he himself didn't like to talk about that part of his life. Once, he'd come close to telling Slim, but the boy had changed the subject, leaving Paddy to wonder if his friend already knew.

Lefty was just getting to the part where he would describe in mouthwatering detail the meal they'd eaten on the train, when the most beastly noise he'd ever heard rang out through the night and sent chills up the spine of everyone near.

Paddy and the others sprang to their feet, each scanning the dimly lit graveyard for the source of the sound.

Slim ran to the front gate, and Paddy followed, his heart beating so fast, he could feel it in his throat. Voices sang out in the darkness as people filed into the street, offering guesses as to the origin of the sound. A siren blared in the distance. Soon, several others joined, and neighborhood dogs wailed in sorrowful harmony as even more sirens blared an eerie echo throughout the neighborhood.

Paddy worked to steady his voice so the others wouldn't know he was afraid. "Something's mighty wrong."

"It's the train," someone yelled. "My sister lives on Flatbush and phoned to tell me about it just now. Said how it shook all the china off the dinner table."

The news spurred people into action as many raced toward the scene of the crash. Calmer now, Paddy looked to the others. "I ain't never seen a train wreck."

"What about the gangs?" Tommy asked.

"It's still early." Paddy said. "Besides, they'll be too excited about the train to pay us any mind. What do you think, Slim?"

Slim bobbed his head. "I think Paddy's right. But I don't think we all should go."

Paddy nodded his head in agreement. "Tommy, Slim, and I will go."

"Who put you in charge?" Lefty asked.

Slim held up a hand to silence the boy, and the others backed down. They walked to the side fence, tossed their coats over the spikes, and carefully made their way over the spiked rails. Once outside, they tugged their coats free and followed the sound of the sirens and hopped on the trolley to go into Brooklyn. They could hear the murmur from the crowd even before they reached the site of the crash. Paddy looked on with eager excitement at seeing the night sky lit up with hundreds of lanterns. They tried to push their way through the crowd, but with everyone vying to see, it was no use. Paddy hopped up and down, trying to get a glimpse of the wreckage. "It's no use." He tugged on Slim's sleeve. "Let me on your shoulders so I can have a look-see."

Slim squatted, and Paddy hoisted his legs over his shoulders.

"Move to the left," Paddy called from his new vantage point. He craned his neck, but it was no use. "Okay, a little more. Ah, phooey, let me down."

"Well, what'd you see?" Tommy asked when Paddy slid off Slim's shoulders.

"Nothing. Because there's nothing to see. The whole tunnel is blocked. If there's anyone left alive, I don't know how they're gonna get 'em out."

A horn blared behind them. Paddy turned to see a firetruck and watched as police and firemen poured from the back of the truck, barking orders, telling those in the crowd to move out of the way. A man stepped off the truck, and Paddy's breath caught in his throat. If not for the fact that the man was dressed in a fireman's uniform, he would have thought the man to be his papa, mostly because the man sported the same brilliant red hair as he.

"My husband has not come home," a woman wailed. "I've got to see if he's alive." Several others chimed in, each naming the person they were looking for.

The man with the red hair approached the crowd with the confidence of a king and pushed through the gawkers, seemingly unfazed by their pleas. "Yeah, well, you better move back and give us room to work."

Struck with an idea, Paddy removed his hat to showcase his own red hair and followed the man through the crowd as if he, too, belonged. Once through the throng of bystanders, Paddy stepped back to keep from being noticed as the workers went to work with axes, shovels, and picks, clearing the debris. After what seemed like forever, they broke through the pile of rubble, and two men disappeared inside. Paddy held his breath until he could hold it no more as he stretched his neck to see into the opening. The man with the red hair motioned him back but surprisingly didn't send him away as he and two other men took turns continuing to clear debris. The man with the red hair had just pushed his shovel into the mix when he pulled it out and flung it aside.

"Get some more lanterns over here," he bellowed while looking into the tunnel.

Without thinking, Paddy took hold of the lantern near where he was standing and raced forward, handing it to the man. As he did, he looked into the opening and saw a faint light flickering in the distance. The light grew closer, until the two men who'd went inside came out carrying a man who looked as if his clothes had been burned from his body.

Paddy sucked in a breath at the sight of the man, who seemed to be missing his left shoe. Paddy stepped into the opening, thinking to help the fellow out by retrieving his shoe. As he did, hands gripped his shoulder and pulled him back out into the open. He looked up, saw the man with red hair looming over him, and for the briefest of seconds, thought his papa had found him. He brought up his arm, blocking the blow he was sure would come next.

His papa released him, and the image cleared. Paddy saw that it wasn't his papa standing over him but the man with the red hair, who now frowned as he looked at him.

"You okay there, boy?" the man asked.

Paddy nodded.

"Don't you go wandering in there. It's not stable, and we have enough to worry about without trying to dig you out as well."

"Here comes another," someone yelled.

Paddy looked to see another body, this one covered in blood. Those were the first of many who were pulled from within the tunnel. Paddy tried to count how many but quickly gave up as he couldn't count that high. He'd never seen so much blood and hoped when all was said and done, he'd never have to see more. While he wanted to look away, he couldn't quite manage to stop gawking at the sorry souls that trickled out of the opening one by one.

"We need a stretcher. We've got a kid in here."

A kid? Paddy recalled the story Lefty had just told about him and his family riding the train, and swallowed. *Poor dumb sap was probably eating dinner with his family when the train was wrecked.* They brought the boy out of the opening and placed him on the stretcher. Paddy moved in for a closer look and gasped. "Mouse!"

The man with the red hair turned toward him. "You know this kid?"

Unable to speak, Paddy nodded his head.

The man took hold of the guy holding the stretcher's arm. "Where are you taking him?"

"Ebbets Field," the man said as they hurried away.

Paddy felt the color drain from his face as he pushed his way through the crowd, tears streaming down his face. He had to find Slim and Tommy and tell them what he saw. Relief washed over him as he saw them. "We've got to go!" he said the second he reached them. "It's Mouse; they're taking him to Ebbets Field. I think he's dead."

"What was Mouse doing on the train?" Tommy asked as Paddy took off leading the way.

"Dipping. I've followed him there a couple of times," Paddy said, racing toward the ballfield. Paddy stopped just inside the gate, sucking in his breath at seeing the massive field littered with bodies.

Slim blew out a whistle. "How will we ever find him?"

"We just have to look," Paddy said, leading the way. The ballfield was lit up, making it easy to scan each body as they walked through the first row looking for their friend. Doctors and nurses wearing white aprons tinged with blood tended to the injured and paid them no mind as they turned to the next row and continued their search.

"He's not dead!" Slim cried out and took off toward a small fire burning in the middle of the field.

Covered in blood, Mouse sat just beyond the fire, slumped over with his eyes closed.

"Is he dead? He looks dead," Tommy asked when he and Paddy neared.

"Don't be ignorant. Dead people don't sit up," Paddy said, letting out a long sigh.

Mouse opened his eyes, blinking several times.

Slim smiled a relieved smile. "I told you he wasn't dead."

Paddy leaned in close. "He don't look much better than dead. Look at all that blood."

"Yeah, that's a lot of blood," Tommy agreed. "You were on the train, huh, Mouse. We heard it all the way to the chapel. Climbed over the fence to come see. Sumptin makes that kind of noise be worth g'tting a stake in the belly."

Paddy couldn't quit staring at the blood. "Are you hurt, Mouse?" His words came out in a whisper.

"Naw, most of this blood ain't mine," Mouse said, looking at his shirt.

"It's a good thing. I don't think you'd be livin' if it was all yours," Tommy said.

"Leave him be," Slim said, shooing Tommy away. "What happened, Mouse?"

Mouse closed his eyes then opened them once more. "Someone said the conductor was driving too fast. The train took the curve like the driver was late for a Thanksgiving feast. It all happened so fast, I saw a man fly through the air, and then the lights blinked and everything went dark. When I woke up, I had a dead man sleeping on me."

"Woke up? How could you sleep with all that noise?" Slim

asked, echoing Paddy's thoughts.

"I didn't know dead men could sleep," Tommy said, scratching his head.

Mouse shrugged. "All I know is a man caught me dipping in his pocket and told me he was going to take me to jail. Next thing I know, I'm waking up and he's on top of me, but he ain't moving. I think his eyes were open staring at me, but I can't be sure 'cause it was dark."

Paddy couldn't believe his ears. Mouse was the best there was. If he could get caught, then they were all in danger of being discovered. Paddy opened his mouth to say as much when Slim beat him to it.

"You got caught?" Slim whispered.

"Ah, don't be looking at me like that. It wasn't my fault. The train was going too fast, and the whole train was in an uproar. Someone yelled about it, and when he did, the man turned to look. That's when he saw me with my hand on his wallet."

Tommy blew out a slow whistle. "Bet he was mad."

Mouse's face paled, and he closed his eyes. Opening them once more, he vomited.

Mouse looked as white as a ghost, and Paddy was sure the boy was going to die right there in front of them. He felt his stomach flip and took a step back. "Boy, Mouse, you don't look so good."

"Just a little headache from the crack on the head," Mouse said and tilted his head toward the fire so the boys could see.

"So it is your blood," Paddy said, moving in to inspect the bump. "Would you look at the size of that lump! You got a melon on your melon!"

Tommy moved in for a closer look. "Wowzers, Mouse. Someone done went and sewed your head shut."

Slim smacked Tommy alongside his head. "Well, they

couldn't let his brains spill out now, could they?"

"Now why'd you go and pound on me? I didn't do nothing wrong. I just ain't never seen anyone with their head sewn up is all," Tommy whined.

"I need to get out of here before they take me someplace." Mouse stood and studied each boy in turn.

Paddy gulped when the boy singled him out, then frowned as he watched the others walk away.

Mouse reached into his pocket, pulled out a handful of coins and offered them to Paddy.

Paddy rocked back on his heels. "What are these for?"

Mouse winced and placed a hand to his head as if to ease the pain. "I got a job for you."

Paddy didn't know how to react. While he and Mouse had gotten along well enough since their fight, it wasn't as if they were friends. "What kind of job?"

Mouse smiled a slight smile, then winced once more. "Nothing that'll get you tossed in jail. I just need you to shadow someone until I get back."

Shadow someone. Does this mean he knows I've been following him? Paddy worked to keep his face unreadable and focused instead on the fact that Mouse needed him. "Where're you going?"

"None of your business. I'll be back when I can. If you don't want the dough, just say so, I'll give the job to one of the other guys," Mouse said, reaching for the coins.

Paddy cupped his fist and placed the coins in his pocket. "I'll take the job, but if you're gone too long, it will cost you more 'an a few coins."

Mouse closed his eyes, wobbled, then opened them once more. "You just go where I tell you and shadow the girl until I come back."

The girl. He wants me to shadow his sister. Only I'm not

supposed to know. Paddy started to call him on it, then decided not to let on that he'd been able to tail Mouse without him knowing. Instead, he smiled. "Got yourself a girlfriend. That splains a lot."

"She's not my girlfriend, and you'll keep your grubby hands off her as well. I just want you to watch over her and see she's okay."

Paddy wanted Mouse to confirm his suspicions; that the boy hadn't confirmed the girl to be his family irritated him. "What's so special about this girl?" *Come on, Mouse, just tell me the truth.*

Mouse narrowed his eyes. "You just do your job and see she's safe. You need anything, you find Slim. The boy's no good at staying in the shadows, but he sure can throw a punch."

Mouse rattled off the Ludlow Street address, turned to leave, and threw up once more.

Paddy started to go after him to make sure he was okay, then decided against it. The last thing he wanted was to further irritate the boy, especially when Mouse had entrusted him with the honor of looking after his mother and sister.

Not wishing to be caught on the street unaware, Paddy ran all the way to Ludlow Street. While he ran, he thought about Mouse and how he could have picked anyone to watch over his family. *Mouse doesn't want to admit it, but he trusts me. He could have picked Slim or Tommy. Either of the boys would have gladly done anything he asked. But he didn't – he picked me.* By the time he arrived at the tenement building, Paddy was convinced that Mouse actually liked him more than he'd bothered to let on. It had to be true. It was the only explanation as to why Mouse had picked him over the rest of the fellows.

Paddy stood in front of the building wondering what to do next and chiding himself for not having asked Mouse if he was supposed to stay there until he returned or sleep in the cemetery like before and arrive before Mouse's mother and sister went out for the day. He thought about returning to St. Paul's Church to spend the night with his friends, but he'd already chanced running into a gang by being on the street alone once. He wasn't about to do it again. No, he'd stay and do the job Mouse was paying him to do. Paddy shoved his hand into his pocket, felt the coins Mouse had given him, and beamed at his good fortune. This was even better than he thought. He'd heard Mouse give orders many times, but never had he heard him pay anyone to do it. Mouse was paying him, and he had the coins to prove it. Once word got out, they would know him for who he was— Mouse's favorite.

Chapter Thirteen

Even in the dark, Paddy had no problem finding the tenement building where the woman and girl lived. The problem was, he'd always watched Mouse from a distance. As such, he hadn't been inside, nor had Mouse given him their name or apartment number. Thankfully, he had had the presence of mind to tell him they lived on the fourth floor, so it was a place to start. Paddy counted the windows on the front of the building. If he knew which window was theirs, he could climb up and have a look-see. The problem wasn't in the climbing; it was in the getting caught. Folks didn't take too kindly to people peeping in their windows, especially when those windows were on the fourth floor. He paced in front of the building, debating his next move. Though he had yet to see any gangs, Paddy knew he was at risk of being discovered if he stayed out in the open.

Dang it, why hadn't he thought to ask Mouse? The boy had stayed away from the cemetery on many occasions and went to great lengths to stay hidden. He had to have stayed someplace close that would keep him safe. *If only I'd asked.* Paddy sighed. *Nothing to be done about that now.* He slipped a hand into his pocket and felt the coins Mouse had given him. *I'll stay inside, and if anyone has a problem with it, I'll give them a coin for their troubles.*

Paddy opened the door, looked to make sure it was clear, then hurried up the stairs. He opened the door to the fourth-floor hallway, breathing a sigh of relief at finding it empty. He pulled his hat low and stepped into the hallway, jumping at each sound.

C'mon, Paddy, quit being a scaredy-baby. Mouse is counting on you. The inner pep talk worked, as he felt his shoulders relax. Sticking his hands in his pockets, he walked down the hall as if knowing exactly where he was going. He gave a second's thought at sleeping in the stairway, then pushed it aside. He'd not felt comfortable in stairways ever since Milo and his gang nearly killed him. Instead, he walked the length of the hallway twice before opting to sleep at the end, furthest from the door to the stairs. Not only would it offer the least chance of being seen, but it also had a radiator heater whose placement provided a small alcove that he could just squeeze into and would allow him to sleep while sitting up. He settled in and waited.

Paddy couldn't recall drifting off, but he knew he had been sleeping as he woke to the sound of a door closing further down the hall. He looked to see a man ambling toward the stairs and closed his eyes once more. As the morning wore on, more people filed out of the doors that lined both sides of the hallway. Sometimes, it was a single person; others, it was more. The door to the middle apartment opened multiple times with men, women, and children leaving. This scenario repeated itself several times before the woman and girl exited and headed to the stairs without glancing in his direction. Even without seeing their faces, he knew it to be them as, when tailing Mouse, he'd followed them enough to recognize them. Each wore a long dark dress and had matching hair that hung well past their shoulders. If not for their difference in height, they would have looked identical. Paddy waited a good minute before following, then made his way down the stairs and cautiously opened the door, scanning the road before continuing.

The route they took was no surprise, as it was the same route taken when he'd followed Mouse. It was a route that took them to another, more affluent side of town, where single families lived in brownstone houses that boasted large rooms and even larger backyards. A place a boy of his standing could only dream of living in. As he waited outside, he wondered what it would be like living in a house with a yard such as this, then chided himself for even thinking of the possibilities. Kids like him roamed the streets fighting for food; they didn't live in sprawling houses where the occupants never went to bed hungry.

***

Paddy soon lost count of the days spent following Mouse's mother and sister. Their routine was simple. They visited three houses during the day and always stopped at the market for a meat pie on the way home. On Saturdays, they went to the library, and on Sundays, they stayed home. He hadn't seen Mouse or any of the others since the night of the trainwreck. He was grateful to Mouse for having paid him in advance, as it allowed him to get the occasional apple or meat pie from a vendor cart without losing sight of the duo who had yet to do anything worth noting. So much so he had nearly grown weary of following them and struggled between keeping his promise to Mouse and his desire to return to the cemetery to see his friends. He was just pondering that very thing when the door to the apartment opened, and both mother and daughter filed out. As always, each remained closed-lipped as the woman took hold of the girl's hand and practically dragged her from the apartment.

Once outside, the woman released the girl's hand, and they chatted while strolling up the street. Paddy had often wondered what they had to say to each other but was too afraid of being caught to move close enough to hear. They'd walked about a block when the woman bent her head and said something that made the girl hesitate. As he followed, his curiosity got the better of him. He pulled his hat lower to hide his hair and moved closer.

The woman said something in another language, the girl answered in the same tongue, and Paddy felt his jaw drop. It wasn't that they spoke a foreign tongue; it was that Mouse did not. *They are not his family!* The discovery was shocking, as he had long convinced himself it was the reason Mouse had been following them and had insisted he do the same. It was all he could do not to run up to them and ask. Instead, he dropped back and pondered the questions now swirling in his head. *If they are not family, then why? And what connection did Mouse have with them?* He recalled a comment Slim had made when he'd returned to the cemetery. *Mouse has a dame. A dame?* It was the same question he'd asked that had raised the boy's ire. *No, that's not true,* Paddy reminded himself. *You called him a dope.* Thinking of Slim and the cemetery had him longing to return. He watched as the woman and girl turned and followed the same route they always took, knowing their next stop would be the trolley, which he'd have to cling to the outside to keep from being discovered.

"I'll not do it! I'll not follow them today!" He realized he'd spoken out loud and turned, running in the opposite direction. His brain yelled for him to stop and go back, but his legs refused to listen. He ran down the street, ducking into alleys and back into the street once more until he saw the steeple of St. Paul's Chapel. He ran into the cemetery, expecting to see his friends, and was surprised not to find them there. Hearing voices, he looked to see a man and woman strolling up the sidewalk.

He laughed and spoke aloud. "Of course, they're not here, it's the middle of the day. They won't be back for hours." He debated his options. As he did, he realized he hadn't changed clothes since he left and decided his first order of business was to find something to wear, then decided if he was going to do that, he should go to the bathhouse. While he didn't particularly like spending money so frivolously, it was much too cold to go to Coney Island and wash in the bay. Mouse liked to gather clothes from backyards; he preferred searching rooftops. While windows overlooked the yards, the lines on the rooftops were often left unattended. He made his way to Cherry Street, hoping to find something suitable to wear on the roof of a tenement building he'd had luck with in the past. As he approached the building, he saw a clothesline stretched across to the next building on one of the upper floors. On the line were several shirts and pants that looked promising, but what really caught his eye was a black coat whipping in the wind. From the distance, it looked to be the right size.

Paddy stood in the street smiling as he peered up at the coat, which looked so new, there weren't even any patches. None that he could see anyway. The issue was the building was taller than any he'd climbed, and the line looked like it was extending from a sixth-floor window. He walked to the building, tilted his head back, and looked up. Paddy blew out a whistle, debating his options. *The Human Fly wouldn't be scared.* Unfortunately, he wasn't the Human Fly, and the thought of climbing that many floors had him plenty scared. It wasn't the height that scared him; he could jump a roof without a second's hesitation. It was knowing he would be too tired to make it all the way up and safely back down again.

The bigger problem was winter was coming, and he really wanted that coat. Paddy studied the building some more, then went inside to find a better solution.

Arriving at the sixth floor, he walked down and stood outside the door of the apartment. After several seconds of debating, he turned the doorknob and stepped inside as if he belonged. It was a bold plan, wherein he was caught, he'd claim to have been distracted and ended up on the wrong floor—

chancy, but better than sneaking inside and getting pegged as a thief. One could get him shooed away with a broom or rolling pin, the other could land him in jail.

The apartment was set up like most tenement buildings he'd been in, with a small living area off to one side and a cooking stove, sink, and table with chairs on the opposite side of the room. The room was tidy, and unless someone was behind one of the two closed doors, he was now alone in the apartment. There was a watch on the table surrounded by several silver coins. Paddy thought about taking them, but it didn't seem right. Dipping pockets was one thing, but stepping into a person's home to rob them felt wrong. It didn't dawn on him to feel guilty about the coat. He was cold, and it could take days of dipping pockets to get enough money to buy one on his own.

He thought back to when Mouse was teaching him and the others how to steal. One of the twins had gotten cold feet, and Mouse had assured them it was okay, saying the owner could have easily hung it inside to dry. By hanging it outside, it was as if they were asking for it to be stolen. Of course, he had gone further by asserting that they were doing the person a favor by stealing whatever it was, as they would be more cautious about leaving things out in the future. That was the thing about Mouse, like him or not, the boy always had an answer for doing things that seemed to make doing them less bad.

Paddy thought about that as he walked to the window. He'd originally thought to steal a complete set of clothes from the line, but now it didn't seem right. Instead, he pulled the line toward him and plucked each garment from the line, placing the wooden pens in a small basket just under the windowsill. As he brought in each item, he folded it the way he'd watched his mother do and set them on the table in a pile. It didn't look quite as neat as if his mother would have done it, but it would do. He repeated the process until he retrieved the coat and shivered as he pulled it on. It was slightly larger than he'd thought but would keep him warm until he grew into it.

He started for the door, then turned and returned to the pile of clothes. Pulling the coins from his pocket, he left them on top of the pile. Reconsidering, he pulled out enough to pay for his shower, the use of a towel, a much-needed haircut, and a meat pie for dinner afterward. He looked at the meager offering of coins that now lay on top of the pile and sighed. It wasn't enough to pay for the garment, but was still enough to ease the guilt that wasn't entirely staunched by Mouse's words.

Instead of going down to the street, Paddy made his way to the roof and was rewarded by several clotheslines full of laundry. He pulled a shirt, pants, and socks that looked to be the right size, then started to go back inside and thought better of it. He'd been lucky thus far; the last thing he wanted was to run into the rightful owner of the clothes he'd just pilfered. He walked to the edge of the roof to judge the distance, then returned for a running start and jumped to the next roof. Once there, he walked to the outer door and took his time descending the stairs then made his way over to Rivington Street Bath.

Not surprisingly, there was a line outside the building waiting to use the bath. Having worked his way through a crowd like this on many previous occasions, Paddy stuck his hand in his pocket to protect his change and kept it there as he waited. He scanned the crowd, watching for the dipper – he hadn't seen any sign of one, but he knew one to be there. Anytime there was a crowd gathered, it was safe to assume someone was up to no good. He found the dipper a few moments later, but to his surprise, it was Dorthia, the girl he'd seen selling flowers on the corner before.

Intrigued, Paddy watched her move through the crowd and held his breath on more than one occasion when he thought she would surely get caught. It never happened. Perhaps it was because she only targeted men and wore the front of her shirt open in the most scandalous way.

Look away, Howard, that girl is nothing but trouble. His mother's words were as clear as if she were standing right beside him. But she wasn't, and he rather enjoyed looking at the girl's bosom, so he didn't feel the need to heed his mother's ghostly warning.

As if feeling his stare, Dorthia looked in his direction and bent low. She smiled a most wicked smile, then turned and strolled away, never once looking to see if he was still watching. He recalled sitting at the dinner table one night and hearing one of his brothers talking about a girl such as this. His momma had said something about her being of easy virtue and told them all to stay away from the likes of her. He wasn't sure why his mother had warned them away, as the girl didn't look the least bit dangerous to him. The door to the bathhouse opened. To his surprise, the woman and girl who he'd been following stepped out into the sunlight. He moved back behind the man in front of him and pulled his hat low. There was no need, as both looked at the ground as they hurried past those waiting outside.

***

Something about a clean body, fresh haircut, and new – to him – set of clothes had Paddy whistling as he made his way back to the cemetery. Then again, it could have been that he was just eager to see his friends and return to life in the streets as he knew it. He dipped a few pockets on the way and returned to the cemetery at dusk feeling better than he'd felt in weeks. He went inside the yard, instantly disappointed not to find his friends already there. *There's no reason to worry; you're just a bit early is all.* Only, as the minutes ticked by, he did worry. It wouldn't be long before the caretaker locked the gate. Not only would Slim and the gang have to worry about the gangs, but it meant he would be sleeping in the cemetery alone. *They're coming, I know they are.* He walked through the graveyard, checking the spots where each boy had lain, and found nothing. Not that they would leave their belongings in the open, but there was no sign anyone had slept there recently. *It's getting cold out; perhaps they have moved into the Newsboy's Lodging House.* Possible, but he doubted it. Mouse had already put his foot down, saying they wouldn't go until it snowed. Paddy walked to the fence and looked out into the street. Nothing. He looked at the empty graveyard, and his mouth went dry. *You dope. Don't be a scaredy-baby. You've slept here plenty of times. Yes, but never alone.*

Something caught his eye and he looked to see the caretaker coming down the path with the keys to lock the gate. Paddy swallowed. *I can't do it. I can't stay here all alone!* He bolted, running through the grass and slipping out the opening just as the man was closing the gate.

The caretaker shut the gate, placed the key into the lock, and hesitated. "Are you sure then, son?"

No. Paddy nodded. "Yes, sir."

"Okay, then. I wish you well." The man clicked the lock, pulled out the key, and turned without another word.

Paddy took off running like a rabbit being chased with no other thought than to get inside before the gangs caught him on the street. It grew darker with each block. He heard voices and cut through the alley, holding his breath until he made it through to the other side. A dog stood in the street eating something. Paddy started to cross, saw another dog standing in the shadows, and gave both a wide berth. The one who'd been eating raised its head and growled a warning. Paddy started to run, remembered something his brother had said and thought better of it. Instead, he kept watching as he made his way slowly down the street. He heard someone cough and looked to see a man in a long black coat watching him. Not able to control his feet, he took off running once more and soon found himself on the stoop of the tenement building on Ludlow Street. Once inside, his emotions caught up with him, tears streaming down his face as he climbed the stairs to the fourth floor and pushed his back against the wall near the radiator. He heard ticking and realized that someone had turned on the heat. While it wasn't warm in the hall, it was enough to break the chill. He took off his coat and draped it over him as his mind retraced the events of the day. He thought about the flower girl he'd seen near the bathhouse and how she'd smiled when she saw him. Then, of the girl he'd been following and how he'd yet to see her smile. It didn't make sense to him. She got to see her momma every day; what could she have to be sad about? He was still pondering that question when sleep came for him.

Chapter Fourteen

The night was filled with dreams that he could not fully remember. He recalled searching for Slim and sleeping alone in a yard where noises on the other side of the iron fence left him frightened and sad. Paddy woke early and sat watching as everyone went about their business. He pressed his back into the wall, carefully counting each person who left the middle apartment. As he did, he thought of the dark-haired girl and her mother and wondered what they did to occupy their day. While he had followed them to each house, he always followed Mouse's example and waited for them across the street to keep from being seen. Now, as he sat here waiting, he wondered what went on inside those brownstones and further wondered if it was why the girl appeared to be so sad. As if thinking about them made them appear, the door to the apartment opened, and mother and daughter hurried toward the stairs.

He stood and started to follow but stopped in front of their door instead. He glanced toward the stairs, debating his next move, but he'd counted as he'd done in the past, and according to his calculations, the apartment should be empty. Also, because he'd never seen anyone actually use a key to enter, he thought the door to be unlocked. He took a breath and tried the knob, letting out the breath when the door opened. He stepped inside, stilling when he saw a man sitting in the far corner.. The man looked at least a thousand years old and sat on a tall wooden chair grasping a piece of wood in one hand and a knife in the other, He rocked back in the chair and brushed wood shavings from his lap with the back of the knife blade as he held Paddy's gaze.

Paddy started to back out.

The man leveled the chair and pointed the knife at him with a gnarled hand. "Come inside." The words were spoken with a thick Polish accent.

"Th-that's okay. I must have the wrong apartment," Paddy stammered.

The man threw the knife toward him. Paddy sucked in a breath as the blade struck the door just beside his shoulder. "I said come inside," the man said firmly.

Paddy gulped a fearful breath and stepped into the room.

"Close the door and bring me my knife. Be mindful of the blade; it'll cut you to the bone."

Then why'd you throw it at me? Paddy kept the question to himself as he pulled the knife from the door and walked closer.

The man held out his hand, and Paddy hesitated.

The man eyed the knife. "You're not aiming to stick me with my own knife, are you, son?"

Paddy shook his hand. "No, sir. But I'd like the same promise from you before I hand it back."

The man smiled for the first time since he'd entered the room. "If I were going to stick you, the knife wouldn't have landed in the door."

Paddy figured that to be true and handed the man his knife.

The man looked him up and down. "What's your name?"

"Paddy."

The man glanced at Paddy's hair and nodded. "Could have guessed it."

"What's your name?" Paddy asked while keeping an eye on the knife.

The man's mouth twitched. "My given name is Dobrogost,

though no one has called me that in a number of years."

"Then what do they call you?"

"Dobs. It's easier, I guess. Now tell me, what did you come here thinking to steal?"

Paddy felt his eyes bug. "I wasn't thinkin' to be stealing nothing. I told you…"

Dobs cut him off. "I wasn't born yesterday."

Paddy frowned and studied the man's heavily wrinkled face. "Of course, you weren't. You're probably one of the oldest fellows I've ever seen."

Dobs chuckled. "I meant I can tell a lie when I hear one. You knew what you were doing and had that lie already made up in case someone was to catch you coming in here. Look me in the eye and tell me I'm lying."

Paddy sighed. "I wasn't gonna steal anything. I just wanted to have a look around."

"Why?"

Paddy wasn't expecting such a straightforward question. "I just was, is all."

Dobs shook the knife at him. "Tell me another lie, and I'll cut that tongue right out of your mouth."

Paddy swallowed, knowing the man was telling the truth. "I wanted to know more about the girl and her mother," he blurted when the man leaned forward.

Dobs eased back against the chair. "Girl? You're speaking of Mileta?"

Paddy shrugged. "I don't know her name. She and her ma left just before I came in."

Dobs nodded. "That'll be Mileta and her mother Milena. What do you want with them?"

Another shrug. "Mouse paid me to follow them to keep them safe."

Dobs raised an eyebrow. "You're not doing a very good job.

You should give the rodent his money back."

"He's not a rodent, he's a boy. And I did follow them, but that money's long gone on account of I've been following them a long time."

"This boy, this Mouse. He's sweet on the girl?" the man asked as he dug the knife into the piece of wood he held.

"The devil if I know. I thought maybe the woman was his ma, but then I heard her talk and knew it wasn't true."

"You didn't ask him?"

"No, on account of I was afraid his brains would spill out. He was hurt in the train crash, and they'd just sewed up his head," Paddy said by way of explanation. "He might be dead because he ain't come back, and Slim and the others aren't at the cemetery. I looked for them, but they weren't there and I didn't have anywhere else to go, so I just came back here. I was going to follow Mileta and her mother again, but then I thought maybe I'd just come inside and have a look around. I wasn't planning on stealing anything, honest. I just wanted to look."

Dobs nodded as if the explanation made perfect sense. "Have you eaten?"

"Not yet today. I'll go get a meat pie for supper." *Providing you don't cut out my tongue.* He kept the last part to himself. Better not to remind the guy in case he'd forgotten.

Dobs waved the knife toward the far counter. "There's some cheese. Go on and cut yourself a small chunk."

Paddy didn't want to rile the man, so he went to the counter and sawed a hunk off the end. He looked over at him. "Do you want some?"

Dobs shook his head. "No, I've already eaten."

Paddy brought the cheese back into the room and stared at the chunk of wood the man was holding. As he did, he could just see the outline of an image within the grain. "Why, it looks like a bird."

Dobs smiled. "You have a good eye. I've just found it myself."

Paddy scratched his head. "You found it? You mean the bird was hiding in that wood all along?"

Dobs set the chunk aside and groaned as he stood and used a shaky hand to pluck a dog off the shelf behind him. He handed it to Paddy, who turned it from side to side.

Paddy blew out a long whistle. "You made this?"

"I made this chair and most of the other furniture in this room. The dog showed himself to me, and I helped him see the light of day."

Paddy nodded toward a basket with several small pieces of wood. "Do they all have animals inside?"

"They all have something inside: an animal, bird, person, or even something else. It's up to the carver to discover what is inside."

Paddy examined the dog for another moment and then handed it back to him. "Boy, I'd like to be able to do that when I grow up."

Dobs returned the dog to the shelf and sat with a heavy sigh. "Why can't you do that now?"

Paddy wrinkled his brow. "I ain't got no knife."

The man thought on this for a moment, then pointed to the table. "Pull one of those chairs over here."

Paddy did as told.

"Now, look in that basket and find yourself a piece of wood. Don't take the first one you come to. Look them over and let them call to you."

Paddy sighed when none of them actually spoke. Instead of admitting he couldn't hear them, he rifled through the pile. "How do I know which one to pick?"

"You'll know it. It'll just feel right in your hand."

"But I thought you said they all have something in them."

"That they do. You need to find the one that you wish to set free. Take your time and look at the possibilities."

Paddy studied the pile a bit longer before choosing a smaller piece that seemed to fit best in his hand, then sat in the empty chair, further examining it.

"What do you see?" Dobs asked.

As Paddy peered into the wood, the image of a mouse came to mind. He smiled. "A mouse!"

"Just because of its size?"

Paddy shook his head and pointed to his forehead. "No. I really saw it. Right in here."

Dobs pulled a second pocketknife from his pants pocket and handed it to Paddy. "If he's in there, you best get to work letting him out."

Paddy wasn't sure what surprised him most, that the man had two knives or that he actually trusted him to use them. "How do I start?"

Dobs slid his own knife into the piece of wood he held, showing how to slowly carve away the smallest of slivers, something that must have been difficult to do with the way the man's hand was curled. "Just be careful not to cut your finger off."

Paddy set to work, sliding the knife along the wood.

"What is it you wish to know about Mileta?" Dobs asked after a while.

Paddy shrugged. "I wanted to know why she doesn't smile." It was a silly request but one that plagued his mind.

Dobs pointed across the way. "See that blanket pallet by the far wall?"

There were several piles of blankets scattered about the room, so Paddy merely nodded.

"That is all the girl has to call her own."

Paddy, who'd spent most of his life sleeping on the floor at the foot of his brother's bed, didn't see anything wrong with sleeping on blankets. "And?"

"And she and her mother come in here each day and stay there until it's time to leave again. Mileta is not allowed to leave her mother's side."

"She can't even come to watch you?" Paddy asked as he shaved off another sliver of wood.

"I am but an old man. No one has paid me no mind for many years until today."

"Are you her grandpa?"

"I have no children. At least, no more." He continued before Paddy could ask what had happened to them. "Mileta has no one but her mother to care for her. She lost her papa coming to America."

"Lost him?"

"He died," Dobs clarified. "The child knew English, but the mother did not."

"She does know English, I heard her. She speaks Polish better, but I did hear her."

"A woman who lives here is a schoolteacher. The people who live here get lessons from her for a couple of pennies each day."

"Is that where you learned to speak it?"

Dobs shook his head. "No, I've been in this country many years. I used to own a furniture store off Water Street. It was close to the piers, and I didn't have to haul my wood very far once it came off the ship."

Paddy blew out a whistle. "You mean you were rich?"

A sadness crossed the man's wrinkled face. "I was once everything."

Paddy frowned. "What's that supposed to mean?"

"I was a husband, a father, a businessman, and had the wealth that went with it all. Now, I am a waste of a man who earns his place on the floor by whittling a few animals the woman sells to pay for my keep." He paused for a moment, looking over the bird he was working on before continuing his story. "I opened the furniture store not long after my wife and I came to this country. My wife bore me a couple of strong sons who worked with me in the shop when they were old enough. We made fine furniture carved with exquisite etchings. People came from all over the city to buy our wares. Then the war between the states began and took my sons from me. They went south to defend the flag. I kept waiting for them to come home, but they never did. Maybe it was for the best, as most of the ones who did return were never the same."

Paddy glanced over at the man. "What is a war?"

"War is death. Death to those who fight in it. Death to everything it touches and death to the hearts it leaves behind," he replied, then turned and spat in a bucket beside his chair as if to rid his mouth of the filth he'd just imagined before dipping his knife and carving into the wood again. A few minutes passed before he continued his story. "We lost a lot of men in that war and those wars that followed, but ships brought in new men each day. Those men needed jobs, and some had the means to open their own shops. Soon, there were many furniture stores in the area, and we were all fighting for business from people who didn't have much money to spend. A man came into the shop one day and offered to buy my business. I was tired and agreed to sell. I woke up the next day, and my wife was gone. So was the money."

"Did you try to find her?"

"I put an advert in the paper asking her to come home, but she never did, and I never thought to try again."

"Wow, that's bad luck," Paddy said.

"That's the way of it." Dobs agreed. "I went to work for an Italian fellow, carving pipes by hand after that. He didn't seem to mind that I was Polish, and I didn't care that I could only understand half of what he said. He liked the work I did, and I liked the money he paid, so we got along just fine. I worked for him for a number of years until my hands slowed me down. I'd sold my house by then and had moved into this tenement. I was paying on time, but the landlord didn't seem to care about that. He moved a family in here with me and said if I complained, he'd throw me out on the street. The family moved my things to the smaller bedroom. Later, they moved another family in and moved my things to a spot in the corner. I heard them talking about sending me away, so I picked a log from the basket used to fuel the stove and carved a little doll for her girl to hold. When that woman found out I could carve things, she started bringing in wood for me to work. Not just logs but actual pieces of nice scrap wood, which she got from a woodworker in town. She'd take those things to the market once a week and sell them. One night, she found me sitting in a chair near the window, working on a piece of wood. Soon after that, she moved my bedding under the window so I could work by the light of the moon whenever I wanted. About a year ago, Mileta and her mother, Milena, showed up with not more than the clothes on their backs. I overheard the other two women whispering, saying how they were some kind of distant kin. I'm not sure if that's the truth of it, but they allowed them to stay. Milena is right to keep that girl close. I don't like the way the menfolk look at her. If I ever see them near her, I'll make sure my knife doesn't miss." Dobs looked at Paddy and winked.

Paddy narrowed his eyes at the man. "You mean you tried to stick me with that knife?"

Dobs smiled. "Sure I did. I thought you were here to take what little I have left."

Paddy swallowed. "I'm glad you missed."

"So am I," Dobs said solemnly. "I can't recall a day that I've enjoyed more. I haven't left this building in longer than I can remember, and no one here has time to listen to an old man tell his stories."

They sat in comfortable silence for some time before Paddy finally asked a question he'd been pondering. He held up his piece of wood that was starting to take shape. "How'd you come to know how to do this… what's it called?"

"Whittling. My papa showed me," Dobs replied.

"Who showed him?"

"His papa did. He learned from his papa before him. I guess it was something our family was born to know. 'Keep your hands out of your pockets,' my pa used to say. 'It only wears out your clothes and never gets you anywhere.'"

Paddy looked at the wood in his hand, which was getting smaller with every stroke of the knife. "Do you think I was born to know?"

Dobs glanced in his direction and smiled a wrinkled smile. "Time will tell, son. That's starting to take shape. We'll see if you can find the mouse tomorrow."

Paddy couldn't believe his ears. "You mean I can come back?"

"Unless you've got anything better to do."

Paddy shook his head. "No, sir, nothing at all."

The man's face turned serious. "You just make sure everyone is gone before you come in, understand?"

"Yes, sir," Paddy said, bobbing his head.

A smile creased the old man's face. "Good, now hand back that knife and get on out of here before the others get home. Run on now, and don't be looking so glum. It'll be here for you when you come back."

Paddy stood and reluctantly turned over the knife along with the slender piece of wood where he was just seeing the outline of the same mouse he'd seen in his mind before he started.

Chapter Fifteen

If not for his fear of getting tossed from the building, Paddy would have spent the morning pacing the hallway instead of crouched in the corner waiting impatiently for the occupants of the apartment to leave. He felt only a slight bit of guilt when he made no move to follow when Mileta and her mother left the building. While still curious at how they filled their time in the brownstones they visited, he was a great deal more interested in visiting with Dobs and releasing the mouse from the wood, so much so that he'd spend most of the night carving away at wooden mice that filled his dreams.

The door to the apartment opened, and the last family left, heading to the stairwell. He was just getting ready to head to the door when the woman returned, stepped into the room then left again a moment later. He made a mental note to see them fully down the stairs in the future. He started to knock, then turned the handle instead. A smile spread across his face when he saw Dobs sitting in the same chair where he'd left him the day prior.

The man returned his grin and motioned him in. "Come, bring the chair."

Paddy retrieved it and set it beside Dobs, who pulled out the knife along with the piece of wood. Paddy had hoped Dobs would offer him another hunk of cheese, but he did not. Instead, Dobs turned Paddy's carving and pointed to the last side he had worked.

"This side is coming along; start on the other side today,"

he said, handing Paddy both the wood and the knife.

Paddy unfolded the blade and hacked at the mouse.

Dobs laid his hand on Paddy's arm. "Easy, son, keep that up and you'll lose a finger. You're not chopping a tree; you're creating life. Concentrate on the mouse and let the knife find its way. Think of the wood as a block of butter that must be carved out gently to keep the butter from sliding off the knife. The thing to remember is there's no turning back. Once you cut it off, you can't put it back."

"Have you ever cut off something you weren't supposed to?" Paddy asked, slowing his hand.

"Of course I have. Anyone who works with wood has, and they'll be lying if they tell you differently," Dobs said, picking through the basket and choosing a hunk of wood for himself.

Paddy glanced at the shelf and saw a bird sitting next to the dog the man had shown him the day prior. "You finished your bird!"

"Stayed up half the night working on it by the light of the moon." Dobs nodded toward the shelf. "Go on, take a look."

Paddy placed his things in the chair and went to the shelf. Picking up the bird, he traced a finger over the bird's wings and blew out a whistle. "How'd you get it so smooth?"

Dobs pointed his thumb to a small stack of papers on the shelf next to the dog.

Paddy returned the bird to the shelf and picked up one of the papers. "Sandpaper?"

Dobs raised a brow. "You've heard of it?"

"Sure, my momma used to use it to sharpen her sewing needles."

"You said used to. Your ma doesn't sew anymore?"

Paddy shook his head. "My momma's dead."

Dobs nodded his understanding. "And your papa, is he dead too?"

"I'd be better off if he were," Paddy replied.

Dobs had been in the process of inspecting the hunk of wood he'd selected. He lowered the wood and looked at Paddy. "How so?"

"Your papa taught you how to make things. The only thing my papa ever taught me was how to hate him. That's why I ran off." Paddy returned the sandpaper to the shelf and went back to his seat. He studied the small block of wood before placing his knife and carefully scraping away the thinnest of shavings. "My brothers ran off too. Only they went out west to find my other brothers, who left when I was born. Momma told them to go but told me not to go with them, saying they needed to find their own way."

"I have a brother. He was a number of years younger than me. He came over on a ship shortly after my wife and I arrived. I tried to get him to stay, but he said he needed to find his way. I suppose that's what brothers do. He stopped in for a visit for a month or so, then took the train to Philadelphia and opened his own furniture store there. We used to write letters, but I guess after my wife left, I was too ashamed to let him know what had happened to me. I thought to mail him a letter when my situation changed here, but by then, my hands were too mangled to do anything but hold the knife. I can only do that because I've been doing it so long that my hands kind of turned in that direction. I asked the woman who lives here to write one for me, but she laughed and said she didn't have time for that. I know the truth. She doesn't want to part with the money my carvings bring her."

Paddy looked up from his task. "Philadelphia? Is that west?"

Dobs shook his head. "No, it's south. Why do you ask?"

"Oh, on account of my brothers went west." Paddy eased off another sliver of wood. "I can do it."

"Do what?" Dobs asked.

"Write your letter for you."

Dobs leaned forward in his chair. "You know how to write?"

Paddy nodded. "I had some schoolin'. I might need help with the spelling, though."

Dobs sighed and pushed back in his chair. "It doesn't matter. I'd have to have paper and an envelope and money to post the letter."

"How much do you need?" Paddy asked.

"A penny or two for the stamp." Dobs looked toward the desk in the far corner. "We could probably find a piece of paper and an envelope in that desk over there."

"Won't the woman be mad?"

"She uses my desk and my table; I think it's worth a measly piece of paper and envelope. I think she'd miss the stamp, though, so it doesn't matter anyway."

Paddy wanted to tell the man he could easily get the money by dipping pockets but decided against it. He liked talking to Dobs, and he didn't want the man to get sore at him for stealing and run him off. He thought about it for a moment, trying to think of a better solution, then smiled. "I can get you money for a stamp."

"You can?"

"Yep," Paddy said, bobbing his head. "By fishing in the grates. I do it all the time."

"No," Dobs said at last. "You'll need that money to eat."

"The grates where I fish in have lots of coins. Why, I bet if I were to go there now, I'd find a pocket full of change," Paddy lied. He could find the change, but it would be by dipping pockets, not fishing in some old grate like a baby.

Dobs leaned forward and pointed to Paddy's hand. "I'll make you a deal. You bring me a stamp the next time you come, and I'll trade you for that knife you're holding."

Paddy looked at the knife in awe. "Why give it to me when you could get way more than two pennies if you sold it?"

"I don't want to sell it," Dobs said firmly.

"Why not?"

"Cause it belonged to my pop."

"Then why do you want to give it to me?" It was not that he didn't want it; it was just no one had ever given him anything so special before.

"I gave it to my oldest son when he was a boy. He didn't want to lose it, so he left it in his dresser before he went off to war. I've carried it around for a long time, but think both my pop and my boy would be happy if you had it."

Paddy studied the knife. "They would?"

"It would give them pleasure to know someone was going to carry on the family tradition."

"You mean carving wood?"

"I mean bringing the wood to life."

Paddy looked at his little block of wood and smiled. "I wish the mouse would come to life."

"It will, just not in the way you're thinking. But if you bide your time and do it right, it'll make you smile. Even better is when it makes others smile. Then you'll know you did a good day's work."

Paddy stared at the block. "You mean this is work?"

"Of course it is. And that's why people pay money for it."

Paddy frowned. "It doesn't feel like work."

"That's the best kind of work there is," Dobs replied.

"Are you really going to give me this knife?" Paddy asked, hoping it was true.

"No, we're making a trade. You never give someone a knife."

Paddy looked up from his carving. "Why not?"

"Because it's bad luck. Some say it will sever the friendship.

You always make them trade you a coin, or, in our case, a stamp for it."

"I'll go get it now," Paddy said, fearing the man would change his mind.

"No," Dobs said, waving him off. "It's waited this long. It can wait a little longer. Now finish that mouse so I can teach you some more."

As Paddy worked the knife along the wood, he couldn't remember a time he'd been this content. Okay, maybe when his momma was alive, but even then, he always had to worry about his papa. But sitting here with Dobs, he could almost imagine that he lived here and Dobs was his papa showing him how to work the family business.

As if reading his mind, Dobs leaned over and pointed his knife to where the mouse ear was just coming through. "Be mindful of your strokes there. One wrong swipe and you'll be left with a mouse that can't hear."

"It's a good thing you didn't cut off the bird's beak, or he wouldn't be able to sing," Paddy said without looking away from the mouse.

Dobs chuckled, then blew out a sigh. "You are a quick study, Paddy."

Paddy slid a glance at his new friend. "My name's Howard."

"That's a fine name," Dobs replied.

As Paddy worked, he thought about what Dobs had said about his brother and wondered what his brothers were up to. He wished he knew where they were as he wouldn't mind sending them a letter to tell them about Dobs and learning about the family business. "What was in the letters?" Paddy asked after a bit.

"What letters?"

"The ones you used to write to your brother."

"Oh, the usual things people put in letters, I suppose. I

would write about things that were going on in my life. And tell him about a large order I received. Once, I wrote a whole letter just to boast about a deal I got on some beautiful teak that came in on a ship from Africa."

"What's teak?" Paddy asked.

"A fine wood which makes beautiful tables and such." Dobs smiled at the memory, then continued with his story. "I'd tell him about the weather, tell him the wife said hello, or give him an update on the boys and the things they did as they grew. I'd regale him with a story I'd heard or something I might have read in the paper that seemed interesting enough to share. Then I'd send it off, and a week or three would pass, and my brother would write me back and tell me of things in his life. One time, he wrote and told me of a big brewery fire that had happened not far from where he lived. He said how that fire started all the way over on Shackamaxon and how it burned some of his furniture store on Frankford Avenue. I guess they must have gotten it mostly settled by the time it reached his place on account of that brewery ended up costing the insurance company fifteen hundred dollars, and he only lost five hundred. They had insurance to cover all of that, which is a good thing, because that's a lot of money."

Paddy had so many questions about insurance and how he remembered the names of the streets and such, but now that Dobs started talking, he seemed to be enjoying the telling, so he just let the man talk.

"He said he was scared for the fellow who owned the building next door on account of he got himself burned trying to help put it out. I don't recall him ever following up on that, so I don't know how the man made out. Another time, he told me how they went and… well, would you look at that, I believe you have found yourself a mouse. And in only two days. Well done. It took me nearly a week to find my first animal."

Paddy beamed under the praise and once again wished the man were indeed his papa.

"Okay, Howard, now for the final part. Grab a piece of the sandpaper from behind my chair and give that varmint a good rub."

Dobs calling him by name caught Paddy off guard. Even though he himself had said it only a short time before, it was the first time he could recall anyone else actually calling him it since leaving home.

"Right behind my chair," Dobs repeated.

Paddy hurried to get the paper and started rubbing the mouse.

"Easy, you're not trying to remove a stain. Relax the pressure and just glide it along the surface to remove any rough edges."

Paddy spent the better part of the hour sanding and tweaking the mouse until, at last, it was nearly as smooth as glass. "I'm finished!" he said, grinning and holding it for Dobs to see.

"You sure are! I do believe that's the finest mouse I've ever seen, aside from a real one. Why, I wouldn't be surprised if it doesn't bring a dime or two at the market tomorrow."

All the pride Paddy had been feeling drained in an instant. "The market?"

Dobs nodded. "Yes, I told you the woman here takes everything I make to the market each Saturday."

Paddy worked to keep his voice from cracking. "But you didn't make it. I did."

Once again, Dobs nodded. "But you used the wood she brought, and she'll know if any is missing and will hold me accountable."

Paddy batted at a tear. "Can't you tell her you put the wood in the fire?"

"I'm sorry, Howard. I thought you knew." Dobs blew out a

sigh. "No, how could you? Mrs. Bronski, the woman who lives here, likes things a certain way. She keeps track of everything I do and everything I eat. You remember the hunk of cheese I told you to take yesterday?"

Paddy glanced at the counter and nodded. "Yes."

"Mrs. Bronski saw that I'd had a piece and was none too happy about it. She told me I'd had my dinner for the day."

"You mean she sent you to bed without any supper?" Paddy was incensed and not a little upset that he had been the cause of the man's ill fortune.

Dobs nodded. "And deprived me of my morning meal as well."

"But you're not a kid," Paddy said, for lack of a better argument.

Dobs sighed once more. "No, I am an old man who has to bide what time I have left on this earth and pray my body gives out on me before my hands do."

"Why?" Paddy asked.

"Because if my hands give out, I will be of no use to her, and she'll send me to a place worse than this."

"What kind of place could be worse than this?" Paddy whispered.

"An almshouse," the man said, matching his tone. "That's where they take people with no means of supporting themselves. They also take the crazies there. I knew a man who had his wife sent there when she developed a case of hysteria."

Paddy swallowed. "What's hysteria?"

"The woman went mad. The man said the woman wouldn't cook or clean and never did another thing around the house. He had her committed and found someone else who would."

Paddy thought about his own momma and how his brother told him the doctor wanted his papa to have her committed, but his father refused. Paddy had to give the man credit; his papa had faults, but he always did right by Momma. "I never knew the name of it, but that is what happened to my momma. She said something was broken inside, and they wanted to take her away, but Papa wouldn't let them. I guess maybe he knew she'd be better off with him."

"I guess some men have more patience with their wives than others," Dobs mused. "Too bad that patience didn't extend to the children she bore."

"Yes, sir," Paddy agreed.

Not having anything else to say, they each returned to their whittling and spent the rest of the afternoon in comfortable silence.

Chapter Sixteen

Paddy sat in the alcove, watching the door to the middle apartment. Dobs had warned him not to come by for the next two days, as he was not always alone on Saturdays and Sundays. While Paddy would miss seeing his friend, he had other plans and was glad he wouldn't have to make up a lie as to why he didn't plan on stopping by today. The door opened, and a woman and man left the apartment and headed toward the stairs. The man was carrying what looked like a small folding table, and the woman carried the crate he had seen sitting on the floor under the shelf that held the carvings Dobs made. *It's her!*

Paddy waited for them to enter the stairwell and then followed. While he was taking a chance at being seen, he would be taking a bigger chance at losing them in the Saturday market crowd. Though there were vendors on the street every day of the week, the Saturday market always proved to be more crowded than the rest. It also proved to be a prime day for dipping pockets. While Paddy planned to do just that, he also planned on taking back what was his.

He followed his marks close enough to keep an eye on them without them making him. Once at the market, the man unfolded the wooden table, set it in place, and pressed on it to test its sturdiness. He then said something to Mrs. Bronski before heading into the crowd. Paddy made no move to follow, as it was the woman and the carvings that she was busy placing on the table that he was interested in. When Mrs. Bronski finished setting out her wares, she turned the crate over, using it as a stool.

Paddy debated his options. He could pay for the mouse, and she'd never be the wiser, or walk right up, take it from her, and be done with it. *Don't be a dope. She'd have you thrown in jail for even looking at it.* No, he was going to have to be smart and bide his time waiting for the right moment to take what was his. He moved in as close as he dared, keeping himself out of the woman's line of sight, and saw the small mouse sitting in the middle of the table, surrounded by the larger items that Dobs had carved. A lady stepped up to the table, inspected several of the sculptures, then reached into her pocket, pulled her coin purse free and handed the woman a coin. Paddy breathed a sigh of relief when the woman left without the little mouse. As the market filled with shoppers, Paddy held his breath each time someone approached the woman's table.

A woman wearing a beautiful deep blue dress approached the table. As she did, Mrs. Bronski stood and began pointing to all the figurines left sitting on the table. As the lady in the dress pondered her choice, Mrs. Bronski rounded the table and stood next to her. Paddy watched with utter fascination as Mrs. Bronski stealthily dipped her hand into the unsuspecting woman's purse and relieved her of her coin purse. She then turned, pretending to cough, and stuffed the woman's coin purse into her bosom before returning to the backside of the table once more.

Paddy couldn't believe his eyes. *Mrs. Bronski is a thief!* Why that came as a shock, he did not know, but the knowledge of it firmed his already low opinion of her. Sure, he was a thief, but he had no other viable option at the moment. That wasn't the case with Mrs. Bronski. She had a roof over her head, food on her table, and according to Dobs, she worked as a schoolteacher and had a husband to provide for her. Plus, she had things to sell even if she hadn't come by them properly. The more Paddy thought about it, the angrier he got. It just wasn't right for her to take money that could be going to honest thieves like himself.

Deciding he'd had enough, Paddy stormed toward the table. As he neared, his eyes drifted to where the mouse had been only seconds before. It was gone! Paddy surveyed the table once more to be sure. It was true; the mouse was nowhere in sight. How could that be? He'd been watching the table all along. He looked at the lady in the blue dress with a fresh set of eyes. It was she who took it; it had to be, as it was there when she approached. Looking closer, he saw the mouse wasn't the only figure missing. The dog with the folded ear was also gone.

Paddy started to blow out a whistle, then he caught himself. *Don't draw attention, ya dope.* Listening to his own advice, he casually browsed the table. Walking away without slowing down, he stopped a short distance away and pretended to tie his shoe. When the woman in the blue dress moved away from the table, he followed. She stopped at a cart selling scarves and smiled as the man showed her a brilliant blue printed scarf. She chatted with the man, holding his attention as she casually slipped a bright red scarf into her right pocket.

Paddy breathed a sigh of relief. Now that he knew which pocket to target, it would be easy to retrieve the little mouse.

The woman waved the man off and started to turn away.

Paddy stepped up beside her and smiled at the man behind the cart. "Maybe the lady would like it more if you tied it around her neck so she could see how nice it looks with her dress." It was an old ploy Mouse had taught them to help distract a mark and prevent them from leaving.

The woman started to object, but the man was too quick. He was at her side in an instant, draping the silk around her neck.

Paddy took that opportunity to dip his hand into the

woman's pocket and retrieve the little mouse. He thought about lifting the dog as well but didn't wish to press his luck. He started to put the mouse in his pocket but decided against it – there were too many thieves in the market today. He lifted his hat and tucked the mouse inside for safekeeping.

Paddy spent the rest of the day drifting through the market dipping pockets. It had been nearly a week since he'd done so, and it felt good to feel the weight of coins in his pocket once more. Seeing a man selling jerky, he stopped.

The man glared at him. "Don't you even think of stealing any."

Paddy pulled out a coin and handed it to the man. "I got money to pay."

"My apologies, son. I'm tired of those street urchins stealing me blind," the man said, handing him several strips.

Paddy started to walk away and reconsidered. He pulled out two more coins, handing them to the man. "I'd like some more, please."

The man pocketed the coins. "You are going to eat them now, or do you want them wrapped."

Paddy smiled. "Wrapped, please."

The man pulled a handful of strips, wrapped them in parchment paper, and handed them over. "Anything else?"

Paddy started to shake his head, then stopped. "Can you tell me the way to the post office?"

"Up that street a couple of blocks." The man turned his back and pointed toward where Paddy already knew the post office to be. As he did, Paddy plucked a fistful of jerky from the cart and added them to the ones he'd just paid for.

Paddy thanked the man and left the market feeling rather pleased with himself. He'd walked about a block when he saw a sign for a furniture store. Though he'd seen the store before, he'd never paid it any mind. He moved closer to the building and stood reading the flyer on the window, which boasted of selling the finest chairs in town for the low price of $1.99. Paddy blew out a whistle. "A person has to be rich to shop here!" He read a little further and saw a box offering a teak table for $2.99. This elicited another whistle. Curiosity got the better of him and he found himself opening the door and stepping inside. A couple stood with a salesman looking over a desk; they each turned in his direction, then continued their conversation, making him glad he'd decided to shower and change clothes earlier in the week. While his coat was slightly baggy, it was devoid of holes and apparently kept him from looking like he lived on the street.

He moved through the building, paying close attention to the various shades and designs within the wood, stopping when he saw a bed that boasted a headboard taller than himself and had what looked to be leaves and flowers carved into the wood. "It looks like a bed a king would sleep on!"

"I'm sure a king could afford a much bigger bed than this," a man said, causing him to jump.

"Sheesh, you nearly scared me to death!" Paddy scolded.

The man was tall with a stocky build and had a smile that lit up his brown eyes. He wore dark pants and a black tie over a neatly pressed white shirt with its sleeves rolled halfway up his forearms. The man chuckled. "I'll try to be more mindful of sneaking up on people. It wouldn't bode well if we have people dying in our showroom."

Paddy wrinkled his brow. "What's a showroom?"

Another chuckle as the man spread his arms. "This. It's where we display the pieces we make."

Paddy looked about the room. "You mean you made all of this?"

"Not by myself, but I helped."

Paddy smiled and rocked back on his heels. "That means

you're in the business too."

The man looked him over. "The business?"

"Yeppers. My grandpa used to be one of the best furniture carvers in the business. Now he's teaching me."

A smile played on the man's lips. "You're telling me you carve furniture?"

Paddy shook his head. "Not yet. But I'm gonna learn because my grandpa says I've got the eye." Paddy removed his hat and pulled out the small mouse, showing it to the man.

The guy looked it over, and his smile widened. "You made this?"

Paddy nodded. "Only took me two days. That's why my grandpa says I have the eye."

"Your grandpa is right," the man said, handing it back. "What brings you in today? Sizing up the competition or here to steal my designs?"

Paddy looked around the room. "I'm not here to steal anything. Besides, none of this stuff would fit in my pocket even if I was."

The comment elicited another chuckle from the man, who extended his hand. "Fair enough. My name's Patrick Murphy. What can I do for you, then?"

Paddy shook the man's hand. "I guess I wanted to know about teak wood."

"What do you want to know?" Murphy asked, releasing his hand.

"Dobs…I mean, my grandpa told his brother he got a good deal on teak. I thought maybe I'd like to see what it looks like so I'd know it if I see it."

Murphy smiled. "You've already seen it."

Paddy scratched his head. "I have?"

"That bed you were looking at is made from teak."

Paddy blew out a whistle. "You mean it looks like every

other wood?"

"To some, yes. But give it time and listen to your grandpa, and he'll show you the difference. What's the matter?" Murphy asked when Paddy frowned.

"My grandpa is old and doesn't get around so much anymore. He only gets whatever wood the woman in the house brings him so she can steal his carvings."

A frown flitted across the man's face. "That doesn't sound right."

Paddy shook his head in agreement. "It's not. She tried to steal my mouse, but I got it back." He realized what he'd said and clarified. "I didn't steal it from her or nothing. I stole it from the woman who stole it from her."

"I see," Murphy replied.

Paddy blew out a sigh. "I wish Mrs. Bronski wasn't so mean. I wanted to learn how to carve more animals, but there's no sense in doing it if she's just going to steal them from me."

"Can't you hide them from her?" Murphy suggested.

Paddy shook his head. "No, sir. She might get mad at Dobs again. She brings in the wood scraps and Dobs said she counts to make sure he's doing his job."

"Is this woman his daughter?"

"Nope, Dobs has a brother, but he don't live around here. She's just a mean lady that lets him live in the apartment until his hands go bad and she sends him to an almshouse."

Murphy leveled a look at him. "Your friend is not really your grandpa, is he, son?"

Paddy retraced the conversation and realized he'd slipped. He sighed and hung his head. "No, sir, but I wish he were."

"You say this Dobs fellow has a brother?"

Paddy bobbed his head. "Yep. Lives in Philadelphia. We're going to write him a letter and let him know the way of things. That's what Dobs said. He's going to trade me a pocket knife for a stamp. He said he can't just give it to me or I'll have bad luck. I have enough of that, beings I'm a redhead and all, so that's where I was going when I saw this place and decided to have a look-see."

The man glanced at the clock on the wall. "I'm afraid the post office is closed."

"Closed! How am I supposed to get a stamp?"

The man considered this for a moment. "Do you have money for the stamp?"

"Course I do," Paddy said, patting his pocket.

"Then how about I sell you one?"

Paddy eyed the man. "How much?"

The man chuckled once more. "The same as the post office."

Paddy followed as the man walked to the back of the room. Rounding the counter, he pulled open a desk drawer and pulled out a stamp. Then he retrieved an envelope and piece of paper, which he folded and slid inside.

Paddy waved him off. "I wasn't planning on buying no paper. Dobs said the lady might have some."

"The paper and envelope is on me," the guy said, handing it to him. He pulled a square from the desk and added it to the envelope. "It's a seal for closing the envelope. This brother, you say he lives in Philadelphia? Do you know his name?"

Paddy shook his head. "No, only that he owns a furniture store on Frankford Avenue. I remember because Dobs said the guy in the brewery nearly burned it down. But it was okay because he had insurance, whatever that is."

The man wrote something on a separate paper, which he folded and stuck in his own pocket. "It's a smart investment. Sounds like Dobs' brother is a smart man. Where does Dobs live? In case I ever want to pay him a visit?"

Paddy rattled off the address on Ludlow Street, then

frowned. "You don't even know him. Why would you want to visit him?"

"Just thought maybe he could use a friend."

"I don't think Mrs. Bronski likes it when people visit him," Paddy warned.

"No, I don't suppose she would," the man agreed. "Follow me for a moment. I want to show you something."

Paddy slid an eye toward the back room. "Is this on account of I haven't given you the money for the stamp yet?" He pulled the change from his pocket, counted out two pennies, and placed them on the counter.

"You're not in trouble, and I'm not playing tricks." Murphy walked to the door and opened it. "You're free to come take a look or go. It's up to you."

Paddy shrugged and followed him into the back. As soon as they entered the room, the aroma of fresh wood filled his nose. He looked about and saw furniture in various degrees of construction and smiled a wide smile. "It smells so good in here!"

Murphy matched his smile. "Dobs may not be your real grandpa, but I think he's right. Woodworking is in your blood."

Paddy wrinkled his brow. "How can the wood be in my blood if I didn't cut myself?"

The man laughed a full belly laugh. "It's just a figure of speech that means you'll be good at working with wood."

Paddy eyed a barrel overflowing with an assortment of wood chunks near the edge of the room. "Mister?"

"Yes?"

"How much for one of those chunks of wood?"

The man walked to the barrel, and Paddy followed. "Normally, I would charge for those. But since wood is in your blood, I don't think it would be right."

"Oh," Paddy said, struggling to hide his disappointment.

"No, sir. I think yours should be free. Not all of them, mind you, but just enough to get you started."

"Really and truly?" Paddy asked.

"Yep, and I'll do you one better than that. If you find you ever want to part with any of your carvings, and you certainly don't have to, mind you, but if you do, I'll pay you for them. No, that won't work."

"It won't?"

The man put his finger to his chin as if thinking. "No, I'll tell you what. When you get something to sell, you bring it in, and I'll give you your own shelf out there in the showroom."

Paddy narrowed his eyes. "Who will get the money?"

"You will, of course. Less a penny or two to keep it all legal."

"How will I know what to charge?"

"Don't you worry about that just now. You bring something in, and we'll figure it out together."

"Mister? How come you're being so nice to me?" Paddy asked.

"Why, I'm not being nice at all. This here is a business arrangement, pure and simple. I figure I'm the lucky one."

"You are?"

"Sure I am. When people find out about your carvings, they'll be rushing in here to buy them. When that happens, I expect they'll have a look around and maybe even buy something of mine. I'm telling you, it's a win-win situation. What do you think?"

"Sure," Paddy said, bobbing his head.

"Fine. Real fine. We're going to have to make it legal, though."

Paddy swallowed. "You mean like a blood oath?"

The man turned away for a moment before answering. "I

was thinking more of a handshake."

Relief washed over Paddy as he stretched out his hand once more.

The man shook it and pointed toward the barrel. "Care to pick out a couple of blocks?"

Paddy rooted through the barrel, studying each piece. Finally, he chose one that seemed to feel right in his hand.

The man peered at the wood. "That's a nice piece of cedar. Any particular reason you picked that one?"

Paddy wanted to tell him that he saw something or knew exactly what it was he planned to carve. But the truth of the matter was he wasn't sure why he'd chosen that particular hunk of wood other than it just felt like something was in there that wanted to get out, and it smelled good. "It just seemed to call to me," Paddy said, hoping the guy wouldn't think him a fool.

"Sometimes that is the best reason," the man agreed.

Chapter Seventeen

The block of wood felt warm in his hand, but that could just have been because he'd been holding and peering at it for quite some time, trying to find the animal inside. While the wood had felt right when he'd chosen it, he now felt as if he'd picked the wrong one. He wished he could ask Dobs, but he wouldn't get his chance to see the man until after sunrise when everyone left. An image of his momma came to mind, and he knew she was reminding him to be patient. After all, it wasn't like he could do anything about it even if he knew, as he had yet to give Dobs the stamp. He double-checked to make sure it was still there since the last time he looked a few minutes earlier. It was. Just as it had been each time he looked earlier in the day and the evening before.

He had been patient, he reminded himself. He'd wanted nothing more than to pound on the door, tell whoever answered he was there to see his friend, and hand Dobs the stamp in exchange for the knife. He thought about the knife and pictured the shiny blade scraping against the wood and carving out…what? That was the problem: even if he had the knife, he still wouldn't know what to carve. He clenched his teeth, trying desperately to think of something to make from the fine piece of wood he'd pulled from the barrel. His breathing quickened as he held the piece up, surveying it the best he could in the dimly lit hallway while willing the image to show itself. Nothing. In a fit of frustration, he flung the wood down the hallway, only to scramble to his feet and race after it before it even stopped moving. The block hit a doorframe, and he snatched it up, hoping the noise didn't alert anyone inside. As he walked under the single bulb that lit the hallway, he saw the block had been dinged when it hit the wall. He turned it and saw a hint of pink. He rubbed the wood with the meat of his thumb, brought it to his nose, inhaled the woodsy scent, and wondered how they put that smell in there. The door to the apartment, whose door jamb he'd just hit, clicked, and Paddy raced to the alcove, holding his breath as a man exited the apartment. The man looked in his direction, and Paddy closed his eyes. A second later, he heard footsteps walking away and peeked to see the man stepping inside the washroom.

Geez, Paddy, keep that up, and they'll chase you away with a broom. The last thing he wanted was to be tossed into the street, much less during the night. Deciding he'd be better off sleeping, he snuggled into the alcove as best he could and closed his eyes for real. Sometime later, he heard a door, looked up to see the man return to his apartment, and then drifted off once more. He slept a fitful sleep filled with frustration, dreaming he was awake and still trying to find the image in the wood. How could woodworking be in his blood when he couldn't even find a simple image?

Paddy stood in the street, brandishing the piece of wood while holding it up to the sky. All at once, the wood became a sword, and he eased the blade back and forth in the moonlight, trying to see his reflection. There was nothing there, though he knew for certain he should be able to see it. He started walking, still holding the sword to the sky, when he tripped and looked to see the street littered with swords. He reached to retrieve the one he'd been holding, and it was cold in his hand. He tossed it aside, knowing it wasn't his. He picked up sword after sword, only to have them turn into a mirrorless block of wood. It wasn't fair. The man had told him he could have all the wood he wanted as long as he was using it to carve. How could he carve without a sword, and furthermore, how could he carve if he couldn't find the face? As if the word were the answer he'd been seeking, the block of cedar he'd chosen appeared at his feet. He grabbed it, held it up to the moonlight, and saw the face within the wood.

Paddy woke from the dream, reached for the cedar plank, and concentrated on the spot where he'd seen the face within his dream. He sighed a contented sigh. While he couldn't see it, he knew it was in there. Tucking the cedar under his arm, he drifted off to a dreamless sleep.

***

Dobs greeted him with a wide smile and waved him in.

Paddy pulled up a chair without being told and pulled a meat pie from his pocket, handing it to the man.

Dobs' eyes grew wide. "Where'd you get this?"

"I bought them at the market. I got one for me too!" he said, pulling a second one from his pocket. "I got us some jerky too."

"You say you bought them?"

"Yes, sir."

Dobs raised an eyebrow. "Fishing must have been good."

"Yes, sir. Got me a whole pocket full of change." Technically, it wasn't a lie.

Dobs worked to unwrap the meat pie, took a bite, and closed his eyes as he chewed. He finished the pie in a few short bites, then wiped his mouth with his thumb. "You didn't happen to make it to the post office, did you?"

Paddy shook his head. "No, sir. They'd closed by the time I got there."

Dobs sighed. "Ah well, perhaps another time."

"But I still got one." Paddy dug into his coat pocket and withdrew the envelope. "A man at the furniture store sold me this for two pennies. It even has a stamp and piece of paper inside."

"What furniture store sells stamps?"

"I don't recall the name. It's the one on the same street as the post office. And they don't sell stamps; the man just found out I needed one and had an extra. I was on my way to the post office when I saw an advert on the door of the furniture store. I stopped to read it and saw that they had a chair that cost nearly two dollars. My curiosity got the best of me, and I had to see what kind of chair would sell for that much." Paddy sighed. "I didn't know the post office would close so early, or I would have gone earlier."

"It's no matter. You brought it, so there was no harm done. Did you find out?"

Paddy cocked his head. "Find out what?"

"What kind of chairs."

Paddy bobbed his head. "Yes, sir. They were right fine chairs at that. They had teak tables too. I know on account of the man showed me one. I saw a bed that had flowers carved in it. I was looking at it when the man showed up. I didn't want him to think I was trying to steal the bed, so I told him I was interested because I was a carver, and you were teaching me about wood and how you said I have the eye." Paddy purposely left out the fact that he'd showed him the mouse he'd stolen and had told the man that Dobs was his grandpa.

"What'd the man say?"

"He said since I have the eye, we are the same. He even took me in the back to show me some of the furniture they were building. He had a barrel full of scraps and told me to take some." Paddy reached into his pocket and pulled out the cedar plank. "It's cedar, see."

Dobs took the wood from him, sniffing as he pulled it under his nose. "Splendid. What did he charge you for it?" he asked, handing it back.

"Nothing."

"He gave it to you?"

Paddy grinned. "He did. Said I can have all I want. You know what else he said?"

"What?"

"He said he'd give me a shelf in the store, and how if I want to sell my sculptures, I can."

Dobs leaned back and crossed one leg over the other. "That man said all that just on your word?"

Paddy gulped.

"Sounds a little hinky if you ask me – him offering to give you a shelf in his store without seeing anything you've done. Do you think that maybe the guy is up to something?"

"No, he was a nice man. Plus, he gave me the wood without making me pay," Paddy reminded him.

"I think it best for you to stay away," Dobs said firmly. "It's just bad business. Now, if you'd shown him the mouse and he knew what kind of work you could do, now that would be different."

"But I did show him," Paddy said, removing his hat and pulling the mouse from within.

Dobs snatched the mouse from Paddy's hand with a gnarled thumb. "Ha! Mrs. Bronski came in here ranting and raving as to how someone had stolen all of her sculptures and pointing her finger as if she were actually accusing me. She even threatened to withhold my supper again until I reminded her that she took them with her to the market, and I could not possibly have taken them as I could not physically make it down the stairs. I saw how upset you were at her taking your mouse and knew it was you!"

Paddy pushed from the chair, shaking his head. "I didn't steal them from her. I swear it."

Still holding the mouse with his thumb, Dobs wagged it in

front of him as proof. "Then explain how you came to have this."

Paddy knew he'd been caught; he just wished he'd been able to trade for the knife before it happened. Not only did Dobs have his mouse, but Paddy had also given him the stamp and envelope. He wasn't worried about the stamp, but he was pretty partial to the mouse and would have liked to have the knife. While he thought he'd be able to steal another, that one had special meaning, and he liked how it fit into his hand. "I stole it," Paddy said simply.

"Do you know how dangerous that was?" Dobs fumed.

"It weren't dangerous at all. I dip pockets all the time."

"Just like a kid," Dobs growled. "Only thinking of yourself."

"Who am I supposed to think of? I was the only one there," Paddy asked.

"What if the woman had seen you take it from her? She may have recognized you from hanging around the building and thought I put you up to it. Why, she would have had me hauled off to the almshouse without a moment's hesitation. Heck, for all I know, she did see you and will be fetching them here yet today."

"She didn't see me," Paddy assured him.

Dobs lowered his hand. "How can you be sure?"

"On account of I didn't steal it from her."

Dobs blinked his surprise. "What do you mean you didn't? You just sat there and admitted it."

"No, I said I stole it. I never said I took it from her," Paddy reminded him. "A woman stopped; she was a real lady. You know, the kind who look like they have a lot of money? Anyhow, she was wearing a pretty blue dress and stopped to look at the carvings. Only when she did, Mrs. Bronski come around the table and took the woman's coin purse. Then the lady left, only when she did, my mouse and the dog with the folded ear were gone."

Dobs wrinkled his brow. "Are you sure that's all she took? Mrs. Bronski said someone stole everything."

"Mrs. Bronski is lying. She sold some of them. I saw her," Paddy said adamantly. "She's a liar and a thief. I saw her steal the woman's coin purse."

"Did she sell anything after the lady left?" Dobs asked.

Paddy shrugged. "Don't know. I wasn't watching her no more, as I had to follow the lady who took my mouse."

"So you stole this from the woman in the blue dress?"

"Yep," Paddy said, nodding his head. "And I don't feel the least bit bad about it because she stole it first."

"Did you take the dog?"

"The one with the folded ear? No, I could have, but figured she deserved to keep it since Mrs. Bronski took her coin purse."

"I suppose she does at that," Dobs agreed. "Did you really pay for the meat pies, or did you take those too?"

"I told you I paid for it, and I did." Paddy said, bristling at the accusation. He pulled the jerky he'd bought for Dobs from his sock and tossed it to the guy. "I paid for this too." Most of it anyway.

Dobs bit at his bottom lip. "And where, pray tell, did you get the money to pay? And don't tell me fishing. Ain't nobody finds that much money in the grates."

Paddy rocked back on his heels. "I was dipping pockets in the market. But only from those who looked like they wouldn't miss it."

"You mean like Mrs. Bronski?"

Paddy was incensed that the man could sit there and compare him to Mrs. Bronski. "Mrs. Bronski has a roof over her head. She has food on her table, yet she steals from you and doesn't share."

"What you're telling me is you're an honest thief."

Paddy liked the sound of that, so he nodded his agreement. "I could have taken my money and bought my own knife and never bothered to come in here again, but I didn't. I spent it on food so you and I could share a meal together. And brought you some jerky to hide in your sock so you don't have to go to bed hungry no more."

"Why did you come back, Howard?"

Because I didn't have anywhere else to go. No, that was only part of it. Though Paddy had only known the guy a handful of days, he felt like they were friends. Obviously, he'd been mistaken, so he kept that to himself and went with the truth. "Because we had a deal. I know we didn't shake on it or nothing, but I promised to help you with the letter, and you promised to trade me the knife for a stamp. I gave you the stamp, but you still have hold of the knife."

"Oh," Dobs said softly. "I thought maybe you came back because we are friends."

Paddy stared at the man. "You mean you're not sore at me?"

"For taking back what is rightfully yours, no. I'm still on the fence about your dipping pockets. I realize a boy such as yourself has to do things they might not otherwise do if they're going to survive in this city. I'm just thankful my boys never had to face that reality. I would have done it myself if it meant feeding my family."

Paddy heaved a sigh. "You're talking about Mrs. Bronski, aren't you?"

"No, I'm talking about myself. Mrs. Bronski does many things I cannot explain and won't even venture a guess as to why. You know what I would venture to guess on?"

"What?" Paddy asked.

"That woman you made mention of."

"The one in the blue dress?"

"That's the one. I'd be willing to bet she knew what she was doing when she stepped up to that table."

Paddy scratched at his head, pretending not to know what Dobs was talking about. While the man knew him to be a thief, he didn't want to let on as to how much he knew about stealing. "What do you mean?"

"You were watching the whole time, and yet you didn't see her steal either of the carvings. My guess is she knew what Mrs. Bronski was up to and used her coin purse as a decoy while taking what she really wanted."

Dobs was right, of course; it was the same thing he'd done to get more jerky without paying for it. "If she had money in the coin purse, why not just buy the dog and the mouse instead of stealing them?"

"I don't know," Dobs mused. "Perhaps she didn't have money in the purse. Perhaps it was filled with pebbles instead of coins. Or perhaps the woman is sick?"

Paddy frowned. This was the last thing he'd expected Dobs to say. "She didn't look sick."

"Not physically sick."

He remembered what the twins had said about his momma. "You think the woman is daft?"

"I once knew a woman – a woman of means who was very dear to my heart, and she would steal because she couldn't help herself."

Dear to his heart. Paddy blinked his surprise. "You mean your wife?"

Dobs nodded. "It was an illness – one that had no cure. She would go to stores and steal jewelry and trinkets that she could have easily bought. Then, once a week, I'd make a trip to the stores and pay for what she'd taken."

Paddy started to call him a dope, then recalled Slim's words and reconsidered. "If you knew her to be a thief, why did you leave the money where she could get at it?"

"Because she always knew where I kept my money, and until that time, she'd never stolen anything from me."

Paddy blew out a whistle. "Dames."

"Dames," Dobs agreed. He bent, reached into his pocket, dug out the pocket knife with the thumb of his right hand, and handed it to Paddy. "Any idea what you are going to do with that chunk of cedar?"

Paddy nodded. "I've thunk on it some, but what about your letter?"

"There will be time enough for letter-writing tomorrow. I think I'd like to do some of my own thinking so I know what words I'd like to have you put on the paper."

Paddy thought about that for a moment. "Dobs? Is your wife the reason you didn't write your brother before your hands went bad?"

Dobs chuckled. "You're pretty smart for a kid."

"That's what my momma used to say. But she said it got me in trouble because I was a redhead and didn't have any patience."

"What's being a redhead got to do with it?"

"I don't know, but it's what she said. Is that the reason?" Paddy asked, circling back to the question.

"My brother learned of my wife's affliction when he stayed with us after coming to America. He told me I should have her committed to an asylum, but she was the mother of my sons, and I couldn't do that to her."

Paddy frowned. "My momma wanted me to go to the asylum."

Dobs raised his head. "The kind I would have sent her to was a different asylum where doctors would have looked after her."

"It doesn't sound that bad."

Dobs leaned forward and looked him directly in the eye. "Neither does a place that is meant to look after kids and keep them from going to prison for dipping pockets or stealing food, and that's what will happen to you if you are to get caught."

Paddy didn't try arguing with the man as, once again, Dobs wasn't saying anything he didn't already know. But something the man had said weighed on him. He returned Dobs' gaze. "Do you think that's why I steal? On account of I have an affliction?"

Dobs shook his head. "No, Howard, I think you steal because life dealt you a bum hand."

Paddy sighed his relief and lowered his gaze to Dobs' gnarled fingers. "Looks like life dealt you two bum hands."

"That it has, my boy, that it surely has," Dobs agreed.

Paddy didn't fully understand what an affliction was, but he wondered if perhaps Dobs was wrong. Maybe he did have one, and that was why his mother had wanted him to go into the asylum.

Chapter Eighteen

Paddy placed the last word on the paper and looked at Dobs. "What's next?"

The man considered this for a moment. "I guess you should just sign it *your older brother Dobs*. Hang on," he said when Paddy placed the pencil lead to the paper. "Maybe you should use my full name."

"You'll have to spell Dobrogost," Paddy replied. "I think I can spell Dobs good enough, but not that."

Dobs spelled his name out, waiting for Paddy to finish each letter before saying the next. "I think that just about does it for the letter. Now you have to address the envelope. There's a box of letters next to my blanket pallet. Pull one of them out. It'll have his name and address on it." Paddy walked to the window, moved the bedding aside, and saw the box. He picked it up, ran his fingers over the smooth surface, and admired the intricate scroll carved on the outside of the wooden box." He blew out a whistle. "This is some box. Where'd you get it?"

Dobs chuckled. "Where do you think I got it? I made it. Lift the lid."

Paddy did as told, sniffing the air as the aroma of cedar filled his nostrils. "It has cedar inside!"

"It does. Cedar is good for chests and letterboxes, as it keeps the bugs away. I made the box of hickory, and then later, when I figured out what I wanted it for, I lined the inside with thinly shaved cedar. If I'd have known earlier, I would have made the whole thing of cedar. But by then, I'd already carved out the design and didn't want to bother. I thought maybe I would make another one someday, but it seemed I was always busy making things for everyone else and never found the time. It is fine for what I use it for. I have another for my journals. People like to use cedar on wardrobes too, as it keeps the moths away. You get a moth locked up with a quilt, and you'll soon find holes in your fabric."

Paddy looked up from the box. "Moths eat paper too?"

"Perhaps, but there are other bugs that eat paper as well."

Paddy pulled a letter from the box and brought it over, copying the address from one envelope to the other. "Dobs?" Paddy asked, studying the return address. "What would you do if you didn't know where your brother lived?"

"Thinking of your brothers again?"

Paddy nodded.

"I suppose if a person wanted to find someone and he had a little money to spend, he could take out adverts in all the big papers in big cities and tell who you are looking for."

Paddy wrinkled his brow. "How do I know which papers to take out the adverts in?"

"You don't, but the newspaper guys do. All you have to do is tell them."

"How do you know so much about adverts?"

"Easy, I was a businessman. I didn't make all my money from people who lived in the city. Why, once I had a gentleman come all the way from the city of Chicago just to order a desk for his office."

Paddy blinked his surprise.

Dobs laughed. "Do you even know where Chicago is?"

Paddy shook his head. "No, sir, but it sure sounded good."

Dobs chuckled once more. "Truth be told, I'd heard of it but had to look at a map to see where it was. Anyway, he'd seen one of my adverts and wanted to buy a desk from me."

"Dobs?"

"Ain't there no place to get a desk in Chicago?"

"Sure there was. Plenty of places. But I'd talked these desks up real big and said as how there weren't any finer in the land and billed them as secret keepers."

"And he believed you?"

"He must have, as he came straight here on a train just to see them. He must have liked what he saw too, as he bought it, had us wrap it, and took it home on the train with him that very day. That's the thing about people, they get it in their head that they have to have something, and they'll do just about anything to get it."

"It sounds silly to come all this way for a desk when they have those there."

"No sillier than risking going to jail over a little carved mouse," Dobs replied, then winked. "It is all about priorities. Mr. Shively said he was getting married, and his fiancé was a woman of means who lived in Chicago and enjoyed telling her friends she'd acquired something all the way from New York City. I don't know what exactly he did for a living, but whatever it was allowed for galivanting across the country to get something to impress the woman."

"If she likes New York so much, why not just move here?"

"See, you and I are logical thinkers. I asked the same question. You know what the gentleman said?"

Paddy shook his head. "No."

"He said if she lived here, it wouldn't sound as impressive when she told her friends she bought something from here."

"What a dope," Paddy replied.

"Indeed," Dobs agreed. "Are you done copying that address?"

Paddy nodded. "Yes, sir. Want to check it?"

"No, I suppose you can copy the print well enough. Go ahead and put the seal on it and stick it in your pocket. We don't want you to forget it and take a chance on Mrs. Bronski finding it."

Paddy placed the stamp on the back to seal the envelope and slid it into his pocket. "Dobs, what are journals?"

"They are kind of like a diary where people write down what happens to them. Why do you ask?"

"On account you said you have some, but I didn't see another box."

Dobs pointed to the desk. "Over there."

Paddy went to the desk but didn't see a box. "Where? I don't see no box."

Dobs pointed a knuckle. "Pull out the third drawer."

Paddy did as told but still didn't see a box.

"Now reach inside and flip that panel."

Paddy slid his hand inside and felt the board move. As it turned, he felt a key and smiled a wide smile. "A magic hiding place!" He pulled the key from its hiding place and held it up for Dobs to see.

"Good, bring it here." Dobs stood and pointed a knuckle at the chair. "Turn it over."

Paddy turned the chair but didn't see a place for a key.

Dobs pointed at the chair once more. "See that plug there in the back?"

Paddy shook his head. "Nope."

Dobs smiled. "That's because you're not supposed to. A good carpenter can hide things in plain sight. Look just to the left of the center. See where the color is just a shade different?"

Paddy studied the chair and smiled. "I see it."

"Good. Use the key to dislodge the wooden plug."

Paddy did as told, beaming with delight when the plug came free, showing a place for a key. He stuck the key inside and turned, watching as the bottom of the chair opened to reveal the wooden box. Paddy pulled the box free, noting that it was nearly the size of the seat that hid it. In that moment, he knew the withered man standing next to him was a genius, who, through a labor of love, had managed to protect what was his when everything else had been taken from him. Paddy took a moment to fully appreciate the deep-seated high-back chair, which was not much different from any of the others scattered about the room except for the secrets it harbored. "It's fantastic," Paddy said, wishing for better words to describe the way he felt.

"People came from all over to buy my special furniture."

Special furniture? Paddy recalled what Dobs had said. "Secret Keepers!"

Dobs nodded. "It was my specialty and what made men with something to hide travel on a train when they could have bought a desk right in their own hometown."

"Boy, Dobs, you're the best."

"There was a time," the man agreed.

Paddy ran his hands over the box, smooth except for a carved smoker's pipe, which fit snugly within the lid. He tried to open it. "It's locked."

Dobs shook a knuckle toward the box. "Pull out that pipe."

Paddy used his finger to dislodge the pipe. As he did, a tiny key revealed itself. He smiled. "Boy, Dobs, you sure do like puzzles."

The man grinned, and his eyes held a twinkle Paddy hadn't seen before. "What good is a treasure hunt if there is no discovery?"

Paddy unlocked the box, opened the lid, and saw a second wooden pipe lying beside a stack of papers. He plucked out the pipe and glanced at Dobs. "You said you were a pipe maker. Did you make this?"

"I did," Dobs said, licking his lips. "What I wouldn't give

for a taste of tobacco."

"I can bring you some," Paddy offered.

Dobs shook his head. "No, it's too dangerous. One whiff and Mrs. Bronski would know."

"What are the papers?"

"Those are the journals. Stories of my life."

Paddy frowned. "You're old. Shouldn't there be more papers?"

Dobs chuckled. "There is a difference between journals and a diary."

"What's the difference?"

"People tend to write in a diary every day. Most of it doesn't account for anything, and if you read them long enough, the words often repeat themselves. A journal, on the other hand, is usually used to tell of something that happened. In my experience, diaries can be rather dull, whereas journals are exciting. Think of it this way: a diary is the story of a life, and a journal is a life's story."

Paddy was about to ask him what the difference was when the man continued.

"I want you to have this," Dobs said, handing him the pipe.

Paddy blinked his surprise. "You do?"

Dobs nodded. "You don't need to smoke it now; maybe you never will, but if you ever decide to, this pipe will allow you to fully enjoy the flavor of the tobacco."

Paddy glanced at the box. "What about the journals?"

Dobs shook his head. "Nah, I think I'll hang on to them for now."

"Okay," Paddy said, trying to hide his disappointment.

Dobs smiled. "I expect you will write your own journal one day, and perhaps when you do, you'll light that pipe and have a smoke and remember your old friend Dobs and all that he taught you. Now, let's get this put back together so we can get down to business. Don't forget to put that drawer back in the desk."

Paddy secured the box, replaced the secret panel to the chair, and pressed the plug back into place. "Do you want me to put the key back in its hiding spot?"

Dobs considered his question, then held out a gnarled hand. "No, I think I'll keep it with me for a while."

Paddy fixed the panel and then replaced the drawer.

"Have you given any thought to what you want to do with your plank?" Dobs asked when he'd finished.

Paddy had, but he didn't want to say it just yet. "I'm still thinking on it."

Dobs reached into the basket and pulled out a chunk of wood. "While you're thinking, I want to show you something." Dobs placed the wood on his leg and used his left hand to steady it as he wielded his knife in the other. As Paddy watched, the blade glided through the wood, creating crevices that soon gave way to leaves. Paddy recalled the design on the headboard of the bed and realized Dobs was creating vines. The man lifted the knife and blew at the shavings before lowering the knife once more. The blade cut into the wood, and soon, a rose appeared. He connected the vine, added a few more leaves, then blew at the shavings once more before turning it for Paddy to see.

Paddy admired the carving. While it wasn't exactly like what had been on the bed, it was close, and Paddy stared at it, dreaming of the day he'd be able to duplicate it. "It looks like what I saw on the bed in the store."

Dobs nodded. "It is a classic scroll. The key is to have patience. As I've told you before, you can't rush the process. If you mess up, the best you can hope for is that your mistake was not so great that you can't fix it. Let me show you." Dobs turned the plank around and started the same process. As he did, he purposely pushed the knife so the blade skipped and marred the wood.

Paddy gasped.

Undeterred, Dobs lifted the blade and placed it back in the original path. Next, he created a new vine that branched off and joined the errant mar. Within minutes, he'd added a few leaves and a small rose bud that looked so fresh, Paddy almost thought it would soon open to show a full bloom.

Paddy smiled. "I can't even tell it was there!"

"Yes, but if it were your mistake, you would know. Then, each time you look at the piece, you would see that bloom and know the reason it is there. It's best to see the beauty of the piece and not the error of your haste. Want to give it a try?"

Paddy very much wanted to, but he was afraid of messing up and having Mrs. Bronski punish Dobs for his carelessness. He shook his head.

"Why not?"

"Because I don't want you to get in trouble."

Dobs held up the jerky Paddy had given him. "Thanks to you, I'll not be going to bed without my supper this night."

Dobs was right. Besides, Paddy felt learning this skill would help him with what he wanted to make on his own plank. "Okay, I'll try."

Paddy set to work recreating the vine, only while he could see what he wanted to make, it didn't fully translate to what was appearing on the wood.

"You're fond of whistling, aren't you?" Dobs asked.

Paddy looked at Dobs. Of course, he could whistle; the man had to have heard him multiple times. "Of course I can; you've heard me."

"I know you know how to whistle, but can you carry a tune? Songs, can you whistle a song?"

Paddy started to whistle the tune to "Johnny Comes Marching Home," then recalled Dobs telling him how his sons had died in the war and blew out the tune to "The Old Grey Mare" instead.

"Splendid," Dobs said with a nod to the wood. "Now whistle that tune while you slide that knife."

"It works!" Paddy said after a moment. "How come?"

"It calms the brain." He winked. "I've also found it helps to whistle when you don't have anything else to say. In regard to this, I don't know the why of it other than it gives the brain something better to do than worrying about making a mistake."

"Boy, Dobs, you sure are probably one of the smartest fellows I know."

Dobs waved him off. "I don't suppose I'm any smarter than the next guy, I've just lived long enough to learn from my mistakes and figure some things out to make life a bit easier."

"If it's easier to whistle while you work, then why don't you do it?" Paddy asked.

"I used to, but Mrs. Bronski doesn't like it, so I stopped."

"Why doesn't she like whistling?"

"She never did say. Only said if God had intended people to whistle, he'd have given them wings," Dobs replied. "I used to do it while she was away, then I'd slip and do it while she was home, and she'd give me a whack upside my head. I decided it was just better to stop altogether so I wouldn't forget."

Paddy wanted to tell him that he didn't think very highly of Mrs. Bronski but kept it to himself, as he knew that even though Dobs hadn't said it, he didn't care for the woman either. Instead, he began whistling and digging his knife into the wood.

"Let me see how it's looking," Dobs said sometime later.

Paddy handed him the wood and watched as Dobs ran his thumb along the carvings.

Dobs smiled his approval. "Very nice."

"If it's so nice, why don't you sound happy about it?" Paddy asked.

"Because I wish I'd found you earlier. It's not often a man gets such a gifted apprentice. An apprentice is someone who wants to learn the job," Dobs said before he could ask.

"Is that what I am? Your apprentice?" Paddy asked.

Dobs smiled. "Yes, sir, and a fine one at that. Now, let's see what else this old man can show you before it's time for you to go." Dobs set the knife to the wood, describing each method as he went, then handed it over so Paddy could give it a try. Every now and then, Dobs would stop him and redirect until, at last, they'd filled the entire front of the piece with vines and flowers. They were still working on the block when the door opened, and Mileta and her mother stepped inside. Both stared in their direction before heading to the spot Dobs had said was reserved for them.

Paddy swallowed back his fear. Mouse wouldn't be happy he'd let them see him. He looked at Dobs, surprised to see the color had drained from the man's face. "What's the matter?"

"I'm sorry, I should have watched the time more closely. Hurry, you must go."

Paddy returned the chair and started to hand Dobs the knife.

Dobs waved him off. "No, it is yours now. Make sure you take good care of it. Leave the mess. There is no time," Dobs said when Paddy started to clean up. "You go now."

Paddy hurried from the room and had barely returned to his spot in the hall when Mrs. Bronski came through the stairwell door. He gulped, realizing how close he'd come to getting caught. He settled in and brought out his block of cedar, pulled the blade from his pocket, and began to carve. He'd only been at it for a moment when he realized he was making a mess that he had no means to clean up. He returned the knife to his pocket and was heading down the hall when he heard a woman's voice yelling from inside Dobs' apartment. Holding his breath, he turned the doorknob and peeked inside to see Mrs. Bronski standing over Dobs' chair, brandishing the jerky in her hand.

"I said, tell me where you got this!" she shrieked.

Paddy started to go inside when he saw the girl rush past.

Mileta stepped up beside Dobs and placed a hand on his shoulder. "I brought it to him." The conviction in her voice was so strong, even he would have believed it to be true had he not known otherwise.

"I don't believe you. Why would you bring him food when you can barely feed yourself?" Mrs. Bronski chided.

"Because you are a mean woman who does not allow him to eat. Why, my papa would…"

"Your papa is dead!" the woman spat. "And you are only living here due to my good graces. Now get over there and mind your manners."

Mileta started to walk away when the woman caught her under her chin and pulled her face up to look her in the eye. "And you are not to ever bring him food again, or I will kick you and your mother to the street. Do you understand?"

Mileta nodded and the woman let her go and walked to the back room. As Mileta passed, Paddy was surprised to see a defiant smile on her face.

Paddy still pictured her smile as he quietly pulled the door closed.

***

"Oh, that woman!" Cindy said through clenched teeth. "Why couldn't she leave that poor old man alone?"

"You should give her some credit," Linda replied.

Cindy narrowed her eyes at her mother. "Credit for what?"

"You read what he wrote. He may not have known it at the time, but I do believe that is the moment Howard fell in love with your grandmother."

"You're probably right. Hang on a minute. I want to check something." Cindy pulled out her phone and scrolled to find the e-mail she was looking for. "It's him!"

Linda gave her a quizzical look. "David?"

Cindy frowned. "What about him?"

Linda pointed to the phone. "You said it's him, and I thought Mr. Wonderful had sent you a text."

Cindy shook her head. "No, not that him. Shively!"

"The guy Dobs said came over from Chicago."

"Think, Mother!"

It took Linda a moment, but then her eyes grew wide. "Wait, wasn't that the name of the sleaze that tried to take Mileta home?"

Cindy nodded. "And if you recall, when I had Bruce research the couple, he said the man had married into money. And that it looked as if he just appeared. It makes sense that he'd want a desk with secret compartments if he had secrets to hide." She sighed. "Somewhere in the world, someone has a desk that could give us so many answers."

"And sitting in your lap are papers that could enlighten you even more," Linda said, rustling her own stack of papers.

"Touche, Mother," Cindy said, returning to her journals.

Chapter Nineteen

Paddy opened the door to the apartment, surprised not to see Dobs sitting in his usual chair. He heard a noise and looked to see the man rifling through the desk.

"What are you looking for?" Paddy asked, stepping up beside him.

Dobs looked up and stared at him blankly. "How'd you get in here?"

"Through the door like I always do," Paddy replied.

Dobs blinked. "Oh, I figured the old bat locked it. She threatened to. Said she was going to make sure no one came in here until she was home so she could make sure no one fed me but her. Can you imagine that? Danged old fool."

"Yes, she is," Paddy agreed.

Dobs shook his head. "I was talking about me, not her. I should have collected my things and moved out the moment the landlord moved her in, but I was too stubborn and wanted to stay just for the principle of it. Well, you take note of this in case you ever find yourself wanting to buck back just because someone is trying to tell you what to do."

"What are you looking for?" Paddy asked, ignoring the rant.

"The jerky you left me. Dang woman took it from me then left without leaving me anything to eat. Treating me like a dog is what she's doing. Why, if I could walk more than a few feet at a time, I'd just stroll on out of here."

Not knowing what to say, Paddy brought a piece of jerky

he'd saved for himself out of his pocket and handed it to Dobs.

The man stared at the offering. "I can't take your breakfast."

"I brought this for you. I already had one this morning," Paddy lied. Actually, it was his last piece that he'd planned on saving for supper, as he usually stayed too late to go to the market to get more.

Dobs took a bite and ate without arguing, then shuffled to his chair. "Bring your seat; there's no time for idle hands."

"What's the rush?" Paddy asked, retrieving the chair.

"You'll not be coming here after today."

The words were so matter-of-fact, Paddy wondered if he'd heard them right. "Why not?"

"Because I've taught you everything I can," Dobs replied.

"Yesterday, you said…"

"Yesterday is done and gone. Today is a new day," Dobs said curtly.

"You're scared of her!" Paddy's words held a bite.

"What of it if I am?" Dobs replied. "A man's got to eat."

"I can bring you food," Paddy replied.

"You're only in here today because she forgot to lock the door."

Paddy shrugged. "Oh, that; if she locks it, you can unlock it for me."

"Dang it, boy, you're not listening. I don't want you around here and that's just the way of it."

Paddy couldn't believe his ears. "Have I done something to make you mad at me, Dobs?"

Dobs was quiet for a moment. When he finally spoke, his voice cracked. "I don't want you coming here because I like you. I let the time get away from me yesterday and that woman nearly walked in on us. I ain't worried about myself so much. But I couldn't bear knowing it was me who got you sent to prison."

Paddy gulped. "Prison?"

Dobs nodded. "She wouldn't just run you off; she'd hold on to you until the police came to haul you away."

"Even if I just tell her I didn't mean no harm, that I was here visiting you?"

"Especially if you told her that. She'd use punishing you to torment me, and I'm telling you, my soul couldn't bear knowing it was I who'd done it to you. Do you understand?"

He understood all right – understood that just when he thought his life was getting better, everything he cared about was being taken away. Unable to articulate that, he merely nodded his head.

"Good. Now let's get to work. I have a lot of techniques to show you before you go."

"Dobs?"

"Yes, Howard."

"Is this one of those times people journal about?"

Dobs nodded his head. "Yes, son, it surely is."

"I think maybe I'd like to try it, but I'm not sure how to begin."

Dobs plucked a block of wood from the basket. "Do you know what's better than whistling when you're whittling?"

Paddy shook his head.

"Storytelling. Pull that chair over here so you can see what I'm doing, and we'll have a little chat."

***

Unable to visit his friend, Paddy soon took to following Mileta and her mother once again. Though everything in his world had turned upside down, their routine remained the same, and he found himself getting careless while following. He'd also taken to peeking in the window of the brownstones. At first, it had been mere curiosity, but then after he'd seen both mother

193

and daughter sitting at the piano playing a tune, he'd taken to listening every chance he got. He was sure Milena had seen him following on more than one occasion, but he'd grown bored and long past caring since he'd now convinced himself Mouse was either dead or in prison – the only two explanations he had for the boy not returning. As Mileta and her mother neared the tenement building, they were approached by a dandy of a man dressed in clothing best suited for the other side of town. Paddy wondered what the fellow was doing there and moved closer, thinking to follow the man when he left. The man wore an overcoat, and Paddy knew men like that were often easy pickings. The man must have heard him coming as he moved to allow Mileta and her mother to pass and peered directly at him.

Realizing the guy wasn't as easy of a mark as he suspected, Paddy started to slip past him and go inside.

"Hey there, boy. Come over here so I can have a word with you."

Paddy thought about running, but the man looked like he'd be willing to give chase if he did, so Paddy stayed rooted in place.

"What's your name?"

Paddy couldn't see any harm in telling, so he did.

The man shook his head. "No, that's not it."

Paddy furrowed his brow. "What do you mean that's not it? What are you, a dope? I should think I'd know my own name."

The man smiled. "What I meant to say is you're not the boy I was looking for."

"Oh. Who are you looking for, then?" Paddy asked.

"A boy that used to hang around here a few months back. Smart fellow, about your height, with dark hair. I believe he goes by the name Tobias."

Paddy took a step back. "What do you want with Mouse?"

The man's smile broadened. "Mouse, yes, he's the one. He

did a job for me, and I never got to pay him for it. I'm sure he could use the dough. Do you know where I can find him?"

Paddy took another step back. "Oh, no you don't. I ain't no snitch."

"I'm not asking you to be," the man said, pulling a bill from his pocket. "I told you I owe the kid some money."

Paddy looked at the dollar bill, which looked real enough, and knew Mouse would be angry if he sent the man off without getting the dough. "I guess Mouse would like to have that, being he earned it and all."

"Of course he would," the man agreed. "Now, if you can just point me in the right direction."

"Can't." Paddy shrugged. "I don't know where he is."

"What do you mean you don't know? We've already established that your friend would want to collect what he's owed."

"I mean I don't know where he is. I ain't seen him since the train crash."

"The one on Malbone Street?" the man asked, looking in that direction.

"What are you, a dope, Mister? I ain't heard of another crash. Have you?"

"No, I am not a dope. I am just looking for Mouse." The man's voice held an edge.

"Yeah, well, I think maybe he's dead or has some other scam going, on account of I ain't seen him round here."

"Thank you for the information," the man said, handing Paddy the bill.

"What'd you give me this for? I didn't do nothing," Paddy said when the man turned to go.

"On the contrary, you were a tremendous help," the man said and left without another word.

"Dang do-gooder," Paddy said under his breath. It wasn't

that Paddy couldn't use the dough, but he would have appreciated it more if he'd picked it from the man's pocket. At least then, he would feel like he'd actually earned it. The thought pulled at him, and he realized that before he met Dobs, he wouldn't have cared about anything but the money.

***

In the nights since Dobs asked him to stop visiting, Paddy grew increasingly antsy. While he enjoyed feeling the weight of the knife in his pocket, he'd yet to use it to pull the image he'd seen from the piece of cedar he still carried with him everywhere. He woke with a feeling of urgency, as if he needed to get the image out before he lost the vision of it forever. He went downstairs and walked to the building across the street and sat on the stoop. He'd used this vantage point numerous times, as he could still see when Mileta and her mother exited the building. He studied the board, trying to decide where to start, then set the knife to the wood, using it to draw the image in his mind, much like he used the pencil to create letters. He was so entranced with his project that he didn't realize he was whistling until a man walked past and blew out a tune of his own. Paddy looked up. The man smiled and tipped his hat as he continued down the street. Paddy bent his head once more, this time whistling with intention. Dobs was right, whistling helped settle the mind.

"Geez, what am I paying you for?"

Paddy blinked his surprise at seeing Mouse standing just a few feet away. "Are you not dead, then?"

Mouse raised an eyebrow. "Do I sound dead?"

Paddy closed the knife and shoved it in his pocket. "No, then again, I don't rightly know what a dead person sounds like."

"I'm not dead," Mouse replied. "But you might wish you were when I get finished with you."

Paddy suddenly regretted putting the knife away. "What did I do?"

"You told Adam about me," Mouse said, narrowing his eyes.

"Adam? Oh, you mean the do-gooder?" Paddy asked.

Mouse doubled his fist. "So you did tell him."

"I didn't tell him nothing on account of I didn't know nothing. He came snooping around a few days ago and said how he owed you money. He even waved a dollar in my face to prove it. He wanted to know where you were, and I told him I hadn't seen you since the train wreck."

"That's all you said?" Mouse asked.

"Sure it was. I ain't no snitch." Paddy purposely left out the part about the man giving him the dollar, figuring Mouse owed him at least that much for his staying here all this time.

Mouse looked over at the apartment. "How's my girl?"

Paddy was surprised at how much the comment grated on him. "She's fine. Her and her mother should be leaving any minute."

"Yeah? You can shove off then, since I'm back."

Once again, the comment smarted. The thing was, Paddy couldn't figure out why, since he never liked following them in the first place. He blew the shavings from the piece of wood and shoved it into his pocket. As he started to walk away, Mouse called to him.

"Slim said you haven't been back to the graveyard since that day. Is that true?"

Not wishing to be caught in a lie, Paddy merely nodded.

Mouse offered him a rare smile. "Thanks for looking after my girl. You're not all that bad for a redhead."

Paddy wasn't sure what to say to that, so recalling Dobs words, he shoved his hands in his pockets, whistling as he walked away.

***

September 16, 1920

Paddy followed his mark as close as he dared, waiting for the right moment to move in and relieve him of his wallet. He and the boys had been working Wall Street for about a month since Mouse told them the lunchtime crowd was easy pickings, as the men always seemed to be in a hurry to get somewhere and were not as vigilant as they were at other times. Mouse had been right as always, as they all had nearly enough dough to pay for a month in the Newsboy's Lodging House when the weather turned. It turned out that was what Mouse had been doing with the money he was collecting. He'd waited until everyone left, then circled back around and placed it in a can he'd hidden near the chapel. Had Mouse been killed in the train wreck, the money would have been buried forever.

Slim and the others left to go back, but Paddy begged off, saying he wanted one more dip before leaving.

The man he'd targeted moved into the crowd, and Paddy made his move. Some of the others didn't like picking when there was a crowd, but like Mouse, Paddy preferred it, as it was easier to disappear if things turned sour.

Dressed in uptown clothes – a black jacket over a white shirt, black pants that stopped just below the knee, and long black socks that he'd procured earlier in the week – he fit in with other boys his age on this side of town. Only most boys his age were in classrooms acquiring an education, not dipping pockets to get enough money for an evening meal.

Paddy moved close, matched his mark's pace, and dipped his hand in the man's pocket. He stabbed the wallet with two fingers and lifted it from the pocket. Just as Paddy was about to call the move a success, the man reached a hand to his pocket. Finding it empty, he looked around and focused on Paddy, who was just in the process of hiding it.

"Why, you little thief!" the man yelled.

Paddy ducked from the man's grasp and bolted across the road, sucking in his breath as he dodged a horse-drawn wagon that was just coming to a stop in front of the J.P. Morgan and Company building. The man holding the reins gave him a wry smile as he jumped from the wagon. Paddy thought the man was going to give chase, but to his relief, the man took off in the opposite direction. In doing so, he nearly collided with the man whose wallet he'd stolen. Paddy was so unnerved, he continued running, not stopping until he'd run nearly half a block.

Just as he turned to see if the coast was clear, the street exploded. He turned as the blast hurled him down the street, sliding on his belly along the sidewalk. Even before he stopped, he heard the screams. Tears stung his eyes as he pulled himself up and watched as heavy metal rained from a fog-filled sky. His palms were raw and bleeding, his ears rang something fierce, and try as he might, he just couldn't seem to stop crying. Instinct told him to run, but morbid curiosity had him walking back into the fray while his mind tried to make sense of what had just happened. It reminded him of the chaos the night of the train wreck, only the sun was shining, and there were no trains. Someone said the word bomb just as Paddy saw an automobile lying on its side. There were people lying everywhere, shouting and crying. He saw a man sitting on the curb, holding his arm in his lap. To his surprise, the man just stared at him as if to say how did this happen. Then the man blinked and held out the arm that was still attached as if asking him to help.

Paddy yelled and backed out of the man's reach and took off running.

***

Paddy stood in front of the door to the apartment, momentarily wondering why he was there. Slowly, the brain fog lifted. He remembered the explosion and recalled thinking Dobs would know what to do. He tried the doorknob, found it unlocked, and opened the door. It took him a second to realize that not only was Dobs not sitting in the chair, but there was no chair for the man to sit in. The shelf above where he always sat was devoid of any of the figurines. *He's gone to the almshouse!*

As he stood in the center of the room, Paddy wept. He cried for his mother, who wasn't there to comfort him. He cried for his friend whose fate he did not know and for the horrors he'd just witnessed, and then he cried solely because he could not stop. Before leaving, he pulled two rags from the basket that once held wood and used them to wrap his hands.

The boys were waiting for him at the cemetery and listened with rapt attention as he told of the explosion and went into great detail about all he'd seen. All the boys hung on every word and asked him to expand on things that weren't clear. All except for Mouse, who looked at him as if to say, *You don't have to explain it to me; I've seen it all before.*

***

Cindy felt her mother staring at her and looked up from the journals. "I can't believe Grandpa Howard was there for the Wall Street Bombing."

"Sounds like he could have identified the man if he'd have known they were looking for him," Linda agreed.

"If I remember right, there were thirty killed and a hundred forty-some injured, and some died later. I remember discussing it with Grandpa after I read about it in school and he never said anything about being there. I'm almost mad at all the history that was lost because he and Grandma Mildred never talked about it."

Linda laughed. "You were a kid. You wouldn't have cared."

"How do you know?"

"Easy. People never care enough to listen to their parents and grandparents until it's too late." Linda peered at her over her glasses. "Tell me I'm wrong."

Cindy sighed. "No, Mom, you're not wrong."

Chapter Twenty

Linda came into the room wielding two cups and handed her one. Cindy could smell the rich aroma of hot cocoa even before pulling the cup under her nose. "Mmm, this smells good."

"Practicing my cocoa skills for my granddaughter." Linda held up a finger. "Before you say anything about taking your relationship slow; I don't care about that. I care about Stella and we both know she needs me as much as I need her."

"Stella is lucky to have you," Cindy agreed. It was the truth. David and his wife couldn't have children and had adopted a then four-year-old Stella, who, through no fault of her own, had already been through several foster homes. Stella blossomed in her new home, only to have her life turned upside-down once more after the unexpected death of David's wife. Cindy and David had been dating for months, and she really liked the man but didn't want to jump into something that would cause Stella any undue stress.

"Are you ready to start the next section of the journal?" Linda asked, pulling her from her thoughts.

Cindy sighed.

"Are you okay?"

"I was just thinking of Stella. She's been through so much, and we have a system designed to help. Grandpa Howard was her age when he ended up on the streets. I just can't imagine how scared those kids must have been." Cindy shrugged. "Oh well, worrying about what's done isn't going to change anything. Let's see what Paddy is up to."

"You mean Grandpa Howard?"

"No, I find it helps when I distance myself a bit. Today, he is just Paddy."

"Is that what you're doing with Stella too?"

Cindy glared at her mother. "That's not fair. What if it doesn't work out between David and me? I will not add to her suffering."

Linda nodded. "I get that. But the truth of the matter is you've always found a reason to distance yourself. I just don't want that barrier you've built around you to get in the way of your happiness."

Cindy nodded to the papers lying next to Linda. "Read your journals, Mother. And leave the psychoanalyzing to the experts."

"The truth hurts," Linda mumbled as she picked up the stack of papers.

Cindy ignored her and began to read….

I wasn't quite myself after witnessing that bombing. I'd been cocky before, but after that, I was cocky and mean. Not mean looking to hurt someone, but I wouldn't back down from a fight. Mouse and I got into a number of brawls until one day he cornered me and told me he knew I was scared. I started to push back, but then he admitted he was scared too and told me that the train wreck had really messed with his head. I told him I didn't want to pick pockets anymore and that I was thinking of going into the asylum. I thought he'd be mad, but then he told me that would be a good place for me. I didn't want to be alone, so I told him I thought it would be a good place for Slim too. To my surprise, Mouse agreed with that too. A few days later, he told me of a plan to get us both inside. I didn't know it at the time, but he had his own agenda. I can't be mad at him, as my going inside set up a snowball effect that turned out for the best. There I go, getting ahead of myself again. I don't remember a lot of what went on in the asylum. I guess that is because, like Dobs once said, boring days repeat themselves, but I do recall a few things I'll share with whoever may read this one day. I knew Mouse had a plan but didn't know how he was going to get us inside.

When the cops nabbed us, and we hadn't done anything wrong, I knew it was Mouse. I didn't want Slim to hold me responsible for getting him locked up, so I decided to make a big show of not wanting to go. The truth of the matter was I would have walked right up to that door if not for Slim, who was pretending not to be upset. But when that Clara, a tall dark-haired girl who matched Slim in height, took me in to see the headmistress, and I saw her sitting behind that big wooden desk, I was relieved. The woman was about as scary as they come, stone-faced and dressed in all black with her dark hair pulled away from her face in a way that seemed to tug at her eyes. I should have feared her, but as I sat there in that office, I was mesmerized by all that wood...

"You'll look at me when I'm speaking to you," she said sternly.

"You shouldn't do that," Paddy said as the headmistress tapped the wooden ruler on the desk.

She lifted a brow. "Do what?"

"Hit the desk like that. You'll ding the wood."

The headmistress sat back in her chair and crossed her arms. "Is that so?"

"Yes, ma'am. I know about wood," he assured her. "Your desk is made of cherry, but the wood on your walls is oak. They are the same color but different woods. The oak is solid, but the cherry is quicker to mar."

A smile played at her lips as she ran her hand across the top of the desk. "That is very astute of you. I'll keep that in mind in the future. Now, if we can get back to the business at hand, what is your name?"

"Paddy."

She wrote it on the card she had in front of her. "And your given name?"

"That is my given name. My papa gave it to me," he replied.

"Your birth name, then?"

"No, ma'am."

"No, ma'am what?"

"No, ma'am, I don't recall my given name." It was a lie, but Mouse had warned him not to disclose anything that could help them find his papa, or they would likely send him home.

"Suit yourself, Paddy. Is there anything you do remember? Like your mother and father's name?"

Paddy grinned. "Momma and Papa."

The headmistress set the paper aside. "Empty your pockets."

Paddy frowned. "How come?"

"It's the way of things. If a child comes in with anything of value, we tag it and put it away for safekeeping."

Paddy thought of the knife and carvings that were in his pants pockets. He reached into the opposite pocket, pulled a nickel free, and placed it on the desk.

She eyed his pants. "Empty your pockets, Paddy."

"No, thank you. I'll be keepin' what I have."

"Suit yourself, but when you leave this room, anything you still have in your possession will be burned when they take your clothes."

Paddy gulped. "Why would they burn my clothes? I just put them on fresh this morning."

"This institution prides itself on its cleanliness. We do our best to curtail the lice." She smiled a disarming smile. "As such, all children get a bath and a new set of clothes as soon as they walk out that door."

While he wouldn't mind a bath, the tone of her comment unnerved him. "If it's all the same to you, I just had a shower on this very day. I'll keep my things and put them in my pockets when I get my new set of clothes," Paddy countered.

"It's not the same," she said curtly. "You will empty your pockets, or I will call someone to empty them for you. I will then walk down the hall with you and take great pleasure watching whatever you are hiding get tossed in the stove."

Suddenly, Paddy was starting to believe the stories the boys had told them about life in the asylum. He stood, dipped his hand into his pocket and pulled free the carving he'd made and handed it to her.

The headmistress turned the carving in her hand. When she next spoke, her tone was light. "This is exquisite. Where did you get it?"

"I made it," Paddy said, looking at the hand-size carving he'd done of Dobs. While he'd carved from memory, he thought it to be a pretty fine likeness of the man, which he'd intended to show him but never got the chance. Not for the first time, he wondered what became of him and prayed he wasn't living out his days in the almshouse.

Her eyes grew wide as she trailed a finger along the wooden face. "You're telling me you carved this?"

Paddy nodded as he brought out his knife and held it for her to see. "Yep. Used this knife to do it."

She eyed the knife. "We can't allow weapons in the asylum."

Paddy looked to the door. "If you're going to throw it away, I speck I'll have to leave."

"Expect," she corrected. "And I'm not going to throw it away. I'll keep it in the back with your carving. Do you have anything else?"

Paddy pulled out the pipe and little mouse and handed them both to her. "I expect," he said, using the right form of the word, "to get these back as well. My friend Dobs made the pipe and I carved the mouse. He gave me that and the knife, and he'd be none too happy to learn that I parted with it."

"I will put them all into an envelope with your name on it and see that you get them when you leave our asylum."

Paddy held out his hand.

The headmistress hesitated. "What are we shaking on?"

"When someone gives their word, it is best to shake on it, on account of a person is only as good as their word." Paddy eyed the knife and took a chance. "Unless you'd rather make a blood oath."

"A handshake is most sufficient," the woman said, extending her hand.

"A person is only as good as their word," Paddy repeated, shaking her hand.

***

Paddy found he was right in being suspicious, as the so-called bath the headmistress promised proved to be nothing more than being dunked into a foul-smelling tub of hot water and scrubbed firm enough to leave one's skin pink and tingly.

The good news was his hair – what was left of it – no longer itched, and he now wore a fresh set of clothes that he hadn't had to steal. Not only that, but they appeared to be new. Having grown up with brothers, he'd never had anything new before. The closest he'd come was the coat he'd taken off the line, and even that had belonged to someone else. The whole process had taken a matter of minutes, and he was finished and rushed out of the room.

Slim greeted him at the door. Paddy lifted his hat to show how they'd butchered his hair. "You know what's good for you,

you'll run. Prison has to be better than this."

Paddy winked at Clara, who frowned as Slim dug in his heels.

"That was mean," Clara said as they walked down the hall.

Paddy shrugged. "I didn't want him to think I liked it."

Clara looked over her shoulder. "You didn't, did you?"

"Of course not; I don't suppose anyone would."

Clara sighed. "No, I don't suppose."

Paddy hesitated when she turned to go up the stairs. "Where are we going?"

"To the dorm."

Paddy knew what a dorm was, as he'd slept in the Newsboy Lodging on multiple occasions when it was too cold to sleep outside. He shrugged his acceptance. As they walked up the stairs, he found they didn't bother him. Perhaps it was because the stairway had large windows and was painted the same bright white that lined the halls or the fact that they smelled as clean as the rest of the building. Clara stopped on the third-floor landing. "Mistress Vivian will help you from here."

Paddy looked at the door. "I'll not get another bath, will I?"

Clara smiled a rare smile. "No, you will wash in the shower room from here on out." "Now go; children are not allowed to dawdle in the hallway."

Clara closed the door behind him as he stepped into a large open room full of single metal-framed beds. The room boasted a wall of floor-to-ceiling windows. The windows were filled with sunshine and opened just enough to allow a breeze. Paddy smiled. It wouldn't be hard to escape if he ever had the mind to do so.

"Come here!"

Paddy looked to see a woman he hadn't noticed until now. Dressed all in black, the woman stood near the far wall. She motioned him forward as she walked to a line of beds and pointed. "This your bed," she growled in a thick German accent.

The bed was just big enough for one person. It had a sheet covering the mattress, a pillow at one end, and a dark grey blanket folded across the other. Of course, he'd seen beds before, but he'd yet to spend the night in one. Even at the Newsboy's Lodging House, he and the others had to sleep on pallets on the floor, as they always arrived too late to procure an actual bed. Even the boys who were lucky enough to get a bed knew it was only temporary, and they would sleep in a different one the next night. Paddy wanted to make sure he'd heard correctly. "This bed is all mine?"

"Yes, for as long as you are here. And don't let me find you in another."

Paddy wanted to ask her why he would want another when he had such a fine bed of his own. Sure, it looked like all the others in the room, but she'd said this one was his and his alone, and that made it special. Afraid she would think him to be sassing and change her mind, he merely nodded. The door opened. Paddy looked to see Slim coming in.

"You may be excused," the woman said, shooing him away and motioning Slim forward.

As Paddy neared the door, he hid his excitement as he looked to see the woman pointing to the bed right next to his.

***

Paddy looked for Slim, but the boy had yet to enter the dining room. He took a seat at the boys' table and wrinkled his nose as he stared at his tray. While Joseph had been right about them feeding him, the meal consisted of a simple bowl of mush, bread, and milk, which was by no means drool-worthy. He lifted the spoon, tilted it, and watched as the mush plopped back into the bowl. As it did, the boy sitting beside him reached onto his tray and took his hunk of bread. Paddy reached for it.

The boy elbowed him in the ribs and leaned in close as

Paddy struggled to catch his breath. "Tell, and I'll pound you into the dirt."

"I ain't scared of you," Paddy lied, staring into the menacing deep-set eyes of the boy who was nearly double his size.

The boy leaned close once more. Just as he started to speak, Paddy headbutted him in the nose. The boy cupped his hand to his nose as he scrambled from the table.

One of the mistresses saw the boy coming and hurried to him. "What happened?"

"Just a nosebleed," he said, narrowing his eyes at Paddy.

The woman led him from the room and another boy slid close. "You came in yesterday, didn't you?"

Paddy nodded.

"You're in for it now," the boy warned.

Paddy doubled his fist. "You want to fight?"

The boy's eyes bugged. "I'm not trying to fight you. My name's Levi, and I'm on your side. I'm just warning you to watch your back."

Paddy looked to the door. "I ain't scart of him either."

"Well you should be. Tommaso is even worse than Anastasia, and she's bad," he said with a nod to an older girl monitoring the girls' side of the room. "Anastasia mostly acts on her own, but Tommaso has some boys that listen to him. They'll steal your food and beat you up if you try to stop them."

"Yeah, well, it looks like I stopped him well enough."

"For now," the boy said and pointed to a girl who was intently staring in their direction. "I'm with Mary – a lot of us kids are. She said for me to tell you that you are welcome to join her little group."

"You mean like a gang?"

Levi shrugged. "Others don't bother you so much when you do."

Paddy frowned. "You're saying you follow a dame?"

The boy bobbed his head. "People don't mess with Mary's gang."

Paddy glanced at the girl. "She don't look so tough."

"Mary is better than tough; she's smart. At least think about it," Levi said. "In the meantime, don't let Tommaso and his friends catch you alone, especially in the play yard."

Paddy shrugged. "I was in the play yard yesterday, and no one bothered me."

"Yeah, that was before you made Tommaso look like a fool in front of everyone," Levi reminded him, then slid back to his place and folded his hands in front of his tray.

***

Paddy lay in his bed, retracing the events of the day and wondering if his momma was smiling down on him now that he was finally in the asylum. He thought about his run-in with the boy with the dark eyes and knew Levi to be correct. The boy reminded him a lot of Milo, and boys like that didn't let people get away with making them look bad. He'd not told Slim about their confrontation as he was afraid the boy would do something to retaliate and get himself kicked out of the asylum in the process. No, it was he who'd acted in haste, so he was the one who'd have to think of a way to make amends.

He thought about the girl they called Mary and how Levi had told him that people didn't bother kids in Mary's gang. He wasn't keen on following a girl, but he was willing to give it a try if it meant staying in the asylum and sleeping in a real bed each night. Not any old bed, he reminded himself as he closed his eyes. As long as he stayed in the asylum, it would be his bed.

Chapter Twenty-One

The tall, gated courtyard the others referred to as the play yard reminded him of the graveyard, only there were no headstones, and the iron gates were locked even though it was daytime. The gates being locked didn't worry him so much, as there were no spikes on the top of the fence, and he knew he could easily climb them if he were to decide to escape. What bothered him was not knowing who he could trust. Clara had plucked Slim out of the line just as they headed outside, and he still hadn't joined the group. Tommaso stood in the corner, speaking with several other boys. Paddy didn't like the way the boys were glaring at him, so he decided to seek Levi out when he saw him and a few others talking to Mary and a small group of girls at the fence.

Just as he moved toward the new group, Tommaso and the boys ran in his direction. Paddy heard a commotion and saw two of the boys who'd been with Tommaso arguing near the door to the asylum. Instantly, he knew it to be a distraction to divert the mistresses' attention.

Way to go, Paddy. You're done for. The thought sent a chill racing up his spine as he quickly realized the asylum was not as safe as his mother had thought. Though he'd lived on the streets for years, he'd never in his life felt so alone.

"You think you're so tough, Leprechaun," Tommaso sneered. "Are you going to fight or run away like a scaredy-baby?"

Funny, when Slim had called him that, it amused him. But hearing Tommaso use the word grated on him. Several of the other boys gathered nearby. The last thing he wanted was to have the boys think he was an easy mark. He'd made that mistake with Milo and thought never to be put in that position again. Instantly, he thought of Mouse and how he'd faced Milo and his gang, seemingly unafraid. Deciding it was his only option, he pulled himself taller and forced a smile. "I wasn't the one that ran off while we were eating."

One of the boys standing beside Tommaso snorted. Tommaso scowled at the kid, who took a step back.

Well, that was one boy he wouldn't have to worry about. Paddy smiled a genuine smile at the victory.

Tommaso must have thought he was sassing him, as the boy's face turned a brilliant pink, and he rushed forward. Just as the guy reached him, Paddy caught a glimpse of Slim standing with the others. He didn't get a chance to weigh the magnitude of the fact that his friend was merely watching as several other boys joined Tommaso in throwing punches. Paddy struck back, punching and shoving best he could, considering there was only one of him.

He wasn't sure when his friend joined in the fray. One minute, Tommaso's fist connected with his eye, and suddenly, Slim was there pulverizing the kid and tossing others to the side like old wet rags. While it felt like the fight went on forever, it probably only lasted a few moments until the mistresses broke it up.

Mistress Vivian snatched him by the ear and shook her head. "What is it about you redheads?"

Paddy started to tell the woman he hadn't started the fight, but she didn't seem to be in the mood to listen as she dragged him inside and pushed him into a chair. Taking hold of his chin, she turned his head from side to side, checking his injuries.

One of the other mistresses led Tommaso and two other boys inside, hurrying past without a word.

"Don't move," Mistress Vivian warned, then stepped back outside and came in a moment later, followed by Slim. She glanced at him as they passed. "Come."

The woman led them to a small room where several children sat on the floor with their backs to the wall. A woman sitting at a desk looked up when they entered. She pointed to two spots along the wall, then went back to the book she'd been reading. Mistress Vivian positioned both him and Slim away from the boys, yet far enough apart that they could not talk to one another. Paddy looked toward the partially opened window, judging the distance, and sighed. While he felt certain he would be able to escape without getting caught, he didn't think Slim, who was sitting further away, would be so lucky, as the woman's desk was between him and the window. Besides, they would probably fare better in prison if they remained together. He was still contemplating this when the door opened, and a girl stepped inside, rolling a cart. The mistress nodded, and the girl began passing out trays to the boys. When she got to him, she gasped. Paddy thought it was because of his injuries, then realized he knew the girl. At least, he thought it to be the case.

He looked again. Though she was dressed in conservative asylum attire with her bosom fully covered, he knew she was Dorthia, the girl he'd met at the flower stand. He started to cover his pocket, then realized he had nothing for her to steal.

She smiled and handed him a tray.

The mistress called out something he did not understand, and the girl hurried off without a word.

Paddy picked up his tray, eating slowly, as he didn't have to worry about anyone taking his food. As he ate, he savored each bite as if it would be his last, for as far as he knew, they would serve him nothing but bread and water once he reached prison.

***

"Dames," Paddy said when they left the headmistress's office. "I just don't get them."

Clara hushed him. "There's no talking in the hall."

"Yeah, well, there's no fighting either, and yet she didn't do a thing about it," Paddy countered. He nodded to Slim. "I'm the one that got clobbered, and she sends him to see the doctor."

Slim frowned. "Do you need to see him?"

"No, but that's not the point. I thought for sure we'd be on our way to prison by now, and yet the woman seemed pleased that we pulverized those kids." Paddy smiled a sheepish grin. "Okay, you did the pulverizing, but I got in a few licks too."

They stopped at the door to the Meeting room, and Clara nodded for Paddy to go in.

Paddy reached for the doorknob and hesitated. "You sure those boys aren't in there?"

"You'll be safe in there," Clara assured him.

Everyone stared as he entered. Paddy fought his insecurities and walked into the room as if Slim was standing right next to him. He saw Levi tug on Mary's arm. She looked in his direction and her eyes grew wide. She quickly recovered and walked to greet him.

"The headmistress did not send you away," she said, stating the obvious.

Paddy shook his head. "Nope."

"And your friend?"

Another head shake. "Nope, Slim is up seeing the doctor."

A frown creased her forehead. "He's hurt?"

Paddy laughed. "Slim doesn't stand still long enough to get hurt."

Mary smiled, and her face lit up. "Yes, I noticed that about him. Does it hurt him?"

"Nah. It's just aggravating, especially when people think

215

he's daft. He's not, ya know."

"I didn't say he was. Now tell me, why did the headmistress not send you both away?"

"Levi said you were smart, and that's why you run this gang. If you're so smart, you tell me."

"I would suppose it is because you are both brave enough to tell the headmistress what happened."

"You mean about the fight?"

"Yes, Tommaso has everyone in here so scared that they won't tell what it is he does. He doesn't get punished, so he and the others keep doing it."

"Why doesn't she punish him?"

"She can't prove it."

"Why don't you tell her or have one of the boys in your gang do it?"

"You saw what they did to you. If your friend hadn't jumped in, it would have been worse. Then, they would have threatened to do it again if you told."

Paddy nodded his understanding.

Mary smiled. "I knew you and your friend would be a good fit for my group."

"I'm okay with it, but I can't speak for Slim."

Mary raised an eyebrow. "He comes too or no deal."

Paddy didn't expect that. "How come I ain't good enough?"

"You're a redhead, and everyone knows redheads are trouble. The only reason we are letting you join is because of your friend."

Paddy narrowed his eyes. "What makes you think I'm trouble?"

"You didn't let Tommaso have your bread. Anyone else would have and that would have been that. But you – no, I can see you have an ornery streak about you. That means you could do something to get us all in trouble. I would think you would be more cautious if you were worried about getting your friend in trouble as well." She held up a finger to silence him when he started to speak. "Tis the way of it. You want to join our group, then your friend must join too."

Paddy knew enough to see through her ruse. The girl wanted something from Slim and was using him to get it. He nodded his agreement. "Okay, but you will owe me one."

Mary bristled. "Owe you what?"

"A favor. I get Slim to join your group, then you will do something for me when the time comes."

"I will not do anything that will get me in trouble with the headmistress," she said firmly.

"Okay," Paddy said, and held out his hand. "Shake on it."

"I'll not shake your hand."

"Then no deal."

"It's not proper," she argued.

"The headmistress shook my hand on my deal."

"What kind of deal would she make with you?"

"None that I'll blab about," Paddy replied.

Before Mary could respond, Dorthia came into the room and motioned for Mary to join her near the far wall. As they spoke, Mary looked in his direction. A moment later, Dorthia left the room. Mary was smiling when she returned. "Dorthia tells me your friend Slim is even more useful than I first suspected."

"I'm not sure I would trust the girl. She is a thief."

Mary laughed an exuberant laugh. "She said the same thing about you."

"Perhaps, but did she tell you she uses her body to…"

Mary's demeanor changed in an instant. "Don't you dare judge her! You do not know what it is like for a girl who lives on the streets."

"She could have joined a gang," Paddy countered.

Mary's anger turned to a haunting laugh. "Would you have allowed her to join your gang?"

"I dunno. We never had a girl ask to join," Paddy said truthfully.

"Well, I know, on account of what she told me." Mary held up a hand to stanch his reply. "And others before her. If they had joined a gang, they would have been made to do what they do anyway without getting anything in return. At least on their own, the money they made went to them."

Paddy wasn't sure what the girls actually did for their money, but after giving money to Mouse all these years, he found himself agreeing that if the girls earned the money, they should be able to keep it.

***

Paddy sat outside the headmistress's office, waiting to be called in. It was the fourth time in as many months he'd been sent to the office for fighting. The door opened, and Clara stepped out. According to asylum gossip, though some lucky children had been adopted since arriving at the asylum, Clara had been living here since her birth and was nearly old enough to leave and make her way in the world. While the girl seemed perfectly content with her role as the headmistress's assistant, he himself was glad he wouldn't have to live here for that many years.

Clara looked him over and shook her head. "When will you learn not to fight with the older boys?"

Paddy shrugged and then grinned, then held out his hand to show her the teeth the boys had knocked out. "They were loose anyway. Now I don't have to worry about them wiggling no more."

Clara chuckled, then hid it with a stern look. "Headmistress will see you now."

The woman frowned and clicked her tongue when he entered. "Oh, my. How big was the boy this time?"

Paddy knew the routine and sat in the chair without being told. "Only a few years older."

She raised an eyebrow. "And what, pray tell, did he say to set you off?"

"He called me a bad name," Paddy said then repeated the word.

She sighed. "Isn't that what the last boy said to you as well?"

Paddy nodded.

"Then you should be used to hearing it," she replied.

Paddy thought about this for a moment. "Headmistress?"

"Yes, Paddy?"

"Do you know what the kids in here call you?"

The woman looked down her nose at him. "I am aware that the children think me stern."

Paddy snorted and told her several names the kids had used.

Her cheeks turned a brilliant pink. "That is quite enough of that language, young man."

Paddy shook his head. "I didn't say it. The others do. Now if you were a kid and the other kids called you that, wouldn't you want to punch them in the nose?"

"What is it going to take to get you to stop fighting?" she asked, ignoring the question.

Three months after having Mouse ask him and Slim for help in protecting his girl and fighting anyone who even looked in his direction to let them know not to mess with him, and this was the moment he'd been waiting for. "My momma used to tell me I had the devil in me. She said how I couldn't help it on account of I had red hair. But Dobs, he said it's more on account of I had idle hands. He showed me how to work the wood to take the anger away. He said I was a natural and how I needed to do things to keep my mind occupied. He even taught me to whistle so I could keep my mind occupied while I work." Okay, it wasn't the complete truth, but he'd been practicing that speech ever since he'd thought up the ruse. "So, I'm thinking if you give me my knife back and find me a piece of wood, that would keep my hands busy, and I'd stop fighting."

A smile played at her lips. "That was a well-thought-out speech, Paddy, but you know I simply cannot allow you to have your knife."

"Aww, why not?" Paddy grumbled. "I need to do my carvings; it's in my blood."

"Because you'd end up stabbing someone in a fight and then I'd have to have you hauled off to prison."

Paddy started to tell her he'd only been fighting so he could have his knife, but she cut him off.

"What if we were to make a compromise?"

Paddy leaned forward. "Does that mean you'll give me my knife back?"

"No, but if you will promise not to do any more fighting, I will allow you to use the knife one hour a day."

"Only an hour?" Paddy sighed.

She nodded. "For starters, and then we'll see how it goes."

"Sure!" The elation was followed by a frown.

"What's wrong? I thought you'd be happy with the arrangement."

"Well, I am, but I don't have any wood to carve. What's the good at having a knife if I can't use it?"

"You can pick a small limb from the tree in the play yard," she suggested.

Paddy shook his head. "No, I didn't learn on no tree. I need wood like they make tables and chairs with."

She raised an eyebrow. "You were living on the streets before you came in here, yes?"

Paddy nodded.

"Then how did you afford that kind of wood?"

Paddy started to tell her about Dobs, then changed his mind. The man was gone, and couldn't help him now. "The man at the furniture store gave it to me. He even said he'd give me a shelf so I could sell my carvings in his store."

She sat back in her chair and tapped her fingers together. "And he gave you those pieces for free?"

Paddy marked an x across his chest. "Cross my heart."

"Okay," she said at last. "Tell me the address of this furniture store and I will investigate your claim. If you're telling the truth, we will get you some wood, and I will allow you to sit in my office for an hour a day – to start," she said before he could interrupt, "as long as you keep up your end of the bargain about not fighting. Do we have a deal?"

"We sure do!" Paddy said, bobbing his head. He couldn't believe his plan had actually worked. The whooping he'd just taken was totally worth it. He couldn't wait to feel the weight of the knife in his hand once more.

***

Cindy laughed and Linda held up a finger.

After a moment, Linda joined in with a chuckle of her own. "I guess your grandpa learned how to game the system."

"Nothing's changed," Cindy said, shaking her head.

"How so?"

"He reminds me of just about every student in my class. I'm serious; I'm never going to be able to look at any of them again and not see the boy version of Grandpa Howard standing there trying to manipulate me."

"Yes, but at least you're smart enough not to let them have a knife," her mother reminded her.

"I know, right? Can you imagine?"

"Personally, I think he's up to something," Linda mused.

"You don't think he just misses carving?"

"It could be that innocent, but it won't surprise me if there's more to it."

"You're probably right. Seems like Grandpa was a master manipulator," Cindy agreed.

Chapter Twenty-Two

Cindy picked up the journals and started where she'd left off...

Shortly after she agreed to let me come to the office to whittle, the headmistress grew tired of having me in her office – I don't think she was fond of whistling. But she liked how I was staying out of trouble, so she moved a chair into the file room, which was set just off her office. That simple act of kindness helped to ingratiate me with Mary, who, until that point, thought she was doing me a favor by allowing me to join her little gang based solely on my ability to bring Slim with me. Now that I had backroom access, I heard and saw things that made me most useful.

I still remember the day Mileta arrived at the asylum. She didn't see me, as I was in the file room, but from my vantage point, I could hear everything.

Mouse had let us know Mileta would be coming soon, and he'd gotten word to Slim the night before to keep an eye out for her. Not having anything better to ask for, I used my favor with Mary to get her to take Mileta under her wing and keep her safe. Looking back, I believe Mary would have done it even if I hadn't asked – it was what she did. While Mary often had her own agenda, she also looked after the kids who wouldn't have stood a chance on their own in the asylum. I'm sure she would have been more accepting of me if she hadn't had a preconceived notion about people with red hair.

Anyway, Mileta came, and I kept the door ajar just enough so I could hear. The headmistress sat with her back to the file room door. And there Mileta stood, looking like a drowned rat, and yet she didn't drop a single tear. She had an answer for every question the headmistress threw at her and I thought, boy, Mouse, you really screwed up asking me to watch out for her. And it was like that each time I saw her stand up for herself or anyone else. She just had this thing about her and had so much compassion for others, and I knew my momma would have liked her.

***

Paddy looked at the clock and knew Mileta would be heading to the dining room after her initial bath. He rushed to clean up his mess then went to the dining room so he could be there when she arrived. He entered the room, grabbed his tray and headed for a table. As he did, he made eye contact with Mary and gave her the signal to let her know Mileta had arrived.

"She's here," Paddy said, sliding in next to Slim.

Slim scanned the room. "Where?"

"No. I mean in the building. She'll be in as soon as the mistresses are finished with her." Paddy shivered, recalling the treatment he'd received the day he arrived. "Poor kid."

Slim nodded his agreement.

Newcomers were easy to spot as they came into the room, with hair cut close to the head in choppy chunks. Mileta was no different as she stood in the middle of the room, scanning the crowd for a friendly face. Paddy looked to Mary, who gave the slightest nod, then watched a smile flitter across Mileta's face.

Even as Mileta sat, Anastasia moved in to harass her. It was the same with all the girls, young or old. It was rare that Anastasia ever got physical, but she was taller than most of the girls and used that to her advantage. The moment Mileta lifted her hands in prayer, Anastasia reached over the girl's plate and took her bread. Though he'd seen her do it countless times, the sight of her taking bread from Mileta, who'd stopped momentarily to lift her hands in prayer, infuriated him. Paddy started to get up.

Slim caught him by the arm. "Don't. You'll only make it worse."

"Mary is supposed to be looking out for her," Paddy said.

"She is," Slim said with a nod to the blonde who'd just taken Mileta by the arm to prevent her from confronting the girl.

Paddy relaxed, and Slim let go.

"She has to find her way," Slim reminded him.

"It shouldn't be that way," Paddy fumed.

"No, but it is. It happens all the time. What's got you so riled?"

"I'm not riled," Paddy lied.

Slim's eyes went round. "You're sweet on the girl!"

"Am not," Paddy said, lying once more. "It's just that we promised Mouse we'd keep an eye on the girl."

"His girl," Slim corrected. "And you'd better not set your sights on her, or Mouse will…"

"Do what?" Paddy said heatedly. "We are the ones in here, and Mouse is living the good life out there."

"I don't know what's so bad about this life. We get to eat three times a day and sleep in a clean bed of our own each night," Slim reminded him. "We're doing alright in here, and I don't want you to screw that up over a lousy dame."

Paddy knew it was sound advice, but he also knew his heart was no longer listening. As Mileta glared at Anastasia, Paddy smiled. Some children came into the room with their spirits broken. He'd seen girls sob and boys cry, but Mileta was doing neither. After the initial burst of tears, she now glared at Anastasia with a renewed strength, which said, *Give it your best shot; you'll never break me.*

***

Paddy was in the common room talking to Slim and a few of the other boys when the door opened, and Anastasia led the girls into the room. He worked to curb his enthusiasm as Mileta came into the room. Her cheeks were flushed, and she looked pretty even though her hair was chopped short and stuck out from her head in enough places most would have laughed had they each not experienced the same humiliation when first arriving.

Mileta joined them when Mary called her by name and started introducing her to the other members of her little gang. Paddy hung on each word, waiting for the moment Mary shined the attention on him. He doubted Mileta would recognize him, but he'd already formed an excuse as to why he'd been in the apartment that day. One that was not needed as when Mary pointed in his direction, Mileta merely bobbed her head.

The disappointment was short-lived as Mary took Mileta by the hand and proclaimed, "This is Mileta. She is going to be part of our gang. She is a smart one. Did any of you see what she did at the supper table?"

Paddy jumped at the chance to sing the girl's praises. "I did! Boy, she showed ole Anastasia who was boss. She saw her coming for her mush and bent over licking her food straight from the bowl like a dog." He bent, taking great pleasure in mimicking her earlier actions. Paddy sighed when, instead of being pleased with his theatrics, Mileta turned a brilliant crimson and turned away from him. He hadn't expected her to remember him, but having her turn away like that did nothing for his confidence.

Music filled the air.

Paddy followed Mileta's gaze as she watched Anastasia pound heavily on the piano keys, something the girl took great pleasure in doing each chance she got.

As he watched Anastasia play, it reminded him of when he'd peeked in a window of one of the brownstones and watched Mileta play. Only the music Mileta produced was pleasant to the ears, not the mangled grating mess that was currently ringing throughout the room.

As if being summoned by the music, Mileta turned. To his and everyone else's horror, she took a step forward, then another, and still another until, at last, she was within inches of Anastasia.

In his mind, he ran to her, stepping between the two. But in reality, he stood gaping along with the others as Mileta tapped Anastasia on the shoulder and asked if she could play. A move so bold even Anastasia was without words. Mileta sat on the piano bench, closed her eyes, and lowered her fingers to the keys. Paddy did not know the name of the tune she played, nor did he care. While he had heard Mileta play before, it was nothing like the song she currently played. Now, as her fingers danced along the keys, it was as if the sorrow of everything in her life poured through her fingers, producing music so haunting that he had no recourse but to cry. He started to wipe the tears away, then realized he wasn't the only one crying and let them flow. By the time her fingers stilled, there were tears in the eyes of everyone in the room, including Anastasia, who whispered something to Mileta.

Mileta tilted her head in their direction and whispered something in return. Anastasia scowled and then nodded her head.

***

Paddy was waiting in the chair outside the headmistress's door when she arrived. She had her satchel over her shoulder and some files in the other hand. She saw him sitting there and raised an eyebrow. "You're early this morning, Paddy. Let me get settled, and then I'll allow you into the back room."

Paddy stood, shaking his head. "I'm not looking to go to the back room this morning. I wish to speak to you."

"Okay, just let me get settled first," she replied and shut the door behind her, giving him no option but to wait.

Paddy returned to his seat, biding his time by swinging his feet under the chair until, at last, she called him in. Wishing to make a formal request, he stepped in front of her desk, shoved his hands in his pockets, and waited for her to call on him.

The headmistress leaned back in her chair and intertwined her hands. "Oh my, but this must be important. What, pray tell, is on your mind? Has someone been misbehaving?"

Paddy shook his head. "No, ma'am, not that I'm aware of." It was true; life in the asylum had greatly improved since Mileta began giving Anastasia piano lessons.

"Good," she said and allowed her shoulders to relax.

"Yes, ma'am, everyone is getting along just fine."

"Then why are you here? Come on, out with it. I have things to attend to."

"I want to ask about getting me a job," Paddy blurted.

A smile played at the woman's lips. "I assume this has something to do with your friend Slim leaving the asylum each day."

Paddy lowered his eyes. "Yes, ma'am."

"Mr. Barsotti has a job and someone to sponsor him," Headmistress said, using Slim's real name. "I'm afraid you do not have the same luxury."

"Oh, but I do," Paddy countered. "The man at the furniture shop said I could have a shelf to sell my wares. I've made a whole basket of stuff, only I can't get them to him."

She thought about this for a moment. "Perhaps I could visit the furniture store on your behalf and ask them if the offer still stands."

"I was hoping to speak with him myself if you don't mind," Paddy pressed.

"This is not about selling things, is it?"

Paddy shook his head. "Not entirely."

"Then stop playing games and tell me what it is," she insisted.

"It's just I've been going to class, and I've been getting better with my spelling, and I have so many things I want to write down."

She smiled. "Write down? So, you would like to keep a diary? I can see that you get one to write in."

Paddy shook his head. "No. This isn't regular stuff that goes into a diary. This is important stuff that goes into a journal."

She sat back and studied him once more. "Just how is it you know the difference between keeping a diary and keeping journals?"

"My friend Dobs told me. He said diaries can be boring since you write in them every day even when you don't have anything important to say. But he said when you write in journals, you are supposed to write important stuff. He said diaries are meant to keep everyday stuff, but journals should be hidden on account of they harbor a man's soul. You're a girl, so I guess it could harbor your soul too," Paddy said.

"I see, but what does any of this have to do with the furniture shop?"

"On account of I need me a box."

"I can get you a box."

"No, this isn't an ordinary box. It is a wooden box with a lock and everything."

"You must have something pretty important you'd like to write down if you need to have a lock. Do you really think it is necessary that this box of yours has a lock?"

Paddy stared at the headmistress, willing her to understand.

"Dobs seemed to think so. His box had a lock, and he hid it in a secret compartment under his chair. I think he only hid it because Mrs. Bronski would have burned it if he did not, so I don't think I need a whole chair, but a box with a lock will do just fine."

"How much do these boxes cost?"

"Oh, I don't intend to buy it. I want it to be special like the one Dobs had. I've been thinking on it a lot, but my mind can't seem to get it right, and I don't have the tools even if I did. That's why I need to go to the furniture shop. I know Mr. Murphy will know how to make it."

"Okay, Paddy," she said, then patted her hands in the air to settle him, "I will speak with him. If he is agreeable to sponsoring you, then we will continue this discussion."

"But."

"That is all, sir."

"Headmistress?"

"Yes?"

"I know I don't have a box or nothing, but do you think maybe I could have some paper so I can start? I won't share my soul just yet, but I think I can get some things written down without it."

The headmistress opened a drawer on her desk and handed him a small stack of papers and two lead pencils.

"It sure would help to have that knife of mine to sharpen these pencils," Paddy said, shoving a pencil behind each ear.

"Don't push your luck, sir," the headmistress said without looking up.

Paddy couldn't be certain, but he thought he saw the barest hint of a smile.

***

Paddy was in the common room when the rest of the

children entered.

"What ya doing?" Levi asked, approaching the table.

Paddy looked up from his writings. "I'm writing a journal."

Unimpressed, Levi left without commenting. Paddy saw the boys telling the others, who also seemed uninterested in what he was doing. Paddy shrugged a hapless shrug and went back to his writings. A couple of moments went by when Paddy heard the chair slide away from the table. He looked up, swallowing his surprise as Mileta slid into the seat beside him.

She smiled. "Levi said you're writing a journal."

"Y-yes," he stammered.

She looked past him as if seeing something only she could see. "My papa used to keep a journal."

Paddy found his voice. "Did he have an exciting life?"

Mileta frowned. "I guess he did right up until he died. Why do you ask?"

"On account of my friend said journals are for important things," Paddy replied.

"Are you writing important things?"

"I'm writing a journal, ain't I?" Paddy replied.

"Well, you don't have to sound so sore about it."

She started to get up and Paddy searched his mind for something that would make her stay. "You should write a journal."

She settled into her seat. "Whatever would I write about?"

"Your life? Coming to America? Your papa dying?"

Mileta frowned. "How do you know about that?"

Paddy was at a loss. He'd heard about it both from Dobs and from listening to her tell the headmistress the day she arrived. Telling her either could have unwanted consequences. He shrugged. "You're in here, I figured your folks died."

Mileta bit at her fingernails. "Oh. How come you go to the headmistress's office so much? I heard one of the boys mention it," she said by way of explanation.

"She lets me use my knife in the back room," Paddy replied.

Mileta's eyes grew wide. "You have a knife? Let me see it."

"She won't let me have it in here. That's why I go to the back room."

"What do you use it for?" Mileta asked.

"To carve things." Paddy could feel where the conversation was heading and knew he should change the subject, but he just couldn't bring himself to do it.

"There was a man in our apartment who carved things. His name was Dobs." Mileta's eyes grew round. "You are that boy!"

Paddy wasn't sure what to say, so he feigned surprise. "What boy?"

"My momma and I came home and there was a boy in the apartment. He had red hair. It must have been you."

"I might recall you coming in once," Paddy replied.

"He got in trouble," Mileta said without telling the rest.

"I miss Dobs. He's the one who gave me the knife. Traded it to me for a stamp. I went back to the apartment one day." Paddy shuddered, recalling the reason for his visit. "Only he wasn't there. I've often wondered what happened to him."

A smile spread across Mileta's face. "He went to live with his brother."

Paddy felt excitement course through his body. "You mean it worked?! His brother actually got the letter I wrote?"

Mildred frowned. "I'm not sure. I don't recall them saying anything about a letter. The man said someone – I think it was someone named Murphy from a furniture store."

Paddy smiled. Even though the letter hadn't reached him, he still had a part in getting Dobs out of that apartment. "That was why he was asking all those questions."

"You knew Mr. Murphy?"

Paddy nodded. "I'm glad he reached him, and that Dobs'

brother came for him."

"No, his brother was unable to travel, so he sent his nephew to take him to Philadelphia," Mileta said. "I remember it so well, as they brought in this wooden chair with wheels. It took two men to carry both him and the chair down the stairs. The lady of the house wasn't at all happy about it, as Dobs made them take his little animals that he'd made and that old chair he sat in. I'm glad he took the chair. I think it would have made me sad to see it sitting there without him in it."

Paddy nodded his agreement. He'd been glad to see it gone because if it were still there, he would have thought the worst. Plus, that meant he took his journals with him. "Did he seem happy to go?"

Mileta bobbed her head. "Oh, yes, he truly must have been on account of he was whistling when they took him out, and I had never heard him whistle before. What are you doing?" she asked when Paddy lifted his pencil.

Paddy grinned a wide grin. "I just thought of something important to write about."

Chapter Twenty-Three

Paddy walked down the sidewalk and through the gates, half expecting someone to call him back and tell him his leaving was all a mistake.

"Jeepers, Paddy, are you okay?" Slim asked. "That's the fifth time you've looked behind you."

"I just can't believe they let me out," Paddy replied.

"Technically, they aren't letting you out," Slim observed. "You're going to work."

"I know, but you do it all the time. This is the first time I've been out since they put me in. Don't say you're sorry for me being in there. I already know. Tell me what it's like."

"What's what like?" Slim asked.

"Working."

"It depends on what kind of work you do."

"Okay, tell me what you do?" Truthfully, Paddy didn't care what Slim did, as the boy had told him a little about it before, and it didn't sound all that fun. But Paddy had a lot of nervous energy, and talking to Slim always helped.

"I am transcribing Mr. Thornton's cases."

Paddy thought about how he'd copied the address off the envelope for Dobs to send the letter to his brother and could not think of anything more boring. "You mean you copy papers?"

"Yes, but I think it is more than that. I think he wants me to do it so I can learn about being a lawyer."

"What's there to learn?"

"I learn about cases and how Mr. Thornton won."

"So, how does he win?"

"According to Mr. Thornton, everyone has a secret. You just have to find out what that secret is, and you've got them."

"Got them how?"

"Because he can use that secret to win the case."

Paddy wrinkled his brow. "Sounds like you found a different way to steal, only you're stealing secrets."

"We're not stealing; we're catching them in lies. Why, just yesterday, I transcribed a case where a man was trying to steal a grocery store from another man."

Paddy laughed. "How could someone steal a whole store?"

"You don't steal the store – not like you're thinking anyway. It's all done on paper. The guy was trying to blackmail the guy."

Paddy blew out a whistle. "I'm surprised you let him do it since you like Big Joe and all."

"What's Big Joe got to do with anything?" Slim asked.

"He's a black male, isn't he?"

Slim laughed.

"What's so funny?" Paddy asked.

"The case didn't have anything about the color of the guy's skin. It just means he thought he'd found something on Mr. Thornton's client and was trying to use it to get what he wanted."

"Man, Slim. Being a lawyer sounds tough, and here I thought all you did was copy papers. You must be real smart."

"Mr. Thornton thinks so," Slim agreed.

"I think so, too," Paddy said and meant it. "Hey, there's the trolley."

"You don't have to steal a ride. The headmistress gave us coins to pay," Slim said when Paddy jumped on the back of the trolley.

"Yeah, but if I use it for the trolley, I can't use it to buy a meat pie." Paddy grinned.

"Good point," Slim said, joining him. "How does it feel?"

Paddy stretched his face into the wind as the car began to roll. "To be riding the back of the trolley again or to be out of the asylum?"

Slim laughed. "Both."

"Then good to both."

"To be honest, I thought you would have climbed out a window by now," Slim said.

"I thunk to do it a bunch of times," Paddy admitted.

"So, you're telling me you like it in the asylum?"

"I guess I like it well enough now that it don't feel like a cage no more. I like sitting in the headmistress's office and working with my knife, and I like being able to eat without anyone stealing my food. I like sitting in the common room and listening to Mileta play the piano. Heck, even ole Anastasia's music is sounding pretty good these days. Hey, whatcha turning all red for?" Paddy asked when Slim's face turned crimson.

"Just feeling the sun on my face," Slim replied. He nodded. "My stop is coming up. Then I take the other one over to West 71st. Do you know how to get where it is you're going?"

"Of course I do. I ain't been locked up that long," Paddy replied. It was a lie. Not the knowing where he was going part, but the part about not being locked up that long. He'd been in the asylum for over a year, which was a long time for a boy used to living on the streets.

"Okay. I'll see ya later, and Paddy?"

"Yeah, Slim?"

"Make sure you come back."

Paddy knew his friend was only saying that as he'd told him the same thing when Slim first started leaving the asylum to go to work. Paddy smiled at his friend. "I'll be there, don't you worry none about that."

The trolley rolled to a stop, and both boys jumped off. Just as it began to roll again, Paddy jumped back on and waved as Slim looked on. Slim turned, and Paddy lowered his arm as another boy jumped onto the trolley, claiming Slim's place. It took a moment for Paddy to recognize the kid. "Hey, you're the kid I gave my fishing string to."

"Yeah, well, you're not getting it back," the boy snapped.

Paddy looked him over and realized that while it was the same boy, the streets hadn't been kind to the kid, who now looked hardened and ready to fight anyone who looked at him the wrong way. "I don't want it back."

"Good, on account of it's mine."

"Have you been living on the streets all this time?"

"Yeah, what's it to you?" the boy snarled.

"You should go to the asylum on…"

The boy cut him off. "I'm not going into no place like that."

"I thought the same when I was first on the streets. But it is not bad at all. They feed us and give us our own bed."

The boy wavered briefly. "You live at the asylum?"

"Yeppers. Little over a year now."

"If you're in the asylum, why are you not there?" the boy asked.

"Because I'm going to work," Paddy said proudly.

The boy belted out a laugh. "Boy, you sure are a dope, trying to tell me life in the asylum is good when they make you go to work."

"They didn't make me," Paddy said. "I asked."

"Then you're an even bigger dope than I thought. I like life on the street well enough. I can do what I want when I want."

"Where do you sleep?"

The boy narrowed his eyes. "What are you, my ma? I didn't think so. So, stop acting like her."

"Just trying to help," Paddy replied.

"Sure you are," the boy sneered. "They're probably paying you to get kids like me off the streets. Yeah, I've heard of that being done. How much are they paying you to be a rat?"

The trolley rolled to a stop, and Paddy got off. "I'm not a rat. I was really trying to help."

"Yeah, well, help this," the boy said and stuck out his tongue.

As the trolley jerked to a start, Paddy wanted to run after it and smack the kid alongside the head. Not because he was sore at him, but because this boy reminded him too much of his younger self. Life inside the asylum might not be the best, but it sure as heck beat living on the streets. He also knew he was once that boy, and nothing anyone would have told him would have changed his mind. As he walked up the sidewalk, he realized how lucky he was not to still be living on the street.

Mr. Murphy was waiting for him when he entered the furniture showroom. "Paddy, my boy. It is good to see you again."

"It is?"

"Of course it is. I was worried about what had become of you and was thrilled when Miss LaRue came to see me on your behalf."

Paddy removed his hat and scratched his head. "You were?"

Mr. Murphy smiled. "Of course. I worry about all my friends. Miss LaRue said you wish to make a box?"

Paddy shook his head. "No, sir. I wish to make two."

"Two?"

Paddy nodded. "Yes, sir. I figure since the headmistress was nice enough to allow me out, maybe I should make her something."

Murphy smiled a sly smile. "And you thought that if you stay in her good graces, she might allow you to keep coming here once you are finished with your project."

Paddy nodded. "You don't have to pay me none unless you want to."

Murphy clapped him on the shoulder. "Let's see about those boxes first, and then we'll figure out how we'll proceed afterward."

"Sir?"

"Yes, Paddy?"

"Is that a fancy way of saying you'll let me keep coming?"

Murphy stopped just outside the entrance to the shop. "I would like to get something out of the way before we even start. I know you are living in the asylum, but I cannot take you in. My wife and I have thirteen children of our own, with another on the way, and it just wouldn't be right to ask her to take in another. But if you're willing to work, I am willing to give you a job. I'll help you make your boxes, and if you still wish to come around after you're done, I'll clear it with Miss LaRue and teach you anything you wish to know. When we are done, you'll know enough to earn yourself a living wage. I know it is not what a boy such as yourself might wish to hear, but it is what I am capable of. Does that sound fair to you?"

Paddy nodded even though he didn't fully understand why Murphy thought he would expect him to take him in when he already had a fine roof over his head.

***

In the two years since beginning work with Murphy, he'd graduated from whittling small animals to helping craft furniture. While Paddy enjoyed working with all types of wood, he still enjoyed carving shapes out of wood and found he truly enjoyed carving the finishing touches on the ornate wooden chests, which Murphy sold to families heading west. Often, after seeing a sampling of Paddy's work, the purchaser would ask for a small matching chest to hold their documents while they traveled.

Paddy was working on one such chest when Murphy opened the door to the shop and motioned him into the showroom. Paddy set the chest aside and hurried to see what the man wanted. He slowed when he saw him standing next to a gruff-looking man wearing a tailored suit.

Murphy palmed a hand in his direction, motioning him forward. "Mr. Schmidt, this is the lad I was telling you about."

Mr. Schmidt bristled. "Why, he is but a boy!"

This wasn't the first time in the two years since he'd been apprenticing at the furniture store that a customer questioned his ability. The first time it happened, Paddy had lost his temper and cost Murphy a sale. To teach him a lesson, Murphy had sent him home early and requested that the headmistress keep him at the asylum for a full week. The punishment had worked in teaching Paddy something his mother never achieved – to be patient. Well, at least when it came to business anyway. Paddy looked at the man and smiled an unassuming smile.

"Be that as it may, young Howard here is all we have to offer."

Paddy smiled again at Murphy's use of his name. While Paddy had danced around the subject, Murphy – whose first name was Patrick – insisted on using their given names, as it helped build customer relations where people felt like family and didn't automatically unveil their Irish origins to folks who would shop elsewhere to avoid purchasing from the Irish. Murphy had laughed after explaining it and branched off into a rant, speaking a mix of English and Irish with words so foul, it made Paddy's ears turn red and ended with the fact that one couldn't find a more Irish-sounding name than Murphy.

Mr. Schmidt looked Paddy up and down, then shook his head. "No, I just can't. The table belonged to my dear old mother, after all."

Murphy nodded his understanding, which let Paddy know

it was time for him to do his thing.

Paddy walked around the small table several times, then squatted and looked at the detail within the wood and blew out a whistle. "It's too bad because just looking at this table, I knew the exact piece of maple I was going to use. It's a perfect match too, as I had my hands on it only an hour ago."

"Now, Howard, that's enough. This gentleman has already made up his mind and we'll leave him to it." Murphy pretended to shoo him away, then turned back to the customer. "You make sure whoever you take it to knows to use the right kind of wood. If they can't tell what kind it is just by looking at it, then have them ring up the store, and I'll have them talk to young Howard here."

Paddy started to leave, and the man called him back. "You say you have the perfect piece of maple?"

Paddy bobbed his head. "Yes, sir. I can get it to look as good as new."

"When should I come calling for it?" Mr. Schmidt asked.

Paddy scratched at his chin. "Well, I have to get it sanded down to match, then carve that pattern into it, stain it to match. I'd say about four weeks should do it."

"Four weeks, you say?"

"Yes, sir," Paddy said, bobbing his head.

"And you have the perfect piece of wood?" the man asked.

"Sure do," Paddy said, looking toward the back room.

Mr. Schmidt turned to Murphy. "Okay, sir. You have my business. I will come back to collect it in four weeks."

Paddy picked up the small table and carried it to the back as Murphy followed.

"I don't recall seeing that piece of maple back here," Murphy said, looking about.

Paddy grinned. "That's why I told the fellow four weeks. If I'd really had it, I would have told him three."

Murphy chuckled a nervous chuckle. "You weren't lying about being able to get the leg to match the table, were you?"

Paddy smiled a reassuring smile and tapped his finger to his forehead. "No, sir. I'm already picturing how to do it in here."

Murphy beamed like a proud papa. "I swear, boy, I do believe you could convince anyone of anything."

Paddy thought of Mileta and frowned. "No, sir. That isn't really the case."

"Well, if that's not the most sorrowful-looking face I've ever seen, I don't know what is. What's troubling you, son? Wait, let me guess, it's that girl you've been telling me about."

Paddy heaved a sigh. "Yes, sir."

"Did you try to talk to her?"

Paddy nodded. "Oh, yes, sir. We talk all the time, but she ain't said how she likes me none."

"You've got some years left before you have to worry about that," Murphy told him.

"Yes, sir." Paddy sighed.

"Chin up, lad. You still have time. They're not going to let you out of that asylum for a few more years. If she's smart, she'll see what a fine young man you are. If not, make her something special that only you could give her, and she'll come around."

Paddy felt a gleam of hope. "Do you really think so?"

Murphy shrugged. "It worked for my wife."

"What'd you make her?" Paddy asked.

"I made her a chest," Murphy replied.

Paddy frowned. "You make chests all the time. I thought you said give her something no one else could give her?"

"See, you are hearing, but you're not listening. I knew what I wanted to give her, but I knew it had to be extra special. So, when I heard her papa was buying a new buckboard wagon, I asked him if I could buy the old one. He, being a smart man and knowing that the old wagon had seen better days, agreed. I took each of those boards off that frame and sanded them down to look brand new. Then, I used them to build my wife the chest. When she found out I'd used the wood from the family wagon, she cried happy tears and said it meant that a part of her family would always be with us. I had enough wood left over that after we were married, I used it to make a cradle for our firstborn child. All of our children are healthy, and my wife feels it brings us luck, so even though I offered to make a new one, she has insisted each of our children use it until they are ready to be in a proper crib."

"How will I know what to make for her?" Paddy asked.

Murphy smiled. "When it is time, you'll know."

***

A smile played at Cindy's lips as she stared at the old piano they'd moved back into the living room. "He did it," she said softly.

"Who did what?" Linda asked, looking up from her reading.

"Mr. Murphy told Grandpa Howard to find something no one else could give her. That was why he returned to New York. What better gift than the piano she once played? She had to have known how much he thought of her to have traveled all that way when he could have easily found one closer to home. No wonder she said yes. How could she not? It is amazing to see how everything worked out."

"They haven't worked out yet," Linda reminded her. "He's still a kid."

Cindy laughed. "Spoiler alert, Mom. He gets the girl in the end."

Chapter Twenty-Four

Paddy pushed his knife through the wood, whittling away the smallest of chips. He lifted the knife, brought the carving close, and blew the shavings away, inspecting his craftmanship. *Perfection.* He smiled.

"You have every tool of the trade at your disposal, and yet you still prefer that battered old knife," Murphy said, entering the room. "I'm sorry I asked the headmistress to allow you use of it."

"I'm not," Paddy said as he folded the blade.

"Why not? These tools are designed to be the best there is. Are you telling me the men who made them don't know their craft?" Murphy asked.

It wasn't the first time they'd had this discussion, and Paddy knew the man was teasing. "I use them some, but when I really need to get into a crevice, this just feels best," Paddy replied.

Murphy held out his hand, and Paddy handed him the knife. Murphy pulled out the blade and moved it back and forth to inspect the blade. "It's because the knife is your first love," he replied.

"Aw, I don't love the knife." It was a bald-faced lie, and they both knew it.

"Yes, you do, and you also love that girl you keep talking about," Murphy said with a wink.

Before Paddy could reply, the bell over the front door rang, alerting that someone had entered the store. Murphy went to the door, pushed it open, and turned to Paddy. "It's Mr. Schmidt. He's here for his table. Since you're the one responsible for the piece, why don't you bring it out?"

Paddy hurried to the other side of the room where the table was sitting among several other finished projects waiting to be picked up. He pulled a cloth from his pocket and gave the table a quick rubdown before carrying it to the showroom and setting it in front of Mr. Schmidt.

Schmidt crouched to look at the table, then duckwalked completely around it, rubbing the legs and peering at the detailed carvings, inspecting it much like a parent would inspect a new infant to see they had all their fingers and toes. "What do you know about that? I can't even tell which one was replaced." He smiled as he stood, then stared at Paddy for a good minute before turning his attention to Murphy. "You'll have me believe that boy did this on his own?"

Murphy nodded and placed his hands on Paddy's shoulders. "Believe what you will. I'm not a liar, neither is the boy."

"No, that's not what I was implying. What I meant was you should be proud to have a son following so close in your footsteps."

"Oh, the lad here isn't my son. My boys are not yet grown enough to help me in the shop. A year or so, and I expect their ma will insist on my bringing them along. For now, she insists on them having a proper education."

Schmidt nodded his agreement. "Your wife is a smart woman. A good education is important. There will be plenty of time for them to learn the trade after that. It is obvious you're a fine teacher." He looked at Paddy once more, his gaze resting on his hair. "My experience is redheads are stubborn and ornery. Seems like you've done a good job with this one."

Paddy enjoyed the compliments but couldn't figure out what the color of his hair had to do with the work he did.

"I'm sure you'll be sad to see him go when your boys come in to take his place."

"To be certain," Murphy agreed.

Any elation Paddy had felt under the compliments dissipated. *Ya dope, he told you from the start. Of course he's gonna make you leave. He has his own sons to carry on his name. Why would he need you and a redhead at that?* Still, the reality of his situation stung. It was his own fault he'd gotten comfortable in his surroundings and assumed things would continue like they were. He swallowed. A year or two and his freedom would be gone, and he would be back in the asylum full-time. He liked the place well enough, but that was because he didn't have to sleep on the streets, and he had friends. In a strange kind of way, it had taken the place of his home. The truth was with the exception of missing his mother, his current arrangement was better than when he'd lived at home. At least now he didn't have to worry about anyone pounding on him. Sure, there were a couple of boys who liked to give him a difficult time for being the headmistress's pet, but they didn't push the issue too much since they knew he had Slim in his corner. And as stern as the headmistress could be, she seemed to have a bit of a soft spot for him. But would he be as happy if he couldn't walk out of that gate each day? Just the act of doing so made him feel somewhat normal even though his world had fallen apart. Not wishing the men to see his unease, he turned and went back to the shop to finish the project he'd been working on.

Murphy came into the shop a few moments later and handed him a silver dollar.

Paddy couldn't believe it, a whole dollar, and it was all his. "Is that what he paid you?"

"No, he paid me a bit more than that, but this is yours. You earned it," Murphy replied.

"Thanks," Paddy said as he pushed it into his pocket.

"What's wrong? I thought you'd be happy with that."

Paddy shrugged. "I am."

Murphy sighed. "You are upset by what was said in there. I told you from the beginning this was temporary."

"I know." Paddy agreed. "Mr. Murphy?"

"What is it, son?"

"Is it because I have red hair?"

Murphy laughed, and Paddy narrowed his eyes. "Well, you don't have to make me feel like a dope about it."

Murphy pulled his wallet from his rear pants pocket and opened it.

Paddy waved him off. "I don't want no more of your money."

"I wasn't planning on giving you any. I wanted to show you this," he said, handing Paddy a small photograph of himself with his wife and a whole string of children. The woman, along with most of the children, all had red hair.

Paddy wasn't sure what amazed him more: that they had red hair or that the photo showed it to be true. "The picture is in color."

"It's called a photograph. It's a thing," Murphy told him.

"I know," Paddy replied. "But I've never seen one with red hair. Someday, I'm going to get myself a photo of me like that."

Murphy smiled and returned the photograph to his wallet. "So you're not sorry you have red hair?"

"Maybe a little," Paddy said, "but seeing that picture helps make it better."

"Good, because the red hair is part of your Irish heritage."

Paddy scratched his head. "You're Irish. How come you don't have red hair?"

Murphy chuckled. "Because I wasn't as lucky as you."

"Aww, now you're just fooling me," Paddy replied.

"No, I'm quite serious. My grandad always said, 'Lucky is a head that is red'."

"What makes them lucky?"

"I don't know. But he had red hair when he was a boy, so I guess he should know."

"Only when he was a boy?" Paddy felt a glimmer of hope. "You mean it changes color?"

Murphy smiled. "Aye, it does at that. His turned a brilliant shade of white, but not until he was fairly old."

Paddy tried to picture himself with white hair, but try as he may, he could only imagine it red.

***

Paddy was still feeling down when he knocked on the headmistress's door. There was no answer, so he opened the door and peeked inside. Finding the room empty, he went in and returned his knife to the counter as he'd done many times before. He'd just placed it on the counter when he heard voices in the hall.

"What about Paddy?" Miss Vivian asked.

What about me? Paddy hurried to push the door, leaving it open just enough to hear what was being said.

"No, Paddy will be staying here. The instructions stated there were to be no redheads. I am on the fence with Master Gideon as well. Then again, while the boy is odd, he is not afflicted."

"Yes, but the instructions stated that Mr. Barsotti specifically named everyone Mary hangs around with," Mrs. Vivian reminded her.

"Fine, Gideon goes, but not Paddy," the headmistress replied.

"Are you sure?" Miss Vivian asked. "He is part of Mary's little group."

"My decision is final. I know what the instructions from Mr.

Vanderbilt said, but I have it on good authority that redheads are not often chosen. It would be better for him to stay here and give the spot to someone who is more assured of a placement."

"Are you ready for the backlash from Paddy? There could be a problem if his friends leave, and he remains here. Especially Slim. They came in together and are close. To be honest, I am not even sure the Barsotti boy will agree to go if Paddy isn't chosen."

Paddy gulped. *Chosen to go where?* He inched open the door, watching as the headmistress paced the room.

"I can handle Paddy well enough. He may be a bit ill-spirited at first, but he'll settle down in due time." She paused. "As for Mr. Barsotti, we will just have to make it look as if all his friends are going. We will include Paddy in the preparations and remove him just before the children are to depart on the trains. There will be so much chaos that Mr. Barsotti will not know Paddy isn't there until it is too late."

It took everything in Paddy's being not to pull open the door and tell them he knew of their plan. The only thing that stopped him was that while he knew the women were doing something dubious, he didn't actually know what that something was.

The headmistress set the stack of papers she was holding on the desk. "We have lots to do to get ready. This here is the shortlist. We are allowed fifty children. Mr. Vanderbilt was adamant that Mr. Barsotti's friends are to go with him. Over the next few days, I will walk through the classrooms and observe the children before making my final decision. We will choose fifty-one. Once we remove Paddy, we will have our final list."

"As you say, Headmistress. Is there anything else?"

"Where are the children now?"

Miss Vivian looked at the clock. "They'll be heading to the dining room shortly."

"Well then," the headmistress replied. "We shall start there."

Paddy waited several moments to make sure they were not coming back, then stepped into the headmistress's office. He went to the door, peeked into the hall, then returned to the desk to read the papers she'd left.

Mistress LaRue,

I'm sure you have heard of the efforts of the Children's Aid Society to help the homeless children of our city find new homes in the West where they can prosper. Our Placing Out Program has been most successful, and to that end, we will be sending out yet another group of children in just a few short weeks. We invite you to select fifty of your most desirable children to be placed onto the trains to head west, where we will do our best to place them with families who will love, nourish, and cherish them.

Paddy flipped to the next page, which had the letter from Mr. Vanderbilt. He skimmed it, then turned the page to see the list of names, which had everyone in Mary's gang, including Little Ruth, who was the youngest member of the gang. While his name was on the top of the names on the Vanderbilt list, it was on the bottom of the one written in the headmistress's hand. Paddy sighed. *It's true; she's going to leave me here!*

Not if I tell Slim. As soon as the thought came to mind, he rejected the notion. The last thing he wanted was to keep Slim and the others from finding new homes where they could be loved and cherished. He replaced the pages, carefully setting them in the order in which he found them, and then went to find his friends.

***

Paddy lay in the darkness, listening to the sobs of one of the boys who'd come in earlier in the day. It was a regular occurrence in the open dorm room after the lights were switched off. Often, those sobs would inspire others to join in, but nothing was ever mentioned come the light of day, for as tough as each boy pretended to be, they'd all cried at one point or another. While Paddy didn't succumb to his emotions as much anymore, he'd shed his share of tears in the four years since being dragged into the asylum.

It mostly hit him when someone spoke offhandedly of missing their mothers. For as much as he tried to forget his, she was always there in something that was said or something someone did, which would stir a memory and have her words of wisdom pop into his mind. He thought of her now and knew she'd be proud of his achievements, in his ability to control his anger, the way he'd settled into learning, and the way he was able to look at a piece of wood and use tools of the trade to transform a simple block into something that truly came to life.

He thought of Mr. Schmidt and how the fellow had raved about the table he'd repaired, then of learning that his work would be ending. While that had hit him hard, he'd nearly thrown up when he went to the dining room and saw the headmistress scanning the room, trying to judge who would stay and who would go – further knowing of her plans to omit him. How could he possibly remain in the asylum without Slim and the others?

Paddy's jaw tensed as he silently cursed his papa. Why did he have to be born with red hair anyway? As he listened to the boy's sobs, he felt his own tears trickle down his cheeks. How had things changed so fast? This morning, he'd felt as happy as he'd ever been, and now, it was all he could do not to scream. It wasn't fair! Not only was he going to be left off the list, but the headmistress was planning on lying right to his face. He batted at the tears, narrowing his eyes, wondering what kind of story she would make up, thinking to keep him in her good graces. He'd trusted her. How could he have been such a dope? This wasn't his family, nor was it a true home, and he didn't belong here.

Suddenly, he thought of his mother and realized he was even angry at her for insisting he come to the asylum in the first place. He hadn't wanted to, and yet, for the last few years, he'd found happiness and a way to get through the day without thinking of everything he'd lost. And now everything was being taken away for the second time, and the only explanation was that people don't take kindly to kids with red hair. He couldn't help it that he had red hair. It wasn't like he'd asked to be born with the affliction. It just wasn't fair.

He deserved to get on that train just as much as Slim, Levi, Geo, Gideon, Mary, and Mileta. *Mileta's leaving!* Paddy's heart pounded with the implication. He'd been so self-absorbed he hadn't thought of her and the fact that she'd be leaving without him. His tears turned to sobs. How would he ever be able to find her and declare his love for her if they took her away?

Paddy wasn't sure when he fell asleep, but he did, and yet, when he woke, he felt as if he'd spent the night running from things he couldn't see. As he lay there replaying everything, he recalled something Slim had once told him. Everyone lies. You just have to find out what they are lying about, and you can use that to win your case. In that minute, he knew all was not lost. He had ready access to the headmistress's office. If she were going to be spending time observing the children, that meant he would have more time to search her office for something he could use to get her to allow him onto the trains. As he lay there devising his plan, he wondered if this made him lucky or confirmed everyone's suspicions in regard to redheads.

Chapter Twenty-Five

The children had nearly finished their evening meal when the headmistress entered and stood in the front of the room as if counting heads. While the other children speculated as to why the woman was there, Paddy was certain he already knew. It had been three days since he'd overheard the conversation between her and Mistress Vivian, and she was there to tell them about the trip and further disclose who'd been selected to go.

"She only comes if someone's in trouble," Mary whispered loud enough for all to hear. At her words, several of the younger children began to cry.

The dorm mistresses moved to the front of the room and clapped their hands for them to line up. Paddy stood and moved to the front of the room with the others and remained silent as the headmistress called Clara and Anastasia to the front and dismissed them. Once they were out of the room, she pulled a slip of paper from her pocket. "If I call your name, you are to have a seat at one of the tables. Mary, Mileta, Rose, Dorthia, Ruth…"

While the rest of the children grew anxious to discover if they were on the list and to what end, Paddy knew his already to be there and would be the last name called. He glanced at Slim and could tell by the boy's face that he, too, was aware of what was happening.

The headmistress continued calling names until, at last, she glanced in his direction. "Paddy, you may join the others. Come along then; don't dawdle," she said when he didn't react. She folded the paper and dismissed the children not selected. Paddy searched the faces of those not selected as they were ushered from the room and saw a mixture of disappointment and relief. He also knew he would be among them if he didn't find anything to use as leverage.

"Quiet down, children. You know there is to be no talking in the hallways," Headmistress said firmly as the children filed out of the room. She turned, facing the tables where he sat with Slim and the others. "Cheer up, children. I have excellent news to share with you. For nearly seventy years, the Children's Aid Society has worked tirelessly to help find thousands upon thousands of children such as yourselves new homes. Most of those placements took place far outside this great city, and the children selected count themselves privileged. Before leaving, each child received a fresh set of clothing and were sent west via trains, where they were then placed with fine families who promised to love and cherish them. In an unprecedented turn of events, the Children's Aid Society has generously offered to allow me to select children from this establishment to join their next Placing Out Program. I am pleased to tell you that, after careful consideration, I have chosen all of you."

Mary and several of the others gasped and began debating the implications. Not everyone was excited, something made all too clear when Ruth began to cry.

It was Mary who dared to raise her hand.

"Yes?" the headmistress asked.

"I believe there's been a mistake. My mother promised to return for me one day."

The headmistress's smile faded. "I'm not in the habit of making mistakes. I assure each and every one of you, if you're in this room, your parents have relinquished all parental rights."

Mary firmed her chin, and Paddy could see she was

struggling to keep from crying.

"Now, if there aren't any more questions, I will continue. "Yes." Headmistress sighed when Rose raised her hand.

"What if we do not wish to go?" she asked tearfully.

"Don't you fret, child," Headmistress said, showing compassion Paddy now knew to be a ruse. "Unlike here, you will have a chance at a real family to love you and see to your needs. Why, if I were a child, I would gladly fill your shoes."

"I had a family once. They were mean to me. What if we don't like the family that chooses us?" Gideon asked without being called on.

"That is a perfectly reasonable question, one I too asked. My contact at the Children's Aid Society told me that all precautions would be taken to find homes that fit each child. People called placing agents will oversee the placements and work to find you the best home possible. Once placed, the agents will check in on you from time to time to see that the home remains a good fit. If you're not happy within your home, the agent will move you to a new home that better suits you. I must also warn you that if your new family is not happy with you, they may return you to this establishment. I shan't have to tell you how unhappy I will be if any of you are returned because of misconduct on your part. I know you must have many more questions," she said, holding up her hands. "I'm told the Children's Aid Society will do everything in their power to see to it that you are each happy and well cared for. You must see this for what it is, an opportunity to grow up outside the walls of this institution. Consider it a grand adventure, one that I expect to hear about when you write telling me of your new family."

Paddy started to raise his hand to ask her if it was so good, why she was planning on keeping him here, when the door opened, and Clara came in, followed by three mistresses who each pushed carts piled high with clothing and shoes.

"Mr. Barsotti, do try to control your legs," the headmistress said when Slim's legs began to dance. "You'll have a difficult enough time being selected at your age without potential families thinking you are damaged."

Slim's legs never stayed still, and the headmistress had no qualms about sending him out, yet she wanted to exclude him simply because of the color of his hair. Paddy laughed at the absurdity.

The headmistress narrowed her eyes at him. "That goes for you too, young man. Why I'm sending you out is a mystery to me, as I've been told it is highly unlikely a redhead such as yourself will be adopted." And there it was, the truth disguised as a veiled threat and the same reason she planned to give when she finally pulled him from the list and told him he wouldn't be going with the rest.

Paddy turned away so she couldn't see how much her words angered him.

***

Paddy took his time getting dressed and followed at the end of the line as the boys made their way down the stairs. Just as they were entering the dining room, he peeled away from the rest and made a beeline for the headmistress's office. He boldly knocked on the door and stuck his head inside when she failed to answer. The room was empty. He peeked into the hall and returned to the office when he saw no one coming. He closed the door behind him, then hurried to the back room and retrieved his knife, his excuse for being in the office if anyone caught him. The room had a wall of files on either side of the room, and the back wall had a counter with drawers underneath and high cabinets above. On the left side of the counter near the chair the headmistress allowed him to use sat the two wooden journal boxes he made. They were nearly identical, except for a long-stemmed rose which he'd carved in the one he'd made for the headmistress. He traced a finger over the rose – something he'd chosen because the woman had seemed so nice at the time. Now, after seeing through her charade, he thought to remove his pocketknife and add a few thorns to the stem. He pushed the thought aside and recalled how pleased she'd been when he gave it to her, admiring not only the beautifully carved rose but the fact that the box had a lock.

He'd smiled and told her it was so she could write whatever she wanted and could protect it with the key, which he'd given her. What he hadn't told her was that while her box did, in fact, have a lock, he hadn't given her the only key – he had the other.

He'd fitted the box with two keys, thinking to give her both, only he hadn't. He didn't know the reason at the time but was now glad he'd had the foresight to keep one. If the woman were harboring a secret, this would be the place to find it.

Using his key to open his box, he lifted the papers and pulled out the spare key. He ran to the front office and peeked out the door once more before returning to the back room. He blew out his breath to calm his nerves as he unlocked the headmistress's box. He knew what he was doing was wrong, but it was the only thing he could think of to make sure he left with his friends. He placed a finger on the stack of papers and began to skim the pages. Three pages in, she first mentioned the trains and how she was excited the children would get the opportunity to leave the asylum. He turned the page and scanned it, looking for his name, and found it halfway down the page.

While Paddy is listed with those chosen, I cannot find it in me to allow him to go. Everyone knows redheads are ill-tempered, and the child has proven himself to be a master manipulator. He has even managed to pull the wool over my eyes on several occasions. I feel it would be better for all involved for him to remain here than to be shipped out, only to be returned to this institution when his placement does not work out. Paddy clenched his jaw. *How does she know it isn't going to work out?* He went back and looked at the other names on the list, including Dorthia. The girl was trouble, and yet there was no mention of keeping her off the train. There were a few more on the list he knew were much worse than him, and yet he was the only name on the list that she made mention of removing.

Paddy started to whistle, as doing so helped calm him, but he didn't want to chance bringing attention to the fact he was inside the office. He thought about taking the page and showing it to Slim as proof the headmistress intended to keep him from the train, but he still hoped to keep his friend from getting involved. No, he needed something else. Something she wouldn't want anyone else to know, so he kept reading. A few pages later, he saw a comment about Clara. He started to read it but knew he didn't have time for idle gossip, so he continued. As he did, something nagged at him. He went back to the original page and saw it. She hadn't referred to Clara; she'd referred to "my Clara."

Paddy stared at the page, knowing he'd found something significant. Just as he started to read, he heard voices. He rushed to put everything back the way he found it and lock the case. He had just returned the spare key to his own box when the headmistress entered the back room.

She frowned when she saw him. "Paddy? What are you doing in here?"

"I came to get my journal box so I could write about going on the trains," he lied.

A blush crept across her face. "Yes, well, you can do that later. I have work to do, so I'll need you to leave me to it."

"I won't bother you," Paddy said, hoping to get another look at her journals.

"I said, that will be all," she said firmly.

Paddy sighed. "Yes, ma'am."

***

Much to Paddy's dismay, preparations for leaving had him and the others so busy, he had not found another opportunity to look through the headmistress's journal. While the others spoke about the trip with eager anticipation, he knew at the last moment the woman would whisk him away, making him return with her to the asylum. Not for the first time, he debated telling Slim, but his friend seemed preoccupied, and it just never felt like the right time. Instead, he decided to stick so close to his friend that the headmistress wouldn't have a chance to pull him away without Slim noticing.

To the headmistress's credit, she'd put on a good show, even going so far as giving him his knife, the carvings, and his journal box to take with him on the trip. All the items were placed into a large suitcase along with a fresh set of new clothes. If not for having read the conviction in her words, he would have thought her to have changed her mind.

"Come along, children. I don't want you to catch a cold in this rain," she said, hurrying them through the iron gates. It was the first time he'd been outside of the gates since learning of the planned train trip. So busy had they been in preparation for the trip, he'd not even been able to speak with Mr. Murphy to tell him why he wouldn't be returning. Then again, if the headmistress followed through with her plan, he would be returning, at least until Murphy's boys were old enough to replace him.

Pushing that thought from his mind, Paddy looked for Mileta, but she was with the girls in line ahead of him. A milk truck lumbered past and sputtered to a stop just ahead of them. To his surprise, the man jumped from the cab and opened the back doors, and the line moved from the sidewalk as the children climbed inside. As they piled inside, the driver began tossing the suitcases on top of the truck.

"Hey, be careful with that," Paddy said as the driver stripped his suitcase from his hands.

"Get inside the truck before I put you up there with it," the man sneered.

Paddy looked to see the headmistress glaring at him and hurried into the sour-smelling truck. He cringed as case after case hit the top of the truck, sounding like a boom of thunder. Chalkie – a boy who got his name for eating chalk and didn't like enclosed spaces – looked green, and jumped with each thud. There was no room to sit, which was probably for the best as the wooden floors were sticky with soured milk.

As the man closed the rear doors, the headmistress stood holding on to a leather strap affixed to the ceiling. Paddy watched her as the truck bounced along its way, recalling the exciting things she'd promised while he and the others were eating a rare meal of sweetcakes and milk. She'd told them they were heading west to live on farms where food would be in abundance. And yards with green grass and trees too big to climb. Paddy had scoffed at that, knowing trees were much easier to climb than brick buildings, not that he would ever find out as she'd made sure to make eye contact with all those listening to let them know she was talking to them. Never once had she looked at him.

As if knowing his thoughts, the headmistress peered in his direction. Her eyes grew wide and he realized he'd been scowling at her. She started to say something when Chalkie groaned a sorrowful groan and released the contents of his stomach in two violent waves. The headmistress tried to move out of the way, but the truck was so crowded, there was no place for her to go.

Paddy looked down to see her legs and foot covered with the mess.

The headmistress turned a brilliant shade of red as she stomped her foot in a feeble attempt to shake the chunks free. She glared at Chalkie, who was also covered in the mess and was looking a lot less green. "You did this on purpose!" she fumed.

"No, ma'am," Chalkie sputtered.

"Of course you did. You didn't even try to turn your head. SILENCE!" she said when the boy tried to argue. "You, sir, will not be going on the train. Instead, you'll be returning to the asylum with me. And that goes for anyone else who soils their clothes. Is that understood?"

Though everyone nodded, no one said a word.

True to her words, Chalkie was made to stay in the truck when they all went inside Grand Central Station. Paddy, along with the rest of the children, quickly forgot about the poor kid's plight as they walked through the massive building. He gaped at the polished marble and grand archways and wondered what kind of tools it took to build such a magnificent place. The windows were so large, they would have let in an enormous amount of sunlight had it not been raining. So impressed was he that he couldn't help but whistle.

One of the mistresses clocked him upside the head. Paddy was getting ready to tell her he didn't mean anything by it when he saw Mileta watching and smiled. It was the first time he'd seen her since leaving the asylum, and while he knew her to be among the group, he was relieved to see her there.

The relief was short-lived, as a moment later, Mouse stepped into the open and motioned him toward the bathroom. Paddy stared at him, barely believing his eyes, then grabbed Slim's arm. "We have to go to the bathroom."

"Then go," Slim replied.

"No, WE have to go," Paddy insisted.

Slim stepped out of line, followed by a boy named Slick, both following him inside.

"Hey, Mouse, what are you doing here?" Slim asked the moment they pushed through the door. Clearly, Mouse was more excited to see him than he was.

"The same as you, getting ready to head out on the trains."

Paddy frowned. The only reason Mouse would ever think to go on the trains was because he'd somehow learned Mileta was leaving. Then again, since he'd yet to find a way to get the headmistress to allow him to go, he was glad that someone would be watching over her. He just wished that someone would be him. Paddy fought to hide his resentment. "How'd you manage that?"

"I have my ways. Funny, you don't seem happy to see me."

Paddy shrugged. "Just didn't expect to."

"More like you thought you'd have Mileta all to yourself now," Mouse taunted.

Slim stepped between them, stretching his hands to keep them apart. "Paddy didn't mean anything, Mouse; we're all excited to be getting out of the asylum. They're going to find us fine new homes with real folks to take care of us."

"You don't believe that?" Paddy asked when Mouse laughed.

"I don't believe a lot of stuff they say."

"Yeah, well you better watch yourself, or they'll send you packing. They just sent a kid back for puking. It's a good thing that truck stopped when it did. A minute later, and we all would've puked," Slim said, wrinkling his nose.

The bathroom door opened. A man stepped inside and went into a stall, closing the door behind him. Mouse lowered his voice. "You guys help me keep an eye on Mileta. Once we get to Detroit, I'll figure out what to do next."

Slick's eyes grew wide. "How do you know we're going to Detroit? They only told us we are going west."

Slim smiled and jutted a thumb toward Mouse. "Mouse knows everything."

Paddy stepped toward the door. "We have to go before they come looking for us. How are you going to get on the train?"

"I've got my ways. You guys get with your group. I'll be right behind you." He gripped onto Paddy's arm, squeezing tight. "And remember, don't let on that you know me."

Paddy started to tell Mouse that it didn't matter as he wouldn't even be on the train, then decided against it. The boy would learn the truth soon enough.

The headmistress was waiting for them when they came out of the bathroom. "Go get in line with the others. I need to speak to Paddy for a moment," she said, waving Slim and Slick away before Paddy had a chance to tell his friend what was happening.

The line was moving, and Paddy knew this was the critical point, especially since his suitcase was sitting on the ground next to the woman. "I should go too. I wouldn't want to miss the train." He leaned in to gather his case.

The headmistress stepped in front of it, blocking his way. "I'm afraid I've had second thoughts about sending you out. I know it feels bad now. But you'll thank me for it one day."

As Paddy watched the rest of the children move away, he thought of Mouse, wondering what the boy would do in his situation, and a plan came to him. "I'm going," he said firmly.

She smiled. "Let's not make a scene, Paddy. You know I have the power to make your life miserable."

"If you don't let me go, I'll tell Clara everything." It was a hollow threat, as he had nothing to tell. He smiled, hoping to further the bluff.

The headmistress's eyes darted from side to side. "What

does Clara have to do with you going on the trains?"

"I know what you wrote in your journals," he said, hoping to sound confident.

The woman's face paled. "How?"

"Because I made the box, and the lock has more than one key."

"You invaded my privacy?"

"Only after I overheard you and Mistress Vivian talking. It's amazing what one can hear when no one knows they are listening." He purposely neglected telling her just what he'd heard, hoping her mind would fill in the blanks.

"You planned this all along? Why didn't you say anything before?"

Actually, he hadn't ever thought about bluffing until the time came, but something told him it was working. He shrugged. "I guess I was hoping you'd change your mind."

She pulled herself taller. "Very well, Paddy, you may go. Just know that if they send you back, our little arrangement of you coming to my office to work on your craft will no longer be in place. And don't even think about trying to bribe me again with what you think you know, as if I hear tell of you returning, I will destroy the journals and your proof along with them," she said, stepping aside.

Paddy saw the last of the line disappear around the corner. He grabbed hold of the suitcase before the woman had a chance to change her mind and took off running.

"Where have you been?" Slim asked when he slid into line behind him.

"The headmistress wanted to tell me goodbye." Paddy shrugged. "I think she's going to miss me."

Chapter Twenty-Six

Cindy's phone alerted her to a text. She picked it up and read the text.

David > Good night, Beautiful.

Cindy smiled and typed her reply. >Good night to you as well.

Linda sighed an exaggerated sigh. "Why do people have to text all the time? How come you can't just call and be comforted by each other's voice?"

"David is being courteous, as he knows we are reading Grandpa Howard's journals tonight," Cindy reminded her.

"And you can't take five minutes for a sappy phone call?"

"I don't make sappy phone calls," Cindy replied.

"Tell me about it! You're missing the whole point. People don't fall in love over texts."

Cindy felt herself blush. "You'd be surprised what people do over texts. And don't ask because I'm not going to tell you."

Linda laughed. "Honey, that blush tells me all I need to know."

Cindy picked up the papers. "Read your journals, Mother."

"Yes, daughter," Linda said, replacing her glasses.

***

Stepping onto that train was both exhilarating and terrifying, as I knew that iron monster would take me away from everything I'd ever known. As that whistle blew, signaling our departure, I felt a freedom I had never experienced before.

While some felt leaving the city to be scary, I felt empowered, as I knew I would never again have to walk down the street and worry about running into my papa. It's true, I had some concerns about what I would find out west, but missing my papa was not one of them.

One of my initial concerns was they'd put Mileta in a different train car. That everyone else had made it into our dedicated train cars let me know that Mouse was the one responsible for her displacement as he had not been on the list. While I was irritated with him, I was pleased that Mileta would be sitting in the forward car with paying guests. Little did I know at the time how dangerous that would be for her. And, if not for Mouse alerting Mary about Mileta's dilemma, I might never have seen her again, so I guess it was good he was on the train. I shudder to think what would have happened otherwise. I know she wrote about that in her journals, and I had no real part in it either way, so I am not going to force you to relive that. With the exception of Mileta's issue, the train ride was everything a child could imagine…

The whistle blew. Paddy and a few others sitting nearby cheered. While he'd been on the trolley more times than he could count and had taken the subway a few times, he'd never ridden on a real train. In fact, after the incident with Mouse and the carnage he'd seen that night, he'd had no desire to ride on one until he heard the headmistress say she wasn't going to allow it. As the train crept its way into the light, Paddy smiled, recalling their conversation. It wasn't the first time he'd channeled Mouse to his advantage, and he knew without a doubt that doing so was the only reason he was now sitting on that train. For someone he didn't care for, Mouse – or at least his persona – proved most useful.

Paddy sat staring out the window, watching as the buildings gave way to an open landscape with houses and large yards with green grass. He elbowed Slim. "If I'd known this was so close, I'd have left the city years ago."

"It's not really that close; it just feels like it since the train is moving faster than the trolley ever did."

Slick stuck his head over the seat. "Ya goof. Even if you made it out here, you would have never survived."

"Why not?" Paddy asked.

"Because there are no pockets to dip!" His comment was met with mumbled agreement.

Paddy decided that the comment had merit and was something he would have to think about if things didn't work out. The last thing he wanted was to go back to a time when he went to sleep hungry each night. While he wasn't sure what he'd do, he knew for certain he would not allow himself to be sent back to the asylum. With the way he'd left things with the headmistress, she'd have no qualms about sending him to prison.

He pushed that thought aside and pressed his face to the window, watching as the train moved further and further away from the city. As it did, the seriousness of the situation weighed on him. His brothers had traveled west, and yet, he had no idea where their path had taken them or what life had dealt them since they'd left the city. He wondered if they, too, rode the train or if they had to depend on their feet to carry them and knew he would probably never know the answer to that question or why he even cared in the first place.

Feeling more apprehensive than he'd felt in years, he sat staring out the window, listening to Slick and his seatmate talking about what the headmistress had said about finding new homes.

"It is going to be tough not seeing everyone," Slick remarked.

"What do you mean?" his seatmate asked.

"I mean, when we get placed, we will all go our own way and won't ever see each other again."

"Yep, you're right about that," the other boy replied.

It was nearly the same discussion he'd had with Mary and the others when they'd first arrived at the train station earlier that day when he'd boldly announced that he would take out an advert in all the papers in the land and find them all. But instead of scoffing at his bolstered claim, they had each clung to the hope they would all someday meet again. As a tear slid down his cheek, Paddy prayed it would be true.

***

On the morning they arrived in Detroit, Slim shook him awake. "Paddy, wake up. We're finally here!"

The fiasco with Mileta the day before had left him unsettled, and he'd been awake most of the night worrying about things he now knew were out of his control. "The train's still moving," he said without opening his eyes.

"Look out the window. We're here!" Slim said, shaking him once more.

"I don't know what you're so excited about. You said yourself that you and I probably won't find a home," Paddy said, sitting up.

"I didn't say that. The headmistress did, and what does she know anyway? She's stuck in New York and probably has never even been to Detroit."

Paddy looked out the window. "Are you sure we're in Detroit?"

"Yes. At least I think so," Slim replied.

"I'm not sure I'm ready. What if we do get adopted, and you and I never see each other again?" Paddy said, voicing fears he'd successfully pushed away until this moment.

"We'll see each other again. You said yourself you're going to put an advert in the paper," Slim reminded him. "It's a good thing you told us because we all know to watch for it."

"Yeah, but not until we grow up," Paddy sighed.

"Don't be sad, Paddy. You're beginning to make me sad."

Paddy looked Slim in the eye. "Aren't you even a little scared?"

Slim nodded. "Sure, I'm scared. But I'm even more scared of going back to New York and spending the next couple of years in the asylum. And it is only a couple. Think about Gideon, Rose, and the little ones. They have years until they grow up enough not to need to be cared for."

Paddy thought to tell Slim he'd made up his mind not to go back at any cost, then decided against it. The last thing he wanted to do was worry his friend and cause the boy's legs to jump so much, he would have no chance at being adopted. He forced a smile. "I guess I can handle anything for a couple of years."

As the train rumbled to a stop, Miss Agana, one of the placing agents traveling with them, stepped in from the forward car to let them know they'd reached their destination. "Okay, children, this is our first official placing stop. Remember to gather your belongings as you exit because even if you're not selected, we will be moving forward on another train. Once outside, you're to line up in single file where Miss Grace, Miss Tany, and I will escort you inside Central Station. There'll be no time for lollygagging. You'll need to wash up and change into your clean clothes before being presented to those who've gathered. I want to remind each of you that this is only the first stop. If, by no fault of your own, you're not chosen today, we will press on. Our – the Children's Aid Society's – goal is to see that each and every one of you receives a home, but unfortunately, that is not always the case."

Slim raised his hand.

Miss Agana hesitated. "Yes?"

"Could you surmise the percentage of children who don't find homes?" he asked, lowering his hand.

Paddy winced. He'd been so caught up in worry about himself that he'd not even considered whether or not Slim would get a home. He was so lost in his thoughts, he didn't hear her reply, except for the woman telling him to wait to make sure everyone got off the train.

Paddy sighed. "Why'd you have to go and make her mad? Now we have to wait back here until the end."

"You don't have to stay. I'm the one she's sore at, not you."

"Sure I do," Paddy said, watching as others departed. "She didn't yell at ya, so maybe she's not all that sore. Could be she just thinks you sounded smart. You got to watch using all those big words you learned from Mr. Thornton on account of they might keep you from getting a home."

"Why would the way I talk keep me from getting picked?"

"Sheesh, all that time on the street, and you still don't know nothing. You know why Mouse gets under my skin so much?"

Slim laughed. "Because he's Mouse?"

"Because he always acts like he knows everything."

"Mouse knows a lot," Slim said.

"Yeah, but he doesn't know everything. Only he don't say that – he just pretends that he does, and that rubs some of us the wrong way." Paddy started to tell Slim that Mouse's method worked but decided against it. "Now you go around using big words all the time, and people are gonna think you're smart."

"What's wrong with being smart?"

"I know you're okay on account of we were friends before you learnt all those words. But if I didn't know ya and heard ya using all those big words, I'd be thinking we couldn't be friends. On account of I don't like feeling dumb," Paddy said, hoping he'd gotten through to the boy.

"Good thinking, Paddy. I guess I should try not to sound so

smart."

"Yeah, sometimes it's good when people don't know you're smart on account they don't watch you so close. They know you're smart, they figure you got to be up to something even when you're not. That's why I try to act dumb. People are already watching me because I have red hair. If they thought I was smart on top of being willful, I'd never catch a break."

Slim clapped a hand on Paddy's shoulder. "I might know more words than you, but in some ways, you're way smarter than me."

Paddy nodded his agreement. "Don't be upset by that. It's on account of I've spent more time on the street than you." He started to add that he'd also spent more time studying Mouse but opted to leave that part out. The last thing he wanted was for his friend to think he admired the kid or anything.

***

Paddy sat chewing his fingernails as he looked over the crowd. After days of fretting, it was time to see if anyone would step forward and speak up for him. He'd spoken to Mileta and the others briefly before the agents called them to sit in front of a crowd who now stared at them as if they were the holiday display in a Macy's window. Dressed solely in black with her hair pulled tight on her head, Miss Agana looked stern as she strolled about the front of the stage, talking to the crowd and speaking of the rules for placement. Pushing back her spectacles, she raised her voice to be heard above the murmurs. "You do not need to adopt the child you choose. You merely have to provide for your charges in sickness and in health."

"I don't aim to take in no sickly child," a man shouted from the crowd.

A child sneezed, and Miss Agana hurried to hand the girl a handkerchief. "No, of course not. Nor would we expect you to. The child just took in too much smoke and dirt from the train.

We only brought the best with us on this trip. I assure you these children are in prime health. Why, you will never see a better group of children than we've brought with us this day. Now, as I was saying, we do not require you to adopt the child. However, if you do, they will get full rights as any child born of your own blood. The rules state that whether you adopt or merely take them in and agree to be their legal guardian, you are required to give them a place to sleep, make sure they are properly fed and send them to school full time."

The murmur amongst the crowd grew.

"Full time? Then who's going to work in my fields while they are at school? How can I afford to feed my family, much less take in another man's cast-off if I have to send them off to school full time?" another man shouted.

Several of the younger children began to sob. Paddy sought out Mileta and was relieved to see her stoically facing the crowd. He wanted to call out to her to remind her he was there, but doubted she would be able to hear him over the commotion.

Miss Agana raised her arms in the air and patted the air to silence the crowd. "You don't harvest year-round, do you? The children can go to school after the crops are harvested. Once the boys reach sixteen, they no longer need to go to school. They can stay at home; however, you must pay the boys for their labor."

"I'll not be taking in the redhead," a man sitting near him said.

Paddy's heart sank as several sitting near agreed.

A man stepped forward, pushing aside those in his way. A child in the audience lost her balance and fell to the floor. "What if the boy is lazy and doesn't want to work? I have enough mouths to feed to be burdened with another," he said, ignoring the child's tears.

"If for any reason things do not work out, return the child to us." Miss Agana leveled her eyes at him. "Someone from our establishment will visit once a year to check on how things are going and to ensure the wellbeing of the child placed. In the meantime, if you need to send the child back to us before our visit, post us a letter or send a telegraph, and we will make arrangements to remove the child from your home, at no cost to you."

The man stared at Paddy for the briefest of seconds before turning away.

For the first time since conniving his way onto the trains, Paddy wondered if he'd made the right decision. The headmistress had made going out on the trains sound like a good thing, but now he wasn't so sure. What if the angry man decided to choose him, or worse, what if he were the one to pick Mileta or little Ruth? The only thing that gave him a little comfort was the train had made several stops along the way, and he was fairly certain that if he were to be sent back, he'd be able to sneak away unnoticed.

"Now, if there aren't any more questions or concerns, I think it is time to make the introductions," Miss Agana said. "We will have you each come up and interview the child that has caught your eye. Remember, there are plenty of children to choose from, so ask questions and take your time. Get to know the child. We have all day to find the child that is right for you and your family and then meet with the committee to go over your application."

Suddenly, the crowd lurched forward as if afraid all would be gone before they had the chance to choose. Paddy tried to see Mileta, but it was no use. A couple came forward, shook their heads, and moved on to another child. The scenario repeated itself countless times, and Paddy knew he'd made a terrible mistake and that the headmistress had been telling the truth.

I'm not going back. He took a step backward, thinking to make a break for it during the confusion, when an older couple, each with white hair, started in his direction. Paddy hesitated and dared to hope they were actually considering him.

The man, whose soft brown eyes reminded him a lot of a somewhat younger version of Dobs, held his hat in his hand and offered him a smile as he approached. "Looks like you could use a friend."

Not knowing how to respond, Paddy merely nodded.

There was something about the woman that pulled at him. Perhaps it was because the woman felt real, with white hair that remained loose and soft around her face and kind eyes that showed the wisdom of her years. When she spoke, her words seemed to float from her mouth. "Can you talk?"

The man chuckled. "Now, Birdie, what kind of question is that? Of course he can talk, isn't that right, son?"

"Yes, sir," Paddy agreed.

"What's your name?" Birdie asked.

"Paddy."

Birdie cocked her head and gave a sly smile. "That isn't your real name, is it?"

Paddy started to lie, then thought better of it. "No, ma'am. My name's Howard."

"Howard." The word nearly floated out of her mouth as she smiled a broad smile. "Such a nice name, and it fits you. Anyone with red hair can be called Paddy, but Howard, now that's a name that says I'm somebody."

There was something about the way she spoke that was comforting. So much so that he didn't mind that she was using his given name. He knitted his brows. "Is Birdie your true name?"

She looked at her husband. "No, it's Waleria. Conall insists on calling me Birdie, and I guess I've just gotten used to it."

Conall smiled. "That's because she can sing and whistle like a canary."

Paddy gasped. He didn't know what a canary was, but he'd never met a woman who actually liked to whistle. "You can whistle?"

Birdie laughed a hearty laugh. "Don't look so surprised. Lots of people whistle."

"I know," Paddy assured her. "I just never heard a lady do it."

Conall's face turned serious. "If you don't like whistling, I guess we can't be taking you home with us."

Paddy couldn't believe his ears. "Take me home? You mean you don't mind that I have red hair?"

Birdie lifted her hand and touched his cheek. "You know, until you mentioned it, I hadn't even noticed."

Chapter Twenty-Seven

After agreeing to go with Birdie and Conall, the three of them now sat in front of Mr. Webber, a member of the committee who was the final overseer of placements. While Birdie and Conall were old, the man sitting across the table from them looked to be at least a couple hundred years old. Webber sat his glasses on his nose and looked over the documents the couple had given him. He removed his glasses and glanced at Paddy before addressing Birdie and Conall. "Your credentials and paperwork appear to be in order. Are you sure you wish to proceed with this placement?"

Birdie nodded.

"We are," Conall replied.

Webber picked up his glasses and pointed them at Paddy. "He's a redhead. They're known to be stubborn and pigheaded."

Conall placed a hand on Birdie's shoulder when she started to speak. "He is a boy, Mr. Webber. I expect he'll act like one from time to time."

Webber glanced at the papers once more. "It says here you own a farm. Will you be using him as a farm hand?"

"We have farm hands. However, the farm is no longer a working dairy. If the lad wishes to change that, it will be his call."

Webber skimmed the paper again. "And you'll see he gets an education?"

Conall nodded. "There's a one-room schoolhouse on French

Line Road not more than a mile's walk."

Webber raised a brow. "One room, you say?"

"Sandusky is a small town," Conall replied. "Our home does not yet have electricity, but I assure you the teachers in our community are most adequate."

Conall's answers must have satisfied the man as he tapped the papers on the table to straighten them and placed them into a file. He placed the file in front of him, intertwined his fingers on top of it, and focused his attention on Paddy. "Mr. and Mrs. Moore here are willing to take you into their home. Are you agreeable to that?"

"Yes, sir," Paddy said, bobbing his head.

"And you don't care that they are old?"

"No, sir. I don't care that you're old either," Paddy replied and smiled when Birdie snickered.

"I authorize this arrangement. Something tells me you three are well suited for one another." Mr. Webber removed his spectacles and peered at Paddy. "Son, don't let me regret this decision."

"I won't, sir," Paddy assured him. He picked up his suitcase and followed his new folks out of the room. As they left, he stepped up beside Birdie. "Ma'am, I sure would like to say goodbye to a couple of my friends if that would be alright."

Birdie glanced at Conall before nodding her consent.

Paddy looked for Mileta, but there were so many people in the room, he couldn't see her. The crowd parted, and he saw Slim coming his way. "Slim!"

"Is this the best you could do?" Slim whispered when he got within earshot.

"They seem alright," Paddy said with a shrug. "Besides, if I get in trouble, they'll have a devil of a time catching me. How about you?"

"I found myself a home too." Slim beamed. "Mr. Gianetti

owns a restaurant across the street and is going to teach me how to cook."

"You're gonna do woman's work," Paddy said, wrinkling his nose.

"Yep," Slim replied, and they both burst out laughing.

"Don't you worry," Paddy said before they parted. "Now that I know where you are, I'll find ya." Paddy saw Dorthia and hurried to where she stood. "Have you seen Mileta?"

"She left."

"She's gone?" His words came out in a whisper.

"Don't look so glum. The people who took her looked nice." Dorthia smiled a reassuring smile. "She'll be okay. I saw Mouse follow them out."

Paddy felt his heart sink. After all this time, had Mouse finally won? He debated his choices – ditch the couple who were willing to give him a real home and try to find where Mileta had been taken, or forget the girl in a bid for a life with the couple who seemed to like him despite the color of his hair.

Birdie approached him. "What's troubling you, Howard? Are you having second thoughts?"

Paddy started to lie, but there was a kindness about her face that pulled at him. "There is this girl, but she is gone now."

"And you're debating about going to find her," Birdie said, guessing his thoughts.

Paddy nodded.

A sadness touched her eyes. "I'll not stop you from going, but I hope you don't. I know you probably think you're a man, but you have a few years left to be a boy. I'm an old woman who never had any children of my own. I know little about children, but I know a lot about love." She slid a glance at Conall and smiled. "If you are supposed to be with a person, something will happen to see that it works out. I sure hope you decide to come with us and have the patience to see what life has in store for you."

Birdie's words penetrated a place in his heart that had not been touched since he'd last spoken with his mother, and in that moment, he knew there was no other choice than to go with the woman whom he was sure his mother had sent to fill the void.

***

Much to Paddy's surprise, he and the Moores traveled to Sandusky by train. Only this time, he rode in a cabin, sitting across from the couple who chatted with him as if they really cared.

"We've been married forty-six years," Birdie told him.

Paddy blew out a whistle. "That's longer than I've been born!"

Conall patted Birdie's hand. "It doesn't feel so long when you find the right person. You'll find that out one day."

Paddy thought to tell him he already had but decided against it, thinking there was no reason to make them sad too.

"Tell us about yourself, Howard," Birdie said, changing the subject.

"What do you want to know?" Paddy asked.

"Why everything, of course! I wish to know your likes. Your dislikes. How long were you in the asylum? What happened to your parents?" Birdie patted her chest with her hand. "I'm sorry, I'm just so excited and want to get to know you better."

Paddy thought about her request for a moment, trying to decide where to start and exactly how much to tell. The headmistress had warned them not to talk about the past, but Birdie really seemed to want to know and the last thing he wanted was to disappoint her.

"You don't have to tell us anything you don't want to, Howard," Birdie said after a moment.

Paddy sighed. "It's not that I don't want to tell you, it's that I'm afraid you'll send me back if you don't like what I say," he answered truthfully.

"Howard, we may look naive, but I assure you we aren't. We realize you may have had a bit of a dubious past, and nothing you could tell us is going to make us want to send you back."

"Promise?" Paddy asked.

"On my honor," Birdie replied.

"Okay," Paddy said when Conall nodded his agreement. "I've been living at the asylum for four years and lived on the streets for four years before that."

Birdie's brows knitted together. "The paper said you were eleven."

"That's because I'm small for my age." Paddy grinned.

"So, how old are you?"

Paddy shrugged. "Not sure. I haven't really thought about it."

"How old were you on your last birthday?" Birdie pressed. Another shrug.

She frowned. "Okay, let's try something else. Do you know when you were born?"

This Paddy could answer. "June 5, 1909."

"You're fifteen," Birdie said with a glance to Conall, who gave a subtle nod.

Paddy felt his heartbeat increase. "I knew it!"

"Knew what," Birdie asked softly.

"Knew if I told you the truth that you'd want to send me back. But I ain't going. Not to the asylum. As soon as this train stops, I'll be on my way."

"So you are going to break our agreement?" Birdie said firmly.

Paddy shrugged. "You wanted a kid."

A smile played at Birdie's lips. "You're fifteen. While you might think you're an adult, you still have time before you need to strike out on your own."

"You mean you don't think I'm too old?"

"Howard, we knew you were older when we chose you. We didn't want a child we would have to chase after this late in our life," Birdie replied.

Paddy wanted to believe her. "Are you sure?"

Birdie looped her arm through Conall's. "I've never been more sure of anything in my life. Now, how about telling us the rest of your story."

Feeling more confident, Paddy started talking. Telling of his momma getting sick and his father's abuse. He told of fishing the grates, meeting Slim, and what had happened to the boy's mother. He told of dipping pockets, jumping roofs, and climbing buildings, though he got the feeling they didn't quite believe that. He told them about Mileta and life in the asylum. When he'd finished, he'd told them nearly everything, leaving out a few details. He didn't tell them about Dobs or Mr. Murphy nor did he tell them that his papa was still alive. "I wasn't supposed to come out," Paddy said at last.

Birdie frowned. "Why not?"

"The headmistress said I wouldn't get picked on account of my red hair."

Birdie ran a hand through Conall's white beard. "It's a good thing they didn't have that mindset when you and I came out, isn't it, Red?"

The implication of what she'd said hit him. "You mean you rode the train?"

"Conall and I both did back in 1875." Birdie smiled a mischievous smile. "It's hard to believe it's been forty-nine years. Sometimes, it feels like it was yesterday, and others, it feels like a lifetime ago. Conall was fourteen, and I was twelve. We met on the train and talked the whole way to Michigan. By the time we arrived, Conall had professed his love."

Conall chuckled. "I tried to get her to run off with me right then and there, but she was too scared."

Birdie leaned into him and smiled a wrinkled grin. "You found me soon enough." She looked at Paddy and winked. "I told you, I know a bit about love. If you're meant to be with that girl of yours, you'll find her when the time comes."

"Unless Mouse finds her first," Paddy replied.

"Patience, Howard. If it is meant to be, it'll be." Birdie frowned. "Are you alright? You look as if you've seen a ghost?"

Unable to speak, Paddy nodded.

"My story is not unlike yours," Conall said, breaking the mood. "My father was a mountain of a man with a heavy hand. My mother bore him eleven children that I know of. I left on my own accord, so there could have been more after I left. Knowing my father, there probably were. I lived on the streets and ran with a pretty bad gang until I was caught stealing a loaf of bread."

Paddy sucked in his breath. "They didn't send you to prison?"

A sly smile stretched across the man's face. "No, it was raining, and I guess my arms were pretty slippery, so I managed to get away. So scared was I that I ran across town, found the first policeman I could, and begged him to take me to the asylum. It was a little rough at first, as I'd been on my own for about five years, but I finally settled in until they shipped me out here on the trains in seventy-five."

"What happened when you got to Detroit?"

Conall shook his head. "We didn't come to Detroit. They let us off in Albion, a town on the west side of the state. I had a family take me in. It wasn't the best life, but it was better than prison."

"Why wasn't it good?" Paddy pressed.

"Because they made me work the farm. I resented it at the

time. I'd been living on the streets and in the asylum and wasn't used to doing a man's job. I took off when I turned seventeen and went to find Birdie. We traveled east, I got a job, and a few years later, I bought us a farm. I guess those years with the Moores taught me a thing or two."

"The Moores? You mean they adopted you?" Paddy asked.

Conall shook his head. "No, but their name was easier to pronounce than the one I had, so I took it as my own."

"What about you, Birdie? What's your story?" Paddy asked eagerly.

"Nothing as glamorous as either of yours. My momma couldn't feed me, so she took me to the asylum, saying she would come back, and never did. I was five and spent seven years in there."

Paddy knew she was telling the truth, as he'd heard the same story many times. He thought of Mary and wondered if she'd found a family in Detroit. He looked at Birdie. "How come you never had any children?"

"I guess I wasn't meant to as I never had any. I can't say I wasn't happy about it." She shrugged an unapologetic shrug. "There were so many children in the asylum that I couldn't imagine having any of my own. Though, I felt bad never having given Conall a son."

"Don't listen to her; she knows I didn't want any kids. Not after having to take care of my siblings for so long."

"If neither of you wants children, why did you pick me?" Paddy asked.

Birdie's answer was simple. "We changed our minds."

"We saw the advert in the paper telling of how the train was coming. Oh, we've seen them before, but something about this one had us thinking that we're not getting any younger, and we have no one to leave the farm to, so why not take a trip to Detroit and get us a boy?"

"We figured it would be good for us all," Conall added.

"We'll deed you the farm in our will. You only have to keep it until we are in the ground. After that, you're welcome to sell it and do whatever you want with the money," Birdie told him. "We just thought that it would be a way to make our life count and that perhaps someone might think about us after we're gone."

Paddy couldn't believe his ears. Until today, having a knife of his very own was the highlight of his life. Now Birdie and Conall were talking about giving him a whole farm. Murphy was right: being a redhead sure was lucky.

***

Paddy wasn't sure what he expected, but stepping off the train in Sandusky, Michigan, was a bit of a shock. With the exception of the train whistle, boisterous greetings from people meeting those exiting the trains, and a few dogs barking as they chased after a horse and wagon, the town was eerily quiet. The streets were covered in dirt; he couldn't see a single building over two stories tall, and there were trees everywhere he looked.

Paddy stared, mouth agape, as Conall stopped at a Model T. "You mean you have a motorcar?!"

Conall smiled and helped Birdie into the backseat. "Yep, she's a 1917 Ford. Bought her used a few years back. Pitch your suitcase in the back, and I'll show you how to crank it. You'll need to know how to start it if you're going to drive it."

Paddy wanted to ask the man if he'd heard him right, but he was too quick for him.

Conall reached inside the cab and lifted a handle just to the left of the steering wheel. "This here is the spark; it needs to be up when you start her." He reached under the steering wheel and pulled another lever forward. "Now, this handbrake is important because if you forget, she'll take off on you as soon as she starts. Got it?"

Paddy nodded.

"Good," Conall said as he reached to the right of the steering wheel and turned a nob to the left. "That's the ignition box I just turned on. Now we're ready to give her a crank."

"Which one is the crank?" Paddy asked, peering inside the cab.

Conall chuckled. "It's on the outside."

Paddy followed as Conall went to the front of the motorcar. "We're going to push in on this here choke, and give that crank a turn."

"I can see why you wanted to take the train," Paddy said when the man turned the crank for the third time.

"She'll take hold," Conall said, giving it another go. True to his word, the motorcar sputtered to life. "Get in and put that blanket across your lap. You don't have a coat, and you'll be frozen nose to toes by the time we make it home."

Paddy worked to hide his disappointment as he started to climb into the backseat with Birdie.

Conall called him back. "I thought you were going to drive us home?" He pointed to the front seat. "Hop on up there and wrap that blanket around you."

Paddy almost told him he didn't need the blanket but didn't want the man to get mad at him for backtalking. Paddy climbed inside, wrapped up in a heavy quilt as Conall did the same, then followed his instructions for backing up.

"Now, bring that spark down and line it up between the ruts and use that lever there to give her some gas," Conall said at last.

Paddy could not believe it. His first time ever in a motorcar and he was the one driving. As they puttered out of town, he wondered what the headmistress would think of his run of good luck.

Going was slow on M-19 as the dirt road was muddy from

the recent rains and full of deep ruts. Several times, the motorcar hopped over a rut and nearly yanked the wheel from his hands. "How far do we have to go?" Paddy asked, trying to hide the fact he was about to freeze from the wind swirling through the open car.

"We are two miles south of town and a mile and a half west," Conall replied as the Ford hopped a rut for the umpteenth time. "Not as fun as it looks, is it, son?"

"Not really," Paddy said, gripping the wheel.

"It's better after they use the grader to smooth the roads." Conall pointed in front of them. "Henderson Road is coming up on your right. Best hold tight to that wheel. That road's pretty bumpy."

***

Paddy stood in the driveway, staring at the white two-story with two large windows on the main floor facing the road. Near as he could tell, there were windows on all sides and curtains in every window. He thought back to his conversation with Slim all those years ago. His friend had told him that his momma always dreamed of a house such as this. He wondered if his mother would have liked this house and instantly knew the answer to be yes. Paddy could almost picture her standing inside, looking out at him. He sighed. She might not be standing in the window, but she was surely smiling down on him.

In addition to the house, there was a huge barn, plus a smaller one and several large outbuildings, built with a mixture of wood and what Conall had referred to as field stone. Paddy blew out a whistle. Now he knew himself to be lucky. His new family was rich! "You mean to tell me you want to give me all of this?"

Conall chuckled. "Eventually, if you stick around."

Paddy looked at the house once more. "And that big old house is just for the two of you, and you don't have to share with anyone else?"

"Well, now we are sharing it with you and Socks," Birdie said. "He's our cat."

"You have a cat in the house?"

"A kitten, actually," Birdie replied. "Came from one of our barn cats. You'll see them out and about, especially around milking time when they're hoping to get a taste. They keep the mice away," she said by way of explanation.

"I knew a kid who had himself this little dog, and he would send the dog in after the mice and rats," Paddy told them. "Said he made a fine living catching rats. Sometimes, he would take them away and let them go into another building, and then those people would pay him to get them out again."

"Sounds like an industrious fellow," Conall said, following Birdie to the house. He pointed to a small white shed. "The outhouse is over there if you need to relieve yourself."

Paddy glanced at the small white structure with a half-moon carved into the door as he followed the man inside. They entered through the back door closest to the building they parked the motorcar in. Birdie stopped to light a lamp and then went on.

"That's the basement," Conall said, pointing to a set of stairs that went down into a black abyss. "The floor is dirt, so it's really nothing more than a root cellar."

They walked through the kitchen, which opened up to the dining room with a table that had seen better days. Paddy smiled, knowing refinishing it would be easy.

The living area was comfortable, with a couch and several chairs. "Our bedroom is through that door. There are three bedrooms up those stairs. They each have a bed, so you can pick the one you want."

"There is a quilt on the end of one of the beds for you to use. I plan on making you one of your own when the weather turns,"

Birdie said. "We'll go to town to the dry goods store in the next few days so you can pick your colors. For now, go on up and have a look around, and I'll start supper. Do you need something, Howard?" Birdie asked.

"I just wanted to say thank you for bringing me home with you." He broke and ran up the stairs so they wouldn't see the tears in his eyes.

***

Cindy hugged the journals to her chest as if doing so would somehow reach the boy and make everything okay. She smiled and laughed inwardly at her silliness, reminding herself that he grew up to be one of the finest men she'd ever known.

Chapter Twenty-Eight

The stairs from the front room led up to a small landing with a window that overlooked the driveway and barns—a second set of stairs led to the second floor. The light was waning, but there was still enough to see a large storage room set off to the right, and a wide hallway that opened to three good-sized bedrooms. The two smaller bedrooms each housed a bed and a single dresser with plenty of space left for sleeping pallets on the floor if the need ever arose.

Paddy looked over the bedrooms – one of which was nearly as big as the tenement apartment he lived in with his parents and brothers – and was at a loss of why anyone needed this much space. After much debate as to whether it was too extreme, he chose the largest of the three rooms. Not because of the size but because it sat in the front left corner of the house and boasted three windows, which not only meant more light, but he could see the front and side of the house without even leaving his room. He stared at the bed, noting it was at least four times the size of the cot he'd slept in over the past four years. It reminded him of the bed his brothers shared, only it would be his alone. He wondered once more about the fate of his brothers and if they, too, would be sleeping in a wonderful bed this night. He pushed that thought aside and recalled the nights he'd slept crammed into the shanty on the top of Big Joe's roof and remembered sleeping under the stars in the graveyard behind St. Paul's Chapel. Next, he thought of Dobs and Mr. Murphy, wishing to figure out a way to thank the men for their kindness and tell them both of his sudden good fortune.

Paddy put his suitcase on the bed and opened it, exposing his travel clothes and multiple carvings wrapped in cloth. He pulled out his travel clothes and debated what to do with them, as they were quite dirty and covered in soot from the trip on the train. Not wishing to soil the bed, he placed them in a pile on the floor, then reached into the case, pulled out one of the carvings, and unwrapped it, exposing the carved mouse he'd made years ago. As he studied the mouse, a black and white kitten jumped on the bed and raised a paw to the sculpture.

"Oh no, you don't. This mouse is for looking at, not for eating," Paddy said, pulling the mouse away. He heard footsteps on the stairs and looked to see Conall heading his way with an oil lamp. Paddy tossed the mouse into the suitcase and turned to face the man.

Conall raised an eyebrow and lifted the lamp so he could see. "Boy, you look like you're hiding something. You even have that kitten all riled. You wouldn't happen to have a snake in that case, would you?"

Paddy turned to look at the case, saw the kitten clawing at the edge, and shook his head. "No, sir."

"Perhaps you picked up a mouse on the train," Conall suggested.

Paddy sighed. "There's a mouse in there, but he didn't come in on the train."

Conall cast a glance over his shoulder. "Son, Birdie will abide by a lot of things, but having rodents in her house is not one of them. That's why she insisted on bringing the kitten in. He's a good mouser, that one."

Paddy shook his head. "It's not that kind of mouse." He turned, lifted the lid on the case, and pulled out the little mouse, holding it in his palm for Conall to see. "Please, sir, I'd like to keep it if you don't mind."

"I don't think Birdie would object to your keeping that one in the house," Conall said, eyeing the mouse. "Is that why you were hiding it, because you thought I would take it?"

"Yes, sir. Headmistress told me I should leave them there because whoever took me in might not allow me to keep them." That was also why he hadn't mentioned Dobs or Mr. Murphy while talking about his past. He knew he could not talk about either of the men without mentioning his carvings.

"Them?"

"Yes, sir, I have more." Paddy turned back to the suitcase, shooed the cat out, and pulled out another carving. He unwrapped it to show a squirrel eating a nut.

Conall placed the lamp on the wall hook and held the carvings under the lamp to get a better view.

Paddy unwrapped the cloth, exposing the pipe Dobs gave him, and showed it to Conall.

The man took it and ran it under his nose, then glanced at Paddy. "Do you smoke?"

"No, sir, not yet. But I'm thinking about giving it a try someday."

Conall smiled and handed the pipe back. "Just make sure never to smoke in the barns. That hay catches fire, and there'll be no stopping it."

"Yes, sir." Paddy took the pipe and handed him the carving he'd whittled of Dobs.

"This is nice work," Conall said, studying the piece. "So good, it's almost like looking at a photograph. I can see the wisdom in the man's eyes."

Paddy beamed under the compliment.

"We'll have to get you a shelf to display your collection," Conall said, handing the carving back.

"If I could get a piece of wood, I can make a shelf," Paddy

replied. Of course, it would take some time since all he had to work with was the knife he'd gotten from Dobs.

"No," Conall said, shaking his head. "It should be a nice shelf. We can see about one when we go to town."

Unlike the previous comment, Paddy felt this one like a punch to the gut.

"Don't look so glum. We should be able to find something suitable in town," Conall assured him. "We have a bit of time before supper. Why don't you set that stuff on the dresser and come give me a hand."

"Yes, sir," Paddy replied.

Conall pointed to the suitcase then lifted the lantern from the hook. "Shoo that kitten out of there and close up that case. That lid closes with the cat in there, it'll suffocate, and Birdie will be beside herself. Bring that pile of clothes downstairs too, so Birdie can tend to them."

Paddy did as told and followed Conall down the stairs. Even before they reached the main floor, the aroma of food invaded his nostrils. Paddy gave the air a thorough sniff. "Something smells wonderful."

"Just wait until you taste Birdie's sausage and beans," Conall said over his shoulder. "Tastes good enough to make a grown man cry."

Paddy's stomach rumbled a reply. He hadn't had a real meal since that time he and Slim gorged themselves. As they passed the table, Paddy saw the worn tabletop and frowned. If the man didn't trust him to build a simple shelf, he would never allow him to fix the table.

"Are you alright, Howard?" Birdie asked when they passed through the kitchen.

"Yes, ma'am," Paddy lied.

"He'll be fine as soon as he gets a taste of your home cooking," Conall said, pulling the woman into his arms and giving her a quick peck.

Birdie peeked over Conall's shoulder and winked at Paddy. "Do you have a favorite meal, Howard?"

Paddy thought about it for a moment, then shrugged. "My momma used to make Johnny cakes."

Birdie smiled. "Johnny cakes it is."

Paddy's stomach rumbled once more. "Ma'am?"

"Yes, Howard."

"Conall said I should give you these. If you show me where the wash pan is, I'll scrub them myself. I used to do it for my momma after she fell ill."

Birdie took the clothes from him. "You help Conall, and we'll see to your clothes in the morning."

Conall kept the lantern with him as he took the four steps down to the back landing. He paused, pulled two brown coats off the hook, and handed Paddy one. "It's Birdie's barn coat. She's not going to need it tonight."

Recalling how cold it was when they came in, he pulled the coat on without complaint and followed Conall.

There was smoke coming from the chimney of the stone building which sat in front of the barn. Conall pointed the lantern toward the building. "That's the bunkhouse. We have a couple of men, Earl and John, who help around here. Every now and then, another soul shows up looking for a place to rest their head. As long as they pull their weight, they can stay. Some of them stay a night, others bunk down for weeks or even months. Earl was passing through on the way to visit his ailing sister in Bad Axe a few years back. He stayed the night, then went on his way. He stopped back a few days later and said his sister had passed by the time he got there. It must have weighed on him because he settled in here and never left. Within days of him settling in, he took it upon himself to milk the cows and do other things that needed to be done. He does a good job of things and keeps the cows milked, and when the occasional stranger comes through, he puts them to work to pay for their supper and sees they get fed."

Conall opened the door to the largest of the red barns and hung the lantern on the hook as they stepped inside. He looked Paddy in the eye. "You bring a lantern into one of the barns, you see it gets hung on a hook. It's the hay; she'll go up quick."

The cows mooed their agreement as Conall moved into the barn, checking on things.

Paddy stood just inside the door, staring at the eight black and white cows that stared out from gated stalls. A dozen or so chickens pecked at the ground as a white and grey bird double the size of the chickens lowered its long neck and hissed at them. Paddy had seen geese and chickens before, but they'd been in wooden cages at the market. Never had he seen one acting like this or heard one hiss. He frowned at the bird. "What's wrong with that goose?"

Conall chuckled. "Gerty's an ornery one. As long as you don't corner her, she'll leave you be. Wish I could say the same about that rooster over there. Don't turn your back on him, or he'll spur you." He pointed to a large turkey. "Tom over there is pretty docile, but he can get riled every now and again."

Paddy stared at the birds and scratched his head. "Why do you have birds that'll hurt you?"

"The goose will be sharing our table on Thanksgiving Day, and the rooster fertilizes the hen eggs."

Paddy watched as the goose made a mess on the ground. "Won't Birdie get mad when he does that in the house?"

"He'll be dead when he comes in the house. That bird is our Thanksgiving goose. You'll understand why we keep him around when you get your first taste of him," Conall said.

Paddy grinned.

Conall smiled. "I take it you've had goose before."

"Yes, sir, at the asylum one year on Christmas day. We knew something was different as we didn't have to go to classes. They gathered us all in the great hall, and we stayed there most of the day while Anastasia and a couple of the others took turns reading to us. Normally, it was just Anastasia who read to us, and we didn't get the whole book, but this day was different. She read *A Christmas Carol*, a book by a man named Dickens. None of the kids liked her much, but I don't think there was a kid in that building who could find fault with the way she read. It didn't matter what she was reading, she had a way of making you see it in your mind. She told of Tiny Tim's family and how they had a meal of goose, potatoes, and applesauce and made it sound so good, our mouths watered. Later, she read where Mr. Scrooge got them a fine turkey, and upon closing the book, the lights came on, and it was announced that we would be having the same meal as Tiny Tim. We all cheered, and that meal was just as good as what Anastasia said it was," Paddy said, remembering.

"Did you ever have a turkey?"

Paddy shook his head. "No, sir, can't say as I have."

Conall leaned in and lowered his voice in a conspiratorial whisper. "Not to worry, we'll change that on Christmas day." He laughed and spoke normally. "Looks like Earl already took care of milking the Holsteins today. Let's go next door and see if Betty can give us some milk for supper."

Betty turned out to be a light brown and white Holstein housed in the smaller barn along with Jenny and Jake, two horses, which snorted and tossed their heads over their stall doors the moment they entered. "Easy, Jenny," Conall said, petting one. He nodded to the other horse, which had a white marking on its forehead. "That's Jake," he said, then picked up a stick with sharp tines and tossed some hay into each stall.

Hay drifted down from the second floor, and Paddy looked

to see several goats staring down at them.

Unable to hide his amazement, Paddy blew out a whistle. "I thought you told the man this wasn't a working farm. It looks like a lot of work to me!"

"There's plenty of work," Conall agreed, "but not near as much as there used to be. We used to have over fifty dairy cows and a string of men to help milk them. Sold all but the ones you've seen about five years back. We keep them for milk, cheese, and butter. And the goats give us milk for soap." Conall walked over to the brown cow, which was tied to a post, and pulled a low stool from a hook on the wall and placed it beside the heifer as he pulled a metal bucket from the shelf and placed it under the cow. He sat on the stool, reached under the cow, and pulled on something that burst, sending white liquid into the pail.

While Conall had spoken plenty about it being a dairy farm and milking, it still took Paddy a full moment to realize what that liquid was. He knelt and watched with rapt attention as the man continued pulling and squeezing the liquid into the bucket. Several cats jumped down from the loft and meowed their desire. Every now and then, Conall would reward them with a taste. As he milked, he continued telling Paddy about life on the farm. "The chickens give us eggs. Some we eat, some we sell. We have some beef cows in the field and a few hogs and sows. We slaughter and cure enough to keep us fed and sell what we don't need at the county fair. We keep our breeding stock, who'll give us more in the spring, and then we will do it all over again next year. We grow a garden in the summer, and we eat what we need and put the rest up to eat when winter hits. Birdie cans a bunch, and what won't go bad goes into the root cellar until it is needed. Birdie usually takes a ribbon or two for her quilts at the county fair. Those ribbons help the price when she goes to sell."

Paddy thought it to be the same as what Murphy had said about his carvings. You do good work, and people will pay the price. He started to ask, then decided against it. He was still stinging that Conall didn't think him capable of building a shelf.

"Farm life isn't for everyone, but if you do her right, she'll provide for you, and you won't have to worry about going hungry," Conall said, bringing him out of his musing. The man gave him a long look. "There was a time I went to bed hungry every night. But that has not happened once since I bought this farm. Sure, we've had lean meals from time to time, but never have we gone to bed without something in our bellies. Promise me you remember that and think hard on what I told you when the time comes for you to decide to stay or sell."

"Yes, sir," Paddy agreed.

Conall gave the udder a final pull, then stood, removed the bucket and patted the cow on her backside. "There, there, Betsy. That's got to feel better."

"Sir? It's probably a silly question, but if a cow is made to give milk, why does it feel better?"

"Silly would be if you had preferred to remain ignorant instead of asking the question to increase your knowledge. To that point, Betsy here produces five to eight gallons of milk a day. If she isn't milked, it could make her sick or even kill her." Conall smiled. "Have you ever had to go to the bathroom so bad it hurts?"

"Yes, sir."

"It's sort of like that. Only eventually, you'll wet yourself on account of you having no choice. Ole Betsy here will leak a bit, but she won't do more than that without help."

Paddy nodded his understanding. As he turned, he caught sight of a neatly stacked pile of wood. As Conall returned the stool to the hook, Paddy moved closer to the wood which lay in both long planks and small chunks. He looked to see if Conall was watching, saw the man's back was to him and picked up two of the smaller chunks, shoving them in his coat pocket. While he felt guilty stealing from the man after he'd been so nice to him, he was afraid if he asked, Conall would tell him no.

***

Unable to sleep, Paddy pulled his chair to the window and peered out at the moon that looked over the house and barns. It was only a half-moon, but still provided enough light to see. True to Conall's words, Birdie was a fabulous cook and he'd eaten until he couldn't possibly eat any more. The Johnny cakes she'd made brought back memories of his mom and had produced a couple tears he'd quickly batted away. But through it all, he'd been distracted by that marred table and the fact that Conall didn't trust him to build a simple shelf. He liked Conall and Birdie immensely, but Dobs was right; woodworking was in his blood, and he wasn't sure he could be happy if he wasn't allowed to do what his heart desired. He went to the dresser, opened the drawer and pulled out one of the chunks of wood he'd managed to sneak upstairs. He pulled out the suitcase, opened it and sat it on the floor. He didn't have to search the wood to find the image; he'd known it the moment he picked it up. Pulling out his knife, he started to carve.

Paddy worked on his project until the moonlight faded then took a pillow from the bed and wrapped himself in the extra quilt. He slept on the floor under the window as he couldn't bring himself to sleep in that bed until he fully made up his mind to stay.

Chapter Twenty-Nine

Three days had passed since he'd arrived in Sandusky, Michigan, and Paddy had yet to decide if he was going to stay. The bed remained unslept in and he continued to hold Birdie and Conall at a distance. While he still hadn't warmed up to the cat, the curious feline seemed to enjoy his company, joining him each evening as he pulled the chair to the window and taking great pleasure chasing the wood shavings as they dropped into the suitcase.

Paddy ran a finger over the carving, then picked up the knife and shaved away the last sliver of wood in a long, thin slice. The kitten caught the shaving and rolled onto his back, clawing at it with his back feet. He laughed, and the kitten took off with the shaving in his mouth. Paddy hurried after him but stopped at the top of the stairs, afraid to go after him for fear of waking Birdie and Conall. *Dang cat, why'd you have to go and run off for?* Time was up, he needed to make a decision, and he needed to make it tonight. Birdie didn't miss a thing. As soon as she found the shaving, his secret would be out.

Paddy went back to his room and sat in the chair, staring out the window at the land which could be his if he wanted it. Then again, he was just a boy; what did he know about farming? He smiled. He knew a lot more than he did three days ago, and it wasn't like Birdie and Conall would be dying soon, so he had plenty of time to learn more. *Besides, if I leave, where will I go?*

Instantly, he thought of Mileta and thought to find her and

beg her to come away with him. *And take her where? What do you have to offer her but a knife and a few carvings? But if you stay, you can offer her a home with plenty of bedrooms to raise a bunch of children.* Paddy had never thought of himself as a father before, but as he sat there, he thought he could be a fine dad – raising his children right and never giving them a reason to be afraid of him. If they wanted to work the farm, he was okay with that, and if they wanted to learn to work wood, he would teach them everything he knew. He recalled Birdie's story of how they'd met on the train and how Conall had come to find her. Then, he remembered the story Conall had told him the first night of how they'd not gone to bed hungry since moving into the house.

Patience, Howard. His mother's voice was clear in his head. *Learn all you can about farming so you will be able to feed your family. There will be time for carving later.* And just like that, he knew he would stay. Not wishing to soil the bed, he once again slept on the pallet on the floor.

***

The sun was streaming in the window when he finally opened his eyes, and he knew he'd slept way past time to begin chores. He hurried to dress, then ran down the stairs thinking to forgo the morning meal and join Conall in the barns. As he passed the table, his heart sank. Sitting in the middle in an etched pink glass bowl was a small pile of wood shavings.

Birdie came into the room carrying a plate with two biscuits and two sausage patties. Absent of the smile she normally carried, her face looked grim and showed her age. She placed the plate onto the table and motioned for him to sit.

"But I have to help with the chores," Paddy said, hoping to bide time.

"Conall has Earl and John to help with those. You'll sit and have your breakfast." Her tone left no room for argument.

Paddy eyed the shavings as he slid into the chair, wondering if he should mention them or just wait the woman out. *Don't be a dope. At least have the sense to have breakfast before she kicks you out.* Deciding to take his own advice, he began to eat.

Birdie joined him at the table, carrying a dainty pink and white porcelain cup balanced on top of a matching saucer. She poured some of the liquid from the cup into the saucer, then lifted the saucer up and took a sip. "It helps the coffee cool," she said by way of explanation.

Paddy had seen her do it before, but it was nice to know the reason behind it, so he nodded.

After several moments of silence, Birdie spoke. "When are you planning on leaving?"

Paddy swallowed the bite he'd been chewing and stared at the woman. "You want me to go?" At least he'd finished the carving he'd made for her.

"No, I want you to stay, but I'll not stop you from leaving." She sighed and pointed at the dish of wood chips. "I've been finding these all over the house since the night you arrived. At first, I didn't know what they were, but when I put them in the bowl, I could tell what it was. I figure if you're cutting kindling for a fire, you must be thinking of taking off."

A fire? Paddy looked at the bowl once more and shook his head. "I'm not making firewood. I was making something for you."

"For me?"

"Yes, ma'am, for being so nice to me." Paddy started to get up. "May I be excused for a moment?"

Birdie smiled. "Of course."

He pushed from the table and raced up the stairs. The kitten ran up after him, beating him to the room. Paddy glared at the cat. "You almost spoiled everything." He pulled open the drawer and pulled out his latest carving, giving it a once over.

Not perfect, but the best he could do without a piece of sandpaper to rub it smooth. He closed the drawer and hurried back down the stairs. As soon as he reached the table, he handed the carving to Birdie.

The woman's eyes grew wide. "A goose! It's lovely. You made this?"

"Yes, ma'am."

"Since you've been here?"

"Yes, ma'am," Paddy said once more.

Birdie's brow knitted. "You've been so busy with all of your chores. When did you find the time?"

"At night."

"You carved this in the dark?!"

Birdie seemed so excited that Paddy couldn't tell if she was happy or upset with him. "Yes, ma'am, I carved by the light of the moon."

"The moon?"

Paddy bobbed his head once more. "It wasn't easy on account of it being only a half moon, and sometimes that dipped behind the clouds, so I had to be careful not to hack off any fingers in the dark." Paddy swallowed. "I'm sorry I took the wood chunk without asking Conall, but I was afraid he'd say no since he didn't think my work was good enough."

She frowned. "What do you mean he didn't think your work was good enough? This goose is beautifully done."

"Oh, Conall didn't see this because I didn't want to make him mad. And it's not so good on account of I didn't have any sandpaper. I could make it smooth if I had some. It's the same with this here table. The first time I saw it, I knew I could fix it and make it look good as new. Only then Conall didn't think I could, so it kind of made me sad every time we sat down to eat."

"Howard, you said that before, but I don't understand. Why do you think Conall disapproves?"

Paddy lowered his eyes. "I showed him my carvings, and he said how I'd need a shelf. I told him I'd make one, but he said that wasn't good enough and that he'd rather buy one from town."

A knowing smile spread across the woman's lips. "When you showed Conall your carvings, did you actually tell him you made them, or did you just assume he knew?"

Paddy shrugged.

The coffee had cooled enough for her to take a sip from the cup. "He admired your work enough to want you to be able to display it. Don't you think if he'd known what you were capable of, he would want you to make your own shelf?" she asked, placing the cup back on the saucer.

"I guess."

"Why don't we ask him? I'll go with you to make sure there isn't any more confusion. But first, I want you to show me your other carvings. If you did this in the dark, I can't imagine what you would do if you could actually see what you were doing. It can wait until after you finish your breakfast," Birdie said softly when Paddy started to get up.

***

Conall had come into the house while Paddy and Birdie were standing at the table looking over the carvings. Paddy remained silent as Birdie explained the confusion.

Conall looked over the carvings then placed a hand on Paddy's shoulder. "Boy, I owe you a deep apology. I knew these must have meant something to you for you to have brought them all this way with the knowledge that you might not be allowed to keep them, but I had no idea you had made them with your own hand."

"Yes, sir," Paddy replied.

Conall picked up the goose. "And you said you made this while sitting in the dark using only that blade?"

"It wasn't too dark. We had a bit of a moon," Paddy clarified.

Conall shook his head. "That's not the point, son. I have you outside milking cows, and here you have a real gift. You don't need to be milking cows and working on the farm. You need to be inside working with wood. We'll get you some tools, and you can make whatever your heart desires."

Paddy couldn't believe his ears; he was finally getting everything he wanted, only he didn't want it so much anymore. He looked at the man, begging him to understand. "Sir, if you don't mind, I'd like to do both."

Conall tilted his head as if he hadn't heard correctly. "You would?"

"Yes, sir. I was upset at first on account of I didn't think you'd let me work with the wood. Then I was thinking about what you said about farming and never going to bed hungry, and I recalled how small your town is and how there aren't that many pockets to pick, and I thought that it would be nice not to have to worry about that anymore. I think having a place to call home and food to eat might appeal to my girl when I go looking for her."

Conall smiled a wide smile. "Yes, I'm sure it would."

"So, if it is all the same to you, I'd like to learn what farming I can," Paddy said.

"Okay," Conall agreed, "but I'm counting on you to find some time for your carving as well. If you are willing to make some to sell, I'm pretty sure George Lever will agree to let you put some in his store."

"Really?" Paddy replied.

Conall slid a glance to Birdie. "Yes, but I think we need to get you cleaned up with some new clothes before we try."

Paddy looked down at his clothes. "What's wrong with these? They were brand new when they gave them to me, and

I've only worn them for a couple of days."

"Your clothes are suitable for the twelve-year-old boy the agency thought they were sending out, but not for the fifteen-year-old we all know you are. Plus, winter's coming on, and you're going to need a suitable coat."

"It's true," Birdie winked. "You keep wearing my coat, and I'll freeze to death."

"Sounds like a trip to town is in order," Conall replied. "I'll hitch up the team."

"What about the motorcar?" Paddy asked.

"No, we'll take the buckboard to save on gas. No sense going all the way into town if we aren't going to get everything we need to hold us for a few weeks. I know Birdie there is itching to get her hands on the fabric to make you a new quilt for that bed of yours."

Birdie nodded her agreement.

"What's wrong with the one I'm using?" Paddy asked.

"Nothing, but winter is coming and it will give Birdie something to do to keep her busy when the weather sets in." Conall looked at his wife and smiled an affectionate smile. "You get to measuring the boy, and I'll go see to our ride."

***

Paddy walked through the aisle of Doyle Dry Goods, trailing his hand across the bolts of fabric as he went. He got to the end of the row and turned to Birdie. "There are so many colors. How am I supposed to know which one to choose?"

She glanced at the fabric. "Just do what I do. Pick the one that makes you smile."

Paddy walked the row again, his gaze landing on one that reminded him of the blue in the stained glass windows at St. Joseph Church. "This one is nice."

She gave a little finger wave. "Okay, now we need one more color to complement it."

Paddy sighed. "It was hard enough to pick one."

Birdie lifted the bolt of fabric he'd chosen and slowly walked the row, placing the blue next to each one. On the return trip, she stopped by several bolts and showed him how they would look together.

Paddy looked at each one and finally chose a bright white.

"Splendid," Birdie said, pointing to the fabric. "Bring it up to the front and we'll have the clerk cut it for us."

Paddy did as she said and placed it on top of the one Birdie laid on the counter. As Birdie chatted up the clerk, he walked through the store, looking at each and every shelf, thinking how easy it would be to take just about anything he wanted. He stopped at a shelf that held writing paper and thought of taking a few pages then realized with everything else he had to do, he would never find the time. He looked over his shoulder and saw Birdie watching him and continued forward.

"Do you need anything else?" the clerk asked.

"Yes, we'll need a pair of trousers and a shirt for my son, and he'll need a new coat as well." Birdie looked in his direction and smiled a sheepish smile.

***

"How come you told him I'm your son?" Paddy asked once they were outside.

"It's a small town, Howard. It would be easier for you if people think you are my and Conall's son."

"Won't they know better?" Paddy asked, following her across the street carrying the packages they'd just bought.

"People around here have better things to gossip about."

"Like what?" Paddy asked.

Birdie was quiet for a moment, then she nodded toward a man who'd just exited Lever's Furniture Store. "See that man there?"

Paddy nodded.

"That's Mr. Anderson. A few years ago, he was clearing some stumps off his farm with dynamite. It turns out his boys had trained his dog to dig up sticks, and as soon as he buried that dynamite, Carlo – that was the dog's name – anyway, Mr. Anderson buried it, and Carlo dug it up, and well, people have been talking about that for years."

"What happened to the dog?"

Birdie slid a glance in his direction. "You've never heard of dynamite?"

Paddy shook his head.

"Good. Let's keep it that way for now. I'm sure Conall will educate you on it this summer. In the meantime, if anyone ever tells you to run, get to it!" Birdie said, pulling open the door to R.A. McPherson Hardware.

A man wearing a long white apron met them at the door. "Good day, Mrs. Moore; what can I help you with today?"

"We'd like some sandpaper and varnish. My son's going to refinish our dining room table." She looked at Paddy and smiled. "He can tell you what he needs."

"Is that right?" the man asked.

"Yes, sir," Birdie said, answering for him. "I'm sure you'll be seeing a lot of him. Howard here is a master woodworker, and he's going to be needing some tools."

***

Paddy sat in his bedroom, carving by the light of the oil lamp Birdie had purchased for him in town. She'd also insisted on getting him a bucket for the shavings so they could properly harvest them for usable kindling for starting fires. While Birdie admitted to having other buckets at home, this particular bucket had a lid to place over it when not in use to keep Socks from stealing the shavings. Paddy yawned, rose from his chair, and placed his knife and carving in the top drawer.

He went back to the window and started to move the chair

back to the corner. As he gripped the chair, he looked out the window and saw a large herd of deer grazing in the field across the street and recalled Conall's words once more. *We've yet to go to bed hungry.*

As he stared out the window, he thought of Mileta and sent out a promise to find her one day. Next, he looked to the ceiling and thought of his mother. *I'm trying my best to be patient, Momma. I hope you are happy for me being here. I hope you don't mind, but I think I'd like to call Conall Pop, as he's a lot better papa than the one I have. I hope Birdie doesn't mind that I continue to call her Birdie, as you'll always be my momma.*

Paddy walked to the bed and started to remove the pillow. He smiled and pulled back the covers instead. As he stretched out his full length, he realized this was his first time sleeping in a proper bed. He was nearly asleep when Socks jumped up beside him, sniffed his face, and then settled down next to him. Paddy thought about sending the kitten away, then realizing there was something comforting in the vibration of the kitten's purrs, closed his eyes once more.

Chapter Thirty

Cindy turned the page, saw her father's handwriting, and gasped. Her mother was the one who'd copied the journals. She had to have recognized the handwriting of the man she'd been married to for years. She looked up and saw Linda grinning and instantly had her answer. "Mom, these are from Dad. How could you have kept this from me?"

"Because if I would have told you, then you would have skipped to the end to see how the story ends."

"This is not a book!" Cindy said heatedly. "They are Dad's journals."

"Only a few pages," Linda replied.

"Which you have obviously already read," Cindy said.

Linda shrugged. "You have plenty of life in you. I'm old; who's to say how many years I have left? Besides, I would've felt bad going to my grave not knowing what happened."

"If you would've died, you could have asked Dad what they said," Cindy said shortly.

"There, you see, I've already read them. Now, if I die, I'll have something to talk to him about."

Though Cindy currently felt like strangling her mother, she didn't like all this talk about the woman dying. "Mom?"

"Yes, dear?"

"I'd like to read these if you don't mind."

Linda smiled. "Go right ahead."

Cindy took a breath and began to read.

My dearest Cindy,

I'm writing these to you as I know how tenacious you are and know you will be the one to find them. If you are reading these, it means I'm no longer with you. I know I should have shown these to you years ago, but after discussing this in-depth with Frank, we decided it best to leave them buried. I can't explain our decision other than feeling if Mother Mildred and Pop went to such lengths to hide these, who were we to dishonor their wishes?

I stumbled upon the journals years ago, as I knew there was something off with the attic. At first, I thought the man had lost his mind because the way he was doing the planking didn't make sense. So, I started snooping, and when I did, I discovered the journals. With them, I uncovered secrets and lies that would have gone to the grave with him had I not found them and hid that key in your grandmother's doll for you to find—good detective work for finding it, by the way.

As you may have figured out by this point, I am my father's son, and I can confirm that Mother Mildred was aware of this.

When I told Frank about finding the journals, he warned me there might be things in there I didn't wish to know. I knew we were brothers born from the same mother, but when I pressed him, he told me about Pop being my true father. He then said he thought Mother Mildred knew, as he'd walked in on them when they were having a terrible fight just before Pop traveled to New York to come for me. I confronted Pop about it after I found the journals, and he admitted the truth. He said he hadn't meant to deceive me, only that he thought it would be easier on everyone if they kept it this way. You see, I was not born out of love. It was a one-time consummation between two desperately lonely people that led to my being here. Pop further explained that he thought that would weigh on me if I knew.

It did for a bit, but then I realized that while my parents did not love each other, they each loved me enough to see I did not fall into peril. How could I fault them for that?

Mother Mildred was the only woman Pop ever loved, yet by the time they married, she was so damaged, she could never fully return that love. She was nice to me but also held me at a distance. I believe I was the constant reminder that another woman was able to give my father something she never could. Pop and Mother Mildred appeared to live a comfortable co-existence, but looking back, I think they both lived with the regret of things that could have been. Pop swore Mother Mildred loved me; she just hated that my mother was able to give him what she could not.

I have so many regrets, and not advocating for you is the biggest one. I was so used to Mother Mildred's aloofness that by the time you were born, it just didn't seem unreasonable that she would be that way with you as well. After reading her journals, I berated myself for not insisting she hold you. Thinking that somehow having her do so would have lit that spark in her that faded so long ago. At least I could have convinced her to get counseling to maybe help her let go of the past. By the time I found the journals, it was too late for any of that. I tried to talk to her about it once, but she shut down and didn't speak to me for months. Come to think of it, I guess we all live with regrets of what could have been.

I know you are reluctant to have children, and I can't help but think that we may have had a hand in that decision. If that is truly your choice, I will abide by it, but my fervent hope is that you find a way to open your heart to a child so that you can feel what a pleasure it is to be a parent. You and Linda are my two consistent joys and supply me with enough love to fill the void I had for so many years. You are both my everything and I love you with all my being.

As Cindy read, she thought of David and his daughter, Stella, and how the little girl pulled at her heart each time she thought of her. While she was afraid of the unknown, the last thing she wanted was to go to her grave with the same regret. Cindy held that thought as she continued to read.

I told Pop that his journals were unfinished. I told him he owed it to the reader to at least speak of his reunion with Mother Mildred. He told me she'd already written of it, but I told him it would be different coming from him. I nagged at him enough that he finally relented and settled down to write a few more pages. This is what he had to say about that.

Cindy flipped the page to find her grandfather's words.

Paul said I should say a few more words, so here goes…

I didn't have much time for journaling after I went to live with Birdie and Pop. I learned everything Pop had to teach me about working on the farm, growing food, and tending what I discovered was over a hundred acres of land, but I wasn't ever interested in growing it back into the thriving dairy farm it once was. I was okay with maintaining what they had left, but as much as I wanted to carry on the family legacy, my heart just wasn't in it for the long haul. Woodworking is where my interests lie, and after seeing my work, Pop Moore agreed. They sold a few acres and used the money to buy me some woodworking tools. I kept up with my chores, milked the cows so Birdie could make and sell butter and cheese, and worked with the wood every chance I got. In my spare time, I helped Birdie.

I believe Birdie and Pop would have made splendid parents. And I think they regretted not having any children of their own, as they doted on me and gave in to my every whim. Had I known just how much that cost them, I would have been a better son.

Not that I was bad to them; I just didn't know what was going on. Instead of paying all of their debt, they were using what they had to spoil me. By the time they passed, the farm was in danger of having a lien against it to pay the taxes. I sold off most of the land to pay off the house and then I used some to travel to New York to get that piano. Sure, it was a foolish thing to do, especially since I could have purchased a new one from Voyle Lever, but I knew Mileta had a sentimental attachment to that one. Plus, if I hadn't gone, I wouldn't have Paulie or my darling granddaughter Cindy. And if not for the piano, I may not have convinced my Mileta to marry me. I had a good life and shared it with a good woman, and a man can't put a price on something like that.

Pop Moore and I talked about the day I arrived many times. On one such occasion, he let on that the reason he'd had me drive home that first day was to strike any notion of my taking the Ford and running away. It worked. Those ruts really beat me up, and I found out that driving that motorcar wasn't quite as fun as I thought it'd be. He also told me they'd spoken with the people in town prior to going down to Detroit to meet the train, which explains why none of them bothered to question my sudden appearance.

I never learned of what happened to my brothers. Maybe someday one of their kin will show up at your door and tell you of their fate. If that happens, tell them my life turned out just about as good as I could have wished for, and I do not harbor any ill feelings toward any of my brothers for not taking me with them.

Mileta and I managed to stay in touch with some of our friends from the asylum, who reached out to me after I ran the advert in the papers. For some reason, they felt obliged to leave us with their journals after Mileta told them we were planning on hiding ours in the walls of our attic. I guess they thought it best to hide them with the hopes of one day being found by someone who cared enough to go looking than to have them fall into the wrong hands or be tossed into the trash with the rest of their belongings. They are hidden under half moons in the attic. I thought that only fitting. My only request is when you read them, know that while they were not our true family, they were the family of our hearts.

I'll leave you with this. If you have children, and I pray that you do, please make sure to distribute your affection evenly, as being a favorite son is a mighty burden to bear.

***

Cindy held on to the journal papers a bit longer, absorbing the words. When, at last, she placed the papers on the table, she knew in her heart that she was ready to explore a deeper relationship with David and ready to embrace a role she never thought herself capable of.

"You will make a wonderful mother," Linda said, reading her mind.

Cindy wanted to remind her mother that she and David were still a ways off from a full commitment but was too caught up in the moment to argue. Instead, she decided to pacify her. "And you will make an amazing grandmother."

Linda looked at her and grinned. "Tell me something I don't already know."

A Note from the Author

"A company of children" is the term used to describe the groups of children sent out on the trains. Each of the books in the saga will follow one child. The first six books are meant to be read in order-each additional book will be a standalone novel which can be read in any order.

The question I get asked most often is are these true stories, meaning, are the children showcased in my books actual children who rode the trains and their stories.

The simple answer to the question is no. With that said, they are the combined stories of many children whose stories I've read. While Ezra is a fictious name, the story that surrounds his early life is true. The child ended up on the street and went to work for a vegetable vendor until his horse died, then he went on to work at a department store. I use the stories I read and add history from the era to give the books depth. I do my best to capture what life was like for children and families of the times: the utter desperation fathers must have felt not being capable of feeding and providing for their children, and of mothers who had to work with what little they had to feed and clothe their children.

There was no medical insurance, no birth control, no money for doctors. People died. Men went to war and either didn't come home or came back a shell of their previous selves. Alcohol was sold in abundance and could still be readily found even during Prohibition.

Parents died. Children died. Multiple families lived in single apartments in rat-infested tenement buildings. I use this history to show what happened and the possible causes of so many children (some orphans, many not) to be in desperate need of help.

Not all homes children were placed in were good, but research shows most of the children sent out were better off than if had they remained in the city.

People are incensed by the fact the children were made to work, but if you research that era, you will find that the majority of children worked. In the cities, they either worked in factories, sitting at the table working with the rest of the family rolling cigars, making paper flowers or countless other tedious tasks families took on to earn enough money to survive.

Did some farmers take it to the extreme? Absolutely. But the bottom line is if a family had a farm, that farm needed to be worked. Unfortunately, people did not have the luxury of adopting children merely out of the goodness of their heart. Another mouth to feed could mean the difference between the family starving or not and that meant everyone – children included – needed to pull their weight.

Most of the time, if a child was working the farm, you can bet the husband, wife, and rest of the family were right out there working alongside them.

My 84-year-old father tells of long hours working on his grandfather's farm when he was a kid. There was no time to play or be a child in today's sense of the word. Again, I acknowledge not every placement was perfect, and I am not trying to romanticize this program, but there were no other options in place during this time in history to help these children. The Placing Out Program was not perfect, but that program, and many like it, saved a lot of lives, and in most cases, the children sent west via the trains thrived and went on to become upstanding citizens who populated our country.

Coming in December, 2024

Book Seven in The Orphan Train Saga

Endurance:
Dorthia's Story

https://www.amazon.com/dp/B0CQTFWQMK

Please find it in your heart to take a moment and go to Amazon to leave a review. Reviews are also welcomed at Barnes & Noble, Bookbub, and Goodreads as well. If you purchased the book at a signing or from my website, please begin your review by including that information. If not, Amazon may not allow the review.

Most importantly, please tell EVERYONE and share in the reading groups! As an indie author, word of mouth is the best publicity I can get.

Thank you for taking this journey with me.

Sherry A. Burton

Please remember to follow me on Amazon and sign up for my newsletter on my website to keep up to date with all new releases.

Please sign up for my monthly author newsletter to keep up to date with all my random thoughts and book updates: https://www.sherryaburton.com/

Follow Sherry on social media:
https://www.facebook.com/SherryABurtonauthor
https://www.amazon.com/Sherry-A.-Burton/e/B005PM6QFG?ref=dbs_m_mng_rwt_auth
https://www.bookbub.com/profile/sherry-a-burton
https://www.instagram.com/authorsherryaburton

About the Author

Sherry A. Burton writes in multiple genres and has won numerous awards for her books. Sherry's awards include the coveted Charles Loring Brace Award, for historical accuracy within her historical fiction series, The Orphan Train Saga. Sherry is a member of the National Orphan Train Society, presents lectures on the history of the orphan trains, and is listed on the NOTC Speaker's Bureau as an approved speaker.

Originally from Kentucky, Sherry and her Retired Navy Husband now call Michigan home. Sherry enjoys traveling and spending time with her husband of more than forty years.